Silver City Reckoning

Silver City Reckoning

J.L. Crafts

SPEAKING VOLUMES, LLC
NAPLES, FLORIDA
2023

Silver City Reckoning

ISBN 978-1-64540-979-3

This book and all those in this series are dedicated
to William Jeffrey Crafts
October 28, 2003 to December 2, 2020.

Acknowledgments

Thanks to my wife of four decades, Colleen, for her patience and encouragement. Advisor, partner, first reader, reviewer, she has always been the initial set of eyes on both story and characters.

Heartfelt thanks go out to my editor, Diane Davis-White. Having worked with her now on multiple books, I cannot imagine getting a manuscript ready for publication without her. Professionalism and experience abound are delivered with gentle yet firm suggestions. She makes what might be tedious enjoyable.

I must also thank Dale Paris, our close friend and farrier for years. Though not an investigator in real life, he is the closest thing to a horse whisperer I've ever witnessed. Fabulous with our horses, he has reviewed all things equine in my books. His advice and approval are much appreciated. I've never seen him wear a bowler hat. But he does make showcase hand-manufactured knives which he sells at shows throughout the west.

All things medical herein came with the review and advice from one of the best diagnosticians I know. In my former life as a trial lawyer, I've cross examined all manner of medical *experts*, but Dr. George Novan is without a doubt the most capable, knowledgeable and inquisitive doctor I've ever met. I made sure the story line surrounding Beth's injury, treatment and recovery met with his approval. Many thanks to both Doc and his wife, Chryl with the funny spelling.

To all my friends and family who volunteered their names. I hope I have done your characters justice.

To my first readers, Wayne Purcell, Dan Frisch, Linda Crafts, I cannot thank you enough. Your input and suggestions make a huge difference.

I again must thank Jim and Nancy Harrell for their contributions in creating a map of the not so fictional Carson Valley and Lake Tahoe to give the reader a glimpse of Will Toal's world.

News from deep within the Consolidated Virginia and California mine about a potential massive new find rose to the surface in late February 1873 as represented here in the story. However, the true extent of the treasure and effect it had on the national economy was not known until late fall of 1873 into 1874.

As you can see in the Fact From Fiction section at the end of the book, I may have compressed some of the true historical timeline here and there to fit the story. Most importantly, though some of those you will read about in this and other books in the series did walk through history, and though many of the events did take place, the story within is mine and pure fiction.

J.L. Crafts

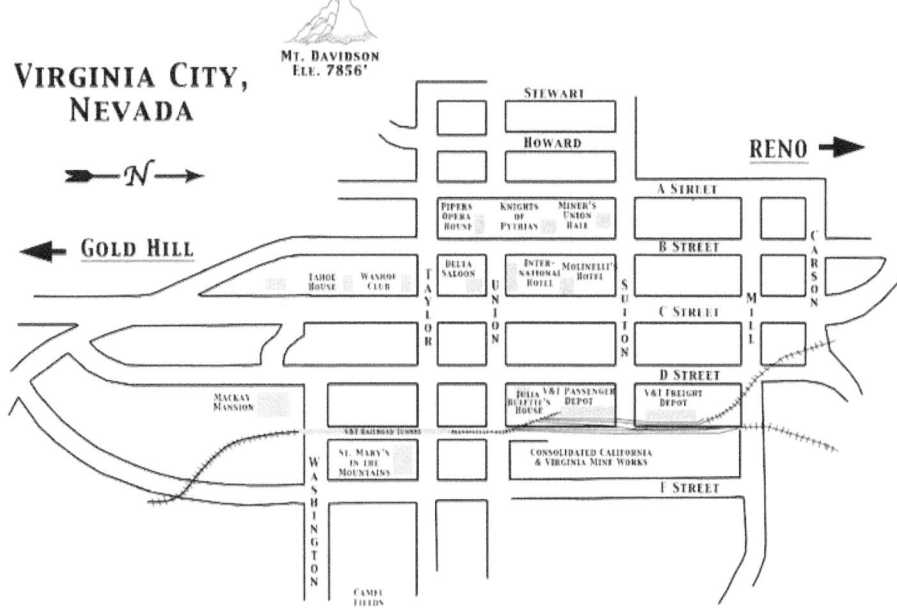

Carson Valley

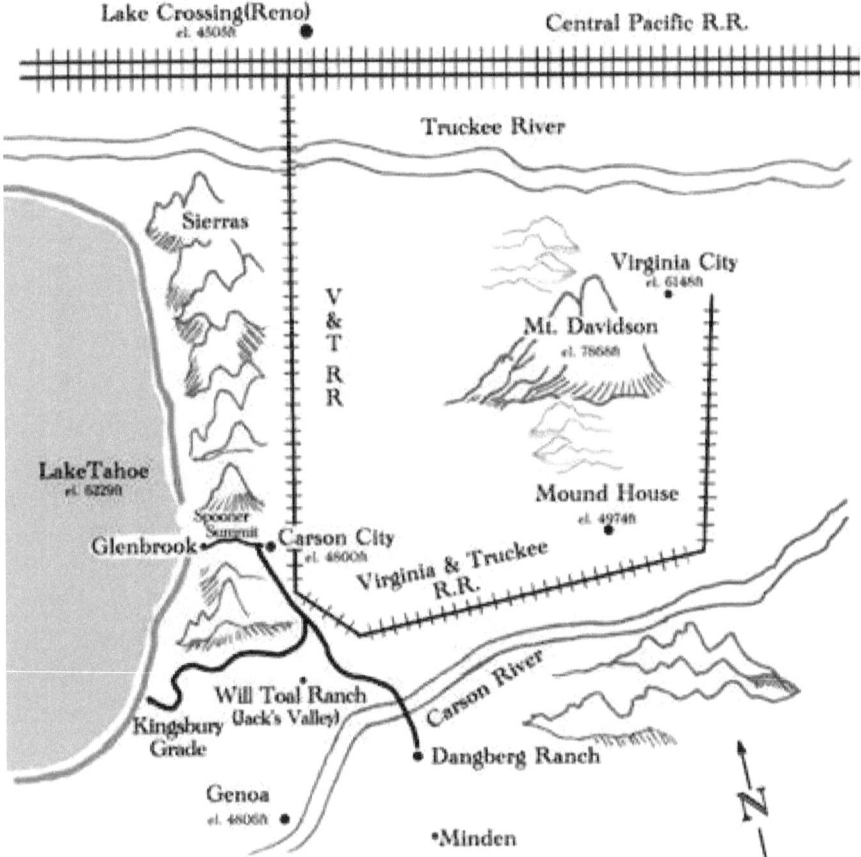

Lake Crossing(Reno)
el. 4505ft

Central Pacific R.R.

Truckee River

Sierras

Virginia City
el. 6148ft

V & T RR

Mt. Davidson
el. 7868ft

LakeTahoe
el. 6229ft

Spooner
Summit

Glenbrook

Carson City
el. 4800ft

Mound House
el. 4974ft

Virginia & Truckee
R.R.

Will Toal Ranch
(Jack's Valley)

Carson River

Kingsbury
Grade

Dangberg Ranch

Genoa
el. 4806ft

Minden

N

Chapter One

The hills in the distance framed a wide expanse of flat desert. Above his head, the high winter sun was not a hot sun, only bright— *very* bright. Life was still.

In the distance beyond the low mountains were dark clouds. Suddenly he saw a tall flash of lightning. It was too far away to hear any thunder, but he knew it was there.

At the base of the mountains near the place where the lightning struck, a diminutive cloud appeared. It started as a spot but grew as it neared. The small billowing flow was the only movement in sight, as if a seal broke in the horizon's visage to let it through. The cloud grew as dust, dust from the hooves of horses bearing riders.

The riders approached at an easy trot, a pace used to cover long distances in the shortest interval. The desert was a timeless expanse where the sands had burned for centuries. Here in the desolate waste, time killed just about everything. The land behind the riders appeared dead.

He sat astride his horse, a borrowed horse on loan from a parishioner, a docile animal now covered in a thick winter coat. Father John Cecconi, a Jesuit of the Society of Jesus, tamped down the broad brimmed hat covering his balding pate. Like his horse, he wore his own coat, a cassock of a thick winter variety similar to the ones predecessors of his order had worn. Years ago, Jesuits wearing these same cassocks had paddled canoes down from Canada to convert natives in the original thirteen colonies. The thick woolen outer shell had kept many a member of the order from freezing.

Father Cecconi was the pastor to a small Catholic community in Carson City. He did not come from Canada but from San Francisco, born into a devout Italian family. They traced their roots back to the Roman legionnaires, but then, didn't all Italian families? His order had started out primarily as missionaries, but now were known for their universities of higher learning. He felt like a missionary here. Carson City hovered in the middle of mountains and desert, like a new Palestine. It was poor, rural, raw, and in need of spiritual guidance.

He was headed to Virginia City. While that city might be rustic and equally in need of guidance, it was anything but poor. Money flowed from the silver mines to all levels of its society. Bishop Manogue, priest at the largest church in the Midwest, had asked that he come say Mass at St. Mary's of the Mountains while the Bishop was away. As a visiting priest, he could have taken the train to Virginia City, but he chose to ride. He liked the peace and tranquility of a ride, even if it did take an additional day or so. A change from his small Carson City parish would be welcome.

He looked again to the east. The cloud grew larger and closer, as if summoned.

He had crested the ridge to the east side of the Carson Valley. Just before he'd seen this vision arising in the east, he had turned to look behind him, marveling at the green grass and trees throughout the valley. Those grasses were constantly fed by snow melting in the majestic Sierras further to the west. The watery succor made the Carson Valley an Eden amid a desert. He again turned back to the east, the path he must travel to his destination. To the east lay the great basin: a barren open land backed by a small string of mountains.

The cloud continued to expand.

Without knowing exactly why, the vision troubled the priest. A scriptural unease. He instinctively made the sign of the cross.

*****

The lead rider straddled a cremello with lots of Morgan blood. A stout, strong, showy horse with long mane and tail. The rider called himself Sam Brown. He was feared and for good reason. By reputation, he was said to have killed eight men. He knew that number to be incorrect. The real number was twelve. People tried to avoid him. Sam could feel their dread. He liked it and used their trepidation in all manner of dealings. He counted on it— nurtured it. At times, he had killed just to enhance the collective anxiety of anyone who stood in his way.

Brown wore a short, light-colored hat with a unique upturned brim and a short crown. He also carried a crossbow strapped to the back of his saddle rig. He found it useful when silence and stealth were needed.

Brown turned to one of the men who rode with him, one of the gun hands he collected depending on need. "Where's Millian?"

The rider next to Brown was Frank Roberts. Roberts told Brown he had served on the Confederate side of the war in Missouri. Depending on those present at the time, Brown had seen Roberts let people think he rode with Quantrill in judgment of Union supporters.

Brown wasn't sure Roberts had ever ridden with Quantrill, but he was ruthless enough to have been one of the Raiders.

Roberts coughed, a rumbling deep in his chest that seemed to stay with him. It never left. Though Brown used the man's talents, he had a consistent fear of being infected by whatever lurked inside Roberts chest. It sounded contagious.

Roberts spit out whatever had risen from his throat. "Millian's a dandy." The words were uttered almost matter of fact. Roberts didn't even turn to face Brown when he responded. Disdain dripped from his voice.

"I've told you before, he's a spineless ladies' man who'll get you in trouble." This time Roberts turned and almost spat the words at Brown. His voice carried his contempt for Millian. It came out just like the contagion that lurked in his cough. Just then his horse, a near black liver bay, stumbled but only slightly. Roberts gently lifted the reins. "Steady, son."

Brown scowled. "You might be right. He does love the ladies. But he knows how to steal. Comes in handy when you're trying to get information on things like payroll shipments."

Roberts shook his head in disagreement, clearly not impressed.

Brown robbed people. He robbed stages, banks, saloons, or individual businessmen. Brown relished taking someone's hard-earned cash and robbing people of their lives. But to date, he had not pursued his thefts within the confines of Virginia City.

There, he enjoyed the reputation of a feared man to the fullest. There, though no sheriff or official law, he tried his best to avoid any overt criminal activity. People had heard of his feats. They'd heard of the men he'd killed. Brown reveled in the distance townspeople kept, all generated by his measure of notoriety. He did not want to jeopardize it; liked townsfolk giving him a wide berth. Brown normally posed as a traveling gambler. He found welcome in the saloons and at the gambling tables. He fit into this city, a place where no one questioned another man's background. Many had even approached to join in his exploits.

"We need to do this quick and get back to Virginia City." Brown's voice held no small hint of longing, clearly a wish to return. He felt a connection to the town.

4

Virginia City was a wide-open collection of hard men and women. Miners, engineers, whores, wranglers, and machinists all worked or plied their trades in one of the most intimidating hillside environments on earth. The whole town sat on a series of bench cuts into the side of Mount Davidson. Townspeople found it an effort just to walk the slopes about town. And that was the nature of things above ground. Life challenged those working hundreds of feet below in the mines far more than folks who toiled above the surface.

Not Brown, though. He liked to find opportunities to take money from people who earned it with hard labor or those successful in their business. Whether at a gambling table or at the wrong end of a leveled gun, Brown excelled at taking money from others. And to do it, he needed information.

The best information on how to take money from others usually came from illegally obtained sources. Sources John Millian knew how to tap. Millian's ability to secure information was why Brown kept him around.

"We don't need Millian for this part of the job. He's no good with a gun, anyways. What I need him for is information, something he provides right regular." Brown hardly ever pushed to justify the existence of anyone. But Millian brought invaluable information regarding shipments of bullion, payrolls, or other avenues Brown could pursue to lighten the load of a target's resources.

"We got Elmer and Charley. They should be good for what we need to do." Brown gazed forward as if looking into the future.

To confirm his thoughts, Brown then turned in his saddle to check the riders to his left and right. Assessing his manpower, he rotated back to Roberts. "Charley's solid. He'll do whatever is needed, but he don't say much. He's always kind of grim."

Roberts nodded. "Charley don't talk much ever."

Charley Waverly rode a small gray roan gelding with short strong legs. Most roans were either gray, red, or the valued blue. But this roan had a different color. The gray spots were muted by the pale white undercoat and held a tint of green in the sun. Brown had never seen a horse of such a color.

Roberts interrupted Brown's thoughts. "Heard Charley fought in the war. Apparently, he was some type of officer because he's carried that sword ever since." Roberts nodded his hat in the direction of the long, thin weapon slapping both Waverly's side and the side of his trotting horse.

Brown chuckled. "Knowing Charley, he might have killed his ranking officer in the middle of a battle and took if from him. He's always talkin' about reapin' what you sow or something like that."

Brown turned to his right to see the last rider in the group.

"The nostrils on Elmer's new horse are already blood red. Almost matches his sorrel coat." Brown shook his head. "The color of fire matches its insane rider. Elmer is twisted."

"Yeah," followed Roberts with another cough. "But Elmer's good both with his gun and the peculiar curved dagger he carries. Said it comes from Arabia. I don't even know where it is, but he acts as if that makes it a grand weapon."

Brown kept the rest of his thoughts about Elmer to himself. The less said the better. But Elmer was crazy, and he knew it. A problem which required regular attention.

Brown was not his real name. He was born Sutton, Samuel Eldridge Sutton. Brown was a convenient identity he'd used for some five years following a murder and a quick move to another town. He just chose the first name that came to mind, and it stuck.

Brown had a brother, an identical twin brother: Drake Sutton. *Had* was the key word. His brother was dead. Shot by a rancher in the Carson Valley, where they were headed.

The rancher's name was Will Toal. Brown heard his brother had signed on to work with the Central Pacific Railroad as a gun hand. Drake had been very quick and very good with his handgun. He'd heard about a shoot-out near Carson City some four years before. The argument started when the railroad tried to serve eviction notices on a group of ranchers who all owned property in the Carson Valley.

In the aftermath of the initial gun fight, this rancher named Toal had shot his brother from a distance with a long-range rifle. To Brown, it sounded like a bushwhacking, a coward's way of shooting someone. He had not heard the reason for the shooting. It didn't matter to Brown. All that mattered was Will Toal had killed his brother, and he would pay.

Looking west up the road, Roberts nodded. "There's a rider ahead."

Brown had seen the figure in a long black cassock and wide-brimmed hat. "It's the priest from Carson City. Seen him there once. Interesting a priest should be here right now."

Brown's gaze turned upward with question written over his face as if the billowy clouds above held some answer to his query. Satisfied with whatever answer might have been delivered, he looked back down in the direction of the cassock-clad rider. "We keep movin'. No one's gonna stop us—certainly not some unarmed religious. He's a meaning-less relic. Ride on by."

Brown's right-hand flexed several times as it moved and hovered over his handgun. He noticed Roberts watching.

"Seen yer hand flex like that before. The next thing that usually happens is you draw, and somebody dies. Thinkin' of killin' a priest?"

"Not today, but you never know."

7

The party passed the priest without slowing or paying any heed.

Roberts looked at Brown again. "We've robbed banks, stages, and payrolls together. But we're headed out to a ranch where you've been told the guy you want dead is gone on some job. Not sure I understand what we're doin' this for."

Brown spoke in a low voice staring straight ahead. "Because he has to feel a loss. If I just shot him from behind a rock out on some road, he'd never know the loss I've felt since he killed Drake. Drake was my twin. Twins are special close. I feel like a piece of me is missin'. This hillbilly rancher must feel the same kind of heavy loss first."

Killing Toal with a rifle had some appeal that was not necessarily out of character for Brown. Not as quick on the draw as his deceased brother, he confronted his targets only on rare occasion. He preferred to surprise his prey when in a position of superiority and they were either caught off guard or unarmed altogether. But if he killed Toal with a rifle, the man would never know why he'd been hunted, no less killed. Will Toal had to know and feel the loss. He had to know the name of the man who'd cause the loss. Sam Brown. He'd know the name.

Brown now turned to Roberts. "So, we are going to take something from him. Something he finds dear. A part of his family. A part of him. Just like he did to me." Anger welled up from deep within Brown, the kind of anger which circumvented rational thought. The kind of anger which led to action without restraint.

Brown could see Roberts' reaction. Roberts physically tensed, probably because he'd seen Brown reach these states of anger before. In such a state, someone usually died, even if the victim had not been directly responsible for the onset of Brown's anger.

He coughed, this time was even raspier than before. "So that's why we're going to this ranch?"

"Yep, we're going to take Will Toal's sons. It's not well-known, but Millian says he found a source who told him Toal has two sons. They're twins. If I take those kids, it should make him feel the loss just like I did. When Toal loses his twins, it will be like me losing my twin brother. Seems a fitting payment to me. We'll ask for a ransom, say twenty-five thousand dollars. According to the information we got from Millian, Toal is doing well with his cattle sales, but he'll have to work at collecting that amount. He'll sweat to get the money. He'll worry. When he comes to pay the ransom, I'll kill the boys while he watches. Then I'll kill him. I want him to see the face of Drake, my face, as it happens."

Chapter Two

February arrived with the bitter bite of cold. It hung at the base of the Eastern Sierras and brought a chill that the sun could not warm. The crisp air smelled great, but the constant wind cut through clothes as if they weren't there.

Will Toal kept his tall, full-bodied gray mustang at a leisurely pace on his way back home. He pulled his collar high and wore his chaps but not because he planned to work cattle today. He wore them as another layer against the winter.

"Steady, boy. We got a late start this afternoon, so we will camp somewhere near Lake Topaz tonight. No sense trying to ride over Simee Pass in the dark. We'll get an early start tomorrow and be home before sunset."

Will often talked to his horse, Powder, as if the animal welcomed the ongoing conversation. He almost anticipated the horse responding.

"Might be a long winter this year. Cold came early and hard. Got to keep a watch on the herd when we get home."

The horse kept his head pointed down the road. No response again.

"It'll be nice to get home to our little Jack's Valley. We did a good job helping those folks on the ranch there south of Topaz. When Henry Millard asked me to help straighten out the resident ranch manager, I wasn't sure I should do it. But I'm glad we did. Turns out their ranch land is at the base of the Eastern Sierras just like ours. I pointed out how we managed the grassland and rotated the beef stock, which should help them with their production over the next few years."

A guttural sound came out of the horse's mouth, probably no more than an equine version of a cough. But Will took it as affirmation of his previous statement.

"I knew you'd agree. It's only a sixty-mile trip home. We could make it in two days if we pushed. In the end, it isn't such a long trip to help out a business partner who'd helped us."

Will paused to look up at the Sierras on his left as he headed north. No foothills leading up to the mountain range. Here, the Sierras rose like a granite wall straight up from the valley floor.

"Yep, son, things are going pretty good right now. Life's moved fast, but it's been a long road from my days as a Reb sniper during the war and then our spell together as a Texas Ranger.

This time, there was no audible response from Powder.

"What, nothing to say? You didn't like those days of riding down Comanches and the lawless with the Rangers any more than I did, right? A year of that was enough. I'm glad those days came to an end."

Powder then issued a standard horse exhale, a cross between a sneeze and a snort.

"Exactly. Never hesitated to make sure the bad guys got what they deserved, but I'd snort too if I had to describe the long days in the saddle heading into God knows what kind of trouble. We never knew what we'd face until it was lookin' at us. We had a lot more fun working cattle after that on the haciendas with Juan and Raúl. Those days were a lot more enjoyable."

The horse lifted his head a little higher than his normal rhythmic rise and fall. Will took it as another affirmative response.

"I knew you'd agree. Then we have the boys. Glad they're in my life, but that ain't quite settled, is it?"

The horse reached around to nip at his side, probably looking to shoo away a fly, but Will took it differently.

"No sense in getting pissy. Don't have to nip me. I know it ain't perfect."

Will then tried to turn his thoughts away from that unsettled aspect of his world and focus back on the business side of his life, cattle.

"Our ranch looks pretty good compared to Millard's ranch south of Topaz back there in Antelope Valley. We run about a thousand head of beef on three thousand acres in the Jack's Valley. We couldn't sustain that many head if we didn't rotate the cattle into different pastures like we do. It's all about how to manage the growth of the grass. Ends up putting more weight on the beef stock."

No response from Powder so Will just kept the thought going.

"Our rotations must have been what Mr. Millard noticed. He felt his ranch in Antelope Valley could do the same. Millard Luce Cattle Company is amazing. The company owns over one million acres, but Millard knows what each ranch is doing. He keeps close tabs on all of them."

Will took it as a nice compliment when Henry Millard asked him to travel to Antelope Valley. But that thought led back to the discussion as to whether he should go. The discussion had been with the mother of his twin sons, Luke and Sean. Her name was Beth.

*****

"Doesn't Henry Millard have anyone else on the planet who can gather up and feed a bunch of cows?" Beth had sounded a bit desperate with her argument.

"He asked and in a nice way. I don't have to go, but Henry Millard bailed us out in the fight against the railroad. He's the one who offered to create the Association of the Carson Valley Ranchers, giving us all access to the San Francisco meat markets when Fort Churchill closed and we couldn't sell our beef. I feel like I owe him. It's only going to be for a month or two, and then I'll be back."

"I still don't see why it has to be you. You know I have to work in town, and I count on you to be here with the boys when I drop them off."

Will shook his head. "Raúl, his son Juan, and Juan's wife, María, can take care of them when you drop them off."

Beth hesitated. "They are all wonderful, but they're not you."

"Beth, you know they can do this for a month or so. Juan, María, and Raúl have been with me since we wrangled in New Mexico. They love the twins. There is nothing they wouldn't do to protect them."

Beth nodded.

"And Mr. Millard offered to pay me to do this. With the extra money, we can expand the bunkhouse, buy more cattle, hire another hand, and maybe even build a new, larger ranch house. All for two months of work."

Will had been trying for over four years to navigate the unique, complicated relationship he had with Beth. He considered his words carefully before continuing. "Beth, we make decisions together, even though we are not married. I run any of my ideas about the boys by you before I do anything. I know this might be a change in our regular routine, but the benefits are pretty big. I have to do it."

Beth didn't respond right away.

Will knew he'd opened the door to a conversation they'd had multiple times over the previous couple of years. Though not married, in many aspects, they acted as if they were. However, they did not live together. "Look, I know it's been tough, but I think we've worked out a good routine."

"You're the one who gets to stay here on the ranch while I live in Carson City and travel all the way out here two to three times a week. I'm the one doing the heavy lifting."

"Beth, I run a ranch. I admire the fact you have kept your job at the land office. You know I have offered and stand ready to pay for all the boys' expenses. But you wanted to work."

Will knew only a limited group of his trusted ranch crew were aware of the whole story. No one else in town knew Will was the father of the twins, now over four years old, who acted as if they were joint kings of the Valley. Will loved them dearly and loved Beth, too, but they had a history. Will had still not arrived at the point where he felt like bending knee and asking Beth to be his wife. While a major bone of contention between them, Beth knew she was responsible for Will's hesitation.

"This all goes back to when I hit you over the head, doesn't it?" Beth sounded defeated.

Will didn't like this as it was the touchiest of topics between them. Her betrayal just under five years earlier, albeit claimed in the name of protection, had left Will with the unease of commitment. He had yet to overcome it.

"Hit me with the barrel of a handgun." Will's voice held anger as well as embarrassment in again reaching back to this same event in their relationship.

Beth had been looking directly into his eyes. "Maybe I should hit you there again." She grinned.

At that point, Will had known two things. First, he felt deeply for this lady. She'd taken his rebuke with humor rather than additional confrontation. Second, he knew he would head off to help turn around Henry Millard's ranch.

"Not sure my head could take another wallop like your last one."

Will felt like reaching out and holding Beth. But he suppressed it. There had been no physical contact between them since the strike on the head. Not that both wouldn't have welcomed it, even longed for it. There had been one evening before the betrayal when both had let their guard down. The twins were the result. But in the years since, both Will and Beth realized they could not fall back there again. At least not until Will bent his knee. Will knew Beth prayed each Sunday for it to happen. But not yet. Up to now, Will thought they'd fallen into a regular pattern of life. The daily routines had become comfortable; at least, he thought so. No need to make any changes.

*****

A gust of wind brought Will out of his reverie. He continued his conversation with Powder, who kept moving on at a smooth, strong pace.

"Those Antelope Valley hired hands seem to appreciate the new barn and bunkhouse we built, too. Thick walls to keep out the winter. Mr. Millard insists on good facilities for the hands. He figures it will translate into good care for the beef."

As in all prior conversations with his horse, the mustang did not respond.

"That's the Walker River we're following off to the right. The river's named for Joe Walker. The snow up top of the Sierras melts, keeping it running strong year-round."

Powder just kept walking.

Will tightened his large neck scarf, trying to fend off the bitter evening wind. While not as strong as the winds in the Carson Valley, the late-day blows here still cut through his clothes.

"Yep, Joe Walker was one of the most respected and admired trappers and trackers among the original mountain men. Those were tough men to impress."

Will gazed up at the cold mountain peaks and thought of times passed.

"I love to hear stories of other people from the Old Country. Did I tell ya my grandpa came from Scotland? Settled in Georgia. That's where I was born. Walker's people were Scots, too. I heard from the longtime ranchers in the Carson Valley that Walker still rides through on rare occasions from his ranch in California."

Will looked out over his horse's head and noticed the animal's ears were relaxed and moved with the rhythm of his walk. Knowing the horse had keener abilities of smell and hearing than his own, Powder's relaxed state confirmed for Will there was no threat of danger nearby.

"The older ranchers tell me Walker came west as a very young man in the Bonneville expedition out of St. Louis in 1832. By the time they got to the Rockies, Bonneville knew Walker to be a quiet, capable leader. After crossing the Rockies, he sent Walker and Old Bill Williams straight west with forty-eight men to find a route to California.

"Walker followed the Humboldt River on to the Carson Valley then over the Sierras at Immigrant Pass and south through California's central valley. In the south of California, he crossed the Sierras back east and headed north back to the Carson Valley. He completed one big loop of the unexplored West."

He had little if any expectations from the horse, who silently plotted on. It didn't stop Will from continuing with his story.

"Walker and Old Bill Williams were the main scouts for the well-known expedition led by John C. Freemont in '42. I've been told that after the expedition Freemont and his wife, Jesse, wrote a flowery picture of the land west of the Rockies, and their description became a magnet and basic map for the coming migration west. Freemont's wife talked about Kit Carson in that report, but not Joe Walker. She must have had a crush on young Carson to leave out naming the experienced scouts who knew the territory that far west of the Rockies. But as a result, Kit Carson got all the dime novel fame as Freemont's guide, but it was Joe Walker and Old Bill Williams who led Freemont to California using the same route they discovered with Bonneville in '32.

"A couple of years later, Walker led the first wagons from St. Louis through the Rockies and over Immigrant Pass on to the gold fields at Sutter's Mill. Walker's the one who showed everyone the wagon path to California's gold. He opened the door to the Gold Rush."

Will looked back down at the animal's strong legs below him continuing their consistent motion up the trail and marveled how Powder could keep this up day after day. At this point, it didn't matter if the horse listened or not.

"More importantly, to the mountain men who followed and traveled with him, in twenty-five years of exploring and leading companies of men through hostile, unexplored territory, Joe Walker lost only one man under his command. The lost man died falling into an abandoned, broken cache, one of those holes dug by the mountain men to store their plews, that had been poorly covered. The mountain men would skin the beaver as soon as they were trapped and stretch the pelt on circular piece of willow. They called it a plew.

"Plews were stacked in a pack of thirty to fifty and kept in a cache until spring when they would pull them out and head to the Rendezvous where most of the trappers would gather in predesignated locations to sell their furs to suppliers. The fur companies would carry flint, powder, and shot along with other necessities over the Rockies and sell those in return for the valuable beaver pelts. The company agents would pay about six hundred dollars for a pack of beaver plews. At a time when the standard wage was a dollar fifty a day for a city worker, six hundred dollars per pack was a lot of money."

Nothing but puffs of misted air came out of Powder.

"See, Powder, we're kinda walkin' along the same trail taken by one of my ancestors. Walker was a humble man, but not many people know about him. Sounds stupid but riding along here feels like a connection to old Joe Walker who did all those remarkable things years ago."

Daylight waned. Will pulled up and stepped off Powder. He camped beneath a good size rock outcropping at the bottom of the mountain slope. The rock ceiling would provide some shelter from the wind or rain. Rain was always unpredictable, especially in the mountains. Also, there was grass nearby for Powder.

He pulled out his set of hobbles and braced up the horse's two front feet. "There, that should keep ya from wanderin' off too far."

Will released the breast collar, main cinch, and rear roping cinch and then pulled off his saddle and blanket. The split reins still hung from the bridle to the ground, but the mustang had not moved in keeping with his training. If one of those split reins touched the ground with Will off his back, the big gray would not move. Will stepped up to the horse's head, opened his palm, and rubbed up and down from Powder's nose to the crest of his skull. Every horse loved having someone rub this area which was so hard for them to scratch themselves. Will undid the bridle and pulled the reins from the horse's neck. He then stood up and gave the gray a tap on his hind end.

"Now, go get something to eat. Be ready to cover ground tomorrow."

Days on the east side of the Sierras ended quickly this time of year. Shadows flowed downslope early and quick as the sun fell below the high mountain crest. With those shadows came another temperature drop. Dinner would be cold jerky. Will started looking for wood to build a fire. He would need a good-sized fire for warmth as he traveled light without a full bedroll. His bedroll tonight would be his horse blanket and chaps. It would not be comfortable. But tomorrow, he'd be back in his own bed.

Chapter Three

1873 February
Washoe Gentlemen's Club Virginia City, NV

"We've come a long way, John."

Jack O'Brien directed his comments to his friend, John William Mackay, who, like himself, came from dirt poor origins in Ireland by way of the most hellish slums of New York. Both had lost parents at an early age, forcing them to find work on the streets to help support their families. Mackay later apprenticed as a shipwright in New York, gaining good carpenter skills which proved invaluable to later mining employers. Their lives had connected after each had sailed around the Horn to San Francisco headed for the promise of gold and quick riches.

O'Brien met Mackay working the gold fields in Downieville, California. They'd toiled there together for more than five years with little success. Gold mining in Downieville took place on surface waterways, otherwise called placer mining. O'Brien remembered how Mackay had demonstrated to his superiors a knack for working with wood sluices and building structures. In addition, he was a natural leader of men. O'Brien had always respected Mackay and his character. They had been good partners.

"Remember how we walked for weeks from Downieville to get here in Virginia City, arriving with only my fifty cents?" said O'Brien.

"Which you promptly threw away before we walked into town," chastised Mackay. He never could abide wasting money. It had been too hard to come by all his life.

O'Brien chuckled. "I thought it only fitting we enter the city the way we looked: penniless."

Mackay shook his head, but O'Brien knew from the look on his face that Mackay realized this conversation was not some offhanded walk through their collective memories. Something more was going on here, and Mackay figured he'd have to wait and listen.

O'Brien took a sip of his beer and sat back in his seat. "We arrived here in Virginia City back in 1859. It was supposed to be a placer gold mining town. We've made it into a below-grade silver mining town. Early on, we noticed the new mining approach at the California Mine here in town. While that mine's main shaft dropped vertically from the opening at the middle of town, the superintendent thought it'd be a good idea to dig a horizontal crosscut from down the slope into the same vertical shaft. The crosscut created a new method to access additional veins of ore. We sold the owners of the Union Mine on the idea we could do the same."

Mackay smiled. "And we got *feet* for that. Our first stake. Our first piece of the ownership value in any mine."

"Yes, we got *feet*. When you first told me we had purchased *feet*, I thought it was food, like some kind of pork in the Old Country. Little did I know at the time a stake or percentage in a mine was measured in *feet*."

Both men sat in wide leather chairs inside the Washoe Club located in the most developed part of the Virginia City. Located at 112 South C Street, the Washoe Club was right in the middle of the most active, diverse, vibrant, and financially crazed town in America. O'Brien looked around. This was a special place: a club within a saloon, reserved for only the wealthiest in Virginia City. Both men had lived hard lives. Though only in their forties, they had seen this town in its infancy when tents and dugouts clung to the side of Mount Davidson housing men desperate to find easy wealth while they held off the immediate threat of starvation. Now thousands of residents and businesses in more permanent structures stretched over this same ever-sliding slope. O'Brien smiled at the thought. He and Mackay had seen it grow from those determined origins to the financial influence it held today.

"Why are we having this conversation about our past?" asked Mackay. "We were both there."

O'Brien hesitated. He looked down and then leveled his gaze at a man whose friendship had been galvanized through distressed winters on the rivers of Downieville and later in the bowels of Mount Davidson when they had no money and barely enough food to survive.

"John, we used our stake in the Union Mine to buy feet in the Hale & Norcross Mine. With the stake in the Union, we made more money than we could ever imagine when we hit a new ore vein. You told me once when we were in California all you wanted was to make twenty-five thousand dollars so you could take care of your mother and your sister back in New York and never have to work again. Well, you've now made close to a million dollars. So have I."

"What's your point?" Mackay said, although O'Brien could sense he knew the exact direction they were now headed and the predictable end to the conversation.

"Why did we have to risk it all, John? In 1871, you pushed me and Jim Fair to join you in buying a series of interests in multiple smaller mines, including the Consolidated Virginia and California. Those mines were distanced from the producing veins in the main portion of the Comstock Lode. The mines in the city were the successful ones, like the Ophir, the Mexican, and Yellow Jacket."

O'Brien watched for a reaction. Mackay always appeared composed. O'Brien could read little on his friend's face, but he continued. "The cost for the Consolidated drained our combined savings, a huge risk. We were forced to combine our capital with two new partners from San Francisco: James Flood and William O'Brien, no relation to myself. While our stake in the Hale & Norcross is still producing, production has waned. You convinced all of us it was a risk worth taking. But unless we strike something soon, the investment could sink us all."

"Jack, if you want out, just say so."

"How are you going to raise the money to buy me out?" O'Brien did not want to ruin their friendship, but he feared losing everything. He did not want to have to start from scratch again. He had tired of the hours of hard labor below the surface. He liked his current status as a mine owner over that of an employee swinging a fourteen-pound sledgehammer hitting solid rock thousands of times a day.

"I'll go to the other partners and raise the money. Bill O'Brien and Flood are really good at it."

Jack nodded. "You have come to a steady separation of the work effort. You and James Fair run the mining operations. Meantime, Flood and William O'Brien handle the stock and place investments for the partnership in San Francisco to raise additional money."

"Jack, if necessary to get you paid, I will personally travel to San Francisco to make sure we collect the needed capital for any buyout. I will go with Flood and try to talk with other businessmen I've met. There seem to be plenty of people willing to buy into our silver mines. You and I know better than anyone why we need to continue the crosscut sideways into the hill to reach the main vertical shaft of the Consolidated and California Mines. We could hit something big. With the crosscut, we'll be one thousand feet below city level. No one is that deep. And you know the signs of quartz coming up from the mine. The potential that far down in the Consolidated and California is huge."

"You might find ore, and you might just dig and hit more dirt."

"Jack, I've known you for too long. We've been through too much together. If you don't want to continue in the investment, you should not do it. We will remain friends no matter what you decide."

This is what O'Brien had wanted to hear. He had already decided to opt out. Mackay had just left him the opening to do so without damaging their friendship. Through straightforward, honest hard work, John Mackay had overcome the stigma of being poor and Irish to become accepted by both investors and miners. A fair and incorruptible businessman, Mackay had never strayed from his aim to make money from producing ore, not from speculating on mining as most in this town did.

"Then I will pass," said Jack. "I think I'll move to San Francisco myself and get away from mining."

"Let's both go to San Francisco soon. I'll get Jim Fair, and we can travel together. You can look for homes to purchase, and we'll look for people with money to buy you out."

"That sounds good, John. The sooner the better. And we need to settle on a price."

"Jack O'Brien, you set the price for your collective interests here in Virginia City, and I'll pay what you ask. You've been at my side ever since we left California. No amount of money could compare to what we've been through."

O'Brien shook his head. "Most people think of you as a solid businessman who can be trusted or as an employer thoughtful of his workers. But John, I know you simply as a good and fair man. Just pay me the current market price for the feet I currently own, and we can separate our interests as friends."

Chapter Four

1873 February
Camp, East of Jack's Valley, NV

Darkness. Dawn had yet to arrive. The black sky was marred by starlight alone. The moon shriveled in a shadowless whisp. The absence of light matched his mood. The darkness fit his intent. He was bent on doing harm, revenge for what had been done to his kin. He lay flat on his back looking up into the ink abyss. He wondered if the cover of black would provide a sign today, instruction as to how he should proceed. He waited but no sign came.

Sam Brown turned inside his canvas bedroll—the outside of which was stiff and hard as if frozen. He looked to the fire, now almost dead, certainly not providing any real heat.

Brown kicked off the top of his bedroll and grabbed his boots.

"Roberts, wake up." The damp, morning chill hit his already cold demeanor. It did not make for a good mood.

Roberts rolled over, looking at Brown. One glance at his boss's dour face he started moving.

"We have to get to Toal's ranch early. We need to look the place over some before we ride in. Millian's contact says the mother drops the boys off about three days a week in the morning. I want to hit the ranch before noon so we can ride out and get to Mound House City before dark."

Roberts rolled out, put his boots on, and walked to where Chuck Waverly slept. He gave Waverly a not-too-gentle shove with his boot. "Chuck, I'll start getting the horses saddled. Get the coffee going and meet me to help finish up."

Waverly woke quicker than most. He immediately rolled out and started to dress. A man of few words, he stood, stretched, put on his well-worn hat and adjusted his ever-present saber. He looked straight at Roberts and dipped his hat brim in wordless acknowledgement.

Brown watched as the group quickly packed up camp. They had been riding light. There wasn't much to load beyond the saddles, bedrolls, and riding rigs. The sun was about to come up. The cold still lingered heavy and sharp in the clear air.

"Check your guns," said Brown. "Might need them."

"My gun is always ready, but I thought we came here just ride into a ranch with nothing but a couple of working hands?"

This comment came from Elmer Lennox, a man of slight, lean build. Dust wafted from his pants as he strapped on his firearm. He was perpetually dirty. Lennox liked to live on the road and hated towns. As a result, he rarely came anywhere near the bathtub. Brown generally kept his distance from Lennox as his odor could be tolerated only in small doses. But Brown kept telling himself, Lennox was very quick with a handgun.

Brown turned to face Lennox. "True, but right now, we don't know how many of them there will be or whether they're on the watch for trouble. Millian says this guy, Toal, is young, but he's known to run a tight ranch with good people. Based on what Millian heard about the shoot-out in Carson City a few years ago, he said we should not underestimate Toal or any of his ranch hands."

Lennox grinned and displayed several teeth brown enough to indicate they'd fall out of his head soon enough. His eyes opened exceptionally wide with one of his grins. The resulting image appeared plain sinister. It fit his personality.

Brown knew all the members of his group including their strengths and weaknesses. Elmer's strength lay in his quick gun. Elmer's weakness lay in the same quick gun, especially because of its connection to a brain with little or no judgment. The combination had led Elmer to take shots he shouldn't. Brown tried to keep his instructions to Lennox simple and direct in order to remove the need for decisions as much as possible.

"Elmer, keep your itchy trigger finger away from your holster until there is gunplay from the other side. And under no circumstances are those two young boys to be hurt. Is that clear? Those boys will be our ticket to getting paid. If they end up dead, all we'll get is people tracking us across the West."

The grin departed. Elmer's mouth now turned down at the corners.

"I'm not waitin' for someone to draw and get a shot off. I'll be clearing leather long before, and their ain't nothin' goin' to stop me, Brown, not even you."

"The boys are not to be hurt. Elmer, if those boys get hurt because of something you do, then you'll be dealing with me. And that goes for the rest of you, too." Brown spun his gaze around to every one of the men now standing around the dying fire. Roberts nodded. Waverly said nothing, as usual. Lennox remained quiet for a change. Point made.

Brown turned on his heel. "Let's ride."

*****

For two hours the group rode through the larger Carson Valley until they came to a slight rise overlooking a smaller adjacent valley which butted right up to the Sierras. Brown turned to see his group as they followed. It had not taken long before the mist from the horses' nostrils began pumping out sideways. Moving at a lope three abreast behind him, the collection of horses looked like some animal locomotive. The aggregate of pulmonary puffs and blows along with the sound of pounding hooves struck him as an equine steam engine heading up a hill. Add to this the four multiply armed men with collars high and hats pulled low, the image was near apocalyptic.

They had moved at a steady pace from their original camp to the present rise. Brown pulled up and dismounted. He stood now overlooking what he thought to be Toal Ranch.

"Millian said the ranch we're lookin' for sits west of a big bend in the Carson River in some small valley right at the base of the Sierras. The ranch has a red barn. The barn down there looks like what he was tryin' to describe."

Roberts swiveled his gaze from the snow-capped mountains to look north. "And didn't you say the mother would drop the boys off in the morning? Well, that looks like a woman with two kids in a wagon coming from Carson City heading toward the ranch house."

Brown followed his gaze. "Yep, looks like we found the right ranch. Let's wait and watch for a couple of minutes. Cinch up tight and get ready."

*****

Beth had a rein in each hand. She drove a single horse pulling what had originally been a wagon designed to haul loads. While functional, it was neither fancy nor comfortable. She glanced at the twins, Luke and Sean, to her right on the seat above the load bed. Both held on tight in case of quick stops and turns. She knew they loved to ride on anything that moved. But she hated their constant fights to sit next to her. On those special days when she'd allow it, the one closest to her would get to drive first. She chuckled at the thought they were so different despite being born at the same time from the same parents. Each tried in his way to maneuver next to her. It never stopped. They had tussled over their seat position the whole way out to the ranch.

"We are almost there. Settle down you two. We are almost to the ranch."

Beth switched both reins into her left hand so she could use her right to try and separate the two attempting to resolve the never-ending conflict. Though she achieved some separation, the adversarial fight for seat position did not end. She pulled into the compound surrounded on its three sides by the ranch house, a barn, and the bunkhouse, respectively.

"Ah, *Señora* Beth."

Raúl walked up to the wagon. Beth had never quite figured out Raúl's age. She knew him to be the father of Juan, Will's other trusted hand, but under his wide-brimmed sombrero, he looked almost the same age as his son. Short and stocky in stature, there wasn't an ounce of fat on the man. Raul, Juan and his wife María had all come west with Will. Raúl never talked about personal things. Beth had come to know Raul as a tireless worker, one who saw what needed to be done before having to be asked or instructed. And she knew he loved the boys.

"Raúl, can you take these two off my hands? They're driving me crazy."

Raúl looked up at the boys with an artificial frown.

"Ah, it is too bad for the little *Niño's*. They want to drive only wagon horses. I was wanting to take a ride and theenk they go with Raúl." The word *think* came out as if there were a series of E's extended in the middle of the word. "But if *el Niño's* just want to sit on some wagon, I guess Raúl must go alone."

Beth could see the contrived and almost humorous false sadness. The boys sat perfectly still, dead quiet. Raúl had grabbed their complete attention. Beth watched as the young brains tried to process what was going on. She tried to hide her grin as she watched the slow-motion deliberation at work. It was if she could see something invisible. Then Sean, in his typical overly loud voice, broke the stillness.

"I want to ride a horse. Can I, Mom? I'm almost five years old now."

There it was. In its most simple distilled essence, a decision made.

"Me too," said Luke.

Both boys jumped up on the running board and grabbed their mother.

"Can we go riding?"

Beth laughed at the brilliant way Raúl had led the two little ones to the planned activity.

He turned to the boys. "Raúl needs two vaqueros to ride his horses. Are you two *Niño's* vaqueros?"

It was Luke's turn to look puzzled. His head spun from Raúl to his mother as if it would somehow solve his quandary.

Finally, Luke looked to Beth. "Ma, are vaqueros good guys or bad guys?" It seemed as if the boys needed to place everyone on this simple scale of status in the world of adults.

"I think if you were the vaqueros, then they would be good guys."

Luke then looked back to Raúl. "I want to be a vaquero. Can I ride?"

"Two caballos are saddled next to the barn. Who's ready?"

Beth watched as the boys climbed down the side of the wagon, instinctively grabbing armrests, seat bottoms, and wheels to drop on the ground, all in an instant. She marveled at the uncanny ability of her two little ones to climb over anything. The boys started for the side of the barn. Raúl hurried after them but turned back to Beth.

"María is in the hacienda. Juan is out with cattle. Be back soon." It was all he could get out before he had to hustle after the boys before they got too close to the horses.

Beth nodded. "Thank you, Raúl. Please keep an eye on those two."

Beth then spoke to the boys, "Come back here you two." She watched as they reluctantly dragged their feet back to within arm's reach of their mother now standing next to the wagon.

Beth then bent down and looked at her boys at eye level, "You both do exactly what Raúl tells you to do, or you will not be able to go riding next time. Understand?"

Eagar to be able to ride, Sean answered, "We will Ma." Luke just nodded already preoccupied with the possibility of getting on a horse.

"Sí, *Señora*. It will be a slow, easy ride. The little vaqueros will be good. "

Beth smiled at both her sons, touched each gently on the head then turned and walked into the ranch house.

Chapter Five

Four men lay flat on a rise to the east of the small valley. Puffed bleached clouds towered above giving notice of potential inclement weather. The same white billows interrupted the sun's weak rays intermittently making long range observation difficult. There was an unearthly quiet.

Brown watched a short interchange between the woman and the man in the sombrero. "Does anyone see any hands other than the one Mex? Damn, could 'a used a sightin' glass. Hard to see em' without one when the light keeps changin' under these clouds."

Roberts shook his head. "I don't see no one else."

"Chuck, you got good eyes. You see anyone else?"

"Nope." Only a one word reply from Waverly.

Roberts waited in case Waverly might say something else. But in keeping with his established pattern, Waverly said nothing further.

Brown spoke. "Okay, get mounted."

Once astride, Brown looked to each in his group.

"Here's what we're going to do. The boys are headed out on horses with the guy in the sombrero. Those horses don't look like they can trot, much less canter. Makes sense since they're small kids, and it looks like they'll be doing nothing but walkin'.

"We'll separate the boys from the sombrero. Roberts and I will take one boy each and put them on our saddles. We'll need to ride hard from here to Mound House, so we dump the two nags the boys ride. We head back to the ranch house to tell the woman where Toal can come to pay the ransom. Then we ride out fast."

"Why don't we pay the woman a visit, a very personal visit?" The comment predictably came from Lennox.

Brown spun around, and leaned out of his saddle to come almost nose to nose with Lennox. "When we ride into the compound, no one gets off their horse. We deliver our message and get out of there fast. I need the woman to pass the message to Toal. Once that is done, we take the boys and ride. That's it."

The veins stood out on Brown's neck. He hoped his tone had been emphatic enough to cut off any further needless thoughts Lennox might have.

Brown tired of Lennox and his constant challenge to authority. Might be time to end their association, but the possibility of current events becoming public knowledge made the risk of a simple parting of ways too high. Any ending of their association was going to have to be a permanent one. So be it. After this job, Elmer would grin his last.

"What if the Mex tries to stop us?" Again, Lennox did the asking.

"Kill him. That ought to be something you can handle, Elmer."

Lennox did not spread one of his eerie grins, but he seemed satisfied.

"Let's go."

Brown spurred his horse and retraced their path down the back side of the rise, staying concealed as long as they could. They headed from there at a gallop to cut off the sombrero and the boys. He estimated they'd meet about a quarter mile from the ranch house.

*****

The sound of the horses caught Raúl's attention. There was no reason for anyone to be riding at a gallop out in the middle of the valley.

33

He knew immediately the riders were trouble. He saw one of the riders, a slender man on the left, move his hand to cover his holster. Raúl knew he had to do something and quickly.

"Boys, hold on tight." He slapped the rumps of both horses, who started to pick up their pace. However, the boys' horses had been chosen because of age and lack of spirit. Their days of moving fast were long since done. The boys had been on several rides, but they were still young and inexperienced. Raúl quickly realized the boys could not stay on their horses at even a trot. So, he told them to hold up. He pulled up his own horse between the two of theirs and looked back and forth between them. "Boys, go to hacienda, now. Raúl is going to talk to these men. Keep going."

Sean looked at the oncoming men. "Are those good guys or bad guys?"

Raúl tried to hide his concern from his voice. "*Vamanos, andele.*" They look like bad hombres. Bad guys. Go."

The boys kept their horses at a walk and headed back to the ranch. Raúl could see the concern on Sean's face. Of the twins, he was more in tune with the emotions of those around him. Sean whimpered just once. Luke kept riding but looked over his shoulder.

Raúl turned and headed straight at the oncoming horsemen. He saw the slender man reach for his gun. Raúl did likewise, lifting the trigger safety on his own weapon. Both men cleared leather about the same time. The distance separating the two horsemen closed fast. Raúl shot first and missed. The slender man had moved slightly ahead of the other three, deliberately raised his gun, aimed and fired. About the same instant Raúl fired his second round again wide. But slender did not miss. Raúl felt a slug hit his left shoulder, and it rocked him violently in his saddle. He did all he could not to fall to the ground and keep hold of the reins. He tried to raise his gun for a third shot, but the separating distance had now closed to a matter of yards. The next shot hit Raúl square in the chest, sending him to the ground. The slender man pulled up, circling the prone body. Raúl tried to roll over, but the man shot him a third time.

*****

Brown and the other two riders pulled up near Lennox. Brown looked down at the body and said, "Roberts, you get one of the boys, and I'll get the other. Charley and Elmer, put the Mex up on his horse and pull him behind us."

Roberts took off at a canter in chase of the boys, who were now only two hundred yards ahead.

Brown spun his horse and followed Roberts. Each grabbed a bridle and then a boy, pulling them onto their own saddles. Luke and Sean both fought. Sean screamed as Brown grabbed him off his horse. "You're a bad guy!"

Brown smiled. "Oh, yes, kid. I am a bad guy. Now stop your screaming." Brown put the boy in the saddle in front of him. He could hold him with his left arm while the reins remained in his left hand. The boy on Brown's saddle got louder. Brown reversed his hand and slapped the boy across his face. Fear spread across the child's face. The boy stopped screaming but continued to cry.

The four riders collected and moved toward the ranch house. They covered the ground in a matter of minutes. As they rounded into the compound, Brown drew his gun. There were two women already running out of the house. One of the women looked Spanish. The second female was a white woman with light colored hair who yelled out the names: "Sean! Luke!"

Brown came around the side of the house with a gun in his right hand. He shortened up his reins and fired a shot about ten feet in front of the light-haired woman who instantly stopped in her tracks. Roberts, with Luke in a similar position on his saddle, came to a stop next to Brown. He had his gun leveled at the second female.

The woman with the light-colored hair looked as if she had seen a ghost.

"That's far enough. I've got your boys. You tell Will Toal it'll cost him twenty-five thousand dollars to get 'em back. He has two weeks. Tell him to get the money and take it to the Delta Saloon in Virginia City. Have him ask for Sam Sutton, brother of Drake Sutton, the man he killed. Tell him if he doesn't get the money, he'll feel the same loss I felt. If he doesn't come up with the money, the boys will die. And it won't be pleasant."

She started to speak, but Brown fired off another shot, this time closer to her feet.

"No need to speak. I got no reason to listen to anything you might want to say. Just tell Will Toal what I've told you."

Waverly and Lennox rode up pulling a horse with Raúl draped face-down over the top.

Lennox snarled. "And you can take this." He reached out and flipped Raúl off the saddle, dropping him in a heap.

María shrieked. "Raúl!"

Brown looked down at the body and then back to the women.

"He was a brave man. He tried to protect the boys. Rode straight at us, one against four. He lost."

Brown's gaze settled back on the blonde.

"Two weeks. Tell Toal it's all he's got."

Roberts fired a third shot. This time, the shot split the distance between the two women.

36

Brown spun his horse and headed out of the compound. The other riders followed.

Sean kept trying to turn back so he could look at his mother.

"Mommy!"

"Sean! Luke! I will come get you."

Brown turned to see the light-haired woman as she sank to her knees.

Chapter Six

A knock came at the door of the home of John Mackay. His butler was busy with something else, so Mackay answered the door himself.

"James Fair, to what do I owe the honor of this visit here in the middle of the day?"

Fair stepped through the front door into what functioned as Mackay's workplace and center of mining operations. The office spread along almost an entire side of the house. A great room on the same floor was accessed from the back of the office, but all other residential rooms were to be found on the upper two levels of the home. The street level entrance presented an atmosphere of business, masking the feel of the rest of the manse.

Fair looked around at the raised ceiling, large stove, and shelves full of ore samples.

"Mark this day here in February of 1873, John Mackay. It will be a moment you will remember for the rest of your time on earth."

Fair now had Mackay's full attention. After closing the door, Mackay sat down in his wooden office chair perched on wheels in front of a massive roll top desk. He motioned for Fair to take a seat. Reveling in the moment and drawing out the drama, Fair was in no hurry.

"John, I have always known you to be the most frugal of men with your hard-earned money. I watched you mind your money for years as we lived in that dugout hole of a home in the side of the mountain while we worked two jobs a day. You never spent a penny more than was needed to stay alive. I marveled at your extravagance when you bought this huge home. It ran so contrary to the man I thought I knew. I never thought the house would fit you, but it does. Now it will fit you even better."

"Jim, you obviously have some news. What is it?"

"Before I get there, hold on for just a bit more. Remind me, when was this three-story brick manor built?"

Fair could see the puzzlement on Mackay's face as he obviously did not know why Fair pursued the question. Fair had been in the mansion dozens and dozens of times before and knew its history. Mackay responded, nonetheless. "As you know, George Hearst, the superintendent of the Gould and Curry Mine, built the house in 1860. The room we now occupy doubled as his office, right here in the front of the mansion. I use it for the same purpose, albeit now the office for the Virginia Consolidated and California Mines of which you and I are principals. Now, you have been reminded of facts you have heard dozens of times; what is the news?"

Fair could sense Mackay's rising anticipation, but being the playful Irishman he was, he continued with his momentary fun.

"And you never felt it strange you have a walk-in, steel encased vault right there at the end of your office. This is a house, not a bank. Do you really think it necessary to hold all our rough bullion from the mills in that vault while it waits for shipment to San Francisco and refinement? How many times have there been robbery attempts here in what is your home? It's probably a good thing your beautiful wife Marie Louise spends so much time in Paris."

"Yes, it upset Marie after the last robbery. It did not go well when security had to shoot a robber here in her own home. The event did prompt her departure. She never liked this town to begin with. But, having the office here works just fine for me. I can and do walk to all six of the mines we own every day, right from here. It is central to everything we run and own. To have the vault here in the house keeps that which is valuable to us both under close watch. It has certainly suited you just fine up to now."

"And she likes to spend your money in Paris. Maybe she will be happy if you generate a little more."

Fair could see Mackay grow seriously irritated. Fair's spreading grin did little to allay his friend's growing distress. But Fair continued with his conversational sport. "Yes, it will be fitting you live in a home with the largest private kitchen and the only residence in the state of Nevada with running water to an indoor bathroom. See, I do remember some of your amenities." Fair was playing the impish Irish leprechaun to the hilt.

"Okay, I am done with the games, Jim. Tell me your news."

"John, the crosscut hit a huge vein in the California."

"How big?"

"Bigger than anything ever found here in Virginia City."

"Jim, careful about what you say. Don't let the blarney get the better of you. The biggest strike in Virginia City so far happened at the Ophir. The strike measured fifteen to twenty feet wide and ran constant for almost a thousand feet. It's a vein they still mine."

"John, the men called me down to see it with my own eyes. It's truly big."

Mackay said nothing, only waited. Fair continued.

"Remember, you and I were in the Consolidated near its connection to the California back in 1869 and noticed promising signs of low-grade ore. We found more low-grade ore in late '72 and decided to start a crosscut. We sent a crew down the slope to start a horizontal shaft into the side of the mountain. The aim was to connect with the main vertical shaft dropping from the city surface. But we planned it such that the point the two shafts would meet would be at least one thousand feet below city street level. That tunnel's deeper than any other crosscut in Virginia City."

Mackay nodded.

"Well, the boys in the crosscut found a vein of what looks to me is high-grade ore. Very high-grade. I had them keep pushing forward to see how wide the vein is. They are now over one hundred and fifty feet across its diameter, and they haven't reached the other side yet. We have started pulling dirt off the side of the vein and its over four to five hundred feet long. So, what we know for sure is that the circular vein is at least one hundred fifty feet around and over five hundred feet long. John, it's huge."

Mackay was now the one smiling.

Fair now tried to drive the point home. "John, no one knew the depths of Virginia City better than us. We've been digging and mining here since '59. We've been swinging hammers since the beginning of the Comstock. This is more than just good."

"One hundred and fifty feet across…are you sure, Jim?"

"There is no sign of the other side. It could be two to three hundred feet. And, John, you must see the ore. It is magnificent. Better than any I have ever seen. The production will be higher per ton than anything we've ever mined."

"Jim, we have to think. Who knows about this? We need to consider how to deal with anyone who knows."

"Our best two crews are working the crosscut. They each work twelve hours shifts. No one else knows."

"We need to keep them in the mine. As soon as this becomes news, the speculators will go wild. Our share price for the Consolidated will skyrocket. But our suppliers will hold us hostage for cost of the timber and supplies they will know we have to buy if we place the order after the announcement. Timber to support the mineshafts will be the key.

For that many twelve-by-twelve inch timbers which make up each square set, we are going to need tons of wood. We will have to get it from the Bliss company up at Tahoe."

"I agree. We'll need more timber than Bliss produces now to support all the mining operations in town put together."

Fair paused as he tried to visualize the needs they faced.

"We will need to square set the mined space. With the solid vein of that size, we are talking about a two or three hundred foot hole. Everything around the vein will have to be removed. Without the square set timbers, there'll be no support for the dirt above. We'd be looking at massive cave ins. It's going to be a lot of eight-foot cubes built out of twelve-inch timbers.

"The price will be steep, and we won't see any profits until the ore can be removed and milled, which will be months after the expenses must be paid. Where are we going to get the cash? And didn't you just tell Jack O'Brien we would buy him out? John, we don't have the money to pay for the combined sums if they hit us all at once."

Mackay had been staring at the wall absorbing the information coming from Fair, but now turned his to meet the man's gaze. "You're right. It's all going to take a great deal of money."

Fair watched as Mackay stood from his chair.

"But let's take this one step at a time. First, how long can we keep the men down there in the mine if we provide food and sleeping quarters? We could tell them this is so big we are going to work back to back shifts until we breach the other side of the vein. Second, we need to send a wire to Jim Flood in San Francisco so he can prepare for the onslaught of activity on the stock and help in any way to generate cash right now."

"To answer your first question, we can probably convince the men to sleep in the mine for about two weeks. After that, they will have to get out. We can send down bedding, water, and food. We'll have pay them extra wages."

"Tell them we'll double their wages for the two weeks."

"If we do that, there should be no problem getting them to stay. But what do we do about having them tell their families why they're not coming home at night?"

"We have to be honest with the boys. Tell them we must keep this secret in order to keep the mine running smoothly so we can attack the ore. We will need supplies and materials. So, they need to tell their families we have a major structural opportunity to access other sections of the mine which might help us find more, and it has to be done quickly to do it right."

Fair nodded. "We might be able to sell that. But you know this town. Everyone will know something is up within twenty-four hours."

"But we can keep the story limited if we keep the men down there. If we let them up, the news will be out with the first beers after their shift."

Fair had to agree. "That's probably right. We can use our normal code over the telegraph to tell Jim Flood the good news out in San Francisco. No one has cracked our code yet. But we need to tell him to keep this between he and Bill O'Brien."

"Jim, we certainly don't have to worry about that. Jim Flood is the savviest manipulator of stock markets that San Francisco has ever seen. He will gleefully lose sleep thinking about how he will want to play the market on this one. I can see his grin now. We could make a million each just on Flood's stock plays."

"Then, John, how do we get to Bliss and place an invoice for timber?"

"That's a much bigger problem. I have no real solution. We've always had a rocky relationship with the Carson Tahoe Lumber &

Fluming Co. Duane Bliss started the company last year in '72 when he saw the huge need for timber as the mines started square setting the open expanses left by the ore removal of our soft soil."

"Shrewd he was. After the Ophir hired the consultant Deidesheimer, the man who came up with the idea of square setting timbers to hold the soft dirt we all mine in, the need for timber skyrocketed. The cost went crazy at the same time."

Mackay shifted in his seat. "The lumber companies know we have money and an unlimited need. Word is Bliss linked up with Darius Ogden Mills to buy over seven thousand acres of timber up on the slopes of Tahoe.

Fair had to agree. "He has the lumber stock and now plans to build his own small gauge railroad pulling lumber up the hill from the Tahoe lakeshore to the crest. He already owns the flume from the crest of the Sierras down the slope to Carson City and his lumber yards. He's made a killing on orders from all the combined Virginia City mines."

Mackay turned to face Fair. "Yes, he had vision, and he's used his old connections with the Bank of California and our competitor William Sharon to get capital from one of Sharon's partners, Mills. We've bought producing mines Sharon also wanted over the last four years. He passed on the Consolidated, and we bought it.

"If Sharon finds out we've hit it big on a mine he passed over, he will do anything he can to block us. He'll just be mad at his own bad decision. Sharon is a master at bankrupting mine owners and then foreclosing on the loans he's made them. It's how his bank became the owner of seven mines here in the city. We must get to Bliss before either Sharon or his joint partner Darius Ogden Mills does. Both will have motive to stop us from developing the Consolidated."

Fair could not contain his concern. "You really can't think of any ideas on how we can approach Bliss?"

Mackay's forehead spread flattening the wrinkles of consternation. An idea struck. "Maybe, now that I think about it. I have a friend and acquaintance from San Francisco in Henry Millard, the Cattle King. He's a huge landowner and very powerful in San Francisco and California politics. When I last saw him, he was trying to get me to invest in Bliss' lumber company. I didn't do it. Should have but we were buying the California and Consolidated and I needed any and all cash on hand. However, maybe I can ask Henry to approach Bliss."

"John, I think we need to do everything we can. I will take care of getting the men to stay down in the mine. You will have to take care of the timber problem. We have two weeks. Two weeks at the most."

"I'll send Henry a wire today."

Chapter Seven

Will rode the final stretch to his property just before dark. A deep blue gloaming blanketed the sharp regal crests on his left clinging to the final vestiges of the day before full darkness descended. The last bits of light reflected off the snow caps as if conveyed by a plethora of mirrors upwards into the darkening inky blue above. The day's dying rays of the sun were being lifted and carried off to some other galaxy.

The last part of his journey had taken a full day to reach home from his overnight camp. The ride had been refreshing, a time away from the regular duties of ranching. The trees along the base of the tall mountains had lost their leaves. The landscape was stark, cold. But he loved riding, especially by himself. There was so much time to think. Riding was easy on the brain, easy on the temperament. Now, he was looking forward to getting warm and maybe even seeing Beth and the boys.

He could see lights already on at the ranch house. He pulled up Powder and started walking to the barn. There was no dust at this time of year. Though the air approached a bitterness of low temperature, the circle of small wooden buildings that now made up his ranch compound gave off something of a warmth. But it was quiet, noticeably quiet. Not necessarily the lack of sound, but he sensed a definite lack of movement, lack of activity. Though not every time he arrived home, usually, either Juan or Raúl came out on his late day arrivals to take his horse for him and brush the mount down while he headed to the house and grabbed something to eat. But no one came out of the bunkhouse. Will sensed things were not right.

Then he heard the crying. It came from the bunkhouse. He pulled off Powder's saddle, turned him into a stall in the barn, and quickly threw him some hay. He started off to the bunkhouse to find the source of the sounds. He saw María.

"Oh, Señor Will, it is terrible. They shoot Raúl. Raúl, he dead."

María had been crying. By the look of her face, she had been crying for a long time. She pointed to an adjacent room.

"Raúl, we put him there." María then burst out in another spasm of tears and abbreviated breath.

Will stood stunned.

"María, what happened?"

"Oh, Señor Will. It was *mucho malo*. Beth, she bring the boys like she always does. Raúl took them out on the caballos. The boys, they love to ride. Then men rode at Raúl and shot him. The men, they take the boys and say you must pay to get them back."

"What men?" Will was trying to process the information but was having trouble taking it all in. He had been a Texas Ranger for just shy of a year before he moved on to wrangling in New Mexico, later coming to Nevada to start his own ranch. He had been confronted with all manner of crimes and criminals while with the Rangers, taking immediate action when needed. But he initially stumbled here in a situation involving his own family. These were his two sons, Luke and Sean. He tried to settle his brain and manage the information.

"Where is Beth?" He struggled with a start at sorting this out.

"Beth, she was here when the bad men come. They shot at her."

"Oh no, was she hurt?" Will didn't think he could handle more potential losses all at once.

"No, they shoot their guns at our feet to stop us from moving. The bad man say he was brother to Drake Sutton. He wanted you to pay."

"Where did Beth go?"

María had to wait for a sob to subside so she could catch her breath and respond.

"She go to Carson City. She say she will tell the sheriff. She also say she stop to get her gun and clothes to ride."

"She's not planning to go after them herself, is she?"

"No, she say she will ride to her home to where she get her clothes. Then she come back to the ranch here and begin to follow Juan."

"Follow Juan? Where did he go?" Still dealing with the shock, Will at least got simple questions out.

"Juan, he come in from checking the cows just before dark. When he see Raúl and hear what happen to the boys, he change horses and start to follow them. Beth say she will come back here to the ranch and change horses then follow Juan to help get the boys."

"How many bad men were there, María?"

Holding up four fingers, María said, "Quatro. They say Raúl see them coming and he waved the boys to the ranch while he turned and rode right at the bad men. He shoot at them, but they hit Raúl first. They rode in and just dump him in the dirt. A skinny one, he grin when he push Raúl off the horse. These are bad men, Señor Will. Bad men."

Will pushed himself to separate from his immediate emotions and think. Thoughts came in blasts the brain can accommodate in a much faster fashion than one can verbalize. *How was Juan going to deal with four armed men alone? Those men were probably good with their guns, too? What was Beth going to do? Would the Carson City sheriff be any help? And most importantly, what about the boys? How could small boys cope with capture and treatment at the hands of men so evil? The thought caught him deep in the abdomen. Those boys get hurt, and there'd be a shame he'd carry forever, a shame that he'd been away when they needed his protection.*

Will had ridden down criminals during his days with the Rangers. He had no hesitation heading out himself to follow this group. He had taken on bad men before. But he now had Juan out somewhere in unknown circumstances and Beth moving between the ranch and Carson City. And he had a dead friend. A dear friend.

Will looked at María. The tears still flowed. He reached out to hug this lady who had been a mainstay around the men over the years as they started from nothing and built a working cattle ranch. It had been their joint dream. And they had been successful in the face of multiple challenges.

Will then pushed María's shoulders back to arm's length. He hoped the hug had settled her at least to some extent. The time and contact had worked to control his own brain. Decisions were now beginning to come with less emotional overlay. He looked directly at María.

"I cannot follow Juan in the dark. You say Beth is coming back to the ranch. I can't see anything else to do right now but wait here tonight for Beth and head out tomorrow. My horse will be rested by then, and I can head out and try to pick up the trails. Beth can stay here with you. But we need to bury Raúl. As soon as I get the boys back, I can talk to Father Cecconi in town, and we will get him to come out and make sure his grave is properly blessed."

Another sob came from María. "Raúl would be happy if the Father would say a prayer over him."

"Would it be okay to bury Raúl here on the ranch? Or should we take him into town?"

María thought, wiped another tear, and said, "I think Raúl, he love this ranch. He would like to stay here forever. If it okay with you, Señor Will, I think he would like to be buried out under a large tree looking over the river."

"I will take him out tonight and do it now. We will get a marker later, so everyone will know where Raúl is at rest."

María seemed to pause and reflect. The fact Will offered to bury Raúl brought a bit of closure to present circumstances, but it ultimately did not make things any better. Will knew that though only a father-in-law to María, she had come to care for Raúl as if he were her own family. She looked back at Will.

"I marry Juan, and I know he and his padre, Raúl, would always be together. We all traveled and worked at the same haciendas and ranches until we meet you, Señor Toal. We all agree to come with you on the way to California and to stop here and start the ranch. I never see Raúl happier. He loved those little *Niño's*, too."

"María, I promise you I will get the men who did this."

"Señor Toal, you have to help Juan. I worry he out there by himself. I no bear it if those men get Juan, too."

"I will get to him as soon as I can. For now, I will take Raúl out and bury him underneath the large cottonwood sitting on the rise near the bend in the river. I think he'd like that spot."

It took two hours for Will to rig up a horse and wagon to carry Raúl out toward the river and bury him proper. He left the shovel standing at the head of the grave as a temporary, if inadequate, marker. He headed back to the ranch house hoping he could get some sleep. His mind was now full of thoughts as to what he needed to take and where to go.

When Will got back to the ranch, María was waiting on the porch. Her tears had not stopped.

"It's done," Will told her.

María nodded. "Is a bad day."

"María, I was thinking while I buried Raúl, which way did the four horsemen ride out?"

María pointed to the north. "Toward Carson City."

Just as they both looked in the direction Maria pointed, a mounted horse came into the ranch. The slender rider moved gracefully under a floppy worn hat. The body of the horseman flowed effortlessly with the gait of the horse. Will could immediately tell the rider was experienced. As the pair got closer, he recognized Beth with her long blonde tresses tucked up under an old floppy hat he'd seen before many years ago. She wore the old second-hand riding pants along with a shirt and hat María had given her five years ago.

"I've seen that outfit on you only once before. That was not a good day back then. This has been a bad day, too."

Beth dismounted. She turned to Will, and he could see anger in her face. He knew this remarkable woman well enough to know she planned to go after those men by herself if needed. She possessed ca-pabilities one would not expect of a woman her age here in the West. Will himself had taught her to shoot. While not quick on the draw, she could aim and shoot remarkably well. But as soon as she saw Will, her entire demeanor changed.

"Oh Will, they've got the boys!"

As soon as she said it, Beth let loose the emotions she had stuffed deep down all day under a veneer of anger. Seeing Will at home, she could not contain the overdue outpouring.

"It was horrible as if a demon had returned. Will, he looked just like Drake. "

Beth reached for Will and fell into his arms.

Will squeezed her tightly to him. He struggled with his own emo-tions knowing his boys were gone and holding the lady he cared for. Here was the mother of his children. It had been his own decision not to marry this woman he loved but could not commit to. His decision hurt her. He had not relished doing that, but he had been open and honest with her as to the root of his continuing hesitation. Now this. More sadness.

"The last time you wore this outfit, you hit me in the head."

Will remembered the events that created the current rift between them. It was the same outfit she was wearing when she and Will confronted Drake Sutton for the first time. Will and Sutton had faced off in a straight draw. Will beat Sutton to the draw, but Sutton's companion got off a shot that hit Will. Beth then shot the companion dead. Though bent over with the pain of his wound, Will had thought he'd survived and had tried looking up at Beth who had been standing next to him. It was at that moment she hit him on the back of his head with the barrel of her gun. He woke up back at the ranch. A man who had heard the gunshots came upon the scene after Beth had left, picked him up out of the dirt, and helped him back home.

Coming back to the moment at hand, Will said, "I will get them back. And the men who did this will be having a close conversation with their maker when I'm done with them."

Beth looked up into Will's eyes. "Will, we have to get them back as soon as we can. There is no telling what those monsters will do to them. I cannot bring myself to think of those two little ones in the hands of men like that."

"I will be riding out as soon as it is light enough for me to follow a trail."

"I'm going too. You know I can shoot."

"Beth, these men…"

"No." She glared at him. "Don't even try. Stop where you are. I am going. There is nothing you can do about it. You know very well if you leave without me, I am just going to follow. So, you might as well agree, and we do this together."

Will looked down. "I suppose I've never had much control over you. You are right; in the face of trouble, you have never heeded my warnings. You probably would follow me."

He hesitated in a multilayered silence hinging on a history they both would like to change but struggled to live with day to day. They both knew his answer would be a large signal for the direction their paths would take in the future.

"Let's do it together."

Beth relaxed into his arms. Will felt the warmth of this lady he felt so close to but had kept at arm's-length for years.

Will lifted her chin so she was looking directly at him.

"Let's get some sleep. We need to ride at first light."

"Will, I couldn't sleep. Just sit here on the porch with me. Hold me."

They sat. The bench on the front porch had its own special place in their relationship. It had been on this bench Beth had tried to explain how she had intended to protect Will when she hit him with the gun. Now they would spend more time seated together on this same bench as the world spun events around them, pulling both down in a vortex of an inevitable bond.

Beth put both her hands around Will's arm. She rested her head on his shoulder. He did not resist. In fact, he shut his own eyes, reveling in the closeness. He felt her nuzzle into his chest. Despite her claims of being incapable of sleep, she was out in a matter of minutes. Drained.

Chapter Eight

1873 February
Virginia City, NV

The sign above the door read "St. Mary's of the Mountains." The elegant yet simple wooden door appeared locked. He heard voices on the other side.

"Bishop Manogue, there is someone at the door of the church."

"Well, Sister, please get the door. I'll be down in a moment."

A nun in full habit with a wide spreading cornette pulled the door back. Fr. Cecconi smiled. "Sister, thank you for opening the door. Might a Jesuit traveling to visit you find some shelter for the night?"

"You must be Fr. Cecconi. Bishop Manogue said we were to have a fully ordained member of the Society of Jesus come to say Mass tomorrow when he must leave. I will be most interested to hear your homily."

"Ordained and Jesuit, I confess to both. As for tomorrow's homily, I hope to deliver my suggestions on the day's readings and conclude before anyone falls asleep."

"Father, please come in. The weather has been threatening all afternoon. You've luckily arrived in time to avoid getting wet." Sister Charity pulled the door fully open to allow the Jesuit to enter. "It is dark out. We are likely to see a good downpour." Just then, an ominous roll of thunder sounded in the distance.

Bishop Manogue arrived moving around the sacristy to the entrance of the nave. "Fr. Cecconi, it is so nice of you to come and fill in for me at Mass tomorrow. It's late, but will you join me for dinner?"

"Thank you, Bishop. A warm meal sounds most appealing."

"Father, did you take the train? I did not hear one travel by. The Virginia & Truckee dug their infernal tunnel two stories below our church's front porch causing tremors throughout the building every time it pulls to its station two blocks away."

"No, actually, I rode my horse. I usually enjoy the tranquility of a day's ride."

"Usually? Do I understand today's ride would not be described as enjoyable?"

"It's interesting you should ask. Something quite unsettling happened on the road here."

Still standing near the entrance to the church, the bishop spread his hands and then asked, "Father, I can see concern in your face. Whatever happened to cause this?"

Fr. Cecconi found it strange to be talking about this so soon after his arrival. But the visage he had seen earlier in the day would not leave his consciousness. He found a mild solace to be able to speak about it to someone else.

"Bishop, I reached the crest of the Carson Valley intending to head through Mound House and then up Six Mile Canyon to Virginia City. Upon reaching the crest, I stopped and looked east. A darkness spread beyond the mountains. Everything was still. A flash of lightning appeared. It was like a hole was burned into the horizon. As if sparked by the lightning strike, a cloud of dust blew out of the hole like smoke. But the smoke turned out to be dust from horses, four horses with riders, the leader of which rode a remarkably white horse. They passed me without stopping, without even acknowledging my existence. It created a deep foreboding I could not shake. I felt I had seen the advent of Revelation."

Bishop Manogue immediately reached across his chest in the familiar movements which comprised the sign of the cross. "Any such vision would be thoroughly unsettling. Let us hope your vision was not scriptural. Come, we must eat. I catch an early train tomorrow to San Francisco, and it would be wonderful if you could bring me up to speed on your parish in Carson City. I will add it to my report to the archbishop."

*****

Sam Brown looked up to the darkening skies. He could see weather coming. He turned his horse to face Roberts. All four riders came to a stop.

"Frank, give the kid you're carryin' to Elmer. Charley, here, you take this one. You all know the plan. Charley and Elmer take the boys to the place we use in Mound House."

"Why'd we ever pick Mound House as a place to stay?"

Again, it was Elmer questioning the strategy.

"Elmer, your brain is not quick enough to understand why we do anything. So, don't keep asking questions about things you don't need to think about." Brown had about reached the end of his rope with Elmer. However, he tried to provide simple instruction.

"The reason you're keeping the boys there is because Mound House is a railroad junction with access up to Virginia City. It's where the Virginia & Truckee Railroad meets a small mining rail line from the south in California."

Brown could see the logic was lost on Elmer. He should probably just leave the comment alone as any further talk would most likely just create more confusion in the man. But he wanted the plan to work. With a sigh, he continued.

"Being in Mound House, we keep the boys away from Virginia City and out of sight. But with the train they'll be close."

Elmer's face told Brown he still wasn't following. Brown took one last chance at driving the explanation home.

"We want Toal to come to Virginia City. I don't want to have the boys with Roberts and me in the same place until I know he's going to show. Too risky if someone sees them. If Toal comes with the money, you'll take the train up to Virginia City."

"How are we going to know if that happens? We're in Mound House, and you're in Virginia City."

Brown looked at Charley Waverly, no longer even attempting to engage Elmer. He knew Charley to be the best chance of having his orders followed.

"Charley, there's a telegraph office in Mound House right next to the train depot. Check for messages each day. Don't go at the same time day by day. Pick different times. Tell the telegraph operator you're waiting on a message, and it could take a week or two, so he should expect you to check each day. Make it sound like it's just a regular routine or something you've done lots of times before."

Brown looked directly at Elmer and said, "And Charley, do not let Elmer ever go to check for the messages. I don't want him to ever leave the house. If he leaves, there is no telling how he could screw this up." Even though he spoke to Charley, Brown never took his eyes off Elmer Lennox.

"Charley, one more thing. If anything happens to these kids, and I mean anything, I am coming after you. So, if Elmer here does something stupid, I am holding you responsible. You'd better keep a close watch on him." Brown still stared right at Lennox.

"Do you hear what I'm saying, Charley?"

"Yep, boss. I heard. But you know Elmer," said Charley, a mouthful for him.

"That's exactly why I'm holding you responsible. It's up to you to not only keep control of the boys, but you hafta control Elmer, too."

Elmer stared back at Brown.

"I'll send the wire when I hear from Toal. If he brings the money, then you can bring the boys up by train. We will meet him out on the field below town where they have those stupid Virginia City camel races in the summer. We will set up at four sides of the field and, ultimately, we will kill him."

"What about the boys?" asked Elmer.

"They die too," said Brown. "But I do that. Shooting the boys is something I will do. It'll be my gift to their mother. I understand she had something to do with Drake's death too."

"What if this rancher Toal don't come up with the money?" More pestering from Elmer.

"He will," said Brown. "He's not the type to just walk away from his kids. Once we get rid of Toal, we will split the money even and head out of Virginia City once and for all. While I really like the place, I can use a change of scenery."

No one expressed any problem with the idea of splitting money. Each's split would be more than any one of them had ever seen in their lifetime.

"Any questions?"

For a change, Elmer did not raise any questions. Maybe he had begun thinking of the money he could make.

"Fine, then let's split up and move out. We waited and watched the ranch. No one came after us right away. It may take them a while to get the money and get to Virginia City. But there's enough food and supplies at the place in town. There's no reason for you two to leave the house where you will be keeping the boys. So, hunker down and stay indoors. Just keep out of sight until you get the wire."

All nodded and exchanged the children, who had been quiet until now.

"My Pa will come to get you." The words came from Luke who, despite being just under five years old, was trying to act much bigger than he was.

Brown chuckled at the show of childish bravado.

"I'm countin' on it, kid."

Chapter Nine

1873 February
Toal Ranch

Darkness covered the morning chill. A sticky moisture clung to the cold air—a dampness that seeped through any outer layer of clothing and into the bones as well as one's outlook on life. His arm was completely numb. But it was a numb that came with pain. It actually hurt. It was the pain that woke him up. Will looked down. Beth had slept in his arms or, more particularly, *on* his arm. She'd barely moved all night, sleeping with her head on his chest just below the shoulder with most of the weight on his arm.

He could feel the pressure down the length of his forearm and into his hand, as if the blood there had been trapped, building with intent to burst. It almost burned. He could only see the blonde crown of her head, a quiet stillness born from a fragment of peace. He moved gently to ease his arm. At first, he'd been unsure of his surroundings. But the blonde tresses below his chin, and the warmth of the lady clutching him told him soon where he was. Beth nestled there on his chest . He knew by the depth of her sleep she had been relieved that he was home.

No sunrise yet, but Will knew the time had come to start getting their horses ready. María would be up soon, preparing some food. They would get a good breakfast and head north on the road to Carson City looking for tracks. Will knew from his time with the Texas Rangers, when following people fleeing the law, the tale would be told in the dirt. You just had to know how to read that language.

"What time is it?" Beth stirred.

"Early. Just rest here, and I will get the horses ready."

"Will, Sutton wants twenty-five thousand dollars for the boys." Will marveled at the fact that Beth seemed to be still asleep by the look of her face, but strangely enough, her brain had awakened, already working at a fast clip. The difference between her drowsy facial appearance when compared to the significance of the conversation struck a chord of mild amazement in Will.

Stunned, he couldn't find any words. Finally, he responded. "I don't have twenty-five thousand dollars. I can't get anything close to that."

"I know," came her reply. "What can we do? Will, I can't tell you how I feel. It's like I've lost a piece of my own body— an arm or a leg. I've lost my boys. They're part of me, and they're gone."

"I know. I feel the same as if someone has carved out my insides."

She looked up at him, lifting her cheek from his shoulder. "Can we find them? Will, tell me we can find them."

"I thought about this last night. We must move fast. But I think our first step should be to get the Carson City sheriff to help."

"I already tried that; he says this is out of his jurisdiction."

"That just isn't true. I'll talk to hm as an ex-Texas Ranger and set him straight. Sheriff Thompson has always struck me as a solid lawman. I have no idea why he would hesitate on this. We must head that direction anyway. If the gang headed north, Carson City is in the same direction. This might take days, and we'll have to get some supplies."

"What if the sheriff does nothing?"

"Whether he does or does not act, I have to get to Virginia City to find this Sutton sibling. If I can send him to his maker, then maybe we can stop this quickly."

"He'll have the boys hidden."

"You're probably right. We must hope Juan has done some good tracking and knows where they took the boys. We will just have to follow those tracks to see if we can come across Juan before he gets into trouble trying to take on the whole gang by himself."

Beth looked away then returned her gaze to Will. "I am so scared I don't know what to do. But at the same time, I am so angry that I want to head out right now and start shooting at the first sight of those men."

Will nodded. "We're both scared. We just have to keep our minds focused on the simple task at hand: get the boys back."

"I will try. I can be ready in ten minutes."

"I'll get the horses. Grab the Enfield rifle from the house and whatever ammunition for it you can find. There won't be much. Getting more ammo is the main reason we need to stop in Carson City; I need ammunition for both the rifle and my handgun. We'll stop in town quickly, talk to the sheriff, and then head off to follow whatever tracks we can find."

*****

"Jim, have you had a chance to calculate how much timber we are going to need?"

Jim Fair had spent the last two days doing his best to estimate the size of the ore body the crew had discovered to calculate the board feet of timber they would need. All of Virginia City mines were in soft soil, not solid granite. When ore was removed, mines had to use the square set method to hold up the unsupported spaces. It was different than any mining done before in the U.S. or anywhere in the world. But the square sets had worked. No miners would go down a Virginia City shaft unless they knew the company was going to use the cubicle wooden structures.

"I've tried to figure this as best I can. The square set timbers are twelve inches by twelve inches and eight feet long. We are going to have a cavern over three hundred feet wide at a length unknown. The final estimates are impossible to calculate. But just to start, we are going to need ten thousand board feet."

Mackay slumped. His body language told the story of how he really felt about this monumental task. The magnitude of the opportunity was more than most men could imagine. But John Mackay had seen ore finds before. Just because you found good ore did not mean that you could turn it into money. His mind narrowed down to one thing: production. They had to start getting the ore out of the mine so they could establish a cash flow.

"There is no way Bliss will have that much timber on hand. The rest of the mines will have a fit. We will probably draw another lawsuit with trumped up charges just to stop us from placing the order until the rest of the mines can figure out how to cope."

"They've filed suit on pretenses for issues of far less importance in the past. You are probably right, John. We'll draw a suit for sure. But that should not stop us. We must get a hold of Bliss. We need a go-between."

"You are right, but at the moment, I canna think of anyone." The Irish accent found its way to the surface, a sure sign of stress. Obviously, even John Mackay felt the pressure.

"To top it off, have you seen the weather?"

Mackay looked up from his desk, puzzled by the question. He had been working steadily in his office since Fair had told him of the discovery. "No, I haven't even been outside since you brought me the news of the recent ore find."

Fair pointed to the dark clouds through the window some ten feet above Mackay's desk. "There are serious thick dark clouds heading our way. It's going to be a heavy rain."

"Better get extra pumps ready. We might also need to protect the primary shaft so no water gets in at the main works. Can't have any water flowing down the shaft. We have to pump enough water as it is."

"Agreed," replied Fair. "I'll take care of it."

*****

Will and Beth had ridden for over an hour heading north on the road from the ranch in little Jack's Valley toward Carson City. The small valley sat just off the path of the Carson River as it ran down the middle of Carson Valley. Kit Carson had left his name on just about everything. It had been the unique setting of waist high green grasses growing at the base of the snow-capped granite walls of the Sierras that ended Will's migration west. His three thousand acres in the small depression nestled at the base of the mountain range was like no other place he'd ever seen.

Will raised his hand, signaling for Beth to stop. "See that?"

"See what?"

Will rode Powder in a circle around a spot at the edge of the road.

"See where the tracks of those four horses take off heading east?"

Beth looked down at the ground and then back up to Will.

"I know you see something you think is important, but to me, it's a lot of marks in the dirt. What is it you see?"

"I have been following four sets of tracks all morning. The horseshoe of one horse has a distinctive bend to the right rear hoof. See, that one there. It's bent to right outside of the hoof wall. The shoe is misshaped. When you re tracking, you look for special signs. Once you have that special sign, then you just keep a watch on the whole bunch riding with it. These have to be the four horses that left the ranch with the boys."

"I'm glad you can see that because I would not know the difference from those marks and the other hundreds out here on a dirt road that gets used a lot."

"The road gets used a lot, true. But these tracks were fresh from the ranch. It must be them. Looks to me that they struck off cross country to avoid town. Didn't want to be seen riding into Carson City with two boys in their saddles that some might recognize. I'm surprised they didn't cut off the road earlier for the same reason. You live in town, and there are plenty of people who might recognize the boys and wonder what's going on."

Will rode back up the trail several paces. "See that set of tracks there? I will bet that is Juan. He has them tracked too and is following."

"What do we do now? We must catch up to them." The distress in Beth's voice had not left since the kidnapping.

"We will, but we need to stop in town, too. It's less than a half an hour to get to Carson City. Let's get there quickly, and I'll talk to the sheriff and send a wire to Henry Millard. You pick up the supplies at the same time. We can then head back out to this same spot and pick up the gang's trail again."

Beth hesitated. "I don't want to waste time. We have to get to the boys."

"Beth, the time we spend now to get supplies for two to three days saves us problems down the road. Once we get started, we can just ride and pursue. The riders are going to stop. Best we are prepared at the outset."

Beth was conflicted. The maternal instincts were competing with any suggested logic.

"Come on, let's get to Carson so we can get back on the trail soon. Juan is following them too, and we need to get to him before he tries to take on that gang by himself."

As they started back up, Will turned in his saddle back to Beth. "We have to get ammunition for the rifle and food for several days. There's no tellin' how long we are going to be out here. It won't take long to get the supplies we need."

*****

Beth was still not convinced, but Will was right; it didn't take long before they were on the outskirts of Carson City.

"You head over to the general store and get some ammunition for my Enfield. Remember, tell him it takes the .577 size ball. I want to stop at the telegraph office to let Henry Millard know that I will give him a report on the Antelope Valley Ranch when I finish getting the boys back."

"Will, hurry." Beth's voice was now approaching desperate. But desperation was understandable.

They split up after entering the main street. Will headed further north through town while Beth turned on to Stewart Street for the general store.

Will pulled up at the telegraph office just as S. Samuel Grande stepped out.

"Will, good to see you. How are Beth and the boys?"

Grande had been Will's lawyer and the person who four years ago solved the legal challenges against the Central Pacific Railroad which followed the shoot-out with the railroad's gun-hands. A special bond had developed between the two as Grande's solution with the railroad effectively saved Will's ranch from foreclosure and solved the lack of a local market for beef.

"Bad right now, Sam. A gang of four men rode on to the ranch, killing Raúl and kidnaping both the boys. The head guy appears to be related to Drake Sutton, the gun-hand I shot in the Carson City shoot-out four years ago. He wants twenty-five thousand dollars to get them back."

Will watched as shock flashed across Grande's face. But the shock was quickly followed by control. As a lawyer used to surprises in court-rooms, Grande was trained to think quick on his feet. Plus, he dearly wanted to help Will, who was more than just a client.

"First, that is horrific. But next, what's your plan? Where are you supposed to obtain that kind of money?"

Grande had also helped Will secure a loan when he purchased his ranch. He knew all the details as to Will's finances: both assets and liabilities.

"I don't have it. But you know that."

Grande had one of the quickest minds of anyone Will knew. He almost expected Grande to express some idea for a solution even though he had just heard about the problem. Will had seen Grande do it several times before. But not this time.

"I wish I could help," was all Grande could say.

"Right now, I was going to wire Henry Millard to let him know I finished the project at the ranch in Antelope Valley as he requested, but I have to go find my boys. It might be a while before I can send him a proper report."

"Where are you supposed to exchange the money?"

"The Delta Saloon in Virginia City," said Will.

"You should ask Millard if he knows anyone in Virginia City who might help. Millard is a very wealthy businessman as you know, and he might have a valuable contact for you in Virginia City. Have you ever heard of this relative of Drake Sutton?"

"No, I've never heard of the man, but that doesn't mean much. I'd never heard of Drake Sutton before he tried to shoot me."

"Send the wire, but I sure would ask Millard if he has any ideas. The man has connections literally all over California and Nevada because he owns ranches throughout both. He could help."

"It's a good idea. Not sure Henry will have anything, but it sure can't hurt. I can tell him to leave me a message at the same saloon. I have to check there anyway."

Grande reached out and grabbed the top of Will's shoulder. As Grande was almost six feet, five inches tall, he was the tallest man in Carson City. Will had never quite become used to the difference in their height. Will was not a small man himself, but Grande towered over him.

Grande looked directly at Will.

"How is Beth doing?"

"Not good, but she is doing her best to keep things under control."

"She has to be upset."

"Oh yeah, that and more. She was there when they rode up to tell us where to bring the money and how long I have to get it."

"There is a time limit?"

"Yep, two weeks."

"That complicates things quite a bit," mused Grande, looking away down the street.

Grande returned his gaze to Will.

"Talk to Henry Millard. I'll bet he will have some idea to help."

"I'm headed into the office to send a wire right now. I'll include the request."

Silver City Reckoning

The telegraph operator sat in a long narrow office fronting the main street in town. The simple wood planked walls looked as if they were left over boardwalk lengths slapped upright in an afterthought. The lumber rose in fragile stance to the forces of weather ready to creak and moan if the winds became too strong. A single man wearing a white, long sleeve shirt with a black ribbon tied around one bicep slumped as if asleep. Will closed the door with an extra push, making just enough noise to wake the man.

Startled, the older gentleman shook off the pangs of sleep and embarrassment. "Things have been slow today. Must have nodded off. Hope you don't go about telling my boss. Wouldn't do well."

"No such intention."

"Much appreciated. What can I do for you?"

Will smiled. "Sometimes, it's good to catch a quick nap when you can. I need to send a wire to the Millard Luce Cattle Co. in San Francisco."

"Write it out and I'll send," came the response. The man must have been long past sixty. He had a garden of recent white whiskers peeking out of each cheek. Will figured it wasn't really a beard, just lazy at keeping shaved.

Will wrote out what he wanted his wire to Henry Millard to say. He rushed a bit as he had to get back to Beth. The telegraph operator looked up and said, "Let me make sure I have this right."

"Read it back to me," said Will.

To H. Millard. From W. Toal. Stop.
Spent two months in Antelope Valley at your Walker River Ranch. Stop. Improvements went well. Stop. Will file full report later. Stop.

Gang kidnapped my sons, and I must track them down first. Stop. Twenty-five thousand dollars ransom demanded. Stop. To be paid in Virginia City. Stop. Do you know anyone in V. City who I might contact for help? Stop. Reply soon. Stop.

Will had listened, checking each phrase. "Yep, that's right. Can you send that right away? I've got to check with someone over at the general store to make sure we have the supplies we need. I'll stop back just before I leave to see if there's any answer."

"If any answer comes, I'll keep it right here so it's ready when you return."

Will walked out and looked to see if he could spot Beth. He began walking up the west side of main street to get back to where they had parted. He seemed alone even here in the city. The sound of his boots and spurs on the wooden boardwalk almost had an echo, as if he were in a tunnel all his own. His boys were gone. There just didn't seem to be anyone who could help. The echoes of boot heels hitting lumber kept ringing in this open-air tunnel of silence, but it began to make him mad. If no one was going to help, so be it. He had to get the boys back.

As he moved past the Nevada Supreme Courthouse opposite the Capitol, he saw Sheriff Zack Thompson coming in the opposite direction.

"Will, I just saw Beth. She says you're headin' out to find the gang."

Will strained to control his temper with the man. His response was terse. "I am."

"Will, from what she told me, it sounds as if you might be dealin' with a man called Sam Brown. She said that money was demanded and to be paid in Virginia City. Brown's activities are well known up there. If it's Sam Brown, goin' after him alone might not be a good idea.

70

You'll be needin' more 'en just you. And there is no way Beth should be goin' after those hoodlums. Sam Brown and his group leave annihilation behind wherever they go. You're gonna need men, lots o' men, to deal with Sam Brown."

"We're going because you didn't." Will's mood remained dark. He did not even try to hide his disgust at the sheriff's lack of action.

"Will, I'm tryin' to git a posse together right now. Should be movin' by tomorrow."

"Tomorrow will be too late. No telling what men like that will do to children. I'm hanging on to the slim hope that they'll feed and care for 'em 'cause they want the ransom money."

The sheriff was almost oblivious to Will's lack of respect. His reputation had never been sterling, but he'd not come to the immediate aid of a woman who'd lost her boys. In Will's eyes as an ex-Texas Ranger, that was unforgiveable. But the man just stood there talking about what he planned to do sometime down the road rather than just doing it.

"What are you going to do?" asked Thompson.

"Tracks veered off the Carson-Genoa road about two miles outside of town. I plan on heading back out to pick up the trail and follow it until I find the boys. The tracks looked like they were headed to the town of Mound House. If I can't find the boys there, then I'll keep going to Virginia City to find this Sam Brown if that's the man who took the boys. Virginia City is in the same direction as Mound House. I'll just continue until I find the source of the evil, this Mr. Brown. We'll have a talk, a short talk. With God's help, Sam Brown won't be alive after that conversation."

At that moment, there was a crack of thunder.

Will looked to the darkening skies in despair. "No, don't do that. I need those tracks to follow. Don't rain, please don't rain." The words were spoken as if to a higher power. The only response was another crack of thunder.

Will turned back to the sheriff. "I need to go. I hafta find those tracks before any rain wipes them out. Where's Beth?"

Thompson turned and pointed. "She was in Benson's general store when I talked to her."

Will did not even bother to say goodbye. His respect for the sheriff had dwindled that far. He just stared at the man and started walking. But Thompson grabbed his arm.

"Will, if you do get to Virginia City, there is no real law there. The only restraint on crime is a group of vigilantes called the 601s. No one knows exactly who runs it or how to get in touch with them. But if you get that far, you might try 'en talk to them."

Will didn't respond. He simply dipped the front bill of his hat and began heading to Benson's general store. He stepped by the sheriff without another word.

The thunder sounded off again. It was getting closer.

A boy then ran up to Will and the sheriff. He looked up at Will. "You Will Toal?"

"Yep."

"You got a message at the telegraph office. Seems you sent a telegram, and it just got answered."

Will reached out and touched the young man's shoulder. "Thanks, I'll head there right away. I need to get on the road, but I think I need that message even more."

*****

Will walked back into the telegraph office.

"Ah, Mr. Toal, the return message came back quick. I sent it to the downtown telegraph office in San Francisco. The Millard Luce Cattle Co. must be located near as the answer came back real quick. Here you go." The man handed Will a folded paper.

Will unfolded the page and read.

Will, got your message. Stop. Sorry to hear about the problem with the boys. Stop. I know of a man in Virginia City who might be able to help. Stop. His name is John Mackay. Stop. Very successful mine owner. Stop. I have sent him a telegram, and he will be expecting you to come by. Stop. Meet him either at the Washoe Club or the office of the California Consolidated Mine. Stop. He is a powerful man in Virginia City and might be of assistance. Stop.

*****

Another crack of thunder. It began to rain. A hard rain. Sister Charity stood still, holding the door open. "Father Cecconi, I heard you and the bishop talking about the Book of Revelation. This rain is the heaviest I've ever seen. Father, it appears as if the heavens are unloading. I do not recall the riders of Revelation bringing rain."

"They brought devastation in many forms, Sister."

He looked up to the uppermost windows of the church through which he could see the heavy sheets of water bombarding the panes of glass. He turned back to Sister Charity. "I may have to change my homily for tomorrow to include a reference to Noah and the Ark if this continues."

*****

James Flood sat behind a massive desk in the middle of his enormous office on Montgomery Street in San Francisco. The desk, the wall hangings, and the entire office were all intended to impress. Flood had come to San Francisco with nothing. He'd worked in a saloon. Pretty soon, he owned a saloon. But tending bar was not his ultimate aim. He started doing all he could to learn about the local stock market. It intrigued him. Stocks were legal gambling. And as things stood right now, the San Francisco stock market was effectively gambling with no laws. He loved the games, the risks, the plays. And, he was good at it. The stock game had made him a very wealthy man.

Flood stared at the telegram in front of him. To anyone else, it was gibberish. But it was in code, he and Mackay's code. Flood had just translated the message and had to sit down. It was a lot to digest.

The decoded message was simple:

New vein found at the Consolidated. Stop. At least one hundred fifty feet in diameter and more than five hundred feet long. Stop. Still uncovering, no end in sight. Stop. Crosscut crew that struck it still in mine for two weeks. Stop. No one above ground knows. Stop.

One hundred and fifty feet! Five Hundred feet long! Flood knew that the Ophir, Chollar, Gould & Curry, and the Yellow Jacket had made the main strikes since 1859. The biggest ore body found in those mines was less than twenty feet in diameter. Each of the owners for those strikes became fabulously wealthy.

A diameter of one hundred fifty feet!

The value of an ore body that size would be millions. On top of that value, the stock play could be additional millions. He had only started to think of how to manipulate that play when the fourth partner in the Flood-Mackay firm, William O'Brien, walked into his office.

74

"Heard we got a wire from Mackay. What news?"

"Have a seat," said Flood. "You're about to become a very happy man."

Flood told O'Brien about the wire.

"One hundred fifty feet! If it weren't Mackay, I'd say he and Fair were both drunk. But John doesn't drink much. And he never plays games in business. Could it be legitimate?"

Flood had been contemplating the financial houses that lined the broad boulevard of Montgomery Street outside his window.

"Oh, we have to play this on the market, Bill. I think we must assume it's legitimate. If true, this is the biggest find in the history of mining. Now it's up to you and me to make this the biggest play in the history of stocks."

"Jim, are you thinking as I am? The timing of this couldn't be more perfect. The Coinage Act is threatening to cause a depression in silver stocks all over the world. Mine values are dropping in anticipation the Act will pass. They are almost at rock bottom right now. We certainly can buy low, but is there a market to sell high? If we can find a market for silver other than the bars of bullion we sell to the government, then we can pull off one of the biggest stock plays in history."

Flood shook his head. He might have spent only a limited time in any formal schooling, but he was constantly trying to educate himself on the markets in general and silver in particular.

"There are plenty of markets for silver outside of bullion. The value of the metal is set by governments, but the metal itself is used in hundreds of different manufacturing operations. Just because governments will not use it to make coins does not mean we have no one to sell to."

"Then we have some work to do. Might as well get started," said O'Brien.

Chapter Ten

1873 February
Deep within the California-Consolidated Mine

"Baker, when can we be a 'goin home? It's been two days. They gonna keep us down here for eternity? First, they be tellin' us we haft a keep drilling on the new vein, then the rains hit, and we do nothing but man the extra pumps. We need to get some fresh air."

Darren Baker had been a miner his entire thirty-one years. He had the perfect build for a miner. He had a barrel chest and forearms of a blacksmith. The muscles in his arms were a result of swinging a fourteen-pound sledge for ten years, striking a four-foot iron drill spike positioned on his partner's shoulder. Hundreds and hundreds of swings a day, day after day. You could see every sinew of every muscle in the man's arms.

"Finn, there is nothing fresh about you. You don't need any clean air."

Taller than most miners at just over six feet in height, Baker felt comfortable as leader of this group. While he met some initial resentment from his collection of European cast offs, over time, they'd become a cohesive group, one relied on by Mr. Fair—time and time again. While Baker had a contagious zest for life, he also got things done. His men loved being in his crew. His smile and never-ending ability to play pranks or jokes kept everyone loose while never giving up sight of the task at hand. But they were down in a tunnel, and James Fair had said it might be up to two weeks before they would come up.

"Look, you mackerel eaters, the girls down in the cribs will be all that more anxious to see you when you get back to the top." The respect and friendship between Baker and his crew could be measured by the fact he'd called his compatriots by a term that, had it been uttered by anyone else, would have ended in a fight.

"Baker, you're not married. You can spend your time in the saloons and cribs, but my wife is going to wonder what the hell's happening."

The comment came from Bill Robinson. Robinson was not Irish, one of the few non-leprechauns in the crew. Baker was well aware that Robinson got along with everyone, but never passed a chance to make sure they all knew he was English and would never set foot on the Emerald Isle.

"Ah, Bill. Your wife's not wonderin' what's happening. She's probably happier than she's been in years that you haven't dumped your smelly arse in her bed for a few nights."

That got a chuckle out of the crew. Baker flashed his best smile. It was all in fun.

But Baker was also deflecting the group's attention from the problem at hand. They would be down here another week, maybe more. It was a bad sign so early for anyone to have a problem with the circumstances.

"C'mon, let's get to work. Fair said we hafta clear a space around the entire ore vein so we know what we be dealin' with. So, let's get to it."

The men went back to their hammers. So far, so good.

*****

"Something's going on over at the Consolidated Virginia Mine. Their crosscut crew has not come up out of the mine for two days. They might have hit something."

"Ralston, you worry too much. It's been raining so hard for the last two days, maybe they just had to pump more water than normal. The rain has been biblical. I heard that visiting priest gave a homily comparing our rain with the time of Noah. Fitting. Look, we checked over the Consolidated when we had the chance to buy. The men we sent down into the shaft said there was nothing but the lowest of low-grade ore."

"Sharon, they could have made a mistake."

William Sharon, president of the Bank of California, suppressed a look of disdain. "Bill, the strategy over the last five years has made our Bank of California the owner of seven different mines, all producing. We've become the premier financier in Virginia City and the main financial force pushing development of almost all mining operations throughout the Comstock. Each of those seven mines went into foreclosure on one of our loans. I made decisions on those foreclosures of what were thought at the time to be failing mines, only to turn them around into producing assets. There were other mines that went under too, but we passed on them for good reasons just like the Consolidated. Those mines we passed on never generated anything of significance again. We haven't made any mistakes."

"Yes, I know your strategy of making loans at two percent per month when everyone was doing five percent per month loans enticed several of the mine owners in need of capital, many of which later failed. We were able to swoop in and foreclose on the seven, and you did a great job of turning those around. But the combined production is waning. Our revenue stream is drying up. We need another strike."

"No, *you* need another strike. Your money and assets are being sucked out in ever increasing volume with the construction of the stupid hotel you got yourself involved with." Sharon did not mince his words.

William Ralston was worried. As a San Francisco investor from the beginning with the Bank of California, he had reaped huge benefits from Sharon's mining manipulations and their partnership. But he had invested heavily in a hotel in San Francisco, the Palace, and the drain on his resources had become critical. He needed another cash infusion and quick.

Sharon's face showed he was tired of Ralston's worries.

"Mackay and his Irish gang of investors are the ones who are going to go bust. Our spies tell me this wonderful crosscut they started is really headed away from the main Comstock vein being worked by all the big mines. They are headed away from decent ore and digging into nothing but dirt."

Sharon now looked across to see if he had finally done enough to allay Ralston's current fears.

But apparently not yet. Ralston persisted.

"Mackay has never played the stock speculation game. Almost everyone else in this godforsaken town has, but not Mackay. Every mine he has invested in has produced. His fame and now substantial fortune came from picking the right mines to invest in."

"He's just been on a lucky streak," said Sharon.

"Lucky streak. Looks like he knows more than the rest of us. First, he bought into the Union, then the Walker followed by the Kentuck, where he hit it big, after which they bought the Hale & Norcross in '69, which has continued to produce since the day they bought it. Now they have sunk a ton of money into the Virginia Consolidated Mine and adjacent California. It doesn't sound like luck to me. He hasn't missed yet."

William Sharon showed no intention of backing down; he did not like to lose even if it centered around a simple argument. He took every chance he could to extol his financial legacy here in Virginia City.

"We haven't done so bad either, William. You and I set up the Bank of California after watching the gyrating opportunities in Virginia mining stocks both in San Francisco and Virginia City. Each time we foreclosed, we had our local spies legitimized each ore vein. We knew when and where we could make money. And we made money, you and me. That wasn't luck either."

"*Made* is the key term, Sharon. Not *making* but *made*. Our mines are petering out. To make matters worse, the entire mining equity market has virtually crashed. Between the Coinage Act and Hayward's ridiculous stock speculation fraud last year in '72 at the Savage Mine, no one has confidence in the markets. Hayward held his crew down in his mine just like Mackay is doing, and everyone thought he'd hit it big. But it was a ruse. The Savage's stock ran from sixty-two dollars per foot up to over six hundred. Every other mine had their stock run up proportionately. But Hayward's play was a hoax. The crash started this year, and we're all down over forty percent."

"I know the history just as well as you, Ralston."

"Well, you've omitted an important piece of the history. You agreed to allow Mackay to use the Gould & Curry shaft to start his crosscut, which now has everyone buzzing."

"That's because he told me he intended to dig in the opposite direction of the Gould's vein. I happily allowed him to dig away. I wanted to let those Irishmen lose some of their Hale & Norcross money."

Sharon sat back down at his desk, a motion of conciliation.

"Look Ralston, I'll admit the markets are volatile."

"What an understatement. This place is usually the personification of financial volatility. But things are outright crazy now."

"Yes, the local markets are normally crazy. But we have seen monumental swings in share prices and mine values over the last ten years."

"But Sharon, this moment in time could be a watershed like never before. Any false step here and businesses could be lost."

"I'll also concede the Coinage Act would hurt. Those damn Germans used silver as a measure to back national wealth for centuries. But they have seen our little city destroy their silver values. They were probably worried any additional flood of new ore into the monetary systems would continue to pound the value of silver. I am sure your banker friends keep talking and fretting about a future reduction in silver value allowing people to buy gold dollars with devalued minted silver coins. They figured how to buy silver dollars at the devalued cost of seventy-five cents then turn around and buy gold coins dollar for dollar, making over twenty-five cents per coin. It is robbing governments of valuable gold resources. So, the Germans reacted. They announced Germany would demonetize silver. But Congress has been playing around with the Coinage legislation for almost three years. They'll never get around to passing a similar law here in the United States."

"Sharon, didn't you see the wires from San Francisco this morning?"

William Sharon lit and took an initial draw on his cigar. "No, I was up late playing poker at the Washoe Club as is my custom on Wednesday nights. It is the only night of the week at the only table in town where the limits suit my need for risk. I stayed long into the evening, looking to recoup my losses of last week. I woke up late and did not have time to read the morning wires."

"William, President Grant signed the Coinage Act into law yesterday, February 12, 1873."

Ralston could see the news stunned Sharon. It was as if the man could not grasp the reality of the news. Ralston took the opportunity to pound his point home. "In signing the Coinage Act, the current mining markets are going to be even more volatile. These markets are already more unstable than any in the history of American finance. Since the Coinage Act is now the law, silver will no longer be used for legal tender, and bullion submitted for stamping into coinage will no longer be accepted. The United States will no longer be a bimetal country. The U.S. financial markets will rest solely on the gold standard.

"Bill, he didn't. Grant didn't sign that damn law, did he?"

"He sure did."

"The crook. I heard the Germans had representatives over here last year spreading around half a million dollars in bribes around Congress to get that bill passed."

"It takes effect on April first. Sharon, I know you hate Mackay, but think carefully about this. If the Virginia Consolidated has really hit a big new find, it could virtually destroy an already fragile silver market. The value is decreasing now; think what an additional flood of silver would do. We could be looking at a financial apocalypse for this mining industry."

Sharon took his time to respond. "You're right. We need to hunker down and carefully manage our seven mines through this. We can find markets for silver other than coinage. But we cannot let Mackay start production on another Ophir or Yellow Jacket type vein of silver. We have to do whatever we can to really make him hit financial bottom."

"How?"

Sharon pondered. "I will get my spies to find out exactly what's going on down in that mine. If there is a strike, Mackay will need supplies and men to start producing ore. We will block all avenues of material supply. Also, the bank will not lend them any money. He'll need money. We won't give it to him. We'll call it too risky."

"That's the Sharon I'm used to hearing. Vicious. It would be a great start if we can block purchase of his materials, especially timber. He'll need timber to excavate. But even if we can block Mackay, we will need to position the sale of silver from our seven mines to maintain the going rate for it. Either way, we still must find new sources of ore."

"Don't worry, the Coinage Act will cause another depression in the market. Just like in 1865 we used a depression to our advantage, fore-closing on loans and taking over mines. We can do it again. The Bank of California might just be the only financial institution in the world that can take advantage of what is sure to be a severe retraction in global financial markets."

"Get those spies to work as soon as you can."

*****

"Sam, where are you? There is a story brewing over at the Consol-idated."

Dan De Quille slammed the door to the Virginia City *Territorial Enterprise* behind him. The *Enterprise* was one of only two daily pa-pers in Virginia City.

The Sam he was referring to was Samuel Clemens, otherwise known as Mark Twain.

"They have a crew that hasn't come up for two days. John Mackay is not one to play the silly stock manipulation game like Hayward did at the Savage. If Mackay is holding a crew down in the mine, he's found something. We have to find out what it is."

"Clemens has been gone for almost ten years," came a voice from a room to the rear of the front office. "And you know it."

The responder was a young typesetter named Robert Bender. He had heard De Quille's verbal musings from the back room.

"You keep talking to Clemens as if his ghost is among us," said Bender. "It's creepy. Last I heard Clemens isn't dead yet."

"I am looking for inspiration. When Clemens *was* here, we never waited to verify sources. I think they have found something big down there. Sam Clemens would just write the story we thought folks wanted to hear and wait to see if it matched up with the facts later. I am hoping that, by invoking his name, I can come up with an angle for a story."

Bender did not let up. "Why call upon the man who is ancient history. He's gone. He actually ran away. As I understand it, Clemens had been employed as the city editor at the *Enterprise*, but he'd left in 1864, avoiding the need to attend a duel he'd committed to in Virginia City. Clemens and his penchant for telling tall tales offended someone in town who called him out. But not being a person of compassion, Clemens kept making fun of the circumstance. In doing that, Clemens enhanced the anticipation for the impending event by use of his byline and following articles. By the time the date arrived, there had been such a buildup it could not be cancelled or avoided easily. So, he left. He's not been back. He ran."

"You did not know the man like I did. He is a genius."

"De Quille, why don't you just go ask John Mackay to let you go down into his mine and see what is going on? John Mackay may be the single most credible, upstanding owner of any mine here in this crazy city. If you ask, he might take you down and show you what is happening."

"Robert, you are brilliant. That is exactly what I will do."

But he had to think. Dan De Quille was not his real name. His real name was William Wright. He'd started out as a beat reporter but moved into what many called humor. De Quille's transformation happened about the same time Sam Clemens took the name Mark Twain. The two wrote scathing articles lambasting everything from politicians to ladies' fundraisers. The two used humor to lessen the blows of their indiscriminate biting assessments. They caused so much consternation that their reputations extended all the way to San Francisco. Part bravado, part personal security, they both decided it would be best if they did a good part of their writing under pen names. Clemens chose Mark Twain after his saloon nickname of "Two Marks" on account of the first two drinks he'd order each day after work. De Quille simply took the name after the old writing utensil. Twain went on to become famous worldwide. De Quille had stayed on at the *Enterprise*. But if he were the first to report some large new ore find, Mackay could make him famous.

"You see in the San Francisco papers that Clemens is actually in Europe traveling around giving his talks?"

De Quille looked at Robert. He saw in the youngster's face a look of admiration that bordered on hero worship.

"Yes, our ex-compatriot Mr. Clemens, now known much better by his nom de guerre of Mark Twain, has made a real name for himself. Who would have thought that the blowhard with a fertile mind for partial truths could have gone so far?"

"But he's funny. That's what the papers say."

"Funny maybe. Sam's real gift is that, in any of his stories, whether he is embarrassing anyone from politicians, enemies, or even himself, he distills a kernel of who we are as humans. People laugh, but what's going on in their brains is that the story he tells could be about them. His crowd feels they know him because they think he's talking about them or someone they know."

"Would that make him a genius?"

"No," said De Quille. "That makes him one of the best liars on the planet. He and I started the group down at the Delta Saloon just so we could have a place to tell our outrageous stories."

"The Liars Club!"

"Yes, Robert, the Liars Club. Mark Twain as the supreme leader of our group made it a point to avoid having the truth ever pass his lips while in session."

"I miss those days. I miss setting the type and laughing while I was reading what he wrote."

"I miss him, too. And what I said earlier is true. We could use him now to ferret out what is going on down beneath the Consolidated. The funny thing is, to be a good liar, you must know where the truth falls so you can avoid it. Twain was good at finding out what the truth was, so he could religiously avoid it."

*****

Outside a storm had hit. Thunder and rain came in liberal quantities.

Little Sean and Luke sat in the corner of a wood sided house which provided little barrier from the elements. Both were cold. Waverly could see it. So could Elmer Lennox. The difference was that Waverly might have cared. Lennox didn't. Neither of the boys had originally ridden out the day they were taken with any heavy coats. Waverly had thrown the boys a couple of blankets, but they did not do much. Both spent a good deal of time crying and asking for their mother.

"Can't we make them shut up?" said an exasperated Lennox. "If they don't stop whimpering, I might just have to shoot one."

Waverly started at the suggestion. "Boss said if you do that he'd come after you and never stop."

"Brown is not the one who has to sit and listen to this."

"They're kids, they're scared. You'd be too if you were in their shoes." Waverly answered.

"I don't care what Brown said, if the taller one don't quit whimpering, I'm going to take him out, and he'll never come back. He won't whimper anymore, either."

"Can't let you do that, Elmer. Boss said I'd be responsible, too."

"Then I have to get out of here. I can't stand it any longer."

"We're supposed to stay."

"Well, Charley, you have a choice. Either I get out of here, or I do something with those kids. Your call."

Waverly considered. Neither was a good option, but he'd rather make sure the boys were in one piece so he did not have to deal with Brown. If Lennox chose to abandon his instructions, then Brown could not blame Waverly.

"Go then. But don't expect me to cover if Brown shows up. You will pay the consequences all by yourself."

"Gladly. I'm not afraid of Brown. Let him try to pull iron on me. He'll never do it because he already knows he would lose if he faced me direct."

Waverly shook his head at Lennox's ability to create chaos and separation. He sat looking at the man without saying another word. But in his thoughts, he knew at some point Lennox was either going to have to leave the group, or he was going to be killed by Brown.

"All right, I'm leaving. Maybe I'll go up to Virginia City and see my girl, Katie."

Waverly had the thought that any girl who would entertain Elmer Lennox would be courting disaster in one form or another. It seemed he created problems wherever he went.

Elmer walked out the door. The boys instantaneously stopped whimpering as if they could instinctively tell an immediate threat to them had left.

Waverly said to both, "Let's see if we can get you something to eat."

Chapter Eleven

Will and Beth left Carson City. They rode anxiously, pushing their horses.

"Temperature is dropping, wind is coming up too. This is going to be a bad one."

Will turned in his saddle to look back to see Beth following behind. He barely glanced up to get some idea as to the severity of the storm without taking the full brunt of the pelting rain directly in his face. He couldn't see much beyond her, but what he did see was a sky full of low clouds, dark and thick.

The thunder became louder and louder. Just about the time they pulled up to the spot that the gang's tracks left in the Carson Road, the skies erupted. A downpour followed, making it impossible to see more than ten to fifteen yards in front of them. More importantly, the tracks in the dirt were washing away as they watched.

"Bound to happen sooner or later. Haven't had any rain for almost a month. But I cannot believe it had to happen right now. Right when we needed some help, the good Lord let the skies open up." Will sat atop Powder with his duster on, which was dripping constant rivulets of water.

Beth, having heard the thunder and not having a duster, had just purchased one back in Carson City. Will looked at her. "How's the new duster working?"

"I'm not getting as wet as I would have, but I am still getting soaked. Is there any place we can go to get out of this until it passes?"

"There is nothing out here on the road up past Mound House to Virginia City. I don't think there is a tree for twenty miles. You leave the Carson Valley, and there's nothing but desert out there."

Beth tried to look up at Will without rain draining on to her face— it was hopeless. "Then, let's keep going after them. We need to get to the boys."

Will shook his head. "Without tracks, there's no tellin' where they went. The tracks we could see before the rain looked like they were headed toward Virginia City. That would fit with the instructions that you told me came from the man who looked like Drake Sutton. But they could have stopped in Mound House, headed up to Gold Hill, or dozens of other routes or destinations. Without tracks to follow, we'd just be guessing where they went."

Will could see that, despite the downpour of heavenly water, Beth's eyes were making some water of their own. She was close to sobbing. So desperate yet so helpless.

"Will, what are we going to do?"

He considered the options, none of which appealed. "Let's find some shelter until the storm blows over. That's the best we can do in this weather. There has to be some kind of shelter in Mound House just up ahead. Once the storm blows over, then maybe we should split. I'll head into Virginia City and see if I can find this brother of Drake Sutton. You can stay in Mound House and look around. If I were going to hide the boys, I would not take them all the way into Virginia City. Too many eyes and ears. I would think of hiding them in one of the towns on the way up the mountain, like Gold Hill or Mound House. Maybe you can find someone who has seen them."

Will saw Beth settle slightly at hearing the beginnings of a plan. The prospect of some positive action quelled the emotions temporarily.

She hesitated but only briefly. "Okay, I'll ask around those two cities. Neither are very large, so maybe someone has seen something."

"Don't forget, Juan has been following them too. He had the benefit of seeing the tracks. If you can find Juan, maybe he'll know where they went."

"You're right, Juan is out there somewhere. Maybe I will get lucky and find him."

Will then changed the topic. "I sent a wire back in Carson City to Henry Millard. Asked him if he knew anyone in Virginia City who might be able to help. Just before I left, I got a response. Henry said I should look up a man named John Mackay. Said he owns mines and is very wealthy but also knows people in Virginia City."

"Do you think he's someone who will even talk to you? He doesn't even know you."

Will shrugged. "Henry said he was going to send a wire to the man and make some kind of introduction. Who knows, wealthy men know other wealthy men. Maybe this Mackay guy owes Henry a favor. Maybe we can get lucky, and he'll give me some idea of where to look for the boys, or Brown, or both."

Beth nodded, but it wasn't a convincing nod.

Will had been trying to keep them moving on the road which was now under inches of water. "If this keeps up, there is going to be serious flooding."

"Yeah," said Beth. "Forty days of this, and I could see how we should start looking for an ark as there would be oceans covering what had been desert."

"We have a bigger problem," said Will. "If it keeps up into tonight, it's cold enough to snow. We will have to stop tonight at Mound House and find some shelter. We can't head up the side of Mount Davidson as it will definitely be snowing up there."

"How far to Mound House?" asked Beth.

"Only a couple more miles. Let's head there and find a place to stay, even if it's only the livery stable. We need to get out of the rain and get ready for the cold tonight."

Beth did not respond. But her look now became steeled to the weather. No more tears. Will saw resolve, a mother's resolve.

*****

Elmer Lennox headed up the Six Mile Canyon road still thinking of meeting his girl Katie. He had been contemplating going or not, but after thinking about it for a few days, he decided he might as well. Wagon traffic on Six Mile Canyon could normally stretch one wagon after another the entire way. But today, it was empty. Probably because of the flooding from the heavens. He pulled his hat low and collar high against the constant rain.

"Sam Brown can't tell me I have to sit in some room with two kids. Hell, it might take him two weeks to get the money from Toal. No way can I sit there for two weeks."

Elmer wasn't talking to anyone in particular. Just venting.

"I'll have to spend one night out on the trail heading up to Virginia City, but I can get close enough before I camp so tomorrow, I'll have plenty of time to circle the upside of town so I can get to Katie's place without using the main road through Virginia City itself. I can't go through town. Someone's liable to see me, and word will get back to Brown. I'll camp out a couple of days and watch to see when might be a good time to ride in and see her.

"Teamsters normally driving their ox-drawn rigs of ore and supplies must be worried about the dark skies. Last time it rained hard, this road became a mud sump. Wagons were stuck for weeks blocking traffic long after the rain stopped."

Lennox looked up at the thick layer of clouds above. The sound of thunder rolled up the canyon behind him.

"Better get a move on before it begins to snow. Have to find an old mine or an outcropping. It gonna be a cold night." Lennox dug his spurs into the sorrel's sides, pushing him up the steep hill.

Chapter Twelve

John Millian stood at the front door to the home of Julia Bulette. He knocked. "Julia, are you engaged?"

The door opened. Before him stood a statuesque woman whose simple dark dress with full skirt did not disguise her broad shoulders, thin waist, and full figure. The high neck of the dress closed around a long graceful neck. Her dark hair was pulled back in a simple bun with a bit of a twist in the rear which he thought must be for a hint of style. Millan considered that the overall image at first glance presented a far more modest picture belying the lady's true profession.

"Good evening, John. No, I am not engaged at the moment. Would you like to come in out of the rain?"

Julia Bulette lived at the corner of D Street and Union, the beginning of the red-light district of Virginia City. While not opulent by any means, it was a high rent neighborhood compared to the cribs occupied by the more common working girls further to the north on D Street. No other working girl had a home like Julia. She was in a class of her own.

"You have such a nice home; a pleasant comfort on a night like this."

"Yes, the house suits me well, but I do not own it. Rent is required each month, which requires a girl to keep working." The comment was delivered with a flirtatious smile. "Can I offer you something to drink?"

"That would be very nice indeed."

"Let me see what I have…any special requests?" This time, the smile was projected over her shoulder as she left the room.

The enticement was obvious to John. "Maybe I could come and assist."

"Please do. We can decide what needs to be served jointly." Her smile disappeared behind an inviting toss of her head as Julia left the main room. Millian needed more inducement.

"I'm right behind you."

*****

Their business having been completed, Julia Bulette lounged on her bed under her sheets. John Millian lay next to her, still catching his breath. Julia had attained her place of special importance in her profession by making sure her customers wanted to return. She was selective as to who she would entertain. Men had to be clean, capable of paying her higher rates, and adhere to what she referred to as "appropriate bed manners."

"John, I hate to rush you, but I have to be at the volunteer fire department fairly soon. They are raising money again for a second fire wagon. I have to make my appearance and contribution before the soirée starts and the respectable women begin arriving."

"I heard you were a regular contributor to our local fire department."

"Those men volunteer in ways most in this town would never consider themselves. Yes, I have always made it a point to contribute what I can. You never know when a fire might start here in town. If there is such a catastrophe, I'd like to think the men would do what they can to save my small abode."

Millian rolled onto his elbow to face Julia directly, speaking in a low tone, "And I am sure it helps secure relationships with clientele too." An insinuatingly judgmental smile spread across his face.

"Why John, I would never reveal the names of my customers to anyone. But, yes, one never knows where the next customer might come from." Julia returned her own smile, a smile a sophisticate would say resembled a woman in a famous French painting, lips of limited expression below ever perceptive eyes.

"Oh, I am sure the money you contribute is returned several times over."

Julia did not really like John Millian. The intention of his comments here did nothing to change her impression. "John, everyone here in Virginia City is looking for ways to support themselves. I am no different. In fact, I go out of my way to please my customers. It seems like you return time and again for just those reasons."

"Julia, please do not take my comments harshly." Reaching out to gently lay a hand on her forearm, he tried to mend the opening rift. "I intend no insult. Much to the contrary. I'm impressed at how you maintain your position of special importance here in town."

With a hint of added coolness, Julia moved to conclude the engagement. "I'd be happy to bring you a cup of water, but we are both going to have to get dressed so we can leave. I am sorry to rush, but today is a little out of the ordinary because of the event with the fire department."

Julia reached back to touch Millian's own forearm as if to say no insult taken, even if it were not true. In the end, he was a paying customer.

"Speaking of supporting one's profession, John, we have the matter of your bill. You owe me for both this visit and your visit of last week."

"Julia, I know I owe you money, but can you wait for just two more weeks? I have always paid you, but it will be two weeks before I will have the funds needed at present. But after those two weeks, I will have sufficient monies to pay you for services coming in the next six months."

Intrigued, Julia pursued. "My, while I hesitate to extend any credit, as I have told you on several occasions, whatever could be happening to provide you with monies for six months of services?"

"The source of the funds is something I cannot reveal."

"You want me to extend credit to you based on your word of some-thing happening in the future but do not feel it necessary to tell me what the event or source of the new funds is going to be? How do you expect me to react? Under the circumstances, I must insist you pay me, John, especially as you do not think this upcoming event is worthy enough to reveal so I can determine if I should extend the credit." Her look was her most enticing, but below the surface, it was forced. She wanted to be paid.

Millian hesitated. He rolled to his back, looking at the ceiling. Julia watched. She had played these games before with many others. She'd already concluded to force a resolution.

Millian rolled back on his elbow, looked again at Julia, and sighed. "You cannot tell a soul. Cannot tell a soul, do you hear?"

"In my business, I hear many secrets. I have no problem keeping a secret."

Millian hesitated again, then waved his arm in front of him as if to wipe some imaginary slate clean and start something completely new. "I am working with Sam Brown on something and stand to make five thousand dollars in two weeks. Then I can pay you the monies owed and for services long into the future."

Julia's face displayed unmistaken dismay. "Sam Brown is a despic-able being. He is so bad, I am not sure he is of this earth. If you are involved in something with him, you best extricate yourself immedi-ately."

"It's already done. All I did was provide him with information. He's going to kidnap two kids from a rancher named Toal in the Carson Valley and hold them for ransom. The plan is for the rancher to ask for Sutton at the Delta Saloon and then get paid. Once the father pays, I will get my cut, and that's the end. I have nothing more to do with it, only information."

"John, how horrible. How could you do such a thing?"

"I didn't do anything, I just provided information."

Julia came close to delivering further admonishment but caught herself. Sam Brown was not only a horrible individual, he was very dangerous. It might be best to stay as far away from this as possible, even if it meant not getting paid for her services today.

"Well, I cannot say I approve. Based on your promise to pay, I will wait two more weeks. But John, there will be no further engagements until I am paid for what you already owe."

"I understand."

Millian stood, dressed, and looked over his shoulder. Julia returned his look not having moved from the bed. "Thank you for appreciating my situation, Julia." Then in a complete change of tone, he added, "And Julia, you cannot tell anyone. I mean anyone."

She only smiled.

Millian continued out the front door, closing it softly.

Julia pulled herself out of her bed. Kidnapping. Someone had to put a stop to Sam Brown. Julia knew she did not have anything approaching the power to do that. But she knew someone who did: the 601s. No one knew who they were. In a town with non-existent law enforcement, the 601s acted as vigilantes, but they were the only justice. They were the only group who could deal with Sam Brown.

Julia did not know who the 601s were, but she knew of someone who did, and she was headed to see him right now: volunteer fireman Kevin Hurley.

Chapter Thirteen

1873 February
San Francisco, CA

William O'Brien looked at the messages in front of him. Across the hall sat Jim Flood. Each sat in their respective office looking at the same documents with the same numbers. Market numbers, and none of them good.

"Do you see what I'm looking at?"

"Yes, Bill, I see what you are looking at."

"The market in mining stocks is crashing. Passage of the Coinage Act is going to kill the business."

"Bill, you are looking at catastrophe, and I am looking at opportunity."

"Jim, how can you think this is a positive development? Consolidated and California stock just went from over seven hundred dollars per share to two fifty. And the only reason our stock hasn't sunk any further is that people think there is something brewing with the men held down in the mine."

"Yes, isn't it wonderful? We can start buying at less than half of yesterday's price per share. We can make it look like we are propping up the company with our own investment. We were going to do the same thing, anyway; now we can do it at less than half the cost. The best part, though, is no one will now think we are starting a run on the stock. We can put out the word we are simply supporting our own investment."

"But the play is all based on the value of the new ore find."

"Bill, the coded messages are now saying the ore vein is over three hundred feet wide. Three hundred feet. That is twenty times the size of the Ophir's big ore vein. When we break news of the size and quality of the ore, our price could go to over two thousand dollars per share. We've seen it happen before on lesser finds."

"Yes, you might be right. I just hope those boys are sure about the size and quality."

"Mackay has never played games with the markets. He leaves that to us. He's even lost money being too honest with information on downturns in production. He's not overstating this one."

"Then you are right; this could be one of the biggest stock plays we have ever pulled off."

"Now you are looking at this in the right light, Bill! Keep buying C & C stock, as much as you can get your hands on. Play up the devastation the Coinage Act is creating."

*****

Father Cecconi looked up at the skies. "Sister Charity, it looks like things have cleared up enough for me to head back to Carson City."

"Oh Father, don't go yet. Bishop Manogue is not back, and we still have several families whose homes were washed away by the flooding."

"The rains were terrible. I never knew there were so many people living in simple tents. How do they survive the winters?"

"Many don't Father. It is a true sadness."

"But in the deluge of water, a tent is not much better than a coat. This whole town is built on a desert slope of loose sand without trees. In a deluge, the dirt and water flow together downhill. It is a poor plan for living space."

"It's all many of them have, Father."

"I will be happy to stay another day or so and assist where I can."

"Father, I keep thinking of the vision you saw."

"Sister, you have to put that out of your mind. This was only a rain. A rain in the desert."

"But there were hundreds of homes lost. And they have yet to determine how many people died. You don't think this is the beginning, do you?"

"Beginning of what, Sister?"

"Of the predictions in the Bible."

"I do not think so. I hope my fears are nothing more than an oversensitive imagination."

Chapter Fourteen

1873 February
Mound House, NV

Will looked up. He laid on his back staring at the roof of a weathered wood building meant for animals, not humans. Beth laid at a right angle with her head on his stomach, still sleeping. Morning had not yet broken. Damp lifted up off the ground in all directions. The deluge had poured down uninterrupted for two days. Travel had been impossible. While he knew finding shelter was the best option at the time, he was two days further removed from finding his boys. Tension hung all around him like vermin creeping down from the cracks in the slap-sided walls. These same flimsy walls seeped responsibility. His sons were in the hands of men capable of almost anything. The rats of his thoughts were not real, but the men who had Luke & Sean were. They were the true vermin.

As if she could feel the concern oozing from his muscles, Beth rolled over and looked at him directly. He knew instantly she was just as concerned as he. But he had to channel that disquiet. He had to act without evidence of unrest.

"Good thing we stayed here in Mound House these last two days. There is no way any horse could have made it up to Virginia City in that rain and mud."

Will sat up now, looking at Beth. The flimsy wooden walls housed a livery stable. They were in an unused stall, the only place they could find on short notice after the skies opened up. They had spent two days in the leaky barn along with several horses and teams sheltered from the rain.

Will looked down at the straw between them and chuckled. "I spend money on only the finest of hotels for you, fifty cents a night for a dry stall."

The comment brought the briefest of smiles to Beth's face. It had now been three days since the boys had been taken. She had not smiled at all until just now.

Beth slowly spun to look around the stall. "I'll have to remember to bring special heavy-duty night clothes to wear if you ever do get around to inviting me on a trip."

Will stood and walked to the large opening of the barn. He pushed the sliding wood door that hung on a rolling track overhead, to open it. Sunlight beamed in. A gust of wind followed, a warm wind.

"We go from a biblical deluge to a hot wind. This is February; rain I expect, hot wind I don't. A day or two of this, and everything will be bone dry again. In New Mexico, they'd call this wind a sirocco." Will turned to see that Beth had not moved. He returned to the stall.

"Will, how are we going to find Sean and Luke?"

"Let's stick to the plan we made. You stay here and look around. See if you can find anyone who has seen Juan. I'll head up to Virginia City and go to this Delta Saloon. If I get lucky, I'll try to confront Sutton. But it's about a two-thousand-foot climb over ten to fifteen miles from Mound House to Virginia City. A good horse can make it in one day, but you'd have to rest it the next. Not knowing what I might find, I should probably take two days on the uphill climb. That means a night out on the trail, but if I have to ride out to pursue, I'm not going to have to wait to rest Powder. Chasing down men in Texas as a Ranger taught me to conserve my horseflesh as you might end up traveling over a hundred miles to get who you were after."

"Will, he'll have other men." Beth stood quickly, moving straight at Will. "You have to be careful. I can't lose you; not now, not ever."

Naked emotion dripped from her words. He paused before he responded. "You're not going to lose me. One of those Sutton's already tried and look where he ended up. I'll deal with the next one just the same."

Beth stood right in front of Will now. He looked down into a face full of multiple worries. He reached out and pulled her close. It was a moment they both needed.

"I'll get going right away. Be careful here. Don't be too obvious. Just ride around as if you know where you are going, but keep your eyes peeled. If you see any of the men who were in the gang, don't do anything. Send me a message from the telegraph office here in Mound House. I'll check for messages in Virginia City. If I get the message, I'll send a return before I head down the hill. Just hold tight until I can get back."

Beth nodded. "But where are you going to check for messages? How will I get word to you if I do find the children?"

"Send a telegram and ask the telegraph office to deliver it to the Delta Saloon, but ask them to give a copy to this John Mackay fella, too. One or the other should know where I am at any given time."

Will then saddled Powder and packed his gear, including bedroll and rifle. He turned to Beth, who was still standing at the barn door. He reached out his right hand and gently cupped her chin. "I'll get them. I'll get the boys back."

He turned, stood in his stirrup, and came to his seat in the saddle. He paused and looked back at Beth. The looks exchanged spoke volumes, but no words came out. Will tried to smile, then touched Powder lightly on the flanks and began to walk out of town.

*****

Charley Waverly looked at both boys. All three were now cold and dirty after two days of rain and sleeping in a shack with a dirt floor. The boys slept a great deal, which was fine with Waverly. He had tried to find things for them to do, grabbing a couple of small sticks for them to play with in any way they could. It had kept them amused for about an hour. The sticks sat on the floor ever since, untouched.

"Okay, I have to go check for messages. You know what I have to do."

Luke and Sean had pained looks on their faces. For the first two days after Elmer Lennox left, Waverly had tied them up so they would not try to run out the door. He also put gags on their mouths. They had cried the entire time he had been gone. He needed to check to see if Brown had contacted the rancher again. The youngsters looked as if they were beyond crying. They took the hand ties and gags without sound or comment.

Waverly walked out the door. He only had two blocks to cover to the telegraph office. He'd established a routine with the telegraph officer, telling him he'd be returning early each day until his message arrived. He didn't know what time of day Brown might send his message, but if he got it in the morning, he had a full day ahead to move his charges if needed. If he checked at night, he would have no such opportunity. He was looking down at the ground most of the way, doing his best to avoid the biggest puddles left by the hard rain.

Then he looked up and saw a rider on a large gray horse. A fine looking animal. The man was headed out of town to the north. Toward Virginia City.

*****

Beth sat atop her horse on one of the several rises circling the city of Mound House. Will had left earlier in the morning. He'd be in

Virginia City tomorrow if his time estimates were right. She looked down at the city itself; what there was of it clung to the railroad depo on the lower, flat ground. Mound House existed and survived solely because of the junction between the Virginia & Truckee Railroad and the Carson & Colorado Railroad in the middle of the city limits. Looking out over the meeting of the rails for both lines, Beth remembered the Virginia & Truckee Railroad had been built by William Sharon and the Bank of California in 1869. The V & T's connection to Carson City and then on to Reno and the Central Pacific had been announced to the entirety of the Carson Valley. Beth could see down to the depot where trains moved tons and tons of ore from the Virginia City mines. The intersecting Carson & Colorado line ran to mines further south both in Nevada and California all the way to Bodie. The ore from all the combined sources collected here at Mound House for transport to the stamping mills along the Carson River.

Then, Beth saw another rider on the opposite ridge across this bowl in the earth's surface where the town was nestled. She could not make out the rider, but she could see the black and white pattern of the Tobiano colored horse he was riding. She knew the horse to be Domino, Juan's horse. The rider looked back at Beth. She stood up in her stirrups and waved. Juan waved back.

Beth spurred her horse, heading off in a circular route and holding to the ridges surrounding the city. Juan started riding the opposite way on the same intersecting route

"Juan, I can't believe I found you."

"Beth. It is good to see you. I do not know what Juan should do. I think I know where the *ninos* are, but I stay out of town during the rains and have not seen the men who brought them here since."

"Oh Juan, what good news. Were Luke and Sean brought here to Mound House?"

"I think so. I follow tracks before the rain wiped them out, and they all came here. The tracks led to a house, *la casa*, over 'dere, close to the house of the railroad." He turned to point toward one of the structures in town.

"Near the train depot?"

"*Sí Señora*. I saw one hombre three days ago walking out of the casa down near the depot, that one with *tres* windows." Juan looked out again at the wooden building he referred to. "But I no see anyone today since the rains stop."

Beth pondered the information. "Will left for Virginia City. I can send him a telegraph. He said he'd check for messages, but I don't know when he might actually stop at the telegraph office and pick it up. We must keep watch. We have to make sure they still have the boys."

Juan nodded. After his own pause, he said, "Maybe we keep watch to see how many men are in the casa. Maybe some of the hombres already go. Juan can sneak up tonight and look into the window and see."

"That might be a plan. I don't think it'd be a good idea for me to head down to the telegraph office in daylight as they might see me and know someone is following. I like the idea of you taking a look in the window tonight. I can slip into town at first light tomorrow and use the telegraph office to let Will know what you find. Maybe he can tell us what we should do."

Juan nodded.

Beth pulled her horse and turned on the trail. "Let's find a more sheltered place where we can keep an eye on the house until dark."

*****

Waverly had a decision to make. The boy called Sean had been vomiting every other hour. Sweat soaked through his clothes. Waverly tried to wrap him in his own blanket in addition to the blanket he'd

106

already given the boy, but he still shivered constantly. The child needed to see a doctor. But he knew he could not bring anyone into the house. It would be obvious what was going on. Waverly also knew that if the boy died, he'd have to answer to Brown. Waverly didn't like his circumstances. But the only idea he'd come up with was to wire Brown and tell him the boy was sick and needed a doctor, then ask what to do. He tied up Luke and told him to sit tight. Luke glared at Waverly. Tough kid. He thought of tying up the other boy, but he looked so sick, he figured he wouldn't be moving anywhere.

Waverly walked out the door and headed to the telegraph office.

*****

"There, see? Can you see that *hombre*? Was he one of the men who took the boys?"

"Yes, that's one of the men who took the boys. They must be in that house."

Juan and Beth watched as the man walked past the train depot and headed into another building. A telegraph wire was strung from the top of the small building to the telltale string of poles running east and west.

"He's in the telegraph office."

Beth pondered. "Probably checking for messages from the others or maybe sending one."

"At least we know it is a good idea for Juan to check out that *casa*."

Beth nodded in accord. "We'll keep watch until tonight and hope my sons are there."

*****

The black ink of night had fallen. Beth had waited just over a ridge behind several boulders while they watched for movement. The man had returned to the house. But no one entered or left after that. Beth strained to keep her body still. The drive to walk straight down to the house where her boys might be consumed all thought. But she kept thinking she should do what Will would do. She had a plan and knew she and Juan had to stick to it.

"It is time that Juan should go?"

Beth looked at the loyal ranch hand and nodded. "Yes, but be careful, Juan."

Beth watched as Juan started down the slope on foot. He stopped frequently to listen and watch. Beth lost sight of him not long after he started. The darkness hung as a curtain spoiling the view of another room. She could only wait.

It took about twenty minutes for Juan to return.

"*Señora*, the boys are there, inside the *casa* we watch."

Beth turned with her back to the rock she'd used for cover and looked away from the city. Her pulse quickened in heavy pounding beats. Her heart felt twice its normal size. *The boys are there. Now what?*

"How many men are there?"

"*Uno*. Only *uno*. I stay and look into the window many times to make sure. The other *hombres* are gone. I no see any other horses."

"Juan, if there is only one man, we should try to take the boys back tomorrow."

Juan did not respond immediately. He considered their position. "Maybe we wait to see if the other *hombres* return. We no want to be surprised by the others and fail to get the boys. If no other men come, then we take the boys tomorrow night."

It was then Beth's turn to consider. "I really want to get the boys as soon as I can. But you're right, we cannot fail. We have to know we can get them and ride."

Juan waited. Conflict showed on Beth's face, but it turned into decision. "Okay, I agree. Let's wait. I'll send a message to Will as soon as we know how many men are watching the boys. If no others arrive, then we move to take them tomorrow night."

Chapter Fifteen

1873 February
Virginia City, NV

Sam Brown and Roberts walked into the Delta Saloon.

Brown stood in the doorway swiveling his head from side to side, taking in the current sights within the bar. "I like upscale saloons. I've always felt right at home in here, the largest of Virginia City's saloons. With its long oak bar with brass running foot stool, it fits the perfect image of what a saloon should be."

Roberts looked at Brown and shook his head. "I just want a drink."

As if landing softly as a bird from some easy flight down to earth, Brown reveled in his return to one of his favorite places, but soon hardened back into focus on the reason they were here. He looked down the length of the bar. Without turning his head to Roberts, he said, "Let's find Mike. We have to tell him about the message we want to leave for Toal."

Brown spied the bartender down at the other end, partially hidden by the line of customers standing at the bar. No matter what time of day or night, the line at the bar of the Delta was just about packed.

"Mike! Bring me a beer," ordered Brown.

Mike Stuart was a giant of men: over six feet four inches tall and a barrel chest. He'd broken up many a fight in the bar with both his fists and the long wooden dowel he kept hidden beneath his side of the bar.

But Mike Stuart did not come right away. He looked at Brown but didn't move.

Roberts took this in and said out of the side of his mouth, "Looks to me that big Mike Stuart doesn't much care for you and isn't afraid to show it."

"Naw, Mike likes me well enough. He knows I'm one of the biggest tippers in Virginia City."

Stuart finally began to move down the line of the bar. He reached up to the tap and filled a glass with beer then wiped off the head with his forefinger. He sent the glass sliding down the smooth top of the bar to where Brown stood. But Brown didn't only want the beer.

"Mike, I need to talk to you."

"What about?" Stuart looked as if it was a huge imposition to have to answer.

"Come closer. I don't intend to be talkin' with everyone in the bar listenin'."

Stuart moved but ever so slowly. He came to a point directly across from Brown, standing up to his full height, looking down at the considerably smaller man. "What?"

Brown was now a bit perturbed at Stuart's behavior. "If a rancher comes into the bar asking for a Sam Sutton, I need you to give them a message. That's all."

"And why would I do this?"

Brown started to flush. Stuart was not the willing friend he'd thought. He stared with no small amount of animosity in the look. "Because I asked, and I'm a regular customer."

Stuart returned the stare, obviously not intimidated in the least. He said nothing.

Brown needed the information passed, so he could not afford offending Stuart. He decided to take another tact. "What if I pay you twenty dollars for your trouble?"

Stuart's demeanor changed, but only slightly more receptive. "What's the message?"

"Tell them to check at the main desk of the Molinelli Hotel on B Street. There will be an envelope for him."

"That's all I have to do, and you'll give me twenty bucks?"

Brown bit his tongue. "Yes." What he didn't say is that he would settle up with Stuart later. The big guy was going to pay for his insolence. But not now. Not yet.

"Okay, I'll do it. Give me the twenty."

Brown pulled a gold coin from his vest and slid it across the bar with his hand covering the money. Stuart picked it up and nodded.

Brown leaned sideways toward Roberts. "Let's go. We need to leave the message at the hotel desk that Toal is to reply as to a time and date he can bring the money to a meeting on the camel racetrack."

*****

"Katie, it's me, Elmer."

Katie Smolders jumped and spun in the air all in one motion. "Damn, don't scare me like that."

Lennox smiled. "I came up from Mound House, spent last night on the road got so soaked it was like taking a bath. Then I camped out uphill from town to watch for ya. I figured I had'ta sneak up at dusk to get ya when you headed to the barn as I know your parents hate me."

Katie looked over her shoulder through the descending afternoon darkness toward her ramshackle wood sided home. The Smolders family barely made ends meet selling eggs and pork to vendors in town. She worried someone might come out and see the two together.

"They're just eatin' supper. Pa told me to feed the animals. If he sees you out here, he be sure to bring a gun. He don't like you at 'all,

111

just as you said. But I do." There was a smile on her girlish face to confirm.

"When can I see you? I got a need that has to be fixed, and only you can do it."

Katie's shoulders swiveled from side to side as she pondered. "Ya'll could come back later tonight in an hour or two and meet me in the barn. If 'en I 'member correct, you didn't mind being out with the hogs and hens."

"I'll be here at seven o'clock. Come out when you can."

*****

Will Toal rode into Virginia City. Despite the recent heavy rains, the unseasonable hot winds had not stopped. The road, town, and everything in it was drying up fast. He'd camped out last night uphill from the main road and made the rest of the climb up the hill from Mound House to Virginia City in the better part of day two. Dry roads had helped. He pulled up Powder in front of the Delta Saloon and tied up.

Will pushed through the bat wing doors and took in the sights and sounds of the bar. As in most western bars, those sights and sounds included smoke hanging low from the ceiling, the smell of liquor, and the sounds of a piano. He thought to himself, you could always tell the quality of the bar from the ability of the piano player. The better the bar, the better the music. If there was no music, then you had hit the bottom of the barrel. This bar had a good piano player. Must be an upscale version.

Will stepped up to the waist-high wooden table with long brass footrest running at the bottom of the structure. The bar ran from the front of the building at its street entrance to almost the back of the building. Tables and chairs were spread on the opposite side of the room. "Can I get a beer?"

A large, very large, man walked over and looked Will over. "Sure, comin' right up."

The bartender carried Will's beer and placed it in front of him. "Never seen you in here before. You look like you work cattle."

Will wasn't wearing his chaps as the weather had warmed with the wind. He couldn't think of any giveaway from the look of his clothes. The bartender's comment surprised him.

"What makes you say that?"

"You're certainly not a miner," came the reply. "Most men in here work below the surface. You don't. Can see it in your face, sun burned in winter. A miner's face shows no sun."

Now enlightened, Will smiled. "You're right; I do own a ranch in a place named Jack's Valley down near Carson City."

Mike Stuart crossed his arms. He now had a pretty good idea of who he was talking to. But he waited for Will to continue.

"I rarely get up here to Virginia City. Forgot how much of a climb it is. Must be almost two thousand feet up from Mound House."

The bartender still waited. He had to make sure.

Will then looked the man in the face. "I'm here looking for a man named Sam Sutton, might also be known as Sam Brown. Said I'd find him in this saloon."

Stuart nodded. "Thought you might be the man I'd been told about. My name's Mike Stuart. I actually do have a message for you."

Will looked relieved. At least there was some connection.

"Yep. You have a message from a man I know as Sam Brown. He's trouble. He told me that if anyone came in asking for Sam Sutton, I'm to send him over to the desk at the Molinelli Hotel here in town."

"I wasn't sure I'd actually get a message. Don't think I can trust this Sam Brown. At least I *got* a message."

Stuart could not hold back when it came to Brown. "A bit of advice. Sam Brown is a dangerous man. I'd be careful in any dealings I had with the man."

Will looked back at the bartender. While still a young man, Will had seen his share of trouble beginning in the war then as a Texas Ranger. With a resolve recognizable man-to-man, Will glared back. "Sam Brown might be trouble, but he's going to find more than trouble with me."

Stuart assessed the man and the comment. "I believe you might be right. Would be good to see a little justice delivered to Sam Brown."

"I intend to deliver more than justice. I'm here to deliver judgment."

Chapter Sixteen

Will finished his beer. Stuart was still standing right across the bar. "Where is the Washoe Club?"

"It's at 112 South C Street, about a block down from the Delta Saloon."

"Okay, I should be able to find it."

"Yeah, it's only a couple of doors down to the left after you leave the saloon. But only rich men are allowed in. It is the most exclusive club in Virginia City."

"It appears I have an invite."

"Good for you. Not many are allowed in."

"Can I ask you another question? Where is the office for the California & Consolidated Mine?"

"That's down in the Mackay Mansion on D Street. It's just down the hill from here. You can't miss it. There are two parts to D Street: the good part is to the south. Then there's the north part, where the ladies of the night work. Mackay's house is in the good section. The mansion is three stories and is the finest house in Virginia City. The office is right behind the front door."

"Thanks, I'll try the office first and then head to the Washoe Club."

Will headed out of the door but then stopped and turned. "Oh, can I ask one more favor? I might be getting a message from Mound House. It may come here. Can I ask that you keep it for me? I'll keep checking with you."

"Sure."

Will tipped the bartender with a five-dollar coin. "It could be important."

"Thanks. I'll make sure you get any message. Town's not that big. I'll find you."

*****

Fr. Cecconi looked up from the group of men and women as they prepared sleeping arrangements in the church. St. Mary's of the Mountains faced west, jutting perpendicular into the slope of Mount Davidson. The church entrance was level with D Street, but the building extended east, descending two stories below the altar at the opposite side of the structure near E Street. The church had taken in fifteen families whose canvas residences had been washed away by the rains. Here they had slept side by side in the church's brick bowels. There was a smell, a smell of humanity crammed into close quarters. The scent was of something almost fluid, a body of unclean water. Like the floods of the last few days, the human flotsam before him drifted in eddies of collected personal loss. Their hope was gone. The looks fathers gave to their families, the attempts of mothers lying prone trying to comfort their restless children, leaked like heavy tears into a small lake here in this sacred brick-sided well. They had all lost their homes, lost their possessions. With futures unknown, the well of dread rose like a rising tide.

"Sr. Charity, do we have any room for more?"

"No, Father. Men, women, and children are jammed side by side as it is. There must be fifty people total."

"This is all so sad. There are so many others who also lost their homes. I suppose we can only do what we can. I hope the others find some shelter."

"The good thing, Father, is the weather is warmer. Last night and today were almost hot."

"It is an odd thing, our weather right now. But, yes, that is a good thing for those who are without a roof or fire to keep warm."

"Father, we received a message from Bishop Manogue. He's delayed and will not be back for several more days."

"Yes, Sister, I heard. I'll stay until these folks are situated or the bishop returns. I will continue to talk to friends of the church to see if we can make other arrangements for those still on the streets."

"Providence brought you here, Father. The Sisters and I could not have managed our current crisis without your help."

Father Cecconi nodded. But he noticed a further hesitation in the nun's face. "What is it, Sister Charity?"

"I cannot get over the sense that something bigger is coming. First came downpours of rain unlike anything for years. Now comes an uncommon heat. It brings me back to your vision. I fear you were placed at that specific spot at that specific moment in time for a reason. But I cannot tell why, yet the confluence of recent events causes great concern. Should we expect more?"

He ran his hand over the top of his hairless head down the back of his neck, holding the hand there as if for support or guidance.

"I know I said earlier that we should try to put those kinds of notions out of our minds. However, I confess, I've lately had similar thoughts. I cannot escape a feeling that my recent sermons are predicting the immediate future rather than simply talking about events in the biblical distance. But we must put those thoughts aside and do what we can for these unfortunate people."

*****

Will tied up Powder in a brass ring hanging from the nose of an iron horse head sitting at the top of a black pipe driven into the ground. He'd walked his horse down the steep grade rather than ride him on such a sharp slope.

"I guess a simple hitching rail is not good enough in this neighborhood, eh boy? At least you have a likeness, albeit an iron one, you can nuzzle up to."

He walked through the gate in the picket fence and knocked on the door of the biggest house he'd ever seen. The size of the front door did not impress but the overall size of the house did. A lady wearing a black dress wearing a white apron and short cap answered the door. "May I help you?"

"I'm looking for John Mackay. My name is Will Toal. My partner, Henry Millard, contacted Mr. Mackay telling him I'd be arriving. I am supposed to meet him either here or at the Washoe Club."

"Mr. Mackay is usually in the mines. But today he said he had business. He's not here, but you will find him at the Washoe Club. Do you know where that is?"

"Yes, I've been told how to find it. Thanks much." Will untied Powder and led him back up the steep slope they'd just descended from D Street to C Street. Though only one block, Will could see how one could get winded in a hurry just walking around this town.

The Washoe Club was one of the smaller saloons in town. Will stepped in the inauspicious entry from the street-side boardwalk to be confronted by two men at the door. Both looked like they'd been cut out of the same picture: tall, broad-shouldered, and completely expressionless. Their clothes were clean, not of a working sort but not altogether fancy either. Both looked at ease in their physicality. He had the thought that this must be exactly why they'd been chosen for the position. Neither said a word, nor moved. Both just stood and waited for him to speak.

"I'm here to see Mr. John Mackay. He told my business partner he'd see me. My name is Will Toal."

The two men looked at each other. One turned to Will and said, "Please wait here just inside the door. My associate will stay with you while I speak with Mr. Mackay."

The second man ushered Will inside and offered one of two chairs at a table. Will had the feeling he was in the middle of a well-used routine.

After sitting, Will looked up at the chandelier and large mirror behind the bar. While the club had the immediate look and appeal of a standard saloon, albeit smaller in size and scope compared to the same items at the Delta, the furniture and fixtures appeared of the highest quality. All meant to impress. It did.

The doorman who had left earlier emerged from an open room at the back left of the saloon. He walked up to Will and said, "Mr. Mackay will see you. Please follow me."

Will walked behind the man through the open portal into a high ceiling room with no windows, a single pool table, two smaller tables, and about eight chairs. Nothing else could fit. The chairs were wide, made of leather, and looked comfortable. The smell of cigar smoke hung like limpid success in the air.

A man who struck Will to be in his mid-forties stood from one of the leather chairs and walked to Will. "Hello, my name is John Mackay. Henry Millard wired me about you. Why don't you have a seat, and we can talk."

"I appreciate you seeing me. Not sure how you might help, but I do have a problem."

Will saw a small sculpture of Mary and the deceased Jesus in her arms. He had seen a picture of the same sculpture in a book his mother had read to him. Will instinctively made the sign of the cross, a movement not lost on Mackay.

"Catholic?"

Startled somewhat, Will had not even given much thought to what he'd done. "Sorry, yes. Raised so in Georgia, but I cannot say I've practiced much. But still remember the lessons from my mother and many Sundays early on. I saw a picture of that statue in a book, and my mother said it was in a sacred place in Rome."

"Yes, it's called the Pietà by Michelangelo, and it is in the Vatican. This is a small, poor copy. Most of the mine owners in the club are Irish, and we placed the replica here as a reminder of what should be one of our foundations. Lots of things have taken place in this room that might make one wonder if anyone knows it's here, but we keep it nonetheless."

Will detected the Irish accent covering what seemed an extra effort to use correct English. Conversation must be an effort for Mackay.

They sat. Will now felt uncomfortable. It must have been obvious. Mackay broke the silence. "Henry Millard told me of your problem. I cannot imagine what it would be like to have my son taken from me. I spent all my early years doing what I could to scrape up enough money to keep my mother and sister Back East and myself here out West from starving. I've worked hard, but I've also been lucky. My wife and I are more comfortable than most. We had our own son only a few years ago. I would do anything to get him back if he were to be taken."

Will had thought about what he'd say to Mackay as he walked around town from the saloon. But the room and the man were intimidating. He was slow to respond, but as he got started, he found the words came in a rush. "Sir, I grew up in Georgia, fought in the war, and came West. Along the way, I worked as a Texas Ranger and then wrangled cows. I have my own ranch near the Carson Valley and run beef, which I sell to Henry Millard and the markets in San Francisco. I have no family other than those two boys. They were taken by a man I've heard goes by the name of Sam Brown when I was away doing a favor for Millard."

Will looked down to the floor in front of his boots then back to Mackay.

"I'd give up that entire ranch to get them back. The men who took them say I have to come up with twenty-five thousand dollars. I don't have that kind of cash. So, I'm here to go after the man who took them. As a Ranger, I've run down men like Brown before. But I'm also told that if I find this man, I'll need help. I'm alone, but I'm prepared to deal with Sam Brown by myself if necessary. I suppose what I'm asking for is help to locate Sam Brown. From what I've heard, he's well known here in the city."

Mackay took stock of the young man sitting across from him. In his years as a shipwright, carpenter, mine foreman, superintendent, and employer, he'd met hundreds of men in hundreds of settings. Some of those settings were inherently dangerous. Mackay always thought one measure of a man is how he'd react with danger present. This young man in front of him did not appear desperate. He did not appear afraid of confronting someone acting outside the law. He admired the independence. He'd not asked for money. After reading the wire from Millard, Mackay had thought the young man would come asking for money. He hadn't and that was another plus in Mackay's eyes. In his current financial status, Mackay regularly had people asking for contributions to one charity or another. But Will Toal had not asked for money or manpower. He asked only for information.

"Will…can I call you Will?"

"Sure."

"There is little, if any, law here in this town. About the closest thing we have to law enforcement is a group called the 601s. No one really knows who is involved. In reality, they're a bunch of vigilantes. They've hung a couple of men who truly deserved their fate. Apparently, they've also run several other deserving souls out of town. But as a result, we really don't need a sheriff or marshal. There hasn't been a killing or robbery here in town since the second hanging, which was over three years ago. The town is rowdy, sure, but there is little crime. I am one who thinks the 601s are responsible for that lack of crime."

Will listened.

"I do not know how to get into contact with the 601s. But I may know someone who can. If we can get word to them, then maybe they can help to locate this man and even help you bring him to justice. More importantly, you have to find your sons."

Will let Mackay finish his thoughts.

"But it might take a day or so for me to establish some contact. My wife lives in Paris. I have a large home with just me in it. Why don't you stay at my house tonight? I should be able to send my message, and we'll hear something in the morning."

"That would be mighty nice, Mr. Mackay. I appreciate anything you can do."

"Call me John." Mackay stood. "Follow me. Let's see if we can get my housekeeper and chef to cook a decent meal."

Chapter Seventeen

1873 February
Virginia City, NV

Elmer Lennox waited in the Smolders' barn. Though he normally liked living life outdoors, he felt good right now drying off under a roof after being out on the trail during the recent downpour. The simple wooden structure had multiple pens for pigs and goats. It also had several open stalls pushed headfirst into the side of the barn. Those open stalls were bordered with low waist high side dividers to separate the larger stock. Lennox leaned up against the outer wall of the barn tucked deep in one of the open stalls. His position provided the most protection from being seen should old man Smolders decide to make a late evening trip to check his animals. Lennox would have plenty of time to draw before any need to shoot. Darkness here in late winter still came early.

He'd been waiting for over an hour when the barn door opened. Lennox covered the handle of his handgun with his palm. He inched his head up above the low separation wall to look down toward the barn door. In walked Katie with a lantern. She had long brown hair hanging in straight sheets from the top of a head covered with a battered hat. She was slight and thin to the point of appearing semi-starved. Her dress was battered and faded green plaid, probably washed only once each week at best. She held a bucket in one hand along with the lantern, which was now raised in the other. Her outward persona was rough and hard, but her face was clean and clear, holding piercing hazel eyes. Elmer figured she was a few years short of twenty, but there was no innocence about her. She'd seen the ways of life raising farm animals, and Lord knows what she'd seen watching human animals.

"Elmer, ya here?"

Elmer quietly whispered, "Yeah, over here." He had picked this particular stall as it was the farthest point away from the pigs. Though on the opposite part of the barn, the smell of the pigs was everywhere. Elmer looked up at Katie and forgot about the smell.

"I laid out my coat."

Katie put the lantern down next to the low wall separating two stalls.

"Ya goin' to turn that out, aren't ya?"

"Naw, I can't. Pa is asleep in his chair. But Ma is still up. She'd know'd if 'en I put out the lantern that somethin's wrong. The light has ta stay on." She lifted the lantern and set it down on the outer support of the low stall separation.

Elmer grinned. "Well, it ain't gonna bother me if it ain't gonna bother you."

Katie folded her hands below her waist. She turned her head down and to one side. "So, do ya'll want to undress me 'fore we lay down?"

The enticement was clear. Elmer needed little encouragement. "Sure, I do. Come 'ere."

When she didn't move, Elmer stood and went to her. He was quick and stumbled in his haste, causing Katie to step back. In stepping back, Katie's elbow knocked her lantern off the wall, the oil spilling out into the next stall, a stall with old, dirty, and very dry straw. It caught fire immediately. The combination of burning oil and dry straw exploded into flames three to four feet high, moving across the stall like lightning. The flames grew to six to seven feet before Elmer reached a full stance. In the short span of time, the entire stall was engulfed. Both Katie and Elmer knew there was no way to put it out. All they could do was run.

Katie shoved Elmer toward the far door on the other side of the barn. "Ya gotta go. Ya gotta go that way. Pa will be up. He sees you, and he'll get his gun."

"I ain't afraid of your Pa."

"Go, she implored. This be bad enough."

"Come with me."

The flames were now up to the second level of the barn, reaching the hay loft. Elmer looked up and knew the loft would only provide more fuel to the flames. He looked at Katie again. He knew this would be his last chance. Their future was done if she didn't come with him.

"I can't. I gotta stay. 'Specially now that I burnt the barn. I got to get the animals out. Go."

Elmer moved to leave, but before reaching the door he turned. In one of the grins Brown had described as a specter of evil, he looked back at Katie.

"Then let it burn. I hope it burns this whole damn town."

Elmer ran out the back door, got on his horse, and rode uphill to the north. It took about ten minutes to get to a point outside of town. He stopped and turned. He couldn't believe how the fire had spread. The hot winds were blowing south down the slopes of Mt. Davidson, picking up flames. The fire had pushed from the Smolders' place at the north end of town right down the middle of Taylor Street and was headed toward the main commercial section of town. Except for the Catholic church, everything in Virginia City was made of wood. Every store, every saloon, the Piper's Opera House; all were made of wood. And now, it was all going to burn.

Elmer reined up and stopped. He watched with a sense close to satisfaction that he could not explain as the flames now rose to towering heights, lifting hailstorms of ash and embers into the air. The light silhouetted the dark outlines of the buildings surrounding the blaze. The black building profiles stood in a line of helpless immovable beings waiting to be consumed in the blaze just as their brethren further uphill. Cries and shouts could be heard all the way up the hill to where he sat astride his mount. The gelding snorted through red nostrils. He held the anxious horse prancing in place while he waited and watched. "You agree then, son. We left our mark on this place. Guess we'll have to head back down to Mound House. Means another night out on the trail. Good, let it burn."

Chapter Eighteen

Mackay and Will sat at the dinner table. Will felt even more uncomfortable in Mackay's home than he did at the Washoe Club. The surroundings of Mackay's home were of a nature and style Will had never seen. Not even hotels looked this fancy.

"Even running water?"

"Yes, the upstairs washroom has running water for the tub and the water closet. They call it a toilet."

"I've never been in a washroom where there was water. Always an outhouse."

"That was my life for years, too. It's the first washroom with running water between the Mississippi and San Francisco."

"This is a wonderful house. Can't begin to think what something like this would cost."

Mackay never liked to talk too much about his wealth. He'd been dirt poor far too long and knew most of the world lived in conditions much worse than his own. It hadn't been too long ago that he'd been in those same conditions. He did not take his present circumstances for granted.

"The house is something I never dreamed I would ever own. I work in a mining world. Fortunes are made quickly, but they are lost quickly, too."

They both looked to their plates, showing beef, potatoes, and some vegetables Will had never seen before. But they tasted good.

"In fact, we are in financial depression. Our government just passed legislation called the Coinage Act. They'd been threatening to do it for months, and markets across the country are falling like stones in water. It has caused a crash in our own mining stock market right now. The values of our main mining operations, the California & Consolidated, have plummeted. I've lost over two hundred thousand dollars in stock value in the past two weeks alone."

Will dropped his fork. "I can't imagine losing that kind of money. Are you broke?"

Mackay smiled. "No, I'm not broke, but I sure hope it doesn't last."

"How long can you hold out?"

Mackay pushed his plate away, which he knew to be a breach of etiquette. But in his own house, the old Irish habits could not be contained. He looked at Will, deciding if he could confide in this impressive, yet young man. He decided to confide.

"We struck a new ore vein in one of the mines. We have men down in the mine excavating what they can. We've already confirmed it is one of the biggest strikes ever in the Comstock, but we cannot announce it."

"Why not?"

"Because to excavate it, we need timber. Lots of timber. We need to make an approach to the Carson and Tahoe Lumber & Flume Company. That company is financially backed by some of our biggest competitors here in town who would love to see us fail. Carson Flume has cornered the market on timber around the nearest points of Lake Tahoe. If word were to get out, they would increase the price to ridiculous levels. I've been trying to figure out how I can approach the owner, Duane Bliss, to make a deal before this all becomes public."

"So, you are not at risk of going broke?"

"Not if I can get the timber to excavate. If we can pull out the ore, it will be one of the richest veins ever discovered."

Will wiped his face. He'd never used a napkin but had watched and mimicked Mackay, avoiding his regular wipe on the sleeve. "I actually know Duane Bliss. He worked at the Bank of California and held the mortgage on my ranch. He sold my mortgage and several others on ranches in the Carson Valley to the railroad. The sales of the mortgages led to the meeting where Drake Sutton started a shoot-out. Sutton shot both men and women during the gunfight. I killed Sutton as he tried to get away. That's what's led to this guy, Brown, coming after me and mine."

Mackay, stunned at the connection uttered, "Then your current situation runs back to Bliss?"

"I supposed it does in a way. But I didn't know Bliss now owned a lumber company."

"Yes, he has done very well. With financial assistance from other investors who had stakes in the Bank of California, Bliss has bought up significant parts of the Tahoe forests and mills lumber for use as square set support timbers in the mines. He is now a wealthy man, but those same investors are the competitors who would like to see our mine fail."

Will listened.

"We need someone who can approach Bliss and place an order for thousands of board feet. I am quite willing to pay a standard price. While it should be discounted, I am willing to pay regular price just to get this started. But I'm worried Bliss will be influenced by his partners who are also investors in the Bank of California."

Will turned away, thought for a moment, and then turned back to Mackay.

"As I said, I had dealings with Bliss. There were news articles at the time about the railroad trying to foreclose on ranches. But no one ever said anything about how the railroad got their hands on the mortgages. Bliss sold them to the railroad. He admitted it to me. Maybe if I were to approach him for you, I could remind him about that little fact and what kind of damage might result to his current business if the newspapers were to find out."

"Will, would you do that? If you did, it would be worth it to me to pay the ransom for your boys."

"You can't do that. Twenty-five thousand dollars is a whole lot of money."

"Will, if I get that timber, it'll be worth millions. Twenty-five thousand is nothing. I'd do it in a heartbeat."

Just then, they heard screams outside the house coming from the direction of town. Both men stood up and went to the front door. Mackay pulled it open.

"Fire!" The word rang out all over the town. Will looked up and saw the mass of flames flying twenty to thirty feet in the air bearing down on the main part of the city.

"Got to get to the mine. There are men down there. If the timbers catch, they'll burn for years in the oxygen trapped below. It happened to the Crown Point Mine some time ago. Timbers burned for over two years. No one could go down. We have to seal the collar, the opening and main shaft of our mine."

Mackay tore off his jacket and expensive shirt as he headed out of the room. "I've got to get my boots and working gloves. I'll be right back down."

Will looked out the door as Mackay returned, now wearing only an undershirt and his well-tailored pants along with a worn set of sturdy looking boots. Will, now seeing Mackay's obvious intent in the change of clothes said, "I'll go with you and help."

"I fear we are going to need all the help we can get. It would be much appreciated if you could lend a hand, but we need to go now."

Both men turned and headed out of the door. Will looked uphill to see fire bearing down the slope, lifted by the hot winds. Both men instinctively started to run, Will following Mackay. The direction of the fire looked like it was heading straight down the fall of Mount Davidson's incline. Assessing what he could see as he ran after Mackay, Will thought the blaze would miss Mackay's mansion and outer buildings, including the carriage house and stable where Powder had been bedded down. But Will could see the tall machinery of what had to be a mine operation directly in the path of the fire. It was also the structure they were headed toward.

Chapter Nineteen

1873 February
Virginia City, NV

The bells clanged from the volunteer fire station on the outskirts of C Street. As head of the volunteer firemen, Kevin Hurley had run knocking on the doors to gather those who would answer his call. But by the time the volunteer firemen collected, the fire had spread down Taylor and branched out both north and south. Hurley and the volunteers raced down C Street, deciding on the run which of the burning structures to pump water on.

Hurley raised his hand, calling to halt the 1865 Button & Lysander side pump fire wagon. "Piper's Opera House and Court House up on B Street look like they're gone. Can't save 'em. We need to try an' save the main section of C Street."

Mike Stuart, bartender and part-time fire volunteer, moved to the side of the wagon. "Let's get this hose unraveled and start pumping, men! Somebody needs to get the syphon going so the wagon's reservoir can be replenished. This is going to be a big job. You heard Kevin."

Stuart, along with Fred Turner, pulled the end of the hose and moved as close to the oncoming fire as they dared. It took two men to hold the hose steady as it shot a stream of water up over a hundred feet. There were two horizontal bars on either side of the rig. Groups of men were positioned on each side. One side would pull down their bar to begin pumping water. At the same time, the horizontal bar on the opposite side would raise up like an elaborate children's teeter totter. Once raised, the men on the other side would then pull down. The combined motions started the flow of water. It took four men on each side to operate the pump. New teams of four stood ready to rotate in and then replace a tired team.

Stuart looked at Turner and said, "God, it'd be nice to have one of those new steam wagons that uses gas to shoot out the water. The boys are going to get tired pumping tonight in this mess."

Turner nodded. "Word is we'd be getting a new Clapp & Jones steamer next year, if there is any town left after this, that is."

The flow started. It took Stuart and his second holding the hose right beside him to pull the hose back and forth across the face of the flames. The aim was to protect an entire block. Stuart and Turner moved quickly back and forth spreading a blanket of water on the ground between them and the oncoming blaze.

Stuart looked at the advancing inferno. Heat lifted everything. Piper's Opera House was fully engulfed. The now ethereal wooden timbers crashed in unison. The structure disintegrated in minutes crashing in a heap. The remnants then rose on waves of heat as nothing but fiery chips and powder to be blown away in a windstorm from fuel driven flames. Labor, toil, and all earlier effort of construction floated to the heavens as molten fireflies of ash and then vanished in the blink of an eye. He'd never seen anything like it.

"How are we ever going to stop this?" Stuart spoke to no one in particular and everyone in general.

Hurley yelled over the sound of burning objects all around. "Aim the hose at the back side of the saloons and banks on C Street. If the fire hits the alcohol in the saloons, this whole town will explode like a bomb."

With hands on the surging hose, Stuart leaned toward Turner and muttered, "And if we save the Delta Saloon, then I'll save my job."

Stuart yelled over his shoulder, "Men, save the Delta, and we'll have a place to suck down a dram after this is over. Drinks are on me."

The water surged through the hose as the men began to pump even harder.

"A little encouragement never hurt," said Stuart as he moved laterally to beat down a series of flames reaching closer to the buildings.

*****

It took thirty minutes of pumping, but the water finally ran out. The fire in front of Stuart had been beaten down. Ashes and cinders still smoked. The smell of burnt wood permeated the atmosphere and caked in his nostrils. His eyes watered. His nose and throat felt singed down to his lungs.

Hurley walked up to Stuart, who was standing with a dripping nozzle in his hands. "We saved the main block of town, Mike: The Delta, the Washoe Club, and the Bank of California still stand."

Stuart turned his grime covered face to look at the businesses behind him. He had focused on the onrushing fire during the fight and never looked to the rear. He saw the block-wide expanse of standing buildings, but he soon glanced to the left and right to see the devastation the fire had caused as it passed to the sides of their position of defense, burning all in its path.

"But look at what the fire's done to the rest of the town, Kevin. One block on either side of what we protected is virtually wiped out. The International Hotel is gone, the Molinelli Hotel is gone, and the Silver Dollar Hotel across the street looks like it's going to be totally lost. The fire just swept down the slope."

Hurley moved his sweat and soot-soaked body in front of Stuart to the right and looked down Taylor Street. The fire had taken the Wells Fargo Bank office and burned over the top of the Gould and Curry Mine. "Hope they sealed off the Gould. Can't afford to lose the mines.

Remember what happened to the Crown Point when the fire broke out down below? It burned for years."

Stuart looked further east and down the slope. "The fire's heading for St. Mary's on one side and the main shaft of the Consolidated Mine on the other. We need to refill the wagon and get down to St. Mary's to see if there's still time to help."

Hurley nodded. "Men grab the wagon and head down to the Consolidated. We need to reconnect to the reservoir and work to save that mine and St. Mary's church."

*****

Mackay yelled at the men to lay more timbers over the top of the mine shaft. They had already pulled the main cage up so that the top of the cage was even with the floor level. Mackay's immediate plan devised on the fly was to bring up the cage, which covered most of the expanse for the main shaft. With the top of the cage spreading across most of the opening, they could lay timbers which had been stacked and ready for shipment down over the top. The cage and timbers it supported completely shielded the main shaft. The plan then included covering the timbers with dirt so they did not burn.

"Men, we have enough timbers; we need to get the wheelbarrows going and bring the dirt. We need to cover the shaft and all this wood before the blaze gets here, or the plan will backfire."

Mackay knew they did not have any wood or metal long enough to stretch over the expanse of the mine shaft itself. He hoped to use the top of the cage as support for shorter beams which could be set side by side and end to end, ultimately bridging the gaps all the way across the shaft.

Will Toal looked at the beams now side by side. "Smart using the cage to fill the shaft. When we first got here, I had no idea how you were going to cover up and seal that opening."

"A calculated risk though," said Mackay. "The fire is not far. If we don't get enough dirt to cover those beams, I've just made things worse as the wood will burn like chimney tinder, taking the fire straight down the shaft. We have to cover the beams with dirt and quick."

With that said, Will spun and ran to help the men shoveling dirt from a nearby open stretch of uncovered ground into a caravan of wheelbarrows.

Sister Charity ran up to Mackay in her habit, torn and streaked with coal scrapings, looking as if she had run a gauntlet of hazards. "Mr. Mackay, the fire is bearing down on the church. You have to come help save the church."

Mackay looked up from his focus on spreading dirt on the timbers. "Damn the church! We can build another if we can keep the fire from going down these shafts."

Sister Charity looked shocked as she moved disappointedly back toward the church and away from the mass of movement around the mine shaft. But Mackay did not stop to console. He returned to spreading the dirt. He knew the focus had to be a thick cover of dirt to prevent any fire from heading down the shaft. Nothing, not even the protection of St. Mary's, took precedence.

"Will, can we get any more wheelbarrows to help move the dirt?"

"No, there aren't any more. But I found some burlap bags. We can fill those and run them over by hand. We have more men than we have wheelbarrows. We can use those extra men to get more dirt on top of the covering timbers."

Mackay nodded. "Do it."

Will turned and screamed above the beckoning abyss of the oncoming inferno. "Fill the bags as fast as you can! Haul them to the mine entrance by hand if you have to. Now!" Men who had been standing while wheelbarrows ran back and forth now jumped into movement.

The collection of men continued to make run after run into the structure surrounding the shaft opening. In a matter of minutes, a level of dirt covered the timbers stretched across the mine shaft. Mackay took a final look out of the mine works and saw the fire now reaching the roof. He yelled to all the men both inside and out. "Enough, men! Time to get out. Leave and leave quick. The roof is now burning. It will collapse soon."

Men began to leave and run further downhill to open space as far away from any wooden structure as possible. When they had all reached a position of relative safety, Mackay stopped and looked back uphill. The Consolidated and California Mine works was covered by a two to three story structure which housed massive pumping equipment and the machinery to raise and lower the cage down hundreds of feet. The structure was wood and now fully engulfed in flames. The roof began to collapse.

Will walked up to Mackay's position. "Didn't you tell me you had men down in the shaft? How are they going to breathe?"

"Those men dug a crosscut tunnel from down the slope into the deeper reaches of the mine. They connected to our main shaft, but it's down over nine hundred feet. They have oxygen from the tunnel they generated downslope. But I already sent a bell message down the shaft when we got here to warn the men below to get out."

"A bell message?"

"Yes, we use a series of messages to communicate down the shaft. I sent a message of immediate warning, which will let them know to leave right away. They can just catch the crosscut shaft at level eight and walk out of the mine down the slope."

Will nodded.

Both men looked south toward St. Mary's of the Mountains. The first story and lower reaches of the structure down to E Street were made of brick and stone. The fire had not affected the foundation or lower portion. The dual brick spires and bell tower would also survive. But the roof was combustible. The roof had been supported by a system of stout filigreed wood braces specially carved in a pattern to look like the flying buttresses of Notre-Dame. But filigreed or not, the supports were wood and their survival was in question. However, they were large and thick like the trunks of trees. Maybe like trees in a forest fire these trunks would live.

Mackay lifted both hands with palms up as if to reach out and lift the structure before him. Speaking more to himself than anyone in particular, he muttered, "Sister came to me and asked us to help save the church while we were sealing the shaft collar. The mine was more important. I told her to let it go. It looks like the roof will char, but the buttresses are not burning and might survive. The lower floor and foundation will be intact as it's all brick and stone. Even if the buttresses do burn, replacing the roof will be far less expensive than internal damage to the mine. I had to make a choice. Not sure she'll ever forgive me."

Will listened but said nothing.

Mackay turned to look at the Consolidated Mine structure. The metal machinery still stood, but the wooden building surrounding the metal had all collapsed. "The structure is gone, but look, the dirt mound is not burning. The seal on the collar worked."

Will could see the relief in Mackay's eyes and the simultaneous release of tension in the posture of his shoulders. A weight had been lifted. Will had no idea exactly how much had been at stake, but he knew it was a lot.

Mackay turned to Will. "I cannot thank you enough for your help. Using the bags was critical. We needed the last layer created by the dirt in those bags."

Mackay reached out one hand and placed it on Will's shoulder. "Young man, you helped save my financial future. Everything I have is wrapped up in that mine. If it had burned, I would have gone broke as you asked me about earlier."

"I was just one of many sets of hands."

"Maybe, but I now still have a mine out of which I know we can pull ore. All I need is the timber. The other mines are going to need wood to rebuild, as will we. If you can get to Carson City and convince Bliss to take our order first, I will happily give you the ransom money for your sons. That way you can bargain or fight. You have the option and choice."

Will was stunned and had trouble coming up with a response. Finally, he said, "Not sure how I can thank you."

Mackay shook his head. "First comes a financial crisis caused by the Coinage Act. Then we have a flood that nearly washes the city down the hill. And now this conflagration. It feels like there is some force doing its best to prevent this ore from coming out of the ground. But the country will need it, especially to help bring it out of this depression."

Will again listened.

"Look at this town. It's like Armageddon. You were here at the exact moment I needed it. It's only fair I try to return the favor."

Chapter Twenty

1873 February
Mound House, NV

"What time do you think it is?"

"Señora, it is after midnight. I see no one else come to the house. I think it is a good time to go try and get *el Nino's*."

Beth sucked in a deep breath. "The lights have been off for hours. The man we saw walk to the telegraph can't keep watch all night. He must go to sleep some time. How do you think we should do this?"

"I go into the front door. You stand by the window. I surprise the man while you make sure he no gets off a shot at Juan."

"If he sees you though, he might just react right away. If I go in, he might make a mistake and think he can outdraw me, even if I have my gun pointed at him. We can't start a shoot-out with the boys right there."

Juan gave this idea some thought. "Sí, then I go to the window and protect you. When you go to the room, *el Niño's* are to the *derecha*, the right. I do not know where the man will be, but I think he'll be across from door. The window is at same wall too. So, he'll be right below the window and out of sight to me. You must be careful. Make him give up his gun and stand up so I can see him through the window."

"I understand. We'll go as quietly as we can. I'll try to work the door. You don't think it's locked, do you?"

"The casa look very old. In bad shape. I no think there is any lock. But he might have a chair against the door. If he does, then knock. Maybe he stand up then."

"Okay, I think we can do this. We must do this. Juan, we have to get the boys."

"*Sí, Señora*. And these men must pay for the death of Raúl. Do not hesitate. If he no give up his gun, shoot him. Do not wait."

Droplets of cold sweat ran down her spine like scurrying insects. Beth didn't know if the shudder that followed was because of the cold or the fear induced perspiration. An infinite moonless black surrounded her and Juan as they started. She could not see in front of her. The only reference was the ground under her feet and a single light at the center of the town. They knew the general direction of the house after watching it for two days. But as she started, she could not escape thoughts of being in the belly of misfortune. Her breath exhaled in small puffs of moist air. *I've got to get the boys.*

As she moved slowly down the slope, strange uncontrollable thoughts kept peeling away at her focus. What a strange name for a town, Mound House. Unlike its name, the town sat in something of a hole. The mounds which gave the town its name surrounded the town itself. But the town existed only because of two intersecting sets of railroad lines. The tracks of the Virginia & Truckee and the railroad coming north from the links to mining towns such as Aurora, Benton Hot Springs, Esmerelda, and Bodie met at a junction of two small canyons splitting an otherwise circular series of low rounded hills on the outskirts of town. It was down one of those heights she and Juan now walked. Both moved slowly, traversing the slope more with side steps than a direct path down. Beth followed the exact path Juan took, placing each step carefully so as not to slide down the hill.

Beth looked to the center of town. The only light was coming from the sole town saloon. While still open, this was a small town, and there was little activity this late.

At the base of the mound Juan stopped. Beth held still behind him. Both listened. Nothing moved. Beth heard nothing but the normal sounds of the night: crickets and sagebrush swaying on the ever-present soft breeze. Hearing no human sounds, Beth waved Juan to continue.

The house, casa as Juan called it, looked more like a decrepit shack to Beth. Maybe it was just the darkness. She leaned against the weather-beaten dried wooden walls and tried to keep her breathing under control. Juan was still directly in front of her at arm's length, which was about the extent of visibility. Juan pointed and waved to indicate the door just around the corner. He then motioned he'd go the opposite way where Beth knew the window would be. But before Juan moved, he looked at her and waited. Beth knew he wanted to make sure she was ready before he moved around to the back of the house. She drew a silent breath and nodded, then moved to the front door.

Beth assessed the front door and its simple wooden latch. A narrow piece of wood fixed to the door pivoted up and down on a dowel away from the door jamb. Another dowel at the opposite side acted as a handle to raise the wood bar. She figured there was a second wood bar inside the house attached to the same dowel pivot so that both bars raised at the same time. The bars crossed the door jamb and fitted into a protruding slot across from the door. When the bar and handle were down, the bar crossed the door jamb and kept the door closed. *The latch might have some type of lever used to hold down the wood bar on the inside, a crude lock. If so, the sound might wake those inside. The only way to find out is to try and lift the latch.* She lifted the latch. It moved. Beth's upper teeth bit into her lower lip as she continued to lift the latch, doing her best to make no sound. The door was free. But what awaited on the other side?

With the latch free, Beth hesitated outside the door. She tried to remember all the lessons with Will shooting cans and bottles. She knew the man inside might shoot first and ask questions second. She had to be ready. Will had taught her that when shooting cans a shot had to be true, but if you're shooting at a gunman, they're a larger target. She did not have to be as accurate.

Beth remembered Will's words: "Don't rush, squeeze firm but controlled. If you jerk, the shot will miss."

Easy to say when you're shooting cans. This was going to be different. And she knew it.

With gun in her right hand, Beth lowered her left shoulder and shoved the door inwards, gun sweeping the dark space. The door swung open with much less resistance than she expected. She lost her balance and half stumbled across the threshold, taking two or three loud steps into the room. She couldn't get a good look around as she struggled with her balance. While her eyes were already used to the darkness, her stumble claimed her focus. She did all she could to keep from falling.

As Juan predicted, a man lay on his back with a hat covering his face at the foot of the opposite wall. At the sound of her entry, the man raised and turned a gun he held on his chest while asleep. His gun exploded. Beth first thought she'd been hit, but the shot missed as she continued to stumble into the room. In the fog of awakening, the man aimed at the door, not anticipating someone flailing their way into the room. She was about to fall and knew it. In a flash moment, she knew she had to fire before she hit the floor and before the man could thumb his hammer and get off another shot. Without any conscious aim, Beth fired in the direction of the supine man. She hit the floor in a heap. Her hat flew off her head, releasing the long blonde tresses that had been tucked up underneath. The man physically spasmed at the waist, his knees coming to his chest, both hands reaching for his neck. His gun banged on the wooden floor.

"Augh!" He rolled back and forth from a fetal position on his side to stretching flat out on his back.

Beth raised up to her knees and crawled toward the man to grab the gun away from his side.

Beth yelled, "Don't try anything! You move again, and I'll shoot." Beth thumbed her own hammer, locking another round into her Pocket Navy five-shooter. But the man continued to writhe on the floor, oblivious to her command.

"A woman, I got taken by a woman…" His eyes glistened with layered astonishment. Blood pulsed through his fingers, which clutched the left side of his neck. Beth could see her shot must have hit an artery in the man's neck as the blood came spurt after spurt. The man must have been doubly shocked. She could see in those eyes his disbelief that her wild shot hit something mortal, but he was equally stunned it was done by a woman.

"It's my neck. I'm goin' to bleed out," his words came with blood welling from his mouth.

Beth could not take her eyes off the man.

"Never meant to hurt the boys. That was Sam Brown's idea."

Beth made no response. She watched as his body began to relax. His end was near.

"The sick boy needs a doc." There was a pause as blood dripped out of the man's mouth. "Brown will get the rancher in Virginia City 'cause he killed his twin brother."

Now it was Beth's turn to be amazed. Here was a man who'd taken part in the kidnapping of small children. But he now tried to tell her they needed care and to warn of the danger confronting Will. The man must have two faces: one horrible and one possibly redeemable. Either way, he was now headed to meet his maker.

"*Señora*, stay back," called Juan as he ran into the room. "I cover the man, find the *Niño's*. Are you hit?"

"No, I'm not hit," she answered. With no small amount of relief, Beth rose up from her knees. The maternal instinct now struck, and she finally scanned the room. There in a darkened, doubly shaded corner were the twins, tied and gagged. She ran to them.

*****

"Those be shots. Sounded like they came from behind the telegraph office." John Murphy stirred from his alcohol-induced stupor and registered his surprise at any activity in this out-of-the-way town late at night. The saloon around him had been quiet. It was quiet this late every night. Most men in this town worked hard in the stamp mills just outside of town, breaking down silver ore and melting it into bars of bullion for shipment. He was out of work. He'd like to think it was because he possessed an independence of opinion that did not always coincide with the judgment of his supervisors. But in truth, he just didn't like hard work. He arrived at the saloon every night and pondered how he could make money in some easy fashion. Pondered as the alcohol filled his body. The possibility of any activity out of the norm brightened an otherwise mundane life.

Richard Adams, the bartender of the Mound House Saloon, had already grabbed his shotgun from behind the bar. "Who'd be up at this hour?" He headed to the door.

Other than Murphy, Adams could see only one other patron in the saloon. He looked at Murphy, a regular customer, who had already stood up out of his chair. Adams did not know the customer in the corner space, but he was asleep with his head on the table. He had not stirred despite the sound of gunfire. He must be seriously drunk. Adams

145

did not have a great deal of confidence Murphy was in any shape to follow directions, but he made à snap decision.

"Go get the sheriff. I'll head down to the telegraph office and see what happened."

"But the sheriff is out of town," said Murphy.

"Then get his deputy."

"Ain't no deputy no more," whined Murphy.

Adams shook his head in doubt of Murphy's information. He took it as an indication that Murphy just didn't want to get involved. "Go down and get the sheriff. He's there. If he's not, ask where he is."

Murphy hesitated, but Adams did not let him off the hook. "Go, now."

Murphy headed out the door followed immediately by Adams. "I'll head to the telegraph office up the street. I'll try to meet you at the source of the gun shots. Hurry."

*****

Beth removed the ties and gags on Luke. By the time she got them off, both boys were crying, and Luke jumped up to hug his mother. Sean was slower. He just reached out. Beth immediately understood the man across the room had been right; Sean was sick. In any other circumstance, Sean would have jumped up, and he'd be standing right next to Luke, holding onto her too.

Luke pulled away but only briefly. "Sean's sick."

Beth grabbed Sean, placing her hand under his head and pulling him to the nape of her neck. She could feel his heat.

"Oh Sean, you are red hot." The young child continued to cry, interrupted only by a deep cough.

"You're right, Luke, your brother's sick. We need to get him home right away." Still holding Sean close, Beth turned to see Juan kneeling beside the man she'd shot.

Juan looked up from watching the gunman. The man no longer moved. Juan looked at Beth, back to the man, and again to Beth. He then moved his head slowly back and forth. Beth knew the man was now dead.

"Where's Pa?" asked Luke.

"He's riding after the bad men," said Beth.

"He's going to get those bad guys." Luke almost shouted the words.

Beth smiled through her tears. "I hope so."

Juan stood. "Señora, we go now. People will come."

"We need to get the boys back to the ranch and get the doctor from Carson City." Beth stood. Another thought now hit. "But we need to tell Will we have the boys. He needs to come back to the ranch too. He has to give up the chase by himself."

"Señor Will, he will no stop. He will keep after these bad men until he find them. Even if the *Niño's* are home, he will no stop until he find the men who hurt his family."

"But he can't do it alone."

Juan did not answer. Beth stood still, holding the sobbing Sean.

"Juan, you have to find Will and tell him to come back to the ranch."

Juan responded not with words. Instead, he simply shook his head side to side.

"Señora, Juan cannot tell Will to stop. He will not listen to Juan when the men try to hurt his family."

Beth knew Juan was right. She knew Will had already reverted to his Texas Ranger days and would ride down these men no matter the consequence. She was the only person who had any chance to convince him to return to the ranch. Even if she got to Will, she might not be successful, but she had to try. The alternative could be Will, dead. Luke had stopped crying, but Sean still sobbed in hyperventilated breaths. Each time he sucked in air his little body shook from top to bottom. Both boys still clung to their mother. Sean had not let go of her neck, and Luke was virtually attached to her leg. The last thing Beth wanted to do right now was to leave the boys. She had just reconnected. But she was not prepared to let Will keep riding after Sam Brown alone. She had to get word to him.

"Mommy, let's go home." Luke leaned out from Beth's leg, now pulling her toward the door.

"Hold on little one. Mommy has to figure out how to tell your Pa to come home."

"Señora, we must go. People hear the guns and will come. We can use the man's caballo for *el Niño's*."

He didn't know it, but Juan had just solved Beth's quandary with his simple suggestion to use the dead man's horse.

"Juan, I have to get word to Will. I'll send him a telegraph and tell him we have the boys, but he won't let Sam Brown go. He'll still go after him. The only chance of getting him to walk away is for me to convince him in person. To do that, I'll have to go to Virginia City. You take the boys back to the ranch. We can put Luke on the man's horse and you hold Sean close to you on yours. You and María have been family to the boys. María cares for them as if they were her own. I have no worry at all that she will take care of them until I can get home. María can easily watch them while you ride on to Carson and get the doctor for Sean. On the other hand, I'm the only one who can possibly stop Will. I don't like to leave the boys, but it's the only solution to a two-edged problem. I'll ride to Virginia City and try to convince Will to return home."

Juan looked at Beth, pleading with his eyes for her to change her mind. "You should no go to Virginia City alone. It is not a place for *Señora* alone."

"I have to go. You take the boys. Go ahead, I'll be fine."

A large man with a shotgun then entered the room. He had on a white shirt, black vest, and apron.

"What's going on?" He held the rifle at an angle midway between Beth and Juan.

Beth held out Sean for the man to see. "This man rode with Sam Brown onto our ranch and took my boys. Brown's mad that the boys' father shot his brother in a gun battle the brother started over four years ago and tried to get revenge by taking my boys. He threatened to kill them both."

"How'd he die?" Adams lowered the gun and pointed the muzzle toward the man lying on the ground.

"I came into the room to get my sons, and he shot at me. I shot back. He missed. I didn't." Beth's stance and tone conveyed the recognizable mode of a mother bear protecting her cubs.

"Mommy, don't let him take us." Luke again grabbed Beth's leg. She reached down to lay her hand on his head.

"No, don't worry, Mommy won't let anyone else take you, Luke."

The bartender took in the scene. "Well, the boys are obviously yours. But how do I know the man died as you say?"

"You don't, but these are the sons of Will Toal. He has a ranch in the Carson Valley; that's where we need to take them. The boy I'm holding is sick. He needs a doctor. These men kept them cold, tied, and gagged for four days. I don't even know if they fed them. They're going home."

Certainty dripped from Beth's voice.

"My name is Beth. If you want, you can find me anytime at Will's ranch. If you or anyone here in Mound House has questions, I'll be happy to answer them, but right now I have to get the boys back to the ranch." There was no reason to try and explain she and Will were not married. In the moment, Beth figured to try and keep this as simple as possible.

Adams paused. Beth watched as he processed a decision. Adams looked at Juan holding his gun at his side. Beth could see the man taking note of the gun rig at her side too. While the man looked, Beth took her right hand from Luke's head and hovered over her holstered gun. He might shoot one, but he'd risk getting shot by the other. Depending on his decision, they would leave peaceably, or there might be more bloodshed. But Beth was leaving. She could see Juan tense with the importance of the moment.

"Our sheriff might be out of town. I'm going to let you go. But I'm tellin' him to look you up and ask any questions he might. I've heard of Will Toal. Got a good reputation. I know he'll be around where the sheriff can find him."

Beth exhaled. Tension released in every muscle. "I thank you. My boys have been through enough. They need to get home."

Beth turned to Juan. "Juan, let's go."

Juan picked up Luke and both walked out of the door, pulled the reins to the dead man's horse, and the group headed back up the slope to where Beth and Juan had left their horses. When they reached the top of the low rounded mound, Beth turned to Juan as he put Luke on top of the horse and rigged a lead rope.

"Are you going to be able to hold on to Sean and still hold the lead rope to Luke's horse?"

"Sí, I tie the lead rope to my saddle. I hold Sean."

Sean's entire body seized in a fit of coughing. The sound of the cough came from deep in his chest. Beth pulled him close until the fit subsided. She smoothed out the hair on his forehead to see his face. He didn't even cry. Beth could see he was too tired or too sick to even do that.

"I'm not sure. Sean looks bad. Maybe I should ride with you down to Carson City. We'll have to camp out tonight somewhere anyway, and I can help you with them overnight. Sean's so sick, I should stay at least until we can get him to a doctor. We can get to Carson City sometime tomorrow morning, and we can have Dr. Williams look at him. From there, you can take them to the ranch, and I'll come back here to Mound House and head up the hill to Virginia City."

"That might be a good plan, *Señora*. I would be hard for Juan to carry Sean and make sure Luke does not fall off in the dark. You could carry Sean, and I will look after Luke."

"I'll lose a day, but I can't leave Sean until I know he's in the doctor's hands. I just hope Will does not find those men before I can get back up to Virginia City."

"*Señora*, when you start ride up the hill, be careful. You go to a big city with many bad people."

Beth shook her head as if to say thanks for the concern. "I'll ride out from Carson City early tomorrow after we get Sean to the doctor. I'll and camp in the hills the next night and head up to Virginia City early the next day. I've got to find Will. He was told to go to the Delta Saloon. That's where I'll start."

"Careful, *Señora*. Do not use the main road. Keep to the ridges."

"I will Juan. Let's ride out. We need to get away from here before that bartender with the shotgun changes his mind about us."

*****

It had been a long day. Beth stopped, looking back at Carson Valley now behind her. The large depression below the Sierras now safely cradled her twins. She watched the sun follow its normal pattern and sink below the tall mountains set in a sky sprinkled with orange and purple pastels. Wispy transparent clouds covered the valley like a clear glass sarcophagus amid the expiring sunlight. The day had been hotter than most this year, but with the approaching darkness, Beth knew it was going to be another cold night out on the trail. She continued to ride for another hour heading northeast toward the canyons that led uphill to Virginia City. She felt exhausted and knew she had to stop and camp soon. She and Juan had camped out last night on the road to Carson City after leaving Mound House. They woke early and got to the doctor's office late morning. Doc Williams said Sean had fluid in his lungs, and that was not good, but with the proper care, he should come out of it. The doctor had given them some medications and said he could go home. Juan had carried Sean on his horse from the doctor's office and headed off to the ranch, leading Luke on green shaded horse once owned by the man Beth shot. Beth grinned. Sean was spent but feeling a bit better that he was headed home. On the other hand, Luke was having the time of his life getting to ride his own horse. He had nothing but big smiles when she kissed him goodbye.

Without any real moon, she let her horse find his own path leading away from Mound House and keeping to the ridges and off the main road. All she cared about at this point was that her horse kept moving in the general direction of Virginia City.

Upon her return to Mound House earlier today, she had left a note with the barkeep and requested that he send a wire up to Virginia City first thing in the morning, asking that it be delivered to Will Toal. He reluctantly agreed to deliver it to the town's telegraph operator. She also asked that it be delivered to John Mackay if they could not find

Will. Will was supposed to meet with Mackay, and maybe he'd know where to find Will if the telegraph operator could not. She told Will in the note that the boys were safe and headed back to the ranch. She also asked that he return to the ranch too. But she knew he wouldn't. She had to find him first.

She dismounted, pulled her saddle off, and hobbled her horse as Will had taught her. She laid down in a patch of soft dirt. As tired as she was, sleep did not come easy. She looked up at what was now a clear dark sky. While she felt the boys were now out of immediate danger, this man named Brown, or Sutton, would not be happy. Would he try to retake them? Was he still waiting for Will in Virginia City? Had Will found him already? If this man was related to Drake Sutton, he definitely had the same evil qualities. But he'd also be intelligent, maybe even educated like his brother. A bad combination.

Beth could not shut down her mind. The events of the past few days kept her emotions churning. This all stemmed from the day she hit Will on the head. She'd made one bad decision, and her life could not settle. Even now, almost five years later, she still paid for that decision.

History kept driving the present. Beth's history with Will had not been smooth. The rough spots kept delivering consequences. Will had killed Drake Sutton just before Drake was going to shoot Beth. It was the second time Will had pulled her from a life-threatening situation. Earlier, she'd taken off with Sutton to escape her marriage. It was a marriage she'd had no say in. She'd been given to a middle-aged man, arranged by her Mormon Bishop. But she'd been attacked by Sutton's men while Sutton was away. Will saved her and took her to the ranch to recover. Then she'd betrayed Will but did so to protect him from Sutton. Ultimately, she returned to Will, who had never quite fully forgiven her. Sutton returned and prompted a gunfight, which ended with

Will shooting him. The saga just would not end. Now, Sutton's twin brother hunted her sons.

Her body was tired but her mind alert. Sleep would not come. Beth then had the thought maybe Will might be right. The only way to truly end this would be to face Sam Brown. How could she ever rest knowing he still might be out there? Next time he might kill the boys when he had the chance.

She needed to sleep. She had to get to Will.

Chapter Twenty-One

1873 February
Mound House, NV

"It'll be nice to have a roof over my head, even if it means we have to share it with two young brats." Elmer Lennox spoke to no one but the blowing wind. He looked west to see a sun falling below the Sierras. At this time of the year, a setting sun sucked the day's warmth out of the air, leaving a brisk chill. The ever-present breeze only increased the bite. Lennox pulled his ragged woolen jacket around his shoulders and fastened it in front. He'd spent the last night on the trail, taking his time to get back to Mound House. He was not looking forward to returning.

Lennox continued with his off-handed mumbled statements, "Hope Waverly has a fire going. The unseasonably warm winds were gone. We're back to regular cold winter."

Reaching the outskirts of town, Lennox kept his horse at an inconspicuous walk. He'd been gone almost five days now. It'd be interesting to see how Waverly had managed with the two boys. He hoped Waverly wasn't too mad. He'd traveled two days up the hill to Virginia City and two more on the way down. There had been a couple of days camping out along with one fateful, fire laden day in between. He stopped and dismounted but didn't see Waverly's pale roan horse.

"Waverly, you in there?"

No answer.

Lennox opened the door. He scanned the one room shack. It was empty. No Waverly. No kids.

"What the hell is going on?"

Lennox walked back outside and circled the entire building to make sure Waverly had not tied his horse up around back. Nothing.

Grabbing the bridle, he looked at his own fire red gelding and said, "Let's head over to the saloon. Someone there should know what happened."

*****

Lennox pushed through the saloon's bat wing doors. His immediate thought was that there was a lack of men for what should have been prime time for any saloon. Too quiet. A newly descended darkness should have brought most of the men in this godforsaken town into the saloon for a drink. But he counted only three men plus the bartender. He walked up to the bar.

"Whiskey."

"Good stuff or other?" asked the bartender.

Mindful of his limited funds, he answered, "Other." He dropped a fifty-cent piece on the bar.

"Not too many people pay for the good stuff around here. Haven't seen you before and thought you might be one to pay."

Lennox looked at the man and came close to a snarl in his response. "It hits you the same way in the end." Lennox then thought he'd best try to suppress his normally prickly tone. He needed information right now, not enemies. Knowing his poor social skills could soon be a problem, he decided he'd better ask his questions before his regular personality put the man off.

"Say, have you seen a man with two young boys anywhere around here lately?"

Lennox noticed an immediate change in the expression on the bartender's face. "Why do you ask?" There was an obvious critical quality to the man's voice, as if the answer to his question might be extra significant. Lennox took note and figured he'd better not let on he knew Waverly.

"I've been told to find the man. He might have taken those two boys."

The bartender's face relaxed just enough to let Lennox know he'd been right not to admit any connection to Waverly.

"He's dead."

"Dead?"

"That's what I said, dead. Shot by a blonde lady. She had me send a wire to Virginia City and told me she'd sent the kids back home with some vaquero who was with her. Said they were connected to a rancher named Will Toal."

Lennox did his best to cover his shock. *Waverly's dead. How had that lady found them? He had to get word to Brown. This was going to cause problems. Brown would not be happy to say the least. Best he send a wire and then head west as quick as he could.*

The bartender continued, "Why do you ask?"

Lennox hesitated to find an answer but not for long. He hoped the bartender did not notice. "I gotta let some people know them kids 'er safe. Me and others been lookin' for them."

The bartender seemed appeased. "The lady also told me as she was writing out the wire that she was going to have to notify the father, Will Toal. Said he was up in Virginia City. Heard her tell the vaquero she was the only one who could stop this Toal fella from trying to avenge the boys by going after the kidnappers. She said she'd have to do that in person if she was going to have any chance of success."

Again, Lennox thought for a moment. He took a sip of the whiskey, giving him some time to think. It burned down low in the back of his throat. Brown just wanted Toal. Them kids were only a means to flush him out. Toal's woman might do the same trick. Maybe he could salvage the loss of the boys in Brown's eyes if he could deliver the woman. He took another sip of his whiskey. Again, it burned down the back of his throat.

"This stuff is miserable snake venom."

"You said you didn't want the good stuff."

"But I didn't order poison, I ordered whiskey."

"You get what the money paid for," came the reply accompanied by a patronizing smile.

Lennox had to check himself. Normally, he'd have shot this irritant behind the bar and his arrogant smirk without a moment's hesitation. But he had better things to do.

"I got to send a wire to the folks I'm workin' for so's to let 'em know the boys is safe."

The bartender turned to start drying a recently washed shot glass. "Telegraph officer usually works late. If you hurry over there, he might still be in."

"Thanks. Might just do that." Lennox downed the last of his drink. It took some real bad whiskey for him not to take it in one gulp. But this stuff might eat a hole in his throat. He felt his face flush. The snarl snuck up to his lips. He could see the bartender take note.

*****

The telegraph office was attached to the train depot. Lennox noted that the depot in Mound House had to be the largest building in this small unremarkable city. It was also the most well-kept building. The rest of the town looked as if it was slowly rotting away, but the depot had a new coat of paint and the walkways out front had recently been replaced. *Must be the railroad taking care of their end of the business.*

The telegraph officer was still in. Most men who worked at such a job were of slight build, someone who could not earn more money with brawn and hard labor. But this man was large and wide. Elmer's first thought was that he must be dense, otherwise he'd be able to make much more working the stamp mills. But no matter, he had bigger things to attend to.

Lennox thought he had an idea on how he'd break the news to Brown. But he didn't know if Brown would still be in Virginia City. He also didn't know if the telegraph office up the hill survived the fire. He'd better ask.

The telegraph operator raised his oversized head and looked up as Lennox entered the small office. The semi-transparent bill of his visor raised upward so that Lennox could see the entirety of his face with puffed cheeks and bad teeth.

"Can I send a telegraph to Virginia City?"

"There's been a huge fire up there."

"Did the telegraph survive?"

"I got several wires over the last two days informing of the damage and asking for help both from here and Carson City. So, yes, the tele-graph is still working."

"Did they say what else survived?" Lennox tried to look surprised even though he wasn't.

"All the hotels burned. I think one bank survived and two saloons, including the Delta."

"Good, I need to send a message to someone named Roberts. If he's still in town, he'll be at the Delta." As he walked over from the saloon, he'd figured sending a message to Sam Brown would cause immediate suspicion. But no one knew Roberts.

"Write it out, and I'll send it right away. It's gettin' late. Like to get home sometime soon."

Lennox pulled out a pencil and wrote on a piece of paper from the box on the counter.

To Frank Roberts at the Delta Saloon. Stop.

Waverly's dead. Stop. Boys back to ranch. Stop. Blonde lady heading up to VC. Stop. I can follow her and help her find our people in VC. Stop. She might like to meet our group. Stop. Reply tonight. Stop.

That should tell Brown what he needs to know but not raise any immediate alarm.

"Here. This is the note. How much?"

The telegraph man looked over the note. "That'll be one dollar."

Lennox flipped the coin onto the counter. "Can you send it right away?"

"It'll be sent in the next couple of minutes. As I said, I need to get home."

"I'll pay you five dollars to wait for a reply."

"That might take more than an hour. It might not come until tomorrow."

"Wait a hour. If there ain't no reply, I'll check back tomorrow." Lennox hoped Roberts would be at the saloon. Lennox figured if the saloon were still standing, that's where Roberts would spend most of his time. Maybe he could get an answer tonight.

Chapter Twenty-Two

1873 February
Virginia City, NV

Brown and Roberts were indeed at the counter of the Delta Saloon when the telegraph operator, Joe Cullen, walked into the tavern. But they did not see him despite his tall, lanky frame and disjointed stride. Cullen walked up to Mike Stuart, who was tending bar as always.

"Do you know a Frank Roberts? Is he here? I got a message for him. Said it was sent with a request for a quick reply. Paid for it too."

"No, I don't know anyone named Frank Roberts," said Stuart. "But I can find out real quick."

"Anybody here named Frank Roberts?" Stuart bellowed out the inquiry. Multiple heads turned throughout the saloon.

One of those heads was Frank Roberts, who looked up from his drink. He and Brown had spent a good deal of time at the Delta as there was almost nowhere else to go in town. They had planned to head out tomorrow. This was to be their last decent drink for a while. A quick glance at Brown received a simple nod of the head in the direction of the bartender. Without saying a word, Brown had instructed Roberts to go find out what he wanted. Roberts walked over and identified himself.

"That'll be fifty cents for the special delivery. It's a standard charge for messages delivered personal."

Roberts reached into his pocket and handed the man the money. He did not glance at the note but walked immediately back to Sam Brown. He then opened the note and read. Stuart watched as the man handed the note to Brown.

Stuart then turned to Cullen and with a frown asked, "What'd that note say?"

"Mike, you know I cannot reveal the contents of a note."

"Oh yes you can. That man sat down next to Sam Brown. If he rides with Sam Brown, he's a problem. Those two are up to no good. I have word that they kidnapped two young boys and intended to hold them for ransom. You're a part of the 601s. You need to tell me so I can tell Hurley."

Cullen winced and turned his head toward the door but then returned his eyes to meet Stuart's and nodded. "The note said something about boys headed back to some ranch but that a blonde woman was headed up to V.C., which I assume meant here. The sender thought it might be good if she met their group."

"Their group," snorted Stuart as he glanced at Brown and Roberts, who were huddled together. "Thugs and murderers. They cannot be up to any good."

Stuart looked back to Cullen. "They will send a reply. After they give you that response, I want you to come back and tell me what the reply said."

"I'll have to wait until they are not watching the office. I don't want any trouble with Brown. If you cross him, you become one of his targets."

"Don't worry, all the boys are in on this. Hurley found out about their kidnapping plan from Julia, that high class lady of the night who looks to him for protection. She got her info from John Millian and then told Hurley. Hurley then told all the boys to be on the lookout for this. We're not going to let Brown take kids and get away with it here in town. And, if need be, we'll protect you in the process."

Stuart turned his head to stare at Brown. "Not in this town."

*****

Brown looked at Roberts in amazement. "Waverly's dead?"

"That's what the wire says. Also says that the blonde woman is on her way here."

"How did Waverly get killed? How is it that Elmer is sending us a wire and not dead too? How did the boys get taken?" Brown's first thoughts were that his plan was completely ruined.

Just as his anger was beginning to really rise, Roberts said, "But Elmer added that he thought the woman should meet our group. Elmer might be telling us we can take the woman in place of the boys. We could use her as the bait. That rancher should be just as interested in her as the boys."

"Maybe. Not quite the same, but if he loses his woman, it might suffice. Like I said, he needs to feel the loss."

"Elmer's note says we should respond right away."

Brown thought a moment.

"Okay, go send a note. Tell him we will take care of meeting the woman before she reaches Virginia City. He and Waverly messed this up. I'm not going to let him spoil it up any further. We'll take care of the woman to make sure we have her in our control here in Virginia City. But, tell him he should come here to the city immediately. We might need him."

"Got it. I'll talk to the operator and send the message right away."

"Come back right after you've done that. We need to saddle up and head out to watch the roads into town. We can set up at the top of the canyons and keep a lookout for the woman. We will have to take her before she gets to Virginia City."

*****

Joe Cullen lifted his head and tried to smooth his grease laden black hair. It'd been four days since his last bath. His hair told him it was time to remedy that. He looked up as the little bell rang on the back of the door. Joe had been dreading what he knew was going to happen. He knew Roberts would be coming. He also knew once Roberts sent his telegram, Cullen would have to reveal the contents to Stuart and the 601s. Any slip up here and he could get killed. He didn't notice his own nervous reaction as his lower teeth reached up and bit into his upper lip.

Roberts strode in and gave Cullen a note. "I need you to send this right away."

Cullen looked at the paper containing the message and then up at Roberts. "That will be two dollars. It's after hours. Not sure there will be anyone there to receive it. The operator in Mound House usually goes home real early. Not sure he's still going to be in his office."

"Just send it and wait for a reply. Do it."

Cullen was all too ready to do whatever Roberts asked just to get him out of the office. The tone of his command to send the wire only made him react with all the more haste.

"I'll send it right now." Cullen thought the possibility of any quick response was slim. Mound House was a small office with only one operator, and that man was never there this late in a day.

The message went out, and to Cullen's surprise, an answer came back in a matter of minutes.

"Message received."

Roberts paid the two dollars and left. The tiny bell tinkled for a suspended moment after the door's forceful closure.

Cullen waited, stood, and looked out the front window. Roberts was not headed back to the Delta. He headed down toward the temporary livery stables set up after the fire. He also saw Sam Brown walk out of the Delta and head in the same direction. Cullen made sure both men were out of sight, and then he darted across the street to the Delta and Stuart, looking down toward the livery the entire way.

"What did the wire say?"

Cullen again gave Stuart a pained look.

"Ah, don't give me that look. You know good and well we need to take care of this. The 601s have run men up the hangman's noose for far less than what these thugs have in mind."

Cullen knew he had to divulge. "The wire said that some man named Lennox was to leave the woman alone, and that Brown and Roberts would take care of her. Lennox was to ride back to Virginia City as soon as he could."

Stuart now leaned back against the back portion of the bar in thought. "They must be thinking of using the woman as some kind of bait in place of the boys they took. I'll bet they're still up to no good. Whatever their plan is, it should not happen here in Virginia City. The 601s are going to have to stop it."

Chapter Twenty-Three

1873 February
Virginia City, NV

Sam Brown stood on C Street in front of what used to be the Moli-nelli Hotel. There was nothing left. His glance spanned across a flat-tened heap of burned out beams and still smoldering ash. A fetid stench of destruction filled the air. Brown pulled his thumbs out of the wide leather belt of his holster rig. His ankle length duster had been held wide by the position of his hands but now draped forward, covering the metallic weaponry underneath. He turned to Roberts who had just walked up with both of their horses.

Roberts sighed. "Horses are saddled and ready. Looks like we need to find a new room."

"Looks like we need to find a new *town*," Brown retorted.

Both he and Brown mounted and turned to leave.

"This city will rebuild. There's too much going on in with all the mining not to. I heard they plan to set up tents for temporary homes and businesses and then rebuild as soon as they can."

"Might be, but not in time for us to get a room. It was a good thing we heard the bells on the fire wagon and were able to get out of the hotel and grab the horses before everything burned to the ground."

Roberts nodded. "We could 'a been fried like the rest of this place."

Brown turned to Roberts. "This place was doomed, only a matter of time."

"Most everything out here is doomed 'cause it's always a matter of time. The desert will take over sooner or later."

Brown shook his head. "Yeah, but in the meantime, we have to get the woman. Let's go. We'll start out tonight and camp. Then tomorrow we'll get an early start. We hafta grab her before she makes it to Virginia City. Without knowing when she left Mound House, we need to travel hard. She could be getting close."

*****

Will Toal descended the stairs and walked into the front room, the office, of the Mackay Mansion. He had awakened yesterday from a conquering sleep following the complete physical and emotional exhaustion after fighting the fire the night before. He had been stiff and sore in muscles not normally used, but he arose determined to spend the day trying to find Sam Brown. He'd figured if he found the man, he could bring this all to an end before he had to go to Carson City and talk to Duane Bliss about the lumber for Mr. Mackay. That would be the quickest resolution to the current situation. Will had walked far and wide through the parts of Virginia City that had not been burned. He'd asked all over about a man named Brown. Nothing.

But despite yesterday's unsuccessful search, he had received great news late in the day from Beth. Great news. She and Juan had found and retrieved the boys. She didn't say, but he assumed she had returned to the ranch. How amazing she had gotten the boys, but then, she was an amazing lady. The news had ended an otherwise frustrating day. He thought he might just have a chance to find Brown. But he'd ridden throughout the town and found no sign of the man. Everyone he spoken to had no idea where Brown might be. Or, maybe they were just too scared of the man's reputation to get involved.

Mackay had told him there were close to twenty thousand people in Virginia City now. Will had tried to ride through the shanty towns spread outside of the metropolis, but though he'd kept at it all day, he hadn't covered a quarter of the outlying sprawl. He'd returned to the mansion late yesterday evening despondent.

His host had insisted he again spend the night in the mansion. As most, if not all, of the regular hotel rooms in town had been demolished, Will had readily accepted access to a good bed and restful sleep. This morning, John Mackay sat across from him at his desk. Will walked down the narrow staircase, knowing he'd have to head to Carson City today for the meeting with Bliss. He couldn't delay that any longer. Mackay had been too gracious in his suggestion to try and find Brown yesterday. But Will knew how important it was for Mackay and his mine to get the lumber. His body felt heavy. He did not know if it was the full day of riding or the fact he'd not found Brown and was no nearer to removing the threat to his family. The weight of no progress pressed on his shoulders. His feet weren't even functioning as usual. He had to consciously lift them or they seemed to shuffle along with his heels, dragging more than rising and falling. But the unusual sound of his riding boots on a wooden floor was now muffled by the covering carpet.

"May I come in?"

Mackay turned in his chair. "Of course, please sit. Let me finish this. It won't take long, and we can talk."

Will sat down on one of the oak chairs positioned for visitors. They were all similar. No padding, just wood. Will thought none of them looked very comfortable. Probably meant that way to keep the intrusions quick. Must have been a way Mackay managed his time. Keep the visitations uncomfortable thus focused and short.

"There, done," said Mackay, now turning to face Will. He showed no evidence of soot and ash from the fire fight. Will thought he'd probably used his upstairs shower or bath in a room with the only running water from San Francisco to Kansas City. He wore a woolen suit and vest of some special weave, which fit him as if made just for his figure. Probably was, considered Will, and expensive too, most likely.

Mackay asked, "Have you recovered from the battle with the fire and then your day of riding around town?" Mackay appeared calm and in control here in his familiar surroundings.

"I have. How do things stand with the mine?"

"My reports tell me that the coverage of the main shaft saved the mine. Had we not done that, the fire would surely have descended into the shaft and timbers below. It would have been a disaster. I have you to thank for that."

"As I said, sir, I played only a small role. There were plenty of others helping."

"We pulled the cover off so oxygen can again flow down to all levels. We won't be doing any mining in the near future. But we are close to connecting the main shaft down from the city level to the crosscut over one thousand feet below. Once we do that, we'll be ready to start pulling ore out of the new find."

Will nodded. "And that is why you need the timber."

"Indeed. That is why we need the timber."

Mackay raised a pointed finger as if aiming it straight up into the sky. The movement was an emphasis of refreshed memory. "There was a telegram delivered for you late last night. In the mayhem of the fire, I gather delivery of many messages were delayed. Did the staff get it to you?"

"They did, thank you for that."

"Good news or bad?"

"It was from Beth. She got the twins. Not sure how she found them, and I'm not sure how she got them back. But her wire says they are headed back to the ranch, and she wants me to go there too."

"That's great news, is it not?"

"Yes, that the boys are safe is great news." Will looked down at his feet. "But it doesn't end there. The men who did this need to pay. If they took my sons, they might come back and try again. I need to deal with them now before it goes any further."

Mackay looked intently at Will. "That's a tough decision. Not sure what I would do, but I can certainly understand your thoughts."

"I'm hoping that Sam Brown is here in Virginia City and doesn't know the boys are recovered. That way I can play along with their scheme, meet them as if they still had them. They'll ask for the ransom, and I just need them to meet me, and we will settle it."

"In the street?"

"If need be."

"I can hear the determination in your voice," said Mackay. "But that's kind of risky, is it not? Sam Brown has a widespread reputation."

"It'd be risky to sit around waiting for them to come again but not knowing where or when."

"True. I see your point."

Will shook his head, "No sense to delay. Better to meet them at a place and time I choose rather than some place and time of Brown's choice."

"Well, if you need to show them the ransom money to get them to come out of hiding, I'll still put that up."

"Mr. Mackay, you offered that before. It is mighty nice, and I cannot thank you enough. But I hope I don't need it now."

"It's still there if you do."

"I appreciate it more than I can say."

"You helped me save my mine. It's the least I can do. The money is nothing compared to what you saved for me and my own family."

There was a sudden anxious rap at the door.

"Mr. Mackay! Mr. Mackay! You have a telegram. It's from the President of the United States."

Will saw question spread across Mackay's face. Mackay gave him a quizzed look and shrugged. "That sounds like Oliver. He's the messenger who normally brings me telegrams from the wire office. Wonder what in the world this could be about."

Mackay rose and headed to the door where the calling and knocking continued unabated.

"Mr. Mackay! Mr. Mackay!"

"Yes, Oliver, I'm coming. Hold on just a minute." Mackay got to the door and opened it. Just outside the door stood a young man no more than twenty-five. His hair flowed to his shoulders but was tied with a leather thong of some sort over which sat a green visor. His face was full of what Will found to be a combination of excitement and concern.

"It's from the president, Mr. Mackay. I thought I should bring it right away."

"That's grand, Oliver. I appreciate it."

Mackay scanned the message quickly and looked back up at Oliver, still standing in the doorway.

"You've told no one about this, right?"

Will could see that Oliver was insulted. "Of course not, Mr. Mackay."

"Oliver, I want this message to be kept absolutely between you and me, is that clear?"

"Absolutely, Mr. Mackay."

"And to make sure, here's a golden eagle twenty dollar piece. Will that help you keep your silence about this?"

"Mr. Mackay, you don't need to pay me. I keep all messages confidential."

"Keep the money. And keep this secret."

Oliver nodded and turned to head back up the slope to town. Mackay turned back into the room but stopped and looked at Will.

"This could affect you as well. I've only just scanned it; let me take a good look, and I'd like to discuss it with you."

Will had no idea how he could in any way be connected to a message from the President of the United States. Mackay's statement definitely grabbed his attention. He waited to see what the news brought.

Mackay sat and read. He then looked up at Will. "Before I read it, I need you to promise to keep it a secret."

"I would have no one to tell who'd believe I had any connection to a message from the president. But I promise anyway."

Mackay held the telegram in his lap. Looking at Will, he said, "President Grant came to Virginia City on a campaign tour of the West before his initial election. He spent several days here. Jim Fair and I took him down into the mines along with all our wives. He wanted to see what the silver looked like before it was mined. I got to know the man somewhat."

Will was more than a little intrigued.

"Here's what it says":

John- Heard about the fire. Stop. Hope you and yours survived in decent shape. Stop. Did the fire damage your mining operations? Stop. My spies tell me you have kept men down in one of your mines for days. Stop. Sounds like you might have another find. Stop. Recently signed the Coinage Act. Stop. It was a mistake. Stop. I should have never signed it. Stop. The press is now calling it 'The Crime of 1873.' Stop.

    Financial markets depressed and vulnerable. Stop. A big silver find would be good news to the depressed economy. Stop. If you have such, announce it and soon. Stop. If you need any assistance following the fire, just ask. Stop. -U.S. Grant

Will was stunned. "He wants you to announce your find. How in the world does a man in Washington, D.C., know about what you have underground?"

Mackay shook his head. "People think Grant is not very smart. They are quite mistaken. We told him how we kept the new finds secret until we could bring the ore up. He obviously listened."

"But how would he even know your men were down in the mine?"

"Grant always had a great spy network during the war. He told us about it. He probably found out from the reporter Dan De Quille. I'm guessing, but De Quille made quite an impression on Grant while he was here in town. We put on several dinners and events for the Grants, and De Quille was at every one trying to get quotes."

The unfolding events amazed Will at how complicated business had become after the war. Information was everywhere, and its effects traveled with it.

Mackay sighed. "I'll have to think about how I'm going to do this, but one thing is clear: we will have to announce the find. If Grant knows about it, the whole world will know about it soon enough. But that means we need those timbers more than ever. And we need them right now. Can you meet with Bliss today? I can wire him to set up the meeting. I hate to drag you away from the situation with your family, but this city and maybe the entire financial markets of the country need the ore. I can't bring it up without those timbers."

"Beth has Luke and Sean. I think Sam Brown can wait one day. If I'm not mistaken, the train to Carson only takes an hour or two. It's still early. I can get on the morning V & T to Carson City, which will arrive before noon, talk to Bliss, and return on the afternoon train back."

"If you do this, Will, I will forever be in your debt."

Will did not have to think long. "Let's go."

"I'll send one of my staff to wire Bliss immediately. Let's walk over to the depot and get you a ticket."

*****

John Mackay stood with Will on the platform of the Virginia & Truckee Railroad. The depot had burned, but the tracks survived the fire, and the train was still running. Virginia City needed the V & T more than ever as it would be the main transport of supplies to rebuild the city. Though the depot itself was in ashes, the platform was relatively intact.

Mackay extended his hand to Will. "If you can convince Bliss to sell the lumber, you will have delivered a second major value to the company. I've telegraphed Duane Bliss in Carson City. He knows you're coming."

Will returned the firm grip and then moved across the depot's heavily wooded walkway toward the steps leading up into the train. "I'll be there later today. I'll try to talk with him right away and then head back."

"I've taken care of your horse. He'll be here when you return."

"We should be able to talk later tonight. I'll do my best to convince Bliss to take your order. As I told you, I have an idea."

"I hope it's a good one. If Bliss didn't already think he held all the cards when it comes to lumber, he will now. With most of Virginia City virtually burned to the ground, he'll know the demand for timber will be even greater."

Will shrugged. "I'll do what I can. You said on the walk over to the depot you'd consider paying more than the standard price. I might have to use your offer to pay a premium."

"Use it if it'll help. We need the square set timbers. We need to get that ore moving out of the mine. The money generated will help put the city back on its feet. In fact, more wires came in this morning about the markets crashing in the East. The move away from silver as coinage won't last long. The gold fields have panned out. Right now, the only ore of value ready to be mined is silver. The entire country needs that ore. The government is getting close to going bankrupt after their ill-advised passage of the Coinage Act."

Will stepped up into the railcar just as the whistle blew. The screeching signal to load stabbed his eardrums. It was hard not to wince. The train began moving slowly, headed to the grades downhill, farther east. The men nodded to one another through the window. No further goodbye was needed.

Will sat on a strong, unbending wooden bench in the passenger section. The train's initial movements were a series of hesitant jerks, as if it didn't know it should begin moving. However, the motion soon settled into a smooth determined pull. Sitting alone, Will had time to think.

The last few days had started with the unknown. Will arrived in Virginia City unaware if Mackay could help him. He rode into this city without means to pay any ransom or any concrete plan to get the needed cash. But he and Mackay had quickly made a connection. Both tended to avoid social situations. Both could lead men and guided their lives from a foundation of right and wrong. Both used words sparingly. As well, the two of them knew what now hung in the balance: Will for his family and Mackay for his mine.

Mackay needed Bliss to sell him the timber. If Bliss would do that, Mackay was willing to put up any ransom. Though Will had said he didn't think he'd need that, it was good to know he had access to the money. But Will must convince Bliss to sell. Then he had to get back to find Brown. Long-term safety for his family depended on an end to this man Brown's attacks on Beth and their children.

Chapter Twenty-Four

1873 February
Mountain Trail to Virginia City

Beth climbed out of her bedroll. The night had been especially cold, and none of her joints felt like they would work. She rubbed her knees and elbows just to generate some heat and mobility. Until she rubbed, she was not sure she could push herself up and stand. Maybe it was the result of the last week too. She lifted onto her elbows and then flopped back down. Everything ached. She looked up into a clear newborn sky. The pale azure canopy above her hung to the sides of the horizon like the hint of sapphire at the edges of an ice cube. Maybe the world had frozen.

She had slept past dawn, something rare for her. Must have been because she'd ridden for more than half the night. Lying flat, she rolled her head back and forth over the hard chilled surface, still looking out into the distant heavens. How was this going to end up? The cloudless blue provided no answers.

Last night, Beth had stayed off the main roads and kept to the ridges leaving Mound House. Keeping high and off the main road would be even more important here in the daylight. There were only two prominent crests leading up to Virginia City. Each paralleled the road. She kept to the east ridge. She worried about reaching Will as soon as she could. She had to get up and get going, but the cold in her bones cried out to stay still. She had no food, but she was not hungry. Her worry pushed away all thoughts of food. She had to make it to town today.

Questions assaulted her thoughts as she tried to find the motivation to rise and get ready for the ride up the hill. Once in town, how would she find Will? More than that, once she found Will, how could she convince him to let Sam Brown go? She wanted the boys, herself, and Will to be together again. For them to be a true unit. If only Will could see that as she did. She didn't need him getting killed in some ridiculous gun battle.

She stood up, working to keep her balance as she stretched. "I am definitely stiff." Then she implored the rising sun, "Hurry up and get warm." Time to saddle her horse. Got to find Will. Got to convince him.

*****

Fr. Cecconi looked at Sr. Charity as she slowly climbed the stairs from the basement. The poor woman was haggard. Her habit carried multiple blotches of dark ash where she'd rubbed against some poor soul downstairs who'd barely escaped the fire. She normally would never have worn an unclean habit. But there had been no time for normal amenities. There was no regular flow of water, which had been temporarily interrupted by the fire. No showers. No clothes being washed. So many had lost their homes. So many were in the church basement, now overcrowded and overrun with local humanity. But it was the only shelter, the only comfort their church could provide under present conditions.

"Sister." She looked up to face the priest. Hers was a face of despair.

Fr. Cecconi stood at the head of the stairway leading down into the basement as Sr. Charity stopped. He struggled again against the feeling that he stood on some border to another world. He saw her expression turn from one of hopelessness to one of question. Behind Sr. Charity, he could hear the confined commotion of people trying to control some minimal space for their loved ones.

"Sister are you alright?"

"Why are these people tested and then tested again?"

From her expression, Fr. Cecconi was not sure the question was directed to him or some higher recipient. He knew many down below these stairs had seen their lives challenged and vexed over and over. The trials seemed to come one after another. Only those of the strongest faith seemed to maintain their upbeat demeanor.

She continued. "Why do those of the deepest faith keep moving forward in the best of spirits despite one challenge after the next thrown at them?"

The question hit hard. Maybe the answer was lost in the events of the last week. He did not attempt to respond as the thought bore deep into his own qualms of faith. He simply remained standing at the top of the stairs, numbed to silence. Again, the feeling struck once more that he was standing on something of a precipice above a chasm leading down to the masses—masses that needed something from him. That something was hope, and hope was in short supply. Not many in the crowded basement below still carried a spirit of hope, a spirit of faith. For most, it had been lost. It was if the flood and then the fire eroded their capacity to believe God brought anything good into the world. Standing above His children, there looked to be precious little faith, if any, left in this town. He felt he was failing in his task, his duty to keep that faith alive, to keep this parish in touch with the presence of God. He felt it slipping away all around him. He had prayed daily for guidance as to how he could balance the gnawing fear that they were all doomed with his sacred duty to support the faith in his collective flock. He confessed to himself that those fears were the result of erosions in his own trust in The Almighty.

"Father, I think there are some new arrivals." Sr. Charity's voice was almost devoid of emotion. She was reciting nothing more than a new fact. The emotional impact of seeing more parishioners arrive after having lost their homes and possessions had been drained from her already.

"Do we have room?"

Sr. Charity seemed to make a conscious effort to push forward and cope with the circumstances as presented. "No. But people are doing their best to add more and more into the limited space of the church's basement."

"The mine owners have been wonderful with contributions to pay for food. And they are doing their best to get some temporary housing for as many as they can."

Sr. Charity's face spread with the slightest expression of optimism. He'd not seen that for some days now. Confirming the priest's comment, she said, "I also heard Mr. Mackay said yesterday that he was having some tents delivered for temporary housing. He felt we could get people into their own spaces in a day or two and out of the church."

Fr. Cecconi nodded. "I'm not sure they will be in any better condition in canvas homes as opposed to what is left of the church."

"But Father, there are so many jammed into such a small space. The basement is covered only by the main floor. The church itself has little left of its roof. The floor of the main church as it covers the basement is the only roof these people have right now. It's not much of a shelter, but we have too many, and more come each day."

"You are right; the roof over the main church was wooden and lost in the fire. Only the brick steeple and bell tower survived," Fr. Cecconi deliberated.

"Father, maybe it's best that these people have their own tents. Mr. Mackay claims it shouldn't be long before wood arrives and more permanent housing can be built. The mines need the workers back on their feet and back on the job," the good Sister said.

He had to acknowledge, "The mines generate the only source of sustenance."

"How strange, Father. It's the mines that provide, but it's also the mines that bring them all here to this place to be continually tested."

Fr. Cecconi lowered his stare to face this lady who was struggling like everyone else to understand why life brought floods and fire.

"God has obviously provided sustenance. Maybe the floods and fires are a warning of what happens if our faith erodes so completely that we cannot feel his presence."

*****

Will stared out the window from his seat. The train was still moving slowly through the hairpin turns down the mountain. He thought of Luke and Sean with relief. He thought of Beth. She was a remarkable woman. She'd found his sons and somehow wrested them from the hold of serious gunmen. He could think of no other woman capable of doing something like that. Only Beth. Though they may have problems in their relationship, she was unique. Maybe he needed to admit her hold on him. He thought about the kidnapping of the twins; how close he'd come to losing them for good. He was not sure he'd have been able to live with that.

They should be close, at the ranch. Luke and Sean and Beth *all* should be at the ranch. If they'd lost their sons, he'd have probably lost Beth too. It would have caused a rift between them that could never be healed. Maybe it already had. Maybe it was time to concede it was his fault they weren't together. Maybe he was the one who should change how things were. He wanted Beth to be near him. He never denied his thoughts and strong fondness for this extraordinary woman. Those feel-ings went back to before the babies were even born. Truth be told, it was his decision that led to how things stood right now. Maybe he should admit that he wanted Beth as his wife.

But he couldn't think of that at the moment. It seemed as though his children were safe. Brown could wait. Right now, he had to get lumber for Virginia City. Then he could take care of Sam Brown. Brown had to meet his justice. That would be the only way he could see any hope of peace in the future for himself, Beth, and the boys.

Will looked out of the window above his simple wooden bench seat. The Virginia & Truckee continued its two-thousand-foot descent down toward Carson City. The initial progress had been slow, allowing the heavy locomotive machinery to make the numerous switchbacks as the rails snaked down the hill. The mountain desert landscape loomed out-side. Truth be known, the expanse mirrored a void of thought and ques-tion of purpose for his upcoming meeting with Bliss. He had to come up with a convincing argument for Bliss to overcome his close associ-ation with Sharon and the Bank of California. But gazing out into the heat seared desert his head remained empty only to be filled with the rhythmic sounds of heavy metal wheels rolling on iron rails. He was only a single man trying to bend the multiple dynamics of recent events into something positive. How could he hope to maneuver the combined forces of nature and wealthy businessmen to work toward a common goal that would benefit the people of Virginia City? The key would be to separate Bliss from Sharon. It was a tall order.

His thoughts returned to his conversation with Mackay last evening at dinner. Mackay had said, "William Sharon built the Virginia & Truckee Railroad to haul ore first and passengers second. Before the V & T we sent our ore down the hill in wagons. Sharon saw a way to maximize his control over the Comstock production by building a railroad to haul the ore down the hill to the reduction mills along the Carson River and then haul supplies back up to Virginia City. He's monopolized the traffic both ways."

Will marveled at what he found to be two different types of men in business: those who work with hands and effort and those who see profit in the use of other's money. Sharon was obviously of the latter type. Then there were men like Sam Brown. That was another category altogether.

*****

Beth sat on her horse, riding a narrow ridge that looked down on the main road up to Virginia City. She was high, exposed.

"Not far now," she uttered. "I'm probably going to have to locate John Mackay if I have any hope of finding Will."

She fretted whether her telegram was enough to keep Will from going after Brown alone. Probably not. She had to be the one to stop Will. She had to come up with some argument he'd listen to. She had to get to Virginia City and soon. If there was any hope of getting Will to come back to the ranch, it would be her personal plea. And that might not be enough.

*****

"You see that? Isn't that a woman? Is it her?" Roberts pointed down the canyon to another ridge below.

Brown squinted to dampen the glare of the sun lifting higher over the mountains. "I think it is. Hard to tell. She's wearing different clothes than when we saw her at the ranch. Elmer said she'd be riding up to Virginia City by herself. Can't imagine any other woman out here alone. That helps."

Roberts turned to look directly at Brown. "How do you want to do this?"

Brown looked over the terrain. "There's a dip in that ridge before it gets to our height. If she holds to the ridge, we can wait for her to get up to the crest and take her by surprise. We can both wait on either side of the path and come up on her just as she passes."

"Then what?"

"Been thinkin' about that. We need to keep her out of sight when we get her back to the city. We will have to set up some meeting with the rancher. We'll need to get a message to him somehow. The woman can be the bait to draw him out into the field below the church, where they have the camel races."

Brown paused in thought, then continued. "But we need to hide the blonde until we can set up the killing of the rancher. It could be a problem doing that in Virginia City right now. The only things left after the fire in the main part of town are the saloons, the church, and the cribs with the working ladies. Maybe we take her to that lady you frequent who runs one of the cribs and ask her to hold the blonde until we need her when we confront the rancher. We can show her to the rancher and then kill him. Once that is done, we'll just let the madame use her for her customers."

"Big Sally? Might work." Roberts turned to look over the lower terrain again. "I'll go to the left side of the depression."

Brown nodded. "Okay, I'll go right. Find some boulder or some tall scrub to hide behind. When you hear me pull out to block the road, you pull out, and make sure she can't turn and head back down."

Roberts shrugged. "We can tie her to her own saddle. If we keep headed north, we can pass by town downslope out of sight to the east side of the city. We then ride to the cribs from the east. No one will be looking at people heading into town from that direction."

"Good idea. The cribs are at the east side of town down the slope anyway. We'll wait until dark and go find that lady friend of yours. What's her name again?"

"Sally, Big Sally. She's a mean one."

"Think she'll be a problem?"

Roberts thought but only briefly. "Naw, the prospect of new good lookin' talent for her customers will be worth any risk she might be takin'."

"Good, let's get into position."

*****

Beth was looking west across the tops of the lower ridges. She had climbed several thousand feet since leaving Mound House. The hard ride uphill spawned a whole new set of aches and pains adding to the stiffness and soreness from her night out in the cold higher elevations. She was not used to long days in the saddle, and the last several days, first headed to Mound House and now Virginia City, had all been long days in the saddle. Here she was, high enough to see all the way across the Carson Valley to the Sierras. She wondered if she could see Will's ranch from here. The twins should have arrived long ago. Juan and María would be taking good care of them.

"Don't move! Keep your hands high where I can see them."

Beth looked forward. Blocking the slim path on the ridge was Sam Brown. *How did he get here?* She pulled her reins and spun her horse, thinking of running back down the ridge.

"Not this way, lady."

Brown's accomplice was now blocking her only exit. There was nothing but steep slopes to either side of the narrow trail.

"Like the man said, keep your hands up high where we can see them."

Beth could not believe these two were here. *How?* How is it she did not see them? It was as if they just materialized. But then she saw the rock next to the path on the high side of the trail that had screened Brown, and another glance backwards and downhill now revealed the scrub trees where the accomplice must have been waiting. Her heart pounded against the inside of her chest.

"I'm gonna walk this horse right up next to you and lift that little pea shooter you have on your hip. You move a muscle and Sam Brown's gonna shoot you right here. You'll never see your sons again."

"I am sure part of your plan is to make sure I never see my sons again anyway."

Brown chuckled. "Smart lady. You might be right. You might be wrong. But for now, Roberts, grab the gun, and tie her hands to her saddle."

Beth tried to hold down the panic. She could draw, but she would never be quick enough. There were two guns already pointed at her. She knew these men were vicious. The pause before her decision felt like minutes had passed. The reality was more like seconds. She resigned to her predicament and lifted her elbow so that the man moving his horse next to hers could remove her gun from its holster. The removal of her weapon left an emotional void. She was truly in their control, vulnerable in every sense of the word. She let him tie her hands, thinking all the while that she'd just have to hope there would be some future chance to get away. The hope was bolstered by the fact she'd recently bested the man who was watching her sons. But something told her these two were different. That hope may be tenuous.

As if reading her mind, Brown looked at her and said, "We're not like the men down in Mound House. We don't make mistakes. If you try anything, you're dead. Understood?"

Then it hit Beth. "You want me alive. You plan to use me as bait for Will."

Brown spoke softly—menacingly. "Like I said, smart lady,"

"Then you're not going to shoot me, at least not until Virginia City."

"You might be right, but that might not stop us from throwing you down on your back right here and having our way with you."

Beth shivered at the mere thought.

"Boss, we could do that. Not many around. We could take our time with this pretty little thing."

"No, we don't have the time. We gotta get back to Virginia City tonight. If we plan to take the low roads past town, those will take more time than the main road. We've got ground to cover. Let's move. No time for personal pleasures right now. We need to get this *smart lady* to Big Sally. Maybe we can think about pleasures later."

Beth had no idea who Big Sally was, but she had a tangible foreboding feeling Sally would not be someone she was going to like.

Chapter Twenty-Five

1873 February
Virginia City, NV

His suit had recently been pressed, as had his shirt. Both carried the sheen of cleanliness that comes at the beginning of the day. He could smell the rosewater his service used on the last rinse. As he lowered into the large executive chair behind his office's seven-foot-wide desk, he felt the day had upside possibilities. William Sharon looked at his door as it opened. He did nothing to hide his disgust once he recognized the identity of the man who entered: Ralston. Ralston had become almost a menace since the fire. Sharon had enough to do outside of holding his weak partner's hand through tough times. The man should grow up. Ralston had fronted the necessary capital to start the banking operations here in Virginia City. It had been a novel and risky idea at the outset. Sharon had needed Ralston because Ralston had money, money his father had made. But that was some time ago; Sharon now had access to all the capital he needed. With the current resources at the Bank of California coupled with the deep pockets of co-investor Darius Ogden Mills, Sharon had plenty of capital. Now, Ralston was simply a nuisance. Ralston being a small man of slight build, Sharon could not help but feel part of his antipathy arose from the man's lack of any significant physical presence. He was not intimidating in any way, either via business acumen or physicality. A nuisance partnership that might need to be eliminated, permanently.

"Sharon, we need to talk."

"Not really. We need to act. All you want to do is to talk, to whine about your worries. I am busy doing something about the current circumstances."

"Current circumstances. That's exactly what we need to talk about."

"Ralston, news flash: there's been a fire."

"Don't be demeaning, Sharon."

"Ralston, like I said, all you want to do is talk. That fire tore into multiple businesses we own. They are now reduced to ash. You can see; open your eyes. You don't need to come here and wail about the devastation. It's done. I've got to put the pieces of our enterprise back in place and start making money again."

"But that's exactly why I'm here. I need to know if we are ever going to make money again. I need to know if I should make arrangements to head back to San Francisco and protect what assets I can there."

"Ralston, maybe you should go. It's going to be a long road before we will be back to normal. As you know, we own seven mines, a bank, and a railroad. Not all were damaged. If we can get the workers back on their feet, we can start thinking about making money. Thank goodness the Ophir's main shaft and works were north of the fire. That mine's still operational as is the Savage and Chollar, both of which were south of the blaze. The Belcher shaft is right on C Street in the only section the raggedy fire department saved. That should mean four out of our seven mines are operational; that is, if we can find workers."

"That fire department saved the offices of the Bank of California. Without them, we wouldn't be sitting here in your office."

Sharon scoffed. "They were probably working to save the Delta Saloon. We just happened to be close."

Sharon looked out of his office window. "Just two days ago, there was a building across the street. And there up the hill on B Street was Piper's Opera House and the Court. Now nothing."

"Sharon, that those buildings were burned is terrible. But we did not own them. What's far more important is that our depot is gone. There is no depot for our train."

"Yeah, but we had no locomotives in town during the fire, and the track is undamaged. The Virginia & Truckee will be needed more than ever. While we can't gouge, we can raise shipping prices. People will need supplies to rebuild. The V & T will be a lifeblood of material needed to rebuild. It's the one business that will definitely generate cash even greater than before the fire."

"How are you going to collect money for tickets? You have no depot."

"A tent, Ralston. A tent if we must. Why are you so negative? We just do what is necessary to get back to business. We can rebuild when the money dictates."

"What about the bank? The Bank of California is going to have a run on its assets."

"My God, Ralston. You really are blind. The bank is going to be our best card in this poker game. Where do you think these people are going to go to get money to rebuild? How do you think they are going to hold off their creditors until their cash flow begins again? Really, you can't see? It'll be the bank. The bank will generate more cash than any of the mines."

"You're assuming that the businesses and mines can pay on your new loans. What if they can't?"

"Ralston, then we foreclose! Just like we did to get the other seven mines."

"But where will you get the capital?"

"We have it on reserve and deposited with affiliates in San Francisco."

"Why was I never advised of these reserves?" Ralston lifted his chin in something of a mock indignation.

"Because you'd have been badgering me day in and day out to spend it on some stupid enterprise like your ridiculous Palace Hotel on Market Street, that's why. There was going to be a day we might need it. That day has arrived. Now we can tap those resources, and lending will go up fourfold. We'll probably have more foreclosures too. Who knows, we might even pick a couple more mines as a result. The bank will be its own little gold mine."

Sharon could see the concern drain from Ralston's face. It was like watching some childlike conversion from punishment to being offered a treat. The adolescent transformation continued as a smile bloomed slowly across Ralston's features. "Really? Then we should be okay?"

Sharon shook his head. *This man was a financier? How did this man survive in the claws of the San Francisco banking world? How could his father have left his fortune to an idiot? Time to separate him from any arguable posture of control.* "Ralston, of course we'll be alright. But there is always risk. Anything can happen. Maybe you should sell your shares in the holding company, the one that holds the interests in both the bank and the mines. You know the markets in San Francisco. It would be a good play for you. Buy shares now as our price is seriously depressed because of the fire. Then wait two months and sell. You'll make a handsome profit because the bank and most of the mines will start generating cash, and the stock prices will go back up."

With any luck, Ralston would take the advice, and he'd be done with the man.

"But then I'd have no further interest in the bank or the mines."

"True. However, the money you make on selling the shares can help with your costs on the hotel." *Maybe I can use some associates to create an immediate demand for cash such that Ralston must sell. There's a thought I should pursue.*

Ralston pondered. Sharon watched him turn back to face him with a look of satisfaction, as if he'd reached a decision or allayed his fear and wanted to pursue another topic. "Word is that Mackay was able to protect the Consolidated's shaft. No fire got down below the surface. He's still got men down there. Have your spies been able to provide any information as to what they're hiding?"

"Now that's the first rational and relevant question you've asked in quite a while."

Ralston looked pleased with himself.

"No, I haven't heard anything. But with all the chaos right now, someone's going to slip, and we'll get word. One good thing about this fire is that there will be a huge increase in demand for wood. It'll be the same wood that Mackay will need for his square sets if he has found new ore but won't be able to get as the city will need it to rebuild."

"Any word back from Duane Bliss as to whether he will hold off selling to Mackay?"

Sharon was a bit surprised that Ralston had remembered their ploy with Bliss on the lumber. "It might be hard for Bliss to say no now as everyone around these parts has been volunteering to help rebuild the city. But it would be a great time to squeeze Mackay if we can."

Ralston pursued. "So, there's no word at all as to why the men were down in the Consolidated so long?"

"None," said Sharon. "And I'm not happy with my sources. The rumor says there's a big find, but I have nothing to confirm it."

"It would be nice to know. If Mackay has some new ore find, then he is going to have an enhanced need for timbers. We could really disrupt his cash flow."

"He hasn't asked for any capital loans," Sharon mused aloud. "If there was some big find, then I'd have thought he'd have come knocking on our door for a loan. That would be the best of all worlds. We hold his feet to the fire on a loan while we squeeze his access to timber through Bliss."

"When was the last time you talked to Bliss?"

"A week ago, but that was before the fire."

"Do you think he'll block the sale of timber to Mackay?"

Sharon grinned. "I told him I'd make it worth his while. But now that the fire has burned every piece of wood in over half the city, he's probably smelling profits galore with people clamoring for his stored timber."

"I've never seen it, but Darius Mills told me Bliss has a lumber yard outside Carson City that stretches over a mile long with stacked timbers."

Sharon nodded. "I've seen it. It's impressive. You wouldn't think there would be enough demand for the stacks and stacks he has. You'd think most of it would just rot. But that was then. With the need to rebuild the city, there is no way Bliss will have enough on hand, even if his yard is over a mile long."

"But will he squeeze Mackay?"

"I think so, but it remains to be seen."

Chapter Twenty-Six

1873 February
Carson City, NV

Will Toal stepped off the train. The Carson City depot on Washington Street for the Virginia & Truckee had only recently been completed. Will looked around at the stone building. "Someone spent some good money to build this," he said to himself. The depot was built of native sandstone which provided the lower foundation and walls below the windows. Next to the capital building itself, the depot was probably the stoutest structure in town. Will had heard that the railroad built a switchyard and engine house big enough for eleven locomotives. The engine house had been built a little further out of town and was also made completely of the same sandstone. He'd never had time or occasion to travel on the train until today, so he'd never seen the depot until now. The thought ran through his mind that it'd be nice to spend time and look the place over but not now, not today. He needed to get to his meeting with Bliss. But there was someone he needed to talk to first.

Will walked through town until he got to the office of S. Samuel Grande. Grande was a giant of a man, a lawyer who'd helped him with advice and counsel during his confrontation with the Central Pacific Railroad several years before. Grande was meticulous in his scruples and ethics, which led him to be highly selective in his choice of clientele. Over the time since the battle with the railroads, Grande had become one of the few people Will trusted without question. He reached for the door and heard the familiar tinkling of the attached bell. He entered Grande's office, lined with perpetual stacks and stacks of books. The piles of volumes were on shelves, on desktops, and even the floor.

They were everywhere, permeating the internal atmosphere with a scent of decaying paper and dust. No matter how many times Will entered this office, most of the stacks remained exactly where they'd been the last time. But he also knew that Grande reveled in his books. He referred to and cited passages and regulations, constantly pointing to the book that contained the information just divulged. The books were a part of his persona, part of the man's confidence to provide advice and instruction.

"Busy?"

"Will Toal, nice to see you. Knowing that I see you on a social basis if, and only if, I make the trip out to your ranch, this sighting must mean you are in trouble again. Are we in risk of jail?"

Grande issued the words like throwing down a gauntlet, but then a smile appeared. Will knew the man well enough to both expect this type of greeting and fend off the challenge.

"You come out regularly on the second Sunday of each month to eat one of my fresh steaks. I don't come into town because I know I'd have to buy you dinner or lunch here too. I can't afford your fees. Better to feed you at the ranch."

Grande waived his arms in a mock scoff. "The only fees I get from you are those I can eat, so I have no guilt in collecting."

"Your waistline is beginning to show that I should renegotiate my fees."

"How is that wonderful lady you treat so poorly with your continued reticence to acknowledge?"

"Why is it you always presume to advise me not only on my legal matters but on my personal life as well?"

"Because you manage your personal life so poorly that you are in dire need of advice. It's a wonder I don't up my fees to include dinners on two Sundays each month."

Will took his hat off to sit. He looked at the ground and then back at Grande. "I told you about the kidnapping. Did you hear we got them back?"

"Yes, I heard they had been brutally taken by some hoodlums, but that Beth had rescued them. Word around town is that she found them in Mound House and shot her way into the room where they'd been kept and killed the captor. I might add, I heard nothing about your involvement. Must have been you sent a woman to do a man's work." Though Grande smiled with the delivery of this barb, Will could tell the humor of their initial greeting had disappeared, and Grande was furnishing a form of judgment. A judgement of Will's conduct that did not meet with his standards or approval.

Will swayed his head side to side as if he'd almost expected the scolding from someone who did not know how plans had developed.

"Beth and I split up. I'd headed up to Virginia City because that's where the gang said they'd taken the boys. Beth went to Mound House to check just in case they were there. We didn't think we could take the time to go to both together. It was faster to split up."

Grande nodded with the new information. Will continued.

"I haven't seen her since, so I don't know how she got our sons, but I'm glad she got them and took them back to the ranch."

Grande looked puzzled. "Beth's not at the ranch."

The comment hit Will like a punch. "What do you mean she's not at the ranch? Did she come back here to town?"

"No, after I heard the rumors from the sheriff and other folks, I went out to the ranch to see what was going on. Juan brought Sean and Luke back. He told me Beth went off to find you in Virginia City. Something about trying to stop you from confronting the gang."

Will had no words. His mind raced with thoughts of immediately changing all plans of meetings and timing. But the V & T did not have a return train to Virginia City for three more hours. He couldn't reverse his day's travels any faster than to simply complete his tasks here in Carson and catch the first possible train back.

"By the look on your face, this is news to you."

"Yes, it is. I thought Beth was safe and back at the ranch. I did not see her in Virginia City before I left. I'm planning on going right back, but knowing she's headed up there, I must get there as soon as I can. The men we're dealing with are truly bad men. If they see her, there's no telling what they might do."

"Why did you come down to Carson City in the first place?"

Will was still thinking of Beth. He forced himself to change his focus. He looked up at Grande with a serious glint. "You are my lawyer, right?"

Grande nodded. "Ah, here it comes. The reason for the visit had to be a legal one."

Will had not broken his stare. "This has to remain confidential."

"All our legal conversations are always confidential."

Will twirled his hat around in a circle, thinking of how to broach the conversation. "As you suggested when I was in town last, I sent a telegram to Henry Millard asking for a reference in Virginia City. Henry Millard sent me a telegram telling me I should talk to a man named John Mackay who could introduce me to whatever law and order might exist in Virginia City. Henry was trying to be nice and put me in contact with someone who might help with any confrontation with the men who took my children."

"Henry seems to have become more than just a business partner."

"He and I get along."

"For a young man, you are running in fast business circles these days. John Mackay is known to be one of the wealthier mine owners at the Comstock."

"I happened to be staying at his house when the fire hit. I kinda helped him keep the fire from getting below ground level into his Consolidated Virginia and California Mine. This is part of what you must keep to yourself. His people have struck a huge new ore find. He had men down in the shaft when the fire hit. Had we not covered the opening at street level, the fire would have run down the timbers holding up the passageways and burned for years. Happened to another mine a couple of years ago."

Grande now listened intently.

"The night after we worked on saving the mine, Beth sent me a telegram saying she'd rescued Luke and Sean and they were headed back to the ranch. I thought she meant that both she and the boys headed back."

"I still haven't heard why you needed to take the train here to Carson City." Grande questioned lightly.

"Mr. Mackay explained that, with this new ore find, his company will be desperate to get the timbers for the square setting so the ore can be removed. He needs that timber from Duane Bliss. But his competition, William Sharon, has some kind of control over Bliss and might try to block any sale of timber to Mackay."

"Now I see where this is going. And you told Mackay you had dealt with Bliss before."

"Yep. I told him that I might have a way to convince Bliss to sell the timbers. Mr. Mackay said that if I could get Bliss to sell, he'd put up the ransom of twenty-five thousand dollars for the boys."

"But you don't need the ransom anymore; you have your sons."

"I thought I'd still might need it to flush out the bad guys. I'd offer to meet and give them the money to leave us alone in the future. But then we would have a *cowboy conversation.*"

"Would a *cowboy conversation* involve guns?"

"Probably. Things would most likely get western. Men like these are never satisfied. Twenty-five thousand would only tell them there's more where that came from, and they'd keep returning to the same well. Beth and I would never be rid of them until they were either dead or so scared of getting dead they'd never return. I intend to make sure they have the opportunity to meet their maker or are sufficiently scared of that meetin'." Will heard traces of the drawl from his old Georgia roots in his own voice. Must be the emotion.

"And just exactly how do you intend to persuade Mr. Bliss to sell his timber to Mackay?"

This was the real reason Will had come in to see Grande. He needed to know how far he could go, how risky his plan was. "I was gonna tell him that there was a legitimate need for the timber."

With a knowing look, Grande answered. "And, what else? That sounds nice, but if Bliss is in league with Sharon, that sentiment will not budge Bliss one inch."

Will hesitated. "I was gonna tell him that if he didn't sell, I'd make sure the newspapers found out about his role partnering with the railroad to generate the bogus foreclosures on all the ranches in the valley a few years ago."

"Ah, now we have it. You intend to threaten him with ruin of his business, is that it?"

"If the rest of the people in town knew about what he did, maybe he'd have a problem or two."

"Maybe?"

"Mackay said he'd also be willing to pay a premium for the wood. There should be a discount for a sale with this kind of volume. But Mackay knows that Virginia City needs to rebuild, and the need for wood goes way beyond the mines right now, so he knows he might have to pay a premium."

"I would strongly suggest that you stick to the offer of paying a premium and stay away from any threats."

"You should also know that the country needs the ore in Mackay's new find."

"How so?"

"Mackay got a telegram from President Grant telling him he knew there was a possible new ore find and that the economy is so bad after the passage of something called the Coinage Act, the government needs the ore, and Mackay should announce right away."

"And how did Grant know about the new find?"

"Mackay thinks Grant became buddies with one of the reporters in town when he visited some years ago, and that's his source."

"No such thing as a secret nowadays, is there? Quite a pickle you've got yourself involved in, isn't it?"

"Yeah, but if Beth is in Virginia City, I need to get back there today, so I need to meet Bliss and get this done. How far can I go?"

"Like I said, stay away from any threat."

"And what if Bliss isn't in a charitable mood?"

"Stay away from the threats."

Will nodded. "I hear you." After a noticeable pause, "I will try not to use it."

Grande stood. "Let me know how it goes. And let me know if I can help with the little ones or anything."

"I appreciate the offer. If you could check in on Juan and María and tell them we'll be home as soon as we can, I'd appreciate it."

"I can do that. Just make sure you come home without any bullet holes in you."

Chapter Twenty-Seven

1873 February
Virginia City, NV

"Hello boys, care to come in? What can we do for you today?"

Beth watched as Roberts stood before a tall and seriously over-weight woman who had seen the last of her thirties. She'd lifted one arm to lean against the door jamb in what she obviously thought was a stance of feminine enticement. The now exposed semicircle ring of sweat underneath her overly ample upper arm coupled with the flimsy, and predominantly transparent, loosely fitted negligee were clear indications of the reputation and business behind the door. She presented herself as if some magical experience awaited on the other side of that portal. Roberts had probably partaken of that magic before. But Beth could also see it wasn't all that magical. The door itself was just a jamb attached to what had to be the dirtiest of tents in town. So much for appeal.

"Sally, I need your help. I need you to take in a woman but only for a short while."

"What's in it for me?"

Beth bit down harder on her gag. She was now downright terrified. The woman standing before them obviously ran a bordello. Beth leaned forward just slightly and could see internal fabric partitions that might possibly block one's view, but the sounds coming from the other sides left nothing to the imagination. And the man she'd heard called Roberts was bartering with the woman to keep her under wraps. Sam Brown stood behind her with one hand on the rope binding her wrists, leading to hands that had long since lost all feeling.

Roberts' face showed no little amazement. "Look at her, she's a good lookin' woman. Tell me you couldn't use her in your string."

"And how am I gonna do that? She's gagged, and her hands are tied behind her back. While I possibly could have some customers who might find that attractive, how am I supposed to feed her and keep her in a tent for the next customer? She's obviously not here voluntarily."

"Sally, keep her. It won't be long. We have the meeting with the man soon and after that you can do with her what you will."

The large woman eyed Roberts. She didn't respond immediately.

"I'm not sure that's gonna work. I don't like the look of this." The big woman's eyes met Beth's as she cocked her head to one side as if to convey the nonverbal question, "How did you get into this, lady?"

Beth softened the rage in her own eyes which had been her only expression up to this point. Now she tried her best to convey a silent request for help. She had no idea if the message was received.

The big woman held Beth's eyes for a moment, then turned back to Roberts. "Nope, don't think I want any part of this."

Beth heard Brown behind her. "I've heard enough. You will take this woman. You will see to it she is kept hidden and away from any of your customers for no more than a week. At the end of that time, I will pay you one hundred dollars for each day she is here. If you don't do exactly as I ask, not only will you lose your business, you might lose your life."

Sally looked at Brown with hard eyes. Beth could imagine that those eyes had seen a lot of brutal things in her life. This woman had probably dealt with a lot of hard men. But had she ever dealt with the likes of Brown? Another pause of silence followed as both stared at each other.

"I don't like you, Brown. Never did. But I don't want no trouble with my business. Got enough trouble right now trying deal with what's left after a fire and no way to get regular food for my girls. We was lucky the fire raged down the hill two blocks from us. But I got enough troubles right now."

"Then take the woman, do as we ask, and you might have some extra money to buy more than just food. And, once we are done, you can keep the woman, turn her loose, or just sell her to one of your customers. Your choice."

Beth could hear an equal portion of threat and negotiation in Brown's voice. Sally still vacillated.

"I can keep her. I know a spot where I can do that. As for what comes next, I can already tell I don't want her near; I want her gone. So, a sale might be the best. Might get five hundred dollars for her."

"Then we have a deal?"

Sally hesitated one more time. "Okay. There's a shed two blocks up north, further away from where the fire hit. It's where I keep my stores. Take her there and keep her gagged. I'll come with you and make sure she is taken care of properly. Don't let any of my girls see her."

Beth felt the tug on her chafed and throbbing wrists. "Come on, we got to get going."

Brown pulled Beth backwards almost causing her to lose her balance. "We need to take care of you honey so we can work on setting up the meeting with your rancher."

After pulling her towards the back, Brown then shoved Beth in the small of the back to push her around the tent, apparently toward the shed Sally described. Around the back of the tent the shed came into view. It was probably three to four paces square with one door and no windows. On the door latch hung an imposing lock.

"Hold right there; you ain't gettin' in without the key." Sally had followed. She sauntered by the two men and pulled on a beaded necklace strung around her neck. From the depth of her ample cleavage slipped a key attached to the necklace. The string from the necklace to the key was an arm's length. Beth saw Sally did not have to take off the necklace to use the key. That string must hang down below her bustline, or maybe that bustline was ample enough. Either way, the string had been completely concealed until she retrieved it. Sally opened the door.

"Put her in the corner. Tie one end of a rope around the binds on her wrist and the other end to one of the braces holding up the shelves. She won't be able to move unless she pulls the entire shed down on herself which will probably crush her in the process."

Beth was jostled into a dark corner. Roberts grabbed her shoulder and pushed her to the ground. A rope was tied around the binding on her wrists and then to a metal brace above her head. The length used would allow her some movement but not enough to get all the way back to the door. Then they all left. Beth heard the lock click. It was all she could do to hold the tears back in the darkness. First the boys, now her.

Chapter Twenty-Eight

1873 February
Carson City, NV

"I am here to see Mr. Bliss. I believe he is expecting me. My name is Will Toal."

He'd entered the rather small office through a nondescript door over which hung a sign. It read: Carson Tahoe Lumber & Fluming Co. The last time Will spoke to Duane Bliss, it had been in the Carson City offices of the Bank of California. He had to keep in mind that Bliss had been—and probably still was—connected closely to William Sharon.

"I noticed on Mr. Bliss' calendar that he had a meeting scheduled with you today. Let me see check with his assistant, Ida, to see if he is available." The receptionist gave Will a cool look, stood up, and walked further back into the office. Will stood hat in hand trying to imagine how this conversation would go. He had already run possible exchanges over in his mind, as he often would do, but those imaginings never seemed to work the same way in real life.

The receptionist returned followed by a petite woman in a proper dark dress. The lady behind the receptionist was barely five feet tall, yet by the tone of her simple instruction, Will could tell this lady was used to being in control. "Mr. Bliss will see you. Please come this way."

Very professional.

Will was ushered into a large, well-appointed office. There had been no other offices or adjacent hallways near the entrance to this room. It was apparently the only office in the small complex. Will looked around, wondering how such a big business could be run from one office. Bliss must have understood his query.

"The main office for the company is in the town of Gold Hill. My home is here in Carson City. My wife Elizabeth and our five children live in a house I built on a street I named for my wife. I take the train most days up to Gold Hill, but the lumber yard is here in town, and there are things I need to look after regularly close to home. So, I maintain this office for use when I am in Carson."

Will absorbed the explanation. "I just came from Virginia City. Might've been easier just to meet you in Gold Hill as I could have walked that distance."

"But you would not have seen me there for several days. Mr. Mackay sent me a note asking me to meet with you at the earliest convenience. So here we are."

"I appreciate it."

"We've met before, have we not?"

"Yep, a few years ago," replied Will.

"That's right, during the railroad's attempt to foreclose on ranch lands here in the valley."

"One of which was mine. That foreclosure effort led to gunplay, and people got killed." Animosity dripped from the comment.

Will could see a slight reaction of surprise in Bliss' face, but he responded shortly.

"I remember it well. It led to my separation from the Bank of California. I had no toleration for the way the bank was treating the ranchers. It was an obvious ploy driven by their need to obtain property along their right of way for their railroad customers which included both the Central Pacific and the V & T. Some of the property was needed for the route of the track as I remember, especially up near Truckee, but their pursuit for other parcels was more out of spite than anything else."

Will was a bit stunned at this admission. Will could tell Bliss appeared to relish a bit in his obvious confusions. Bliss continued with a bit more abandon.

"I had built up a small bank in Gold Hill which later merged with the Bank of California. As part of my duties in that newly combined operations, I was designated by William Sharon to obtain property rights for the V & T Railroad's right of way. I did that, but I was fair with everyone I dealt with paying fair market value for the property needed. Then the Central Pacific had a problem with land up near Truckee to which I believe you had some connection. They approached Sharon and said that if he wanted any chance to connect his V & T to the Central Pacific, he needed to allow sale of the mortgages to their people who would then move to call the mortgages due and payable. Sharon smelled extra profit and decided to have the bank call the notes due and then ask higher prices from the Central Pacific. If the loans were not paid, then the bank should start proceedings to take the land that had been promised as security for the loans. Sharon pushed me to instigate the foreclosures. I refused. Because he had no other operatives here in Carson City, he simply decided to sell the mortgages to the Railroad. The rest is history you know."

"But I met you before lawsuits were filed. You said I needed to come current on my mortgage or the bank would foreclose."

"That was absolutely correct. You needed to come current, or I knew Sharon and the Central Pacific would push the proceedings. I gave you the correct information as per an employee of the bank, but I was also doing my best to warn you of what might happen."

Will was stunned for the second time today. First, he heard Beth was not home and now this.

Bliss shook his head. "I vehemently disagreed with Sharon. It led to a falling out. I took a leave of absence. It was a good time to get away from that activity. I left shortly after the shoot-out you were involved in. I told Sharon it wasn't right. I went back to Massachusetts to marry my fiancée, intending to return and start up another business. While back East, the stock I held in the Bank of California as a result of the merger with my earlier bank and my interests in various mines hit rock bottom. I was bankrupted in abstention. To this day, I believe Sharon orchestrated the whole thing in retribution for my adverse opinion on the foreclosures."

Still a bit skeptical, Will asked, "If you were broke, how did you get the money to start the lumber business?"

"The answer to that question is Darius O. Mills. Had it not been for a loan from Darius O. Mills, a dear friend and ethical businessman who thought I'd been mistreated, I would have never gotten back on my feet and started this company. Mr. Mills is one of my partners along with H.M. Yerington and J. A. Rigby. The Carson Tahoe Lumber & Fluming Co. has no affiliation with Sharon or the Bank of California."

"I thought Sharon would have been the money behind the lumber business."

"No, and he never will be. Not as long as I'm alive."

"But you sell lumber to his mines, don't you?"

"Yes, I have to. That's a simple function of business. But I don't have to be affiliated with the man."

"Isn't Darius Mills an investor in the Bank of California?"

"Mr. Mills is a private man. He doesn't make a point of disclosing the extent of his investments. I am pretty sure he is an investor in the bank and probably the mines, but from my vantage point, he keeps his relationship with Sharon at arm's-length."

Will was now in something of a quandary as to what his next step would be. Feeling that Bliss had been unexpectedly candid, Will felt a bit of a compulsion to be the same in return.

"I come here on behalf of John Mackay and the Consolidated Virginia and California Mine. They need to purchase a large order of square set timbers. A lot. Word in Virginia City was that William Sharon was going to try and block any sale of timber to Mackay and his partners. Mr. Mackay thought you were affiliated with Sharon and might agree with him not to sell."

Bliss remained quiet for the moment. Hearing no response, Will continued.

"I helped Mr. Mackay protect his mine during the fire. He told me why he needed the timbers, and I offered to speak to you. See, I had an idea I could convince you to sell. Mr. Mackay said that if I could convince you to sell the timbers, then he'd help me with a problem I have."

"Interesting state of affairs. I have several questions, but let's start with your immediate problem."

"A gang of four men kidnapped my twin sons, aged four. They demanded twenty-five thousand dollars. I don't have the money. The boys have been recovered, but I don't think the head of the gang knows that. Because of my assistance in the recent fire, Mr. Mackay offered to put up the ransom demand. I was going to use the money offered to flush kidnappers out into the open and settle up with them in final terms."

"Another gun battle?"

"Maybe. Maybe there might be a way to convince them to take the money and never come back. Not sure how that might work out. But the fact is I don't have the money, and Mr. Mackay offered to give it to me."

"My next question would be how were you going to convince me to sell Mackay the timbers?"

Will looked down at his boots and spun his hat around in his hands extra fast. He looked defensively up at Bliss, who was patiently waiting with interest.

"After hearing about your history and current feelings about Sharon, I don't think I need to use my idea. But as you have been open with me, I'll tell you. I was going to ask you to sell the timber and, if you had said no, I was going to let you know I'd tell the newspapers about your role in the foreclosures. In truth, though I'm not proud to admit it, I figured you might have trouble with your business. After thinking about it, you'd agree to sell."

It was now Will's turn to look directly at Bliss, this time with a sense of purpose. "But I don't think I need to do that, do I?"

"No threat is necessary. I'd like to keep a solid business relationship with Mr. Mackay. However, that leads to another question. Why does Mackay need so much timber?"

Will smiled. "You probably already know."

"I probably do. I've heard the rumors about Mackay holding the men down in the mine. That usually means a new ore find. It's also probably one of the reasons he didn't want the fire to get below the surface as the timbers there would have caught, and those men would have been fried."

"True. We worked hard to keep the fire on the surface."

"So, is there a new find?"

"Yep, a big one. But we were hoping you would keep that to yourself until it's announced. I had another argument I planned to use. I had hoped this argument would be convincing enough that I wouldn't have to use my newspaper idea."

"And what was this other argument?"

"Mr. Mackay received a telegram from President Grant. Grant has spies in Virginia City and became aware that Mackay was sitting on a possible new ore find. He asked Mr. Mackay to announce as soon as possible as the national economy is in terrible shape. As crazy as it sounds, the president says the country needs access to the new ore and its value."

"That's because he signed that ridiculous Coinage Act. That act has sent the economy into the dumps."

"He almost admitted that in his telegram. He said he regretted signing it."

"Too late now. Based on what I've read, he bent to the will of foreign countries who were worried about the huge influx of silver coming from Virginia City and wanted to remove silver as an approved metal for coinage. The international financiers and managers of government assets are all trying to protect their investments in gold."

"Glad you know something about it, 'cause I had no idea why this act was such a big deal."

Bliss paused. "I have no problem selling timber to Mackay. How much does he need?"

Will could not disguise his relief. However, relief was immediately followed by a new concern: the amount. "Mr. Mackay's engineers think it will take over ten thousand feet of timbers."

"Ten thousand feet! I don't have anything near that amount on hand. Not to mention the fact that I am getting barraged with orders for boarded wood so Virginia City can rebuild. Does Mackay know the sky's the limit on what I could charge him? There's never been a demand like right now for wood."

"Mr. Mackay knew it would be a tough time because of the demand. But he doesn't need the timbers all at once. He just needs a commitment to deliver regular shipments over the next six months as his men remove the ore. And he's willing to pay a premium for the wood. But he said there should be a value at your end for a regular series of orders in that amount."

"He's right. I like the idea of a long-term steady order. And I suppose over that amount of time, I can add men up at the lumber fields around Lake Tahoe to fell enough trees to fill the additional demand for timber. The bigger problem is whether I have enough capacity at the cutting facilities. But I'll work that out."

"What kind of premium would you charge?"

"Ten percent over the current price that I charge for square set timbers. I would be willing to remove the premium after six months."

Will had been given more leeway than that by Mackay. "Mr. Mackay would agree to those terms. When can you start the deliveries?"

"I can start within two weeks."

"I'll tell Mr. Mackay. You and he can deal with paperwork."

Chapter Twenty-Nine

1873 February
Virginia City, NV

"How are we going to get a message to the rancher?"

Brown stepped from the dirt road otherwise known as C Street onto the boardwalk in front of the Delta Saloon. The wooden sidewalk had extended all the way along both sides of the street for over five blocks. After the fire, there was only one side of one block left, this one, the block in front of the Delta Saloon. Ash and destruction lay limpid on what used to be a vibrant central city. There was little vibrance now. Other than the regular noise coming through the doors of the Delta in front of them, there was an anguished silence.

Brown looked at Roberts. "The only way I can think of is to leave another message at the Delta. He got the last one."

"How are you going to leave a message without everyone in town knowing what we are doing?"

"I've been thinkin' about that. While I'm not too worried about people in this town interfering, as they never have, I think the note should be short and simple. He'll get the message."

"Sam, you may not think anyone in town would interfere, but you can't count on that. You got the 601s, you know."

"No one's going to interfere. The 601s are a bunch of overeager miners who maybe have clubs and rakes. We've got guns. I'm not worried about the 601s."

Roberts shrugged his shoulders. Brown smiled. Standing at the doorway to the Delta, he turned back to Roberts and said, "Let's get this done. The sooner we can get this meeting set, the sooner we can get our money and leave this godforsaken pile of ash."

"You really think he's gonna bring any money?"

"Oh, he'll get the money. Millian told me people in Carson know he's real sweet on his woman. He's not gonna walk away from her. We just have to set it up so that he sees her in a position of real distress. We're good at that. I gotta plan there, too. But let's get the note done first."

Brown pushed through the Delta's bat wing doors.

"Look at this place. It's plum full. 'Suppose it's to be expected. The Delta is the only bar left in the main part of town. They probably got a big increase in business because of the fire. Lots of miners with nothing better to do but drink. C'mon, let's talk to the bartender again."

"Barkeep, I need two whiskeys along with a pencil and paper."

Brown watched as two bartenders spoke together.

"Here's trouble," said Mike Stuart to his fellow bartender, Bill Haluck. "Be careful what you do. That's Sam Brown and one of his thugs."

"I'll take care of it, don't worry." Haluck spun from Stuart and turned to Brown.

"Here come the whiskies. I'll have to go into the back room to find pencil and paper. Not much call for those."

Brown nodded and grabbed his drink, passing the second to Roberts. "Hurry. I ain't got much time."

The bartender stopped and turned back before heading out of the room. "What's the rush? There's no work here in town."

"Hurry, I need to leave a note here for someone. And when I do, I don't want no one readin' it. Understood?"

"Yeah, I get it," said Haluck. "No one's gonna read your note; why would anyone be interested in your note?" He turned, opened a door, and moved away from the bar.

After only a few moments, the door banged open, and Haluck barreled through with a look of open annoyance obviously meant to be conveyed clearly to Brown. "Here you go. It's a simple piece of paper, but it should work."

Brown picked up the pencil and started to write. As he wrote, he spoke out of the side of his mouth to Roberts, who was standing next to him drinking his whiskey. "This has to be just right. Simple but it has to be clear enough that the rancher knows what he's gotta do."

Brown finished and pushed the note to Roberts. "What do you think?"

Roberts looked over the short note and back up at Brown. "It works."

Brown called out. "Barkeep, need you over here."

Mike Stuart grabbed Bill and said, "I'll do this. Something's up and, with Brown, it's never good. Let me do the talking from here."

Brown pushed the note across the bar and looked up at the barrel-chested man across from him. "Ain't you the same bartender we had deliver a note to a rancher named Toal a couple of days ago?"

Brown could not miss the disdain in the man's face as Stuart responded. "Yes. It was me, Brown. I know you're up to no good. Why don't you just leave town?"

"Who's gonna make that happen? You?" Brown returned the disdain in equal measure.

"What'd you do with those children?"

"What children?"

"You know what children I'm talkin' about. The ones you took from their home."

"Don't know what you're talkin' about," retorted Brown. The outward denial did little to mask Brown's inner rage that this man knew about the kidnapping. Had to be Millian. Millian and his big mouth.

"Look, I need a message delivered to that same rancher. Since you seem to know him so well, I guess there's no need to write it out. Just tell him he's got two days to meet me on the Camel Fields with the agreed upon amount. Tell him there is a blonde lady I'd like him to meet. Got that? Two days. Eight o'clock in the morning sharp on the Camel Fields."

Brown stared at the barkeep and then turned on his boot heel and headed for the doors, followed by Roberts.

*****

Stuart held out his towel. "Bill, watch the saloon. I have to go find Hurley."

"No problem. I'll watch things."

"Good. I'll be back as soon as I can."

Stuart pulled off his apron and headed immediately to the Knights of Pythias Hall to get Hurley, thinking that he was the one man who'd know what to do. Hurley was a short ball of fire plastered with an ever-present grin. A surface of playful banter and outlandish practical jokes masked a burning force of competition and drive. The jokes and laughter collected people who were drawn to the man, wanting to seize pieces of what appeared as superficial joy. However, what held men collected around Hurley was his depth of loyalty and commitment. Something more serious than just laughter radiated from his antics. For the most part, those relationships flourished and a good time was had by all in Hurley's immediate vicinity. But cross him or take some posture as an adversary, and the man could draw from a bottomless well of unabated force to drive the opposition into the ground.

Hurley, Irish by heritage, could not join the larger Freemason group. Catholics were not invited into the Freemasons, so most of the Irish men who wanted to join a fraternal organization applied to the Knights of Pythias. If Hurley was not working, he was drinking. Stuart knew that Hurley would do his drinking either at the Delta or at the Knights. As he was not at the Delta, chances were, he would be at the Knights Hall. The Hall was one of the few other buildings left standing in the city after the fire.

Stuart hustled down several blocks of burned businesses and uphill to B Street until he reached the door of the Hall. "Who goes there?"

The speaker was a young man who could not have been more than twenty years old. Watching the door must have been duty for new initiates.

"I need to see Kevin Hurley."

"Are you a Knight?"

"No, but I still need to see Hurley."

"No one but a Knight can be admitted inside." The statement was issued with perfunctory bluntness.

"You probably say that to anyone you don't recognize. I need to see Hurley, it's important. If you don't give him this message, I will wager he'll be quite upset with you."

The youth at the door did not look happy. Stuart figured the consternation stemmed from the fact his request was outside of any standard procedure. He probably did not deal with nonmembers too often, if ever.

"The only thing I can do is to go find out if Knight Hurley is inside the Hall. Then, if he is inside, I'll need to ask if he would like to come out. Who are you so I can tell him?"

"Tell him it's Mike Stuart, and it concerns Sam Brown."

Stuart stood outside the door leaning against the front of the building for what seemed like twenty minutes but was probably closer to ten. Hurley finally walked out of the entrance.

"Mike, what's the problem?"

"Jesus, Hurley, it took you almost twenty minutes to walk out here. What the hell were you doing?"

"Finishing my drink."

"You could have had three in that amount of time."

"Might've been that many. Wasn't counting."

Stuart wagged his large head from side to side to express his disbelief. "We got trouble with Sam Brown."

"Some of the men at the bar told me a couple of days ago that Brown left town."

"Yeah, well, he's back. And he's up to something, and it sure ain't philanthropy. Came into the saloon today and left a message for the same rancher. Wants to meet at eight a.m. at the Camel Fields in two days. Says he's got someone the rancher will want to meet. The man is up to no good, Kevin. We need to make sure he leaves and never comes back."

"But we don't really know what he's up to."

Stuart looked exasperated. "We do know he intends to meet the rancher Will Toal at the Camel Fields in two days. Says he's got some woman Toal will want to meet!"

Hurley mulled over the information that Stuart brought. "I thought we were told Brown had kidnapped some boys."

"That's what you were told. You got that from Julia Bulette, your friend in the red-light district."

"She's just a friend."

Stuart lifted his chin. "Right."

Hurley caught the skepticism. "That's all. There are times when we take steps to protect the girls in the cribs if someone gets out of hand. She is just one of the girls who come to me or one of the other boys simply for protection."

Stuart smirked. He did not need to say another word to convey his suspicion as to the nature and extent of Hurley's relationship with Julia.

The barkeep watched Hurley come to the realization he was not going to win this small argument before he responded. With a hint of resignation, Kevin then said, "There's nothing I'm ever going to be able to say to convince you, so I won't try."

Hurley, the unofficial head of the 601s, then looked away. Stuart figured the man was formulating a plan or at least thinking of one. He also figured if anything was going to be done, it had to start with Hurley.

Hurley lifted his hands and spoke to Stuart. "There's no tellin' what Brown is up to. If he has the kids, why does he say Will Toal needs to meet a woman?"

"Maybe Brown has got both the boys and their mother?" Stuart's voice rose an octave in disapproval.

"If he's got the boys and the mother, then Brown's gonna swing."

"But Kevin, these guys are gunmen. None of our men have guns."

"You're right, but I do. Here's what we should do. We should get as many of the fella's as possible and head out to the Camel Fields at the time the rancher is supposed to meet Brown. We need to tell them to bring any weapons they can. I'll get Dan Frisch and others. You get Darren Baker and anyone else you can roundup."

"I can do that. You think we are going to get involved?"

"Seems unavoidable. This rancher is not going to be able to face Sam Brown and his group of gunmen alone and come out alive. We need to tip the scales a bit."

For the first time, Stuart felt satisfied. "Agreed."

"Let's head back to the Delta. I could use a drink."

"You just had three."

"Anything less than five to an Irishman is merely an appetizer."

Stuart shook his head. "And you are most Irish."

Hurley grinned. "Absolutely and quite proud of the fact."

As they turned on B Street, Hurley looked up and down the block. "Look at this place. Used to be a city. Now it looks like a Civil War battlefield. Nothing left but broken and burned buildings with ash everywhere. We have fires, rain, people getting kidnapped, and people getting killed in their homes. Michael, what's going on?"

"Not sure, but it sure seems like we've been vexed."

*****

They hadn't moved more than fifty feet from the door of the Delta Saloon when Brown stopped right in the middle of C Street. He pivoted on his heel and faced Roberts. Roberts could tell Brown was livid. The kind of livid that usually resulted in someone getting hurt. There was no mistaking the emotion behind the face he now gazed into. A normally undetectable small vein crossing Brown's forehead now stood out and pulsed. *Yep, he is in a fine state of livid.*

"Go find Millian, and tell him I need to talk to him. He's got to be the one who leaked out the business with the two kids. If he did, he won't live out the week. We may need him for the meeting with the rancher, but if I'm right, Millian will never see any payoff. He'll be dead."

Roberts nodded. "I'll go right now. It had to be Millian. Neither you nor I have said anything. Elmer's been gone, and Waverly's dead. That leaves only Millian."

"I know. Go find him. Tell him to come right now. I don't care what he's doin'. I got to keep my temper for now. We'll need Millian to replace Waverly when we meet Toal. He won't be anything close to Waverly's capability with a gun, but we need the best show of force we can muster. Even if he doesn't shoot one shot, just being there might help. We will settle with Millian for his big mouth after we get the money."

"Got it."

*****

Big Sally turned the key to the lock and opened the shed. The blonde was in the exact position as when they left her.

"I'm plannin' on takin' your gag off and let you go to the outhouse, then get some food. But if you start yellin', I'm gonna whack you unconscious and let you wallow here without food and water until Brown comes back for you. Understand?"

The woman nodded that she agreed.

Sally approached and removed the gag. "First, what's your name?"

"Beth." The word came out with unnatural effort due to stiffness in her jaw.

"Face sore?" Sally asked.

"A lot, but nothing like my hands. Is there any way you can loosen the ties on my wrists?"

"Maybe in a bit, but not right now. I need some answers first."

Beth nodded.

"Depending on the answers you give me, maybe we figure out what to do with you."

"They kidnapped my four-year-old twins and intend to kill my husband, but only after they get him to pay twenty-five thousand dollars."

Beth used a simple reference to marriage rather than try to explain the true state of her relationship with Will and how the boys came to be.

Sally could see the primal rage in the words as they came out. "I knew Sam Brown was no good. How in the world did he get you?"

"He first rode onto the ranch when my husband was gone, killed one of our best hands, and grabbed the boys. They told us to bring the money to Virginia City. My husband returned and the next day we both went out after them. Another one of our hands had already set out tracking them, and we tried to pick up the trail only to have the downpour and flooding wash the tracks out. My husband and I agreed to split up, me going to Mound House just to check and make sure they had not taken Luke and Sean there, and my husband to Virginia City to follow the men. The twins were kept in a shack at Mound House."

"Slow down, there's no rush. I'll listen." The words had come out in such rapid succession, it was hard for Sally to follow.

Beth continued. "The other hand is also a dear friend. He's been with my husband for years. He and I found where they had the boys and shot our way in to rescue them. The hand took the boys home. I started on my way to Virginia City to stop my husband from facing these men alone when they surprised me on the trail, tied me up, and brought me here. Somehow, they knew I was coming. It was as if they were waiting for me."

"Did they force themselves on you?"

"Not yet."

"Well, that's a surprise. I would've predicted they'd have mistreated you much worse."

"They seemed to be in a hurry to get back to the city. Can I go to the bathroom somewhere and then get some water?"

Sally ignored the question for the moment. "Look, I know what kind of man Sam Brown is. I can't let you go, or I could lose everything.

He comes back, you hafta be here. I can't even give you to some authority, not that there is any here in Virginia City. Brown would get his revenge."

The large woman could see the despair flow across Beth's face.

"Sorry honey, but I just can't risk it. But I'm not one to mistreat people. So, yes, I can get you food and water, and I'll take you to the outhouse. But I have two men who watch over my girls waiting for me. If I don't come back right away, they'll come lookin'. If you run, they'll follow and get you. Understand?"

"I understand you can only take so much risk. Is there no one who can help? How can a city not have someone who could deal with the likes of Sam Brown?"

"No sheriff to speak of, but there is someone I might be able to talk to. When is Brown to meet your husband?"

"I don't know. I just know it's supposed to be here in the city, and he intends to take the money and kill him. Brown is bent on revenge as my husband killed his brother just before the brother tried to kill me."

"You keep some bad company."

"Oh, you have no idea how one mistake I made led to nothing but pain in so many ways."

The big woman held Beth's eyes in a thoughtful look. "I seen lots of pain here in this world. This is a tough life. Not many escape some kind of pain. Don't care to hear more of yours. But I don't plan to cause you any more pain than is needed to keep my business. Don't think I can stop whatever Sam Brown has in mind."

Beth's shoulders sagged. Sally could see there was little hope left in the woman.

"So, here's what I'll do. Let's get you to the outhouse, and I'll get you something to eat and drink. I'll bring you some blankets, but I'm gonna hafta keep you tied up after I leave. That's just the way it's got to be."

*****

"Did you find Millian?"

Roberts entered the tent Brown had somehow commandeered. "Yeah, he's right behind me."

Brown stood from his rough bench, the only furniture inside the canvas abode, as Millian ducked under the tent flap and stepped in, hat in hand.

"Still wearin' the same suit and vest I see. Not winnin' at the tables?"

"What tables? No one has any money to speak of after the fire. The only players left are the mine owners, and they all play at the Washoe Club."

Brown moved until his face was only a couple of inches away from Millian. He could sense Millian's discomfort at the unexpected invasion of his space. It was exactly what Brown intended.

"You told someone about the kidnappin', didn't you?" Brown's words were tinged with a sneer, and his anger carried palpable intimidation. Again, intended.

Millian's face registered obvious shock as he floundered for a response. "I did not," was all he ended up saying in his defense.

"The bartender at the Delta knew about the kidnapping. That means others do too. We have only two more days to finish this job off, and now it's become a lot riskier."

"Why do you think I told anyone? How does what the bartender knows have anything to do with me?"

"Because there were only five who knew about it: me, Roberts, Elmer, Waverly, and you. Roberts has been with me ever since we took those kids, and neither of us told. Elmer and Waverly been in Mound House. That leaves you."

Brown could see Millian's initial shock was giving way to outright fear. Brown sensed that the man before him now worried about his immediate fate. Then, a thought or idea flashed across Millian's face. "Wait, maybe the rancher told the bartender. Didn't you leave a note for him at the Delta?"

Brown stepped back. He hadn't thought about the rancher. He turned away from Millian, then shot a stare back at the man. "Maybe, but I'm gonna find out one way or another."

Brown sat back down on the bench. "Right now, I need you. I need you to replace Waverly in my plan when we meet the rancher."

"Why do I have to replace Waverly?"

"'Cause he's dead!"

"Dead? How'd that happen?"

"Elmer says the woman somehow shot her way into the shack along with some ranch hand, took the boys, and killed Waverly while Elmer was out doing something, probably something stupid. They took the boys back home."

"So, why would the rancher even think of meeting you now?"

"'Cause we got his woman."

Millian shrugged. "Might still work. Where's the woman?"

"That's no concern of yours. Sit down. Elmer's gonna be here quick, and I want to make sure everyone knows what they're supposed to do when we meet the rancher."

Chapter Thirty

Will once again stood at the front door of the Mackay Mansion. Thinking it would be a while before the butler answered, Will had turned to look away from the mansion and upslope over the city. It would soon be dark. The sun had dipped below Mount Davidson's peak beyond the city. While the mountain blocked the sun itself, the vision left was a burnt half-circle of at the outer edges of the peak colored in a halo of yellow. Despite the high elevation, that same mountain prevented any view to the west. This high on the other side of Mr. Davidson and he should be able to see his ranch, his home. But would he ever see his ranch again? The idea of life returning to normal invaded his thoughts as a fleeting haunt, a ghost of some history that was beginning to feel beyond any immediate grasp. He'd let his mind wander as he knocked on the unpretentious door to the very pretentious manse.

John Mackay himself answered. "Will Toal, I was wondering if you were going to make it back today."

Will turned at the sound of the welcome. "Yep. I got to Carson City and back all in one day. Amazing how much further you can get on a train as opposed to a horse. I think I have good news."

"I like the sound of that. Come, sit, and tell me about your meeting with Bliss."

Will looked for the same seat he had used last time he sat in Mackay's office. It hadn't moved, but this time, it had a stack of papers on it. Not wanting to upset something that might be important, Will moved toward a seat further down the office and further away from Mackay's desk. But before Will could sit down, Mackay voiced another alternative.

"My office is a mess. As the news sounds good, why don't we go out to the back veranda and discuss this as we look east over the canyons and lower mountains?"

"That would be fine."

"Would you take a drink?"

"That would be most welcome after a long day."

"Whiskey?"

"Perfect."

Will followed Mackay as he moved to the back of the office, took a left turn through the main sitting room, and headed toward the back of the house. The pair passed a stairway on their right which Will knew led downs a floor to the kitchens and rooms for the help. Mackay stopped at the head of the stairway.

"Andrew, would you bring two whiskeys out to the back veranda?"

Will and Mackay stepped through the back door and onto what looked like a five- to six-foot deck that clung to the back three sides of the house. Will sauntered down to the end of the back veranda and looked around the corner. Mackay had said earlier that the deck surrounded the entire back of the house. Will could see the deck did extend all the way back to the front wall.

Mackay watched as Will inspected. "Yes, the deck does, indeed, circumvent the entire back of the house."

"You can walk all the way around the back sides of the house and not go back in?"

"That you can. I like the ability to sit back here and look out over the canyons. It is the one feature of the house I really liked. When George Hearst built the house, he made sure the veranda circled the back of the house to take in the view. When I bought it from the Gould and Curry Mine, he handed me the keys and told me he was going to miss this veranda. I soon knew why he was going to miss it. Out here looking over the mountains is about my most favorite spot on earth. And, if Andrew hurries up with the drinks, it will make it just about perfect."

"I would suspect, with the regular position of the sun when it sets, the back of the house is usually in the shade this time of the day."

"Yes, you are right. Most afternoons, the rear of the house is shaded and about ten to fifteen degrees cooler than the front. Another reason why an evening cocktail or cigar following dinner is best taken here."

Will could not help but admire the view over what had to be some sixty to seventy miles of canyons and vistas. With the mansion sitting on the side of a steep slope, there was nothing to block the expansive view.

"So, tell me what Mr. Bliss had to say."

"First, we thought he was closely connected to Sharon. Not so."

"Really? That is something of a surprise."

"I never told you what I intended to say to Bliss in order to convince him."

"I was not sure it was something legal, so I thought it best not to ask."

Will smiled. "I planned to let him know I would tell the newspapers about his hand in pursuing several foreclosures years ago which led to the shoot-out in Carson City."

"The shoot-out you were involved in?"

"Yes, the shoot-out that followed the railroad trying to take my ranch and the ranches of several other men. The same shoot-out that led to the killing of a man named Drake Sutton, who is apparently the brother of Sam Brown."

"Funny how life circles around itself so often."

"I never thought of it that way, but it's kinda true. Almost like a spiral. We think we are moving forward, but it's not always the case."

Mackay looked out over the canyons. "So, did you make the threat?"

"Funny you should use that word. Before I met Bliss, I stopped to talk to my lawyer, S. Samuel Grande, to see if I would be taking any legal risks. He said what I had in mind was a threat too. He told me to avoid any such intimidation because it could have legal consequences. But I'd decided to do what was necessary."

"As a businessman, I certainly would have taken it as a threat. I use that word in the simple form as I'm not sure of any specific meaning that could lead to legal implications. But in the straight business man to business man context, had I been in Bliss' shoes, I would perceive you were potentially going to do harm to my company. A man would react to protect his company's interests. So, did Bliss react?"

"As it turns out, I didn't have to threaten him. Bliss said neither he nor the Carson Flume and Lumber Company are beholden to Sharon."

"Not only did I not know that, I never would have anticipated it, either. I knew Bliss was out of money a couple of years ago. I thought he got his stake for the lumber business from either Sharon or the Bank of California."

"Yes, he was broke. He lost everything while he was Back East getting married. He lost his stock and interest holdings in the bank. He's convinced it was all Sharon's doing."

"Interesting."

"More importantly, it was Sharon who told Bliss to foreclose on us years ago. Sharon was looking to get right of way property for his V & T Railroad. Sharon was also trying to help the Central Pacific so they would look more favorably on a connection with the V & T in Reno.

Bliss told him foreclosing was wrong. He left the Bank of California because of it."

"Funny what happens in the back rooms of businesses that one never finds out about until long after the events are done. But then, where'd Bliss get the money for the lumber company?"

"Darius O. Mills."

"Ah, that makes sense now that I hear it. Mills was—and is—a part of the Bank of California, so he'd know Bliss or at least know *of* him, but I've heard he keeps his distance from Sharon."

"Bliss doesn't much care for Sharon. He is beholden to Mills, who he claims is an honorable businessman. According to Bliss, Mills said what Sharon had done to him was wrong and offered to help."

"And now Bliss is successful and Mills reaps benefits there too." Mackay stated the facts.

"Probably," Will replied.

"Do you want another whiskey?"

"That would go good right now. I'm sure I've never had a drink so smooth."

"It is rather expensive. You get what you pay for."

"I can certainly taste the difference."

"Andrew should be here shortly. He knows I'm usually on the veranda for at least two drinks."

"So, as my fine agent, Mr. Toal, did you and Bliss discuss terms?"

"We did. The fact that Bliss doesn't care for Sharon made it much easier. But he still held off a bit because he's facing a serious demand for lumber due to the Virginia City fire. I told him about President Grant and that you were willing to pay a premium. Both of those were with your permission."

"Yes, you certainly had my permission. We need the wood."

"Bliss still hesitated, but after he heard you were willing to pay a ten percent premium, he agreed."

"You and I both discussed that I would be willing to go fifteen percent."

"I know, but he agreed to ten. I told him you needed ten thousand feet of square set timbers, but that you were willing to take delivery over six months. He said if he had that much time, he could deliver the timbers."

"Well done, young man. I'll get the paperwork completed and send a formal order tomorrow. This calls for another drink.

Mackay turned to the doorway where his butler waited. "Andrew, bring another round."

Will took a deep breath. It had been a long day. He was relieved Mackay seemed pleased with the deal.

Mackay stood, turned, and half leaned, half sat on the railing at the edge of the veranda with his back to the canyons. He spoke directly to Will.

"Young man, you first helped to save what could be the largest find of valuable ore in history from destruction by fire, then you were instrumental in obtaining the timber needed to extract that ore. You probably have no idea how valuable that is to me and my partners. You have earned the twenty-five thousand dollars I previously offered to you. I insist you take it."

Will paused and took another deep breath. "Mr. Mackay, on the train back from Carson City, I had a chance to ponder your offer. I didn't think I'd need the money, but the more thought I gave to it, the more I think I might take you up on the offer."

"I sincerely hope you do."

"I think Sam Brown might just take the money and run. Maybe that is all he wants, and we don't get to gunplay," Will replied.

"If the money can be used to keep you from any such risk, then all the better."

Will nodded gratefully.

"Ah, Andrew, you have arrived. Please take our glasses and give Mr. Toal his second drink, and I will certainly take my second too."

The butler placed the used glasses on a silver tray held in one hand then he delivered new drinks to both. "Mr. Mackay, this is Mr. Will Toal?"

"It is Andrew. Why?"

"There was a messenger from the Delta Saloon who came by earlier this afternoon with a message for a Will Toal. It was Mike Stuart. I had no idea Mr. Toal would be here at the house. Stuart said an earlier message for Mr. Toal found him here, and he just thought there might be a possibility he would be here again."

"What's the message?"

"According to Stuart, a Sam Brown said to tell Mr. Toal to meet him at eight a.m. at the Camel Fields two days from today. That would be the day after tomorrow morning. Stuart also said this Sam Brown mentioned that he had a blonde woman that Mr. Toal would be interested in meeting."

Will jumped up. "Beth! He's got Beth!" He sank back into his seat, staring down the canyon.

Mackay pulled back at Will's reactive movements. He waited, then said, "I gather from your reaction you know the lady he's referring to?"

"She's the mother of my sons."

"Oh my God. First, he takes your boys, now your wife."

Will saw no purpose in explaining the details of his relationship with Beth at this point. He just looked up at Mackay and said, "Yep."

John Mackay sat in his own chair but not until he pulled it right next to Will.

"What can I do to help?"

Will wagged his head from side to side. "Not sure you can do anything. Like I said, the money might help. But if he's got Beth, if he's harmed Beth in any way, I won't need the money because I will spend every day of my life headed after him until either he dies or I do."

Mackay nodded. "Maybe I can be of some help. We don't have any sheriff to speak of, but possibly there is someone I can contact who might be of some assistance."

An idea came to Will. "Is there anyone who might know of a place where they could be keeping a tall blonde lady? After the fire, there can't be that many places left in town. Maybe I can get her before I meet Brown. If she's here, someone should have seen her."

"Will, there's no telling where they might have taken her. She could be here in town, but she could be anywhere out in the hills. I think you told me they kept your boys in Mound House but then lost them. They have probably taken extra precautions with your wife."

Beth, they've got Beth. Will struggled to keep thinking rationally. He verbalized the next thought without specifically addressing anyone. "Do you think they intend to use Beth for exchange in place of the boys?"

Mackay shrugged. "Possibly. No way to tell. If they intended to use the boys for the money but no longer have them with which to bargain, maybe they are using your wife in replacement. Might mean they really want the money, not trouble."

Will shook his head in disagreement. "If I know Sam Brown to be the kind of man I think he is, he's not in this for just the money. He wants me, and he figures he can grab and hurt anything near and dear enough to me to make me show up. No, this probably ends on the Camel Fields in two days."

Chapter Thirty-One

1873 February
Virginia City, NV

John Millian knocked on the door of Julia Bulette's house. This time, he did not remove his hat. He did not feel deferential in the least. Despite the dropping temperature, his entire torso was bathed in sweat. The moisture had all been generated not long ago as he stood in front of Sam Brown, the focus of his anger. Now Millian was mad. Scared mad.

"Julia, are you home?" The knock was anxious as was his tone. His head swiveled at the neck, scanning the immediate neighborhood to see if anyone had taken note of his presence. He saw no one in sight.

The door opened. Julia Bulette stood there before him immaculately attired in a full length dress. The dress was a modest style but made of excellent maroon colored fabric with narrow strips of lace running vertically to the hem. The neckline was high, and as usual utilized a formfitting bodice giving a clear image of the figure beneath. She was beautiful. He stopped. He'd intended to push right past her, but he just stood there absorbing her presence.

"John, I haven't seen you in some time. Would you like to come in?" The coquettish flash of her smile kept him rooted in the same spot, dumb, void of words. It was an effort to lift himself from this realm of abject admiration and focus on the original purpose of his visit.

"I need to ask you a question. Maybe it would be good if we talked inside."

"Is that all you would like to do?" The smile now became outright enticing.

Millian pushed his way past Julia and entered the house. He spun immediately and held his ground. She almost bumped into him after closing the door and turning to follow.

"You told someone, didn't you?"

"Told someone about what?"

"Don't play coy on this, Julia. I let it slip that Sam Brown was going to kidnap some little boys, and you told someone, didn't you?"

"John, I told you the moment you mentioned this that it was a dastardly evil thing, and someone should stop it."

"But I asked you to keep your thoughts to yourself."

"You did, but I never said I would."

"Damn, Julia! Do you have any idea what this could mean? Sam Brown thinks I told someone. If he finds out I told you, I'm a dead man." Millian's voice rose at least an octave. He twirled in place, revolving in a complete circle. The moment had now grabbed him. He could feel the fear, the betrayal rising from within. Deep within. Permeating not only his emotional state but his physical being.

Millian watched as Julia stepped back and away from him with her hands behind her, searching for the now closed door. He stepped toward her to keep the distance between them constant.

"John, what they did was inexcusable. Those were small children you described."

Millian found her response a cross between defensive and taunting. "So, you admit it. You told someone." The pressure in his neck was now expanding against his starched collar.

"I think you should leave." Julia stepped back.

"You don't deny it, do you?" Millian took another step toward Julia.

"Leave, please leave." Now she was pleading.

"I'm not going to get shot because of some tart's loose lips."

Millian grabbed Julia around the throat. He squeezed so hard she could not make a sound. There wasn't a rational thought to it. There wasn't a thought to it at all. All he felt was anger. In his way, he had trusted her. He'd tried to talk to her. But she betrayed him. Brown could not find out. If he did, Millian would die. His eyes were open. It was as if they were watching someone else act as the visions did not register the need for correction. He just squeezed. He barely took any breath himself. But Julia could get none. Eventually, she went limp. He did not let up. He kept on squeezing.

Millian came out of his malevolent mentality and found both he and Julia on the floor. He couldn't even remember the details as to how they got into that position. They were just there. He was out of breath. He had now sweat through all layers of his clothing.

Julia was dead.

The shock hit. He did this. It had not been a conscious, intended action. His anger had taken over both mind and body. It moved without him, even despite him. But she was dead. She now laid right in front of the entry door. He had to get out.

Millian stood, shoved the body away from the entry with his foot, and turned the knob. He leaned out of the door to check for passers-by, and seeing no one, slipped through the sliver of an opening and stepped outside. Turning back, he closed the door and again looked around. No one. He had to get out of town and fast.

*****

Kevin Hurley sauntered his way down Union street. Union sloped downward in a steep drop from C Street all the way to where the V & T depot had been on F Street before the fire. He was headed to the

Camel Fields to get a firsthand view of where the confrontation was supposed to take place between Sam Brown and the rancher.

Hurley chuckled to himself. The road at D Street sloped so steep it almost pushed one's body down in motion by itself. It was in this momentary thought that he saw John Millian leave Julia Bulette's house at the corner of Union and D Street. Yet it was not a normal departure. Millian had spun side to side as if looking for someone. The actions were almost sneaky. And Julia was not at the door. She always accompanied her customers as they exited. Hurley knew; he too was a customer. No, Millian had virtually slipped out as if through a small opening. Then he hustled down toward F Street and looked like he was headed north, away from town. Something did not look right.

Maybe he should check in on Julia.

Chapter Thirty-Two

1873 February
Virginia City, NV

"Does Flood know we are about to announce?"

John Mackay lifted his gaze from his newspaper but had no imme-diate response for his partner James Fair as he had abruptly changed the tenor and topic of conversation. Mackay put down his Bloody Mary on the small table separating their chairs in the Washoe Club. He then looked around and made sure they were alone.

Covering the gap in the exchange created by Mackay's awkward-ness at generating a quick reply, Fair lofted a good-humored jibe, "A bit early to be drinking, isn't it, John?"

"If that isn't the pot calling the kettle black. When have you ever passed on a cocktail, no matter the time of day?"

Fair laughed. "Touché. As for Flood, didn't you send him another coded telegram today?"

Mackay finally responded to the question at hand, "Yes I did. It should have been delivered immediately, so yes, he knows.

"How do you intend to make this announcement?"

"James, we have always tried to conduct our business in the utmost ethical manner. In the past, we just posted a notice on the entrance to the mine telling workers we were looking for minors because of a new find. So many times, other mines tried to oversell or play games with a new find. But I've been thinking; this find is truly much more special than anything ever discovered here in Virginia City, if not the world."

"Special it is. What do you have in mind?"

"It is so enormous I am pretty sure people will not believe us if you or I just announce a find of this scale. The markets might even react adversely thinking we are desperate to create some temporary stock play. The Consolidated Virginia's stock is dangerously low right now. The fire and the long wait for the crosscut to hit something has depressed the stock to levels we haven't seen in years."

"That's true, but those low prices have helped as Flood buys share after share at depressed levels. Once we announce, the four of us stand to make millions, John. Not just thousands, but millions. And that is on the stock play alone. The ore down in that mine will make all four of us wealthier than any of us ever imagined."

"That is probably true. But we need to make this announcement in such a way that it carries weight, carries veracity. We need some outside confirmation of the find's magnitude."

"I think I understand what you are getting at. If we can do what you intend, it might even help the stock play. If the confirmation is solid enough, then the stock prices will soar long before we even start drawing the ore out. The earlier the stock rises, the better. But how do you plan to generate such a confirmation?"

Mackay smiled. "I told you, I've been thinking about it." He let the thought simmer, and he held his tongue, smiling.

"Okay, John, I'm waiting." Fair could not conceal a heighten anxiousness.

Mackay took no small satisfaction in Fair's anxious tone.

"Ah, isn't that a bit of a role reversal? When you came in to tell me about the find, you enjoyed yourself keeping me in suspense. Turnabout doesn't seem to become you."

Fair smiled. "I suppose I deserve that. So, you've had your little revenge. Now tell."

"Dan De Quille."

"The newspaper writer?"

"Exactly. How long has De Quille been here in Virginia City? Ten years? More? How many finds has he had to report in the paper? Dozens upon dozens, right? Over that time, he's come to know a lot about silver mining. He would appreciate the enormity of a find like this and the quality of the ore too."

Fair now smiled in return. "You are absolutely right, John. It's brilliant. If De Quille printed an article about the nature and extent of this find, he'd be believed. The markets would scoop up the news in a heartbeat. The prices would rise astronomically."

"And what better way to satisfy President Grant's request that we properly announce and to do so quickly? A De Quille article would be picked up immediately by the San Francisco papers and, not long after that, the eastern newspapers would pick up the story as well. The news would spread country-wide quicker than any other way we could devise."

"But how are you going to convince De Quille about the size and quality of the find? Do you think he'll take your word on it?"

"No need. We'll show him."

"Show him?"

"Yes, show him. We will take him down to the crosscut and give DeQuille a look at the size and quality of the ore. He'll know it when he sees it. Showing it to him will have much more of an impact than any attempt to just describe it."

"John, you have been thinking about this. I think the idea is diabolical. I cannot recall any mine ever inviting a reporter down to see an actual new find."

"Nor I. But that is because most mines are trying to pull some fast and loose play on one or more of the stock markets. The finds rarely meet the hype. This time, we want the hype to be as big as the find."

"When do you think we should do this?"

"Today, just as soon as we can finish breakfast."

"Then hurry up and gulp down that tomato catastrophe you're drinking."

*****

Will walked into the Delta Saloon. The normal smells of smoke, whiskey, and beer were now mixed with the blowing shards of ash that still covered this upper part of the city. He looked around for the large bartender he'd talked to the day he arrived. It seemed so long ago, just after the flooding and before the fire. Since then, his twins had been recovered, he'd helped Mackay save his mine, sat in the room when Mackay received a message from the President of the United States asking him to help save the national economy, and his Beth had been taken. A week? Slightly more? Seemed like ages. Life was moving at a hell-bent pace right now.

Beth: that was why he was here. He had to try and find her. Maybe this man Stuart could point him to a place or another person who might know something. He hadn't slept last night at all. He couldn't close his eyes without seeing some image of Beth suffering under the control of a man like Brown. He had to find her.

"Is there a man named Stuart here?" Will spoke to the first bartender he came to.

"Mike Stuart is in the back room. Who should I say is asking?"

"Will Toal."

"I'll see if he can come out." The man walked to the end of the bar and through a door in the wall supporting a massive mirror behind the bar itself.

Will stood motionless. Fear that immobilized his muscles for extended periods of time gripped him now. He'd found it hard to concentrate since hearing about Beth. Thoughts of her in pain hit him deep inside his chest.

The large man he'd spoken to days ago came out through the door.

"I'm Mike Stuart."

"I'm Will Toal. You carried a message to the Mackay Mansion last night, correct?"

"I did."

"I'd like to ask you a couple of questions if it's alright."

"You're the rancher Sam Brown is after, right?"

"I suppose that's me. Now I'm after him. The message said I was to be at the Camel Fields tomorrow at eight a.m."

"That's right."

"I was also told the message said Brown had a blonde woman I might want to meet, is that right?"

"Yes, more or less that was the message."

Will did not shrink under the unbroken gaze of the man. He knew he was being measured.

"That woman is dear to me. She's the mother of my sons. If Sam Brown has done her harm, I'll travel to the ends of the earth to make sure he meets his maker."

Stuart did not react. He just kept looking at Will. "Rancher, I don't know you, but standing here, I get a feeling you would go after Brown just as you say."

"Brown is bad. Biblically bad. But I rode down bad men when I was a Texas Ranger. He's no different. Sooner or later, justice finds bad men. I aim to be the one to make sure Sam Brown is introduced to his justice."

Stuart now smiled. "So, what can I do for you?"

"Have you seen the blonde woman Brown spoke of? Did Brown give you any indication where he's keeping her? If you don't know, do you know anyone who might be able to answer my questions?"

"That's quite a list to deal with. With Brown involved, I can understand why you're anxious about the woman. But I can't help you. Brown gave no indication as to where he was hiding out or where the woman was. I can tell you I have friends who've been trying to find him for a variety of other reasons. But no luck. Brown and his accomplices could be anywhere in town or anywhere up in the mountains."

"I've got to look for her. I can't imagine what they've done to her."

Stuart nodded in acknowledgement. "You are right to be worried, and I would help if there was any way I could. But I have no useful information for you."

Will held the bar with his left hand but turned, now facing the door. *What lay beyond those batwings?* "I have to walk around town. I have to try to find her."

"You might get lucky. But I would be careful hunting Sam Brown here in town. He's the type who could just shoot you in the back."

"No, he wants money as well as revenge."

"Then maybe the best thing you can do is meet him at the Camel Fields tomorrow."

"I'm going to look around town anyway."

Will held Stuart's eyes. In some men, a message of determination and resolve can be communicated without any words. It radiates from their eyes. It was not intentional on Will's part. It was just part of who he was.

Stuart must have seen it as he smiled and said, "Best of luck; I have a feeling you might just be more than Brown bargained for."

*****

"Was that the rancher?" Kevin Hurley walked into the Delta, passing Will Toal who was on his way out.

Mike Stuart nodded in the affirmative. "It was. He came in to see if I had any idea where Brown might be. He also wanted to know if Brown gave any indication where the woman is being kept. Hurley, Toal's convinced that they have his wife. First his kids, now they've taken his wife."

Hurley kept looking at the swinging batwing doors set in motion by Will's exit. "We need to make sure Brown leaves Virginia City for good. This is getting out of hand."

"I've been sayin' that for months. No one would listen. Brown is something awful. Known it from the first time he walked into the bar."

"But so many people thought he wasn't that bad."

"They were wrong. Maybe even envious. But Brown is like a disease. It may start off with just a minor irritation, but then it really hits you and, if you're not careful, you could be dead."

"You don't have to convince me now. Julia Bulette is dead."

"How did that happen?"

"I saw that John Millian leaving her home as I walked down to the Camel Fields to see what we might be facing tomorrow. He was leaving her home as if slipping out of a bank robbery. I went down to check on Julia, but she didn't answer the door. It was open so I went in to see her on the ground, strangled."

"Did you go after Millian?"

"I'm startin' to do just that. Figured I'd start here, though he'd be really gutsy to just walk in here and start playin' cards or something after doing to Julia what he did."

"Millian is not here. Haven't seen him all day."

Hurley shrugged. "Didn't think he would be, but I thought I should start here. I've told some of the boys. If we find him, it's not going to be pretty. Julia was a soiled dove, but she was generous and tried in her way to help other folks. Every man I talked to is real upset. Her murder is a loss and their blood's up for Millian."

"Everybody's blood should be up. No one deserves that. She kept to herself for the most part and did what she could to make a living. Isn't Millian part of Sam Brown's little group?"

"I have no idea. I'd think you'd have a better idea than me seein' as you're the bartender. If anyone would know that, it'd be you, not me." Hurley's voice carried a bit of exasperation.

"Don't get touchy," said Stuart. With a smile, he added, "Seein' as you have so many contacts in the world off the edge of proper society like Julia, I figured you might have gained some knowledge and not just temporary satisfaction."

Hurley released a sly grin. "You better be careful, Stuart, or your wife might get a message in the night about your own appetite for temporary satisfaction."

"You do that, Hurley, and you've had your last drink at the Delta, and we know how much that would hurt."

"Guess everyone just has to keep their thoughts close."

"Best if we all do at that," replied Stuart acknowledging a proper standoff. "Good thing we're friends. I might even believe you can keep your thoughts close, Hurley."

"Might be worth a drink."

"Don't you ever let up on the liquor?"

"I'm Irish. No such thing as letting up on liquor. We're bred to sip the Lord's libations." The words were uttered with an accentuated Irish lilt for emphasis.

"Especially alcoholic ones."

"Of course, are there any others?"

245

"Alright, I'll set 'em up, and we'll drink to secrets. Then you can get back to looking for Millian. I'll bet he's going to be out on the Camel Fields with Sam Brown tomorrow."

"If he is, that would be perfect. We can deal with Sam Brown, his gang, and Millian all at the same time."

"Better be careful what you wish for. These are gunmen you're talkin' about."

"Stuart, you have no confidence. We've handled several men who richly deserved the justice we delivered."

"But none of them were gunmen. Only miners."

"We will have numbers."

Stuart stopped and turned to Hurley. "You know that rancher Will Toal told me today just before you walked in that he'd been a Texas Ranger. Said he'd ridden down several men who deserved to meet justice."

"There you go; he's got to be pretty good with a gun if he was a Texas Ranger. We've got numbers and, if Toal is what you say, then we have a gunman too."

A boy of about twelve ran into the saloon and up to Stuart. "Mr. Stuart, Mr. Mackay sent me to ask if you would have a Kevin Hurley meet him in his office later this afternoon."

Hurley looked at Stuart with expectant question written all over his face. "And why would Mr. Mackay think to ask you about my whereabouts?"

"We'll talk about it later, but if Mackay thinks there is something amiss here in town, he's gotten a message to me, and that message seems to find its way to people who can take care of the problem. He's done it before. Probably the same here."

"But he's asking for me."

Stuart broke from Hurley's stare. "Maybe I told him once that you were someone with special contacts."

"So, we're back to my contacts, and you were questioning my ability to keep secrets."

"Might've slipped."

"And we were just talking about keeping our thoughts close."

"We were just about to drink on that. No pact entered until you drink on it. Isn't that the Irish way?"

"Spoken like a true Scotsman."

Stuart turned to the boy. "It's Elijah, is it not, son?"

"Yes, sir. My name's Elijah."

"Well, Elijah, do you know what Kevin Hurley looks like?"

"No sir. I've never laid eyes on the man."

"Well you have now. He's standing right in front of you."

The boy looked startled. He swung his head back and forth, first at Stuart, then to Hurley. "You're Kevin Hurley?"

"That I am. Thought I was downright famous. Guess I was wrong." Hurley smiled.

"Mr. Hurley, Sir. Mr. Mackay wants to talk to you later today."

"You've done well. Go tell Mr. Mackay his message was delivered. I'm going to walk around town looking for someone after speaking further with Mr. Stuart here, and then I'll be right along to Mr. Mackay's office."

Chapter Thirty-Three

1873 February
Virginia City, NV

Will stood on the edge of the wooden boardwalk fronting the Delta Saloon. Behind him was a raucous bar. But stepping out from the doors as he left his conversation with Mike Stuart, he was moving into an apocalypse. The smell of burnt hope hung amid the ruins. Businesses were gone. Homes were gone. Beth was gone. All of this despair clung desperately to the side of a mountain sloping into a burning desert, a desolate sand covered descent toward the underworld.

He had to find Beth. He had to get her away from this outpost of hell. Maybe this city could be rebuilt. Maybe it could be reborn. Maybe the blazed remnants of the city's heart kept a beat or pulse of life that could give rebirth. But he wanted to take Beth back to the valley and leave Virginia City to its future whatever that might be. Yet, to do that he had to find her.

The telegraph office was still standing. Will stepped inside and spoke to the only person there. "Have you seen anyone by the name of Sam Brown?"

The telegraph operator, appearing startled, looked up from something he was reading. "No, no, not lately. Weren't you in here a couple of days ago looking for him?"

"Yeah, now I want to find him even more," said Will.

"Not sure I've ever seen a man named Brown. But I think someone named Roberts got a telegram and I was told he was an associate of someone named Brown. I took the message to the Delta and Mike

Stuart told me Roberts might be involved with this person you call Brown. But I've not seen him since."

"How many days ago?" asked Will anxiously. Brown, at least, had been in town. He couldn't be that far away.

"Not quite sure, mister. It was at least two days ago, might've been three."

"Any idea where he might be stayin'?"

"Can't say. If I remember right, a telegram came in for a man named Roberts. As I said, I gave the note to Mike Stuart at the Delta, who said I should be real careful of both of them. Stuart stepped in and did the talkin' after I gave him the note. No idea where he's staying or where he might be for that matter."

Will dipped his hat. "Thanks. Just lookin' to talk to the man."

"Who should I say is asking if he comes back?"

"Will Toal."

"If I see him, I'll let him know you're looking for him."

"If you do see him, best be careful. I'd ask that you tell a bartender named Stuart over at the Delta. He'll know how to get the information to me."

"I know that bartender. If I hear or see Brown, I'll talk to Mike."

"Appreciate it." Will turned to leave. He stood at the office door and looked first up and then down the street. He stood once again in what had been the center of C Street. How was he ever going to have any chance of finding Beth in all of the humanity living in haphazard rows of tents and lean-tos? Hopeless. But there was no choice; he had to try. He walked down to the Mackay Mansion to gather up Powder and start riding through what was left of the city.

*****

James Flood sauntered into the office of William O'Brien. "Did you see the telegram from Mackay?"

O'Brien looked up from a stack of papers on his desk. "I did. Good news. They're going to announce the find. Any announcement is going to cause a ruckus in the San Francisco markets."

"Only if Mackay can figure out a way to convince people quickly that the find is legitimate. The first reaction could occasion a serious backlash in the price of Consolidated as most will think a find of this size is beyond believability. The markets might think we are trying to pull a fast one."

"That could be more of a result of your own reputation, Mr. Flood."

James Flood, not one to shirk from a gauntlet thrown, retorted, "Anything I've done has been with you at my side, so don't think the reaction is limited to my individual reputation, Mr. O'Brien."

O'Brien laughed. "Yes, we've had some wild rides in our day."

Flood smirked. "But none of those rides will come close to the wild one we are about to start."

"Probably true. How much do you think we'll make on the stock play?"

"The price of Consolidated stands at close to twenty dollars per share. If the find can be substantiated and is as big as Mackay and Fair have said, I think the price will shoot up to over one thousand dollars per share. Could go to two thousand."

"And how many were we able to buy back over the last couple of months?"

"We own over ten thousand shares."

Flood could see O'Brien trying to do the profit computation in his head. Trying to shortcut O'Brien's attempt at the calculation, Flood said, "At only one thousand per share, that's almost ten million dollars to split four ways. If it goes to two thousand, it's twenty million. Not a bad play, wouldn't you say?"

"James Flood, that has to be one of the biggest stock plays in the history of the markets. I can't wait to see all their faces, especially those who thought the Consolidated was a bust. The same ones who really drove the price down."

"And then we start talking about what we can make on the ore coming out of the mine itself. You won't have to work another day, William O'Brien."

"My grandchildren's grandchildren won't have to work."

*****

John Mackay opened the door to the cage as it hovered over the main shaft of the Consolidated Virginia and California Mine. The shaft dropped straight down for over one thousand feet. A lifeless air rose up to invade the nostrils, a smell unlike any other. Oxygen fought to drop down into the depths of any mining operation. The air itself and all things within a mine smelled unique. The smell was cramped, caged, decomposed. Mackay was used to it. He felt almost comfortable within the confines of the stale mine air. But most were repelled. He turned and waived his guest into the cage before him.

"Please step in and grab on to a handle. When was the last time you were down in a mine?"

"Mr. Mackay, I cannot even remember. It's been years."

"And, how far down did you go?"

"Only a couple hundred feet."

"Mr. De Quille, you are in for a treat. You're going to go down over one thousand feet."

"You're taking me to the depth where the crosscut hits your main shaft?"

"You are well informed. Yes, we are taking you down to that depth, the deepest cut into the Comstock Lode that anyone's made yet."

"And did your men come up, the ones that you kept down below just before the fire?"

"Yes, they are all back home. We kept the fire from getting below the surface. The men had oxygen from the other end of the crosscut, down the slope from the city. There were no casualties, and the structure of the mine remained intact."

"But you kept them down there for a purpose. Was that to keep them from revealing the true nature of the new ore find?"

Mackay snorted. "You would have me for the true demon I am. Yes, I chained those men to timbers just to keep their mouths shut."

De Quille turned sharply. "You mock me, sir."

"All in jest, Mr. De Quille. All in jest."

"You kept them down there for a purpose, you cannot deny that."

"Ah yes, there was a purpose. But it was nothing near as sinister as you would like to make it out. Too many times in this city there have been claims of new ore finds. Too many times were those finds claimed to be something spectacular, only to dry up in a matter of months. We kept the men down there to carve out the ore around the vein so we could be sure of what we were dealing with. I had no desire to be a part of another silly game. This is no game, and this is no small find."

"Why me? Why take me down for this viewing?"

"Because you are not me. Because you are not affiliated with the Consolidated in any way. Because if you take one look and confirm what I think you will, then we have sidestepped any claim of hyperbole. I want you to print exactly what you see."

"You may not like what I print."

"It's your healthy skepticism that is exactly what I'm counting on. Everyone in town knows that Dan De Quille prints what he believes he should, not what anyone convinces him to print. So, I'll say it again, print exactly what you see."

At that moment, the downward momentum of the cage rocked to a stop. "Here, let me adjust your candle."

"I appreciate it. I still can't believe the men down here work only with candles."

"Each man takes two candles per day down the shaft. But the men work in pairs, and they share the use of the candles. We make them buy their own candles so they conserve them. More often than not, you'll find two men working using only one of their combined daily rations of four candles. That way, they might conserve enough to only need one new one before the next day's work starts."

"One candle for an eight-hour shift. Remarkable."

"But you won't need to worry about conserving today. Not only do we each have our own candles to help navigate the corridors, we have also lit up the area recently, excavated with dozens of candles and lamps so you can fully see what we are talking about."

"Just as long as I am looking at Mother Earth, the more light you can bring to bear, the better I might see whether you are trying to use my good offices to perpetrate the exact type of rouse you claim to be avoiding."

"We need to move down this tunnel for about fifty more feet, then we'll come to the area we've been excavating."

Before they came to any opening, Mackay pointed out the increased light up ahead. "You can see the upcoming area by the extensive additional light further up."

Mackay entered what seemed like a large room, stood up to full height after walking hunched over in the low ceiling tunnel, and came to a stop. "There, Mr. De Quille, there is our new find. Take your time and look it over carefully."

Mackay stood back and watched De Quille as he moved about the underground chamber. Mackay's men had eliminated the waste dirt around a generally circular roll of ore. The tube was enormous, over one hundred feet high. The cylinder ran almost two hundred feet where the excavation stopped as the process to unveil its length ended there for the time being.

"It's magnificent."

Mackay smiled. This idea just might work as he'd anticipated. "It is big. Bigger than anything Jim Fair or I have ever seen."

"How large is the tube?"

"Over one hundred and fifty feet in diameter."

"And how far does the tube run?"

"We have cut small probe tunnels along the edge and, so far, we have traced it at over one thousand feet. But it keeps going. There's no telling how far it'll run. We haven't hit the end yet."

Mackay watched as De Quille walked up next to the huge roll and touched the ore body itself. "The color looks outstanding. More importantly, the excellent dark tint appears to be consistent throughout the entire diameter. No lesser quality inside the ore body."

"You see, you are approaching this just as I intended. You are right; the color is dark. Most people wouldn't know good looking ore from bad. You've obviously seen both kinds. This is the highest quality ore find I've ever seen."

De Quille did not take his eyes off the ore body as his hand caressed a wide swath. "And have you had the quality assayed?"

"Yes, the quality is as I've represented."

"I might want to have a local assayer confirm that. Can I take a piece?"

"Be my guest. Use anyone in town, but make sure they are independent and qualified."

"I'll take it to three just to make sure they are all of the same opinion."

"As you wish. My aim here is to present you with the most open access you need before composing what I hope will be an article in the *Territorial Enterprise* telling people what you've seen."

"Are you going to have any trouble bringing it out?"

"Of course. We're over a thousand feet down. Getting ore to the surface over that stretch is a problem but not impossible. It only takes money. But the biggest problem is water. It's always the biggest problem. We'll have to rig a whole new set of machines to pump out the water. Not only is it everywhere, but down this far, you must be careful you don't drill into a pocket of hot water that can be under pressure. It almost explodes, spewing scalding water that can take out a crew of men in a matter of seconds."

"Any chance Mr. Sutro's crosscut will be able to help drain the water?"

"You really are well informed. You are even aware of Mr. Sutro's activities?"

"You'd have to be pretty blind as a newspaper man in these parts not to know of Sutro's activities. He approached Congress and proposed a horizontal cut deeper than your own crosscut for the sole purpose to drain the water all you mine owners have spent hundreds of thousands of dollars on your modern-day pumps to remove. He thinks he can just let the water flow out by gravity."

"He might be right. But we intend to use the pumps to lift it upwards and out as soon as we can. There is no telling when Mr. Sutro will ever get his crosscut completed. We cannot wait to pull up such a valuable cache of ore until he drills his tunnel. From what I've heard, his crosscut will be over three miles long. That could take years. Can't wait for that."

"Looking at the splendor before me, I can understand why you wouldn't want to wait."

"I've got investors also. I have to think of them too."

"Mr. Mackay, I've been around the silver mining business for over fifteen years now. I have seen many a new ore find. I have seen many samples of those finds and watched as they were assayed. I will be shocked if the assayers I take this to don't tell me this is the highest quality of ore they've seen."

Mackay already knew the size and quality. He never doubted the value of the ore tube looming over him. But he was relieved it was equally as obvious to a non-miner like De Quille. He had hoped De Quille would see the find for what it was. By his initial reaction, Mackay felt justified in his decision to bring him down the mine.

De Quille finally turned and faced Mackay. "Utterly incredible. It's a bonanza."

Mackay smiled.

Chapter Thirty-Four

1873 February
Virginia City, NV

Brown watched as Roberts pulled back the flap of the tent and hustled inside. He immediately closed the flap behind him, making sure it was secured. Their tent was up on a rise behind the skimpy center of Gold Town, a mere mile from the Delta Saloon. The canvas was old, worn, and barely held out any moisture. It certainly did not hold out much of the cold. But it was far enough from the center of Virginia City so that their comings and goings went unnoticed. They only had to go back to Virginia City one more time to meet Toal. The tent would do until then.

Roberts turned and coughed, the same cough he always had, deep and fluid. He tried several times unsuccessfully to clear his throat.

"Are you always going to have that cough?"

"Seems like it's always been with me."

"Well, keep some distance. I never want to get it."

Roberts finished clearing his throat. "The rancher is in town. He's been looking for us and the woman. That's not all. I just heard that there are other men, miners, who've also been asking as to our whereabouts. We gotta get this job done and get out of here."

"Relax. All we must do is lay low for the rest of today, and then we meet the rancher tomorrow. The good news you bring is that the rancher is in town and, if he's lookin' for us, then he got the message to meet tomorrow."

"Yeah, maybe. But he talked to Big Sally."

"Did she tell him about the woman?"

"She said she didn't. She said she don't want no trouble with you. But she felt bad about doing it and wants the woman gone soon."

"Good thing she didn't tell the rancher where the woman is. I'd come down real hard on Sally for that."

"There is also another buzz in town. Seems like one of the high-class ladies of the night's been murdered. People are looking for the man who did it."

"Do they know who it was?"

"I was at the livery stable. I didn't want to stay too long and ask a bunch of questions. When I heard they were looking for us, I got back here as soon as I could. So, no, I didn't hear who they think did it. But I got a feelin' it was Millian. He saw that lady regular."

"He wouldn't be so stupid to get us all caught up in the murder of some prostitute."

"I told you before, he's a dandy, and he'll get you into trouble someday."

Brown sighed. "Anyone follow after you?"

"Naw, I checked."

"Okay, as long as we can still get the woman, we're still set to meet the rancher. Go find Elmer and Millian. Bring them here to the tent so I can make sure we go over tomorrow's plan one last time. But be careful. Try not to raise any ruckus."

"I'll get them."

"I'm gonna stay here. My face is too well known. Best I just sit here and wait it out until tomorrow."

"Elmer's easy to find. He's sweet on this girl Katie and keeps tryin' to get her to leave with him."

"Elmer's sweet on a girl? That's strange. I thought the only thing Elmer was sweet on was building a fire."

"It just helps when I need to find him. He's always hanging around the girl's home."

"Well, get him and Millian, and get back here as quick as you can."

Roberts nodded and headed out of the tent.

*****

John Mackay walked up to the back of his home. As it set on the side of a slope, the back entrance was two stories below the main floor, which fronted D Street. But after he had been down in the mines, he came to the back door to remove his dirty coveralls before heading up to the living and dining rooms.

He tossed the coveralls into a bin by the door and took off his work boots. The staff would clean both before he left again tomorrow. He began walking up the narrow stairway to the second floor in his stocking feet. This was the life he loved: his mines. But this was also the life his wife left. In fact, she moved as far away as she could. Paris: not only far away but expensive. When she got the news of the new find, she would feel even more comfortable staying away and spending money. Mackay loved his mines. He loved the risk. He loved the men. He loved the effort it took to be successful. His wife loved parties and rubbing elbows with the rich and powerful. He exhaled; truth was, their marriage succeeded this way. It probably functioned because they were each happy in their separate spheres. Funny how that worked.

Mackay's reverie was interrupted by the butler, Andrew, standing at the top of the stairs.

"Mr. Mackay, a man named Kevin Hurley is here to meet you. I was not sure I should let him in, but he said he had a specific message from you to come this afternoon."

"It's alright, Andrew. I do need to talk to him. Please tell him I've just been down in the mine and need to change my clothes, and I'll be right there."

"How did it go with Mr. De Quille? He was very pleasant when he arrived earlier before your trip down into the Consolidated."

"The trip down the mine with De Quille went very well, thank you, Andrew. I think he'll be writing exactly the kind of article I had hoped he would."

"Excellent, sir. I will tell Mr. Hurley you will be up shortly."

There were actually four stories to the house: two below the main floor and one above where the bedrooms and bathrooms were. From D Street, the mansion looked like it was only two stories high, but the other stories fell down the slope to the back. To get changed so he could meet Hurley, he would have to climb all the way to his bedroom, which was on the top floor. He trudged upward, snaking around the turns of the rear staircase which was no more than three feet wide. Narrow and tight, this was the access up and down for the staff. They didn't use the main staircases. Mackay liked this staircase as it gave him some freedom of movement without many knowing where he was going.

After changing, Mackay descended into his office. Hurley was in one of the visitor's chairs. He rose as Mackay entered.

"Mr. Hurley. I am sorry to keep you waiting. I had an extended meeting that required us to drop into the Consolidated which can leave one's clothes a bit messy, so I had to change."

"Not to worry, sir. I am here at your request. How can I help?"

"My sources tell me that you have contact with the group here in town known as the 601s. I am not a believer in vigilante justice, but from what I've heard, the actions taken by this faction in the past have been justified and appreciated by the city. Our law enforcement has been terribly weak, and I think the fact that we have a very law-abiding city is because most folks know the 601s will see to it that bad apples are tossed."

There was no response. Mackay could see Hurley was in something of a quandary as to how he should answer.

"We've never met. You don't know me. But though I cannot be a part of any vigilante band, I'd like to assist anyone who protects the greater good of our community. However, any contribution I might make must remain absolutely anonymous."

Hurley smiled as if his fears were somewhat allayed. "Contributions to our efforts will help keep the peace we've enjoyed. Support would be much appreciated. It is generous for you to even think of helping us."

"I hope we can come to an understanding here that will not only be beneficial to the group but also to the city at large. I would be willing to contribute, but the key would be to have any transfers or contributions made in a way that remain absolutely secret. Can you put me into contact with the right man to have that done?"

"I can personally take care of that."

"How can I be certain the funds will be used in an appropriate manner?"

"Because I will be happy to report back to you as to exactly how the funds have been used. But I need an assurance in return from you."

"And what might that be?" asked Mackay.

"That the involvement of myself or anyone else in the group we are talking about remains just as secret as your contributions."

"I think that is the only way this arrangement will work, don't you agree?"

"Yes, secrecy on both sides is the only way it can work."

Mackay sat down in his office chair. Hurley returned to his seat. With a finger under his chin, Mackay turned to look at Hurley.

"Then I'd like to run a little test. I'd like to ask this group, which we shall refrain from naming any further, to assist someone who has been a great help to me. His name is Will Toal. He's been confronted with a terrible task of facing Sam Brown and his gang to get his wife back. He's to meet Brown tomorrow alone at eight o'clock in the morning at the Camel Fields. I'm worried that if he goes unaided, he could be killed. If the group can assist, then I shall contribute two thousand dollars to what we shall call *the cause*. Would that be something you could arrange?"

"Mr. Mackay, I am amazed you even know of this meeting between Brown and the rancher. Our group is already aware that they are set to meet at the Camel Fields."

"And how did you become aware of this meeting?"

"Brown passed a message to Toal through Mike Stuart at the Delta who told us."

"I thought our good bartender had contacts to the group. That's why I had the message delivered to him that I wanted to meet you."

"And how did you get my name?"

"Let's just say I have many employees, and they hear things."

Hurley smiled. "Maybe I am more famous than I thought."

"Don't get too famous. That might not be good for our new arrangement. So, you were already planning on being at the Camel Fields tomorrow?"

"Some of the group was going to be there. We also believe that the recent murderer of Julia Bulette is a part of Brown's gang, a man named Millian. Julia was a lady of the night, but she contributed to the volunteer fire department and other community groups in her way. Lots of people are upset at her death. We intend to get our hands on him. So, several men in the group will be there to get Millian and Brown or anyone else in his gang that stands in the way."

"I am glad to hear it. If it goes well, come by afterwards, and we can work out the details as to how the contributions can be made."

"I will speak to you tomorrow then."

Chapter Thirty-Five

1873 February
Virginia City, NV

Will walked through the door held open by the Mackay butler, Andrew. "Thanks, Andrew."

"Welcome back, sir."

"You'll probably have me only one more night. By tomorrow, one way or the other, I'll be gone."

"I know very little about what tomorrow holds, but I've heard there could be a great risk to you and your family. I hope it works out in your best interests, sir."

"So do I, Andrew. So do I."

Will followed the butler as he made his way from the entrance through the office and then the formal sitting room.

"Mr. Mackay is on the back veranda."

"Even though it's dark?"

"Yes, it's been a long day. He just finished his dinner and has only been out there for a short time if you'd like to join him. Oh, and we have plenty of food left if you would like to eat first."

"I'm not hungry, Andrew. My stomach doesn't feel like it would accept food well right now."

"I understand, sir. Let me tell Mr. Mackay you are going to join him."

Will waited as the butler exited through the back doors, each of which had plenty of windows in multiple panes. With the movement of the doors, the light from the room's candles refracted through the glass windows, redirecting the beams into momentary flashes without a source. With the doors completely open, the light relaxed and cast a subdued glow out to the veranda. Will could see Mackay sitting in his regular chair looking straight out over the dark horizon. He heard Mackay respond to the butler, "Sure, have Will come out."

"Mr. Mackay will be happy for you to join him."

"Thanks, Andrew."

Will walked out through the doors.

"Will, how was your day?" Mackay inquired in a pleasant tone.

"Not very successful. I walked and rode all over this town asking if anyone had seen Brown or my wife. Nothing. Don't know if they truly hadn't seen the man or if they are just too afraid of Brown to get involved in any way. But the net result is that I couldn't find either Brown or Beth."

"Too bad. So, what do you plan to do at this point?"

"Only thing I can do, head out to the Camel Fields tomorrow."

"You still plan to do that alone?"

"No choice. If I want to get Brown or have any chance of rescuing Beth, it has to start at the Camel Fields."

"I hate to see you go alone. I'd help, but Will, I'm a miner. I've never even shot a gun. I'd be no help."

"Mr. Mackay, I would never let you get anywhere near the Camel Fields tomorrow. You have plenty of more important things to do in this life than any risk on my account."

"Well, I can provide the money. I collected the cash over the last few days and put it in the vault next to my office along with the daily bullion from our stamp mills. I want you to take it. I dearly hope this man Brown will take the money and give you back your wife and let you get back to your life."

"I much appreciate the use of the money. Mr. Mackay, I can't tell you how much that means to me. But I'm not sure Brown is going to let it go at that. Truthfully, I'm not sure I'm going to let it go at that either. He's taken my sons and now Beth. He's got to pay, not get paid."

"What do you plan to do?"

"Walk out and stare the man down. See what he has in mind. I'll keep the money somewhere else until I see Beth and that she's okay. If I can, I'll use the money as a distraction to get to Brown. But it's hard to tell how this will play out. Sometimes you just have to react to the circumstances as they happen."

"I've spoken to some men who might be in a position to help you tomorrow."

"That's mighty nice. I am heading into this thinking I have to do this myself, but if someone else can help, I can sure use it."

"In truth, I can't guarantee they will be there, but it was the least I could do." Mackay looked back out over the horizon. "So dark, no lights but the stars. Almost ominous."

There was a silence between the two men. A comfortable quiet. One that had no need to be filled with words.

After what Will thought was a quarter of an hour during which nothing was said, he stood. "I'm going to head up and try to get some sleep. Might not get much shut eye but got to try to do what I can to be at my best tomorrow. Again, Mr. Mackay, you've been more than a friend. I hope to thank you proper someday."

"Will, there are no thanks needed. After what you've done for me, what I've done in return is minimal. Good luck to you tomorrow."

"Thank you, sir. I hope to be able to sit right here on this veranda someday down the road and join you for another drink."

"Anytime, Will Toal. Anytime."

*****

Fr. Cecconi had made his last rounds checking the church. He saw Sr. Charity on her knees at the kneeler closest to the altar. She had apparently finished her prayers, made the sign of the cross, and stood. When she turned to leave down the main aisle, Fr. Cecconi approached.

"Sister, did we have any newcomers today?"

"I don't think so, Father. There could have been a couple of new folks. There are so many, it would be hard to make them out. But I don't think so. We've reached a kind of teetering balance; a limit if you will. We are at the maximum of our ability to help. We could hold on and see these folks get resettled and the world get back to normal. But, if we have anything else harmful that happens in this town, then I fear we will see a complete collapse. I just spoke to God, trying to impress him of our situation."

"That's the best we can do at this point. People are trying to rally and support those who need it. The mine owners seem to think there's plenty of money to rebuild. It'll just take time," said the priest. "Time and a break from all the evil that has befallen us. We could use a sign that He has listened."

"We could use a sign." Sister Charity glanced up as if to forward another plea to the Almighty.

*****

"Roberts will handle the woman. Elmer, you and Millian know what you're supposed to do."

There was only a small candle lighting the internal confines of Brown's tent. Four men were huddled inside, a collection of moral failure operating under the impression they had some kind of mandate to function as they wished. And, if that function resulted in some measure of pain or destruction, so be it.

Elmer looked completely disinterested. "We've heard this ten times now. Yes, I know what I'm supposed to do. This'll be real simple. Just say when, and I'll shoot the bastard."

"Elmer, you don't say anything, and you don't start shooting until I've shot first. Got it?"

"You want him dead; I can make him dead."

"Yeah, I do want the rancher killed. But I'm going to do it. And I'm not going to do it until we get the money. You want the money, don't you?"

Elmer hesitated but then agreed. "Yeah, I want the money. If I get this money, maybe I can convince Katie to leave her sorry life and head out with me."

Brown shook his head in disgust. What could be sorrier than to go anywhere with Elmer? "I would never let my life be ruled by any desire for a woman. But Elmer, if that is what it's gonna take to make you follow orders, then fine. Just don't take any shots until I shoot first."

Brown turned to Millian. "You understand your role?"

"I do. But don't count on me to do any fancy shooting."

Brown now smiled. "Millian, we would never count on you for any shooting. Just do your part, and you probably won't have to pull any triggers."

"That sounds just fine to me."

"By the way, did you kill the prostitute?"

Brown could see the immediate change in demeanor, the shock. He'd seen it too many times not to recognize a question that hit home.

"No, no I haven't killed anyone. Why would you ask?"

"Roberts says you were a regular customer of hers."

"That doesn't mean I killed her."

"Not sure I believe you, Millian. But right now, I really don't care. As long as you do what you're supposed to tomorrow, that's all I'm worried about." He let his gaze linger on the man in a form of judgment that said Millian's denial wasn't believed.

Roberts had another coughing fit. After it finally subsided, Brown looked around at the collection before him. "Bunk out here in the tent. No one leaves. Can't have anything else happen that might upset the meeting tomorrow. I'll get us up, and we can head out."

*****

"But we got no guns, Hurley!"

"I know we don't have guns. But I think I can lay my hands on one or two before tomorrow. We shouldn't need them. If this rancher was a Texas Ranger, he should be able to occupy one or two of Brown's men. We then concentrate on one of the others and remove him."

"How are we going to even get close if we don't have guns?"

Hurley, Dan Frisch, Tom Gorman, Fred Turner, Joe Cullen, and others were in the back room of the Miner's Hall. All told, there were eight men. Hurley was finding it difficult to muster his soldiers, soldiers without serious weapons.

"Look, we meet at the front of St. Mary's. We watch and see what happens. We react if we can. If we can't, then we can't. But there's a lot of money in it for each of us from Mackay if we can help this rancher. Not only that, if we need help down the road on other events, Mackay said he'd help pay. We've got to try."

No one answered. The quiet lingered. Unity hung in the balance.

Mike Stuart broke the silence. "Kevin's right. We all know this is something new for us. Usually, it's a group of us that just meets one man in an alley or breaks into a house after he's asleep when we have numbers. This is different; but I agree with Kevin, we've got to try. Sam Brown has got to be stopped. Running him out of town won't be enough. He'll just come back. He's like a plague, a pestilence. We have to get rid of it, permanent."

Dan Frisch exhaled. "I'm in. We can't let the rancher face a man like Brown alone. It's our city; it's up to us to do our part to remove the likes of Brown. We shouldn't let the rancher do all our work for us."

Turner looked at Hurley. "Gotta be done. This guy and his gang must be removed. If not from town, then existence itself."

Hurley knew he'd finally convinced the group. "Then we are agreed, we help?"

One man after the next nodded his agreement.

"Okay, we meet early at the front of St. Mary's. I'll see if I can get the guns. Bring anything you can. Knives, axes, whatever. Just come."

Chapter Thirty-Six

1873 February
Virginia City, NV

Will stepped out of the Mackay Mansion under an orange sky as daylight crested over the mountains in the distant east. To his left was the slope up to C Street where the burned and pitted spires randomly rose as testament to the destructive forces that had befallen the city. He looked further up to a complete umbrella of high clouds that blocked the grace of any direct sunlight. The clouds were wispy thin and bore the same color and texture as the underside of an orange peel.

In all the countless cloudy days of his life, he'd never viewed these puffs of vapor as adversarial. But right now, those clouds struck him as a clear barrier separating the chaos here on the surface from any heavenly reaches above their ethereal obstruction.

If I die today, would there ever be any bright light in Beth's life, or that of my boys? Maybe we've been cut off from any higher power. Maybe the clouds are not a barricade but a sign, some kind of separation. If it is a sign, maybe there are times when the deeds of a few are required to break through that ceiling. Not something I can affect. Maybe my mind is only spinning out thoughts just before a confrontation, the outcome of which is unknown. Been there before. All I can do is deal with the evil pursuing my family: Sam Brown. But somehow, this all seems bigger than just Sam Brown, though any light for my own family would be much brighter if Sam Brown were no longer creating his own chaos.

Will turned to grasp Powder's reins. "C'mon, son, let's go deal with Mr. Brown."

He began to walk north leading his horse. The distance was not far. No need to ride just yet. After a turn downslope, he strode out onto the southern edge of what townspeople called the Camel Fields. He had saddled and brought Powder just in case the events required. The smell of leather tack on the horse's back along with his chaps provided something of a comfort, a constancy whenever Powder was around. He had no idea how this would play out. He might need a horse and figured it was best to be prepared. Powder's ears flicked forward. Will knew something moved or someone was coming, drawing the horse's attention. He dropped one of the split reins to the ground and grabbed his Enfield rifle out of its scabbard.

"Stay here, boy." Will knew the gelding would hold his position no matter what took place until he returned and lifted the rein back off the ground.

He stood alone as instructed in Brown's message. Powder was still looking intently across the empty dirt field toward the rear of St. Mary's of the Mountains Church. As was the case with most Catholic churches, the main door was to the west and the altar in the east end of the nave. That worked well on the slope here in Virginia City as there would not have been any other way to position St. Mary's. Maybe it was just meant to be right where it was. Powder's ears flicked again toward the church. Will kept his eyes trained on the same spot. He knew the animal's hearing was far better than his own, and Powder's ears told Will he'd heard something. Will moved the Enfield rifle to his left hand. His Navy Colt was holstered on his right hip. He released the leather safety. The early morning air now felt cold and damp.

To the east, the Camel Fields were bordered by a canyon that dropped quickly from the level surface. To the immediate west was St. Mary's. Further upslope from the church was the platform where the train depot stood before the fire had reduced it to ashes. North from the base of the church was a road leading to the Consolidated Virginia Mine works. That road branched off farther to the east where it snaked in multiple curves to the city hospital, also built with money from John Mackay. Behind Will was the road that led to the Savage and Hale & Norcross mines at the south edge of town. But he now stood completely out in the open, vulnerable. He knew Brown demanded he be right in this spot for just that reason. He could still not see any movement.

Will kept scanning the open field of hard packed dirt covered with a fine coat of dust. Mackay had told him about the history of the fields. Once a year the town all turned out on this same field for a crazy day of racing camels. They had been brought to America years ago with the thought they'd be perfect beasts of burden to carry material up the desolate barren hills to Virginia City and carry the ore back out. They had been a miserable failure. A camel's feet did not agree with the rocky landscape and sagebrush. They turned out to be useless. No one had known what to do with the beasts. Rumor had it that a series of wagers were placed in the Delta Saloon on which camel could run the fastest. The undoubtedly inebriated instigators had nothing better to do that day. The races were on. The tradition was set. Eventually, the races were accompanied with picnics, beer, fun, and games. But there would be no fun and games here today.

"Where's the money?"

Will still looked to the north, the same direction Powder had sensed movement earlier. A solitary man walked out around the base of the church from its far side blocked from Will's view until he strode to the middle of the field opposite him. He hesitated there and then began to walk in Will's direction. Will had never seen Sam Brown, yet he knew in an instant it was him. The figure walking toward Will was the spitting image of Drake Sutton, the man who had attempted to kill Beth as he sought to escape from a railroad instigated shoot-out and massacre in the Carson Valley years ago. Will had killed Sutton just before he would have killed Beth.

While Will kept his eyes directly on Brown, he consciously focused to his sides with his peripheral vision. He could not see anyone else. But he knew they were there. They were probably moving in behind and to the side as Brown moved toward him. Brown was too confident to be alone. He walked with an arrogance that could be rooted only in the knowledge of his men hidden close by. This man had others somewhere around. He would never walk right at him unless he was covered. Will needed to flush out their positions.

"Where's Beth?"

"Wouldn't you like to know?"

"You won't see any money until I see her. Let her walk out where I can see her and let her go. Then I'll tell you where the money is."

"It ain't gonna work that way, rancher. You killed my brother, my twin brother. You either drop the money in front of you, or you won't live to take another step."

Will saw a man rise up over the downslope to the east on Will's right. He had evidently just walked up the slope, but from Will's vantage, it looked as if he rose up right out of the ground. His gun was drawn but pointed down the line of his right leg. He wore a suit. Without even turning his head, Will figured this man was not a serious threat. If he were a gun hawk, the pistol would be pointed right at Will. But instantaneous decisions could be wrong.

"That's one," said Brown.

Will did not respond.

Then to Will's left, another man walked out along the near side of St. Mary's. He held his gun drawn and pointed in Will's direction. He handled the gun with a casual ease. He was too far away for a handgun to be accurate, but like Brown, he was walking toward Will. The man looked dirty, thin, and he had a strange menacing grin. Will could not afford to take his eyes from Brown. But in his limited observation out of the side of his eye, this man looked to be a problem.

"That's two," said Brown.

Will kept his eyes on Brown. "Where's the woman?"

"WILL!!!" It was Beth. The scream came from higher up. There was a primal fear in her voice. Will looked away from Brown this time. It was a reaction more than a decision.

The sound came from the bell tower of St. Mary's. There was little if anything left of the roof after the city fire, but the brick bell tower rose above the level of what would have been the highest pitch of the old wood roof that was now burned away. It appeared as a small observation post at the corner of a fort. There was a low white rail surrounding all four sides. Beth struggled in the arms of another man. The man struck her on the back of her head with the barrel of his handgun. Beth went limp, but he still held her up. He propped her up next to the nearest railing with his left hand while he held a gun to her head with his right.

I can't lose her. As if the thought rebounded inside his head, it jumped back through his brain again. *I can't lose her.* A part of him would be lost. His reaction was not one of pride. It was because of the injustice. No, it was much more than that. Beth was a part of him. His gut clenched. An acidic fluid burned the bottom of his throat. He'd faced off with gunmen dozens of times in his short life and had never felt this way. Then it struck. In this most peculiar of moments, standing here against impossible odds, Will realized that he really did love this woman. Beth was more than just the mother of his sons; he loved her. But how could he save her? He had no idea. He'd faced onrushing Union soldiers and had never felt like this. Oh, he'd been anxious, but this was different. The muscles in the back of his legs twitched, trembled as if they no longer would hold his weight. His brain clouded over obscuring thoughts other than the loss of Beth now confronting him. He'd always been able to mentally slow time in critical situations. It gave him an advantage when he had to react quickly. But Beth's scream floated like a aerial blanket over his ability to think. Slight beads of sweat began to well under his hat band.

Up to now, despite the odds growing against him as every additional man appeared, he was confident he could deal with each and have a good chance of survival. But Beth's vulnerability changed everything. How could he save her with a gun at her head? The fear must have shown.

Gloating at Will's obvious discomfort, Brown said, "She's got to be five hundred yards from you, rancher. I heard you were a good shot. But nobody can shoot that far."

Will knew Brown was wrong. He'd made shots much further than five hundred yards as a marksman in a specialized Confederate sniper corps during the war. The Enfield was loaded. It always was. Brown counted on Beth being out of range. It was a mistake, Brown's first. But how was Will going to take advantage? The gun the man held was virtually pressed against her head. Will had been one of the best in his sniper corps. But even if Will dropped to the ground and raised his Enfield as trained and executed during the war, he couldn't get off a shot quick enough to stop the man who held her.

*****

Kevin Hurley and a group of 601s gathered in front of St Mary's and peered around the front south corner. Hurley moved only his head around the corner to see the Camel Fields while waving his hand behind him for the group to remain quiet and still. He saw Brown and the two men on either side of the Camel Fields and heard the woman scream high above his head.

Hurley pulled back and looked at the group. Before him were Mike Stuart, Dan Frisch, Fred Turner, Tom Gorman, and others. He quickly decided what had to be done.

Hurly whispered, "We were following Millian, but it looks like he's working with Brown to kill this guy Will Toal. Millian's across the field above the down slope. There's a guy right below us near the bottom of the church. Brown is to the north. And I think there's a guy with the woman up in the bell tower."

Stuart insisted, "We can't let Brown get away with this. We were out to get Millian for killing Julia, but this is even worse."

Hurley nodded. "Okay, here's what we'll do. I was able to lay my hands on two guns. Mike, you take one of the guns along with two of the men and circle to the north around to the downslope opposite us here. You got to hurry. Millian's on the other side. You got to get behind him and make sure he doesn't get a good shot at the rancher. I'll take the other gun along with Frisch, Turner, Gorman and three others and deal with this guy at the base of St. Mary's."

It was Turner who first acknowledged the plan. "That sounds okay but who is going to deal with Brown and the guy in the tower?"

Hurley shrugged. "The rancher will have to deal with Brown. But I have no idea how we can help with the woman. Maybe the guy up there will just drop her and try to save his own skin when he sees it's not four against one. Don't know, but we can only do what we can. Now move!"

Stuart and his group ran north around the church and kept below the level of the Camel Fields, holding to the slope that circled to the east.

Frisch got close to Hurly and asked, "What's your idea for the guy just below the church? We've got one gun. I've got an axe handle, and the boys only have clubs."

Hurley looked back around the corner of the church. The brick foundation was only six feet tall here at the top of the slope, but the ground angled downward as one moved east. The man below was maybe twenty to thirty feet beyond the east end of the church which meant he was about one hundred thirty feet from where Hurly stood.

Hurley pulled back and looked again at Frisch, thinking.

"We'll wait and see how the rancher handles this. As soon as any shooting starts, I'll take a shot at the man just below us at the other end of the church. Then we rush him. We can sneak up next to the brick wall of the church. If we're absolutely quiet, maybe we can get close while his attention is on the rancher. Maybe we can even get close enough to use the clubs."

"Sounds sketchy," said Frisch.

"Sketchy at best," said Turner.

"Got any better ideas?"

Frisch hesitated. "Not at the moment. Let's go with it."

Hurley looked at Turner. He shrugged. "Probably the only way to handle it."

Hurley knew he and Turner had a close bond in other aspects of life. But this was a decision that could lead to somebody getting killed. Hurley extended an appreciative look for the support.

Hurley returned to again look around the corner of the foundation. He pulled back to his group. No more talk. No more planning. It was time to act. With hand signals he indicated they should move around the edge of the west side and head toward the Camel Fields hugging the brick wall. All nodded.

*****

Sr. Charity held Fr. Cecconi's head in her lap. She sat at the front of the altar in St. Mary's. She looked down the nave toward the front door as Fr. Cecconi lay unconscious on the ground. His head was bleeding from a jagged rip over his left temple. She was trying to stem the flow when his eyes opened.

"Sister, what happened?"

"A man struck you with the barrel of his gun. He had a woman at gunpoint and was dragging her through the church when you stopped him. He asked how to get up into the bell tower, and you said you were not going to let him take that woman up there."

"That's right, I remember that now. She looked wounded or something. But I have no recollection after that point."

"Because he swung his gun and hit you on the left side of your head. Then he aimed the gun at you on the floor, looked at me, and said that if I didn't tell him how to get up to the bell tower, he would kill you right there. I pointed to the stairway. But I told him no one had been up there since the fire. I said it might be dangerous. He didn't even listen. He just dragged the woman with him and headed up the stairs."

"Is he up there now?

"Yes."

Fr. Cecconi heard voices out in the field below the church.

"Help me up, Sister." He was now on his hands and knees.

"Father, I'll lift under your arms, just get one foot under you at a time."

He moved slowly, getting from bent knees to his feet as Sr. Charity lifted under his armpits. He stood and wobbled initially, but he worked to keep his balance.

"I think I'm coming back. My head feels like it's splitting apart, and the world is spinning. Hang on to me for a moment."

"Father, you should sit. He hit you real hard. The bleeding stopped, but if you move too much, it will open up again."

"Walk with me behind the altar. There's a window out of the back of the church. Maybe we can see what is going on."

The pair walked arm in arm around the altar to the far back of the church. There, a window looked out over the expanse of the Camel Fields. Both could see men. There was no doubt it was a confrontation.

A woman screamed from above their heads.

"Father, that has to be the woman up in the bell tower. We have to help."

Having no idea what he might be able to do, Fr. Cecconi turned and took several steps back toward the rear of the altar. He looked up. He could see up through a hole in the bell tower floor, obviously another result of the recent fire. The man with the gun stood to the rear of the church looking out to the field. He had his back to the bell, which was only three to four feet away. The bell weighed over seven hundred pounds. The brass behemoth had been casted in Pennsylvania and sent via rail and oxcart at the expense of John Mackay. The rope to activate the swinging of the bell dropped down to the floor just in front of Fr. Cecconi.

"Father, we have to do something!" Sr. Charity was nearing panic. "Those men are going to shoot the rancher from Carson."

Fr. Cecconi turned back to look at Sr. Charity. He had no idea what to do and knew time was running out. Despair gripped both. "Another test, Sister."

"But why, Father?"

He looked past Sr. Charity again to the Camel Fields out of the window behind her. He saw a slight opening in the thick cloud cover. A single ray of light broke through and shot in a beeline to the brass bell only to be reflected downward. The reflected ray hit Fr. Cecconi directly in the face. He blinked away the bright blast. But in that blink, he knew immediately what he should do.

He turned away from the window and raced to grab the rope. He pulled down hard, as hard as he could. The bell sounded, and it sounded loud. The floor normally blocked most of the sound between the bell tower and the main body of the church. With the hole in the floor, the sound of the strike was magnified inside the church tenfold. It reverberated off the inner walls like a thunderclap. It had to be deafening for anyone up in the tower. Fr. Cecconi looked up and saw that the man stumbled, grabbed for his ears, and lost his grip of the woman.

*****

Will heard the bell. He looked up to see the man let go of Beth, who fell below the railing and out of sight. Will dropped to the ground, lifting the Enfield up to his shoulder with elbows on the soft dirt all in one smooth motion. As he hit the ground, Will thought that this was exactly why he kept the rifle loaded: for situations like this. His drop to the earthen floor was the same motion he had used time after time during the war to cover the retreating Confederate Army. And there had been many retreats in the face of the ever-driving Sherman on his March to the Sea. Time and again valiant Confederate soldiers charged into the ranks of Sherman's forces only to be pushed back, retreating under the covering fire of the men in Will's special force. He and his group were always the last to retreat. They would cover the main army with rear fire then retreat to another position, drop, and shoot, repeating the process until pursuit stopped, all the while fleeing and dodging Union bullets. This was going to be just like another retreat.

He flipped up his elevated sight. He aimed. He was only going to get one shot. He squeezed off the round. He saw the man's body jerk backwards. He'd hit him. Will had hit Union officers at seven hundred yards with his specially equipped Enfield during the war. Brown's mistake was thinking five hundred yards was too far. Now Will had to take full advantage.

A shot rang out from Will's left. A bullet hit the dirt just to his left and ricocheted upward off the hard-packed terrain. Will felt the sharp hot sting of the bullet searing through the top of his buttock just at his lower back. It hurt, but he could tell it was superficial, and while it might bleed, there was nothing vital back there. Will rolled to his right, away from the oncoming gunman, moving to pull his handgun as he did.

The skinny gunman was laughing.

"Coming to get you, rancher. First, I started the fire to burn this city, and now I'm going to kill you, take your money, and destroy the rest of this town before leaving."

Will rolled onto his back, extending his right hand up off the dirt in the direction of the skinny gunman. He pulled off a round. He missed, but the gunman looked surprised at the accuracy of a quick shot without any real aim. He ducked and was about to shoot at Will again when Will heard a shot come from behind the thin gunman.

The skinny man turned and with only a brief glance saw a group of men charging down the slope at him. Another shot rang out. Skinny began to run north along the base of the church, which took him away from Will.

"You started the fire that burned my city, you son-of-a-bitch! I'll tear you apart single-handed!" Will could see a short solid man running at full speed right at the skinny gunman, red faced and yelling at the top of his lungs with a good Irish accent. There was no caution in the man's action. Will could also see the men that followed the yelling Irishman each waved a club of some sort.

That took two men out of the action.

Another bullet whizzed by Will's head. It had come from Brown.

Will rolled again to let his right arm now point north at Brown. He squeezed off a hasty round just to give himself some time to get a better shot. Brown dropped to one knee and fired again. He missed another time, but not by much. Will took better aim this time. He fired the fourth shot from his Navy Colt, leaving only two rounds. Brown flopped back, grabbing his left shoulder in the motion. Instinct pushed Will to follow up and finish Brown off. He stood to run at Brown who now rolled backwards away from him.

As he started running, a bullet ripped through the meaty portion of Will's left calf. He went down in agony. The shot had come from the man in the suit to his right. Pure luck to hit a man in motion, no less a leg. Will had almost forgotten about the man to the right. Will pulled a shot off in the suit's direction, but he hadn't aimed at all and knew the shot would be wide. His target must not have been a battle-hardened soldier, though. With the one shot in his direction, he turned to head east down the slope. But Will heard voices.

"Hold it right there, Millian. One more step, and you're a dead man. Would not like to cheat the hangman, but I'll kill you right here for the murder of Julia Bulette."

Will had no idea who had gotten the drop on the suit, but he saw the man dangle his gun off his fingers and raise his hands.

The suit's surrender removed a third gun from the battle. It only left Brown. Will struggled up and began to move to the north. His leg was bleeding. He looked up and saw Brown running to the far side of the church's foundation. Will half ran, half limped after him. He had to get Brown. There would never be any peace if he got away. Brown was the kind of man who'd keep coming back to avenge a day like today. It had to end here.

*****

Fr. Cecconi jumped backwards to avoid the falling body. He'd heard the man's body fall back against the bell and hit the floor only to have the burned and frayed edges give way beneath his weight. The body crashed down directly on top of the altar. Blood spurted everywhere. The man laid still. He didn't move.

Sr. Charity screamed. Fr. Cecconi moved toward her to shield her from the sight.

"Sister, you must go up to the tower to see if the woman is all right. But be careful. You cannot trust the floor. This man fell through, and I don't want you to do the same. We don't need any more sacrifices on the altar right now."

Sr. Charity lowered her hand from her mouth, her composure now returned. "That man is part of what has descended upon us these last few days. The altar is a good place for such a sacrifice."

Fr. Cecconi was mildly shocked at the venom in Sr. Charity's voice.

"Go, Sister. Go and check on the woman up there."

*****

Hurley rounded the back of the church to see the skinny gunman headed north past the burned-out train depot. He moved more cautiously as he entered open ground. He was following a man who could definitely use the gun he was carrying.

"Where's he going?" asked Dan Frisch, running alongside Hurley. Frisch was of German stock, thick and wide. He held his axe handle in one hand where it moved effortlessly as he ran along. It were as though he carried a fork or kitchen utensil.

"Looks like he's headed to what's left of the Consolidated Virginia works. There's metal machinery there that survived the fire. He'll probably use that for cover."

Frisch nodded. "We need to spread out. With Tom Gorman and the others, we should have enough to get men positioned all around him."

Hurley nodded in agreement. "Do it. Tell Gorman and the boys to surround him. But go careful. We've got time. There's nothing further north of the Consolidated, so he's got nowhere else to go. He's probably thinking he can pick us off one by one if he has cover."

"So how do we plan to get him? Stuart has our other gun. We have only one gun, same as him."

"Once we get all the boys into position, signal me, and I'll start to move at him while firing, hoping to drive him into one of you. Club him, and we'll drag him to the jail."

"Might work. But the boys will have to stay down if you're shooting. No telling what you might hit. Wouldn't want it to be one of us."

"We need a signal." Hurley paused in thought. "When I yell 601s, you all duck and stay behind cover. Then, if this guy moves, get him."

"But you may get hit. He could just stay behind something and shoot back."

"Maybe, but maybe he'll move looking for better cover. We've got to try. You heard this jerk; he started the fire! We've gotta get this one."

"Alright," said Frisch. "We'll spread out around him. But be careful."

Hurley waited until the men had time to disperse around the metal works, watching for some movement. He had to flush out the man's position. Maybe he'd be dumb enough to answer a taunt. Hurley figured they had nothing to lose so he yelled out, "Hey, skinny, you'll never leave this town alive! Either you're dead today, or the hangman's noose will be tightened around your scrawny little neck within a week."

"Not by you, Mick. You will not be the one to get me. Come and try. I'm waiting."

Hurley had hoped the man would answer. He could now tell he was behind the massive winch that lifted the cage up and down the main shaft to the mine. That shaft was over one thousand feet straight down.

"Oh, I'm comin' for you. Bet on it."

Hurley moved to his left, crawling low to the ground. The outer walls to the works had burned. They had been built entirely of wood. But the machinery that worked the mine was all metal. The metal was intact.

Hurley could see the man behind the large steel wheel attached to the steam winch.

"Six-o-ones are comin' at you, you son-of-a-bitch." Hurley aimed and pulled his trigger. He just missed hitting him in his right shoulder.

Startled, Elmer reached right and fired back at the now advancing Hurley. He lifted and ran to his left at the same time, looking back at Hurley, who was firing off a series of shots thinking it would cover his movement to another defensive position.

But Elmer was not watching his surroundings. As he moved, Dan Frisch stood up and swung his axe handle in a full arc, catching Elmer flush in his ribcage. The force of the blow lifted Elmer up off the floor and sent him flying. He landed on the mine shaft's collar, a smooth cement floor surrounding the edge of the main shaft, bounced and kept sliding. Lennox tried to grab the side of the cement wall as he passed over the edge, but there was nothing to grab on to. He slid into darkness. His scream could be heard for what seemed an infinite amount of time. There was no thump, no end. He just kept falling. Finally, the voice could not be heard.

Hurley stood at the edge of the shaft and looked down. "Fitting."

Frisch, still holding his handle, nodded in agreement. "He's just started his journey, but he's headed in the right direction."

*****

Will followed the trail of blood. Brown was definitely hit. But Will was leaving his own trail. The wound on his back stung but did not really restrict any movement. The leg was another story. There was a continual flow of his own blood from the lower limb. A steady flow was not something you liked, but it was not pulsing, which would have indicated an artery had been hit. Will stopped at the rear of the church, bent down, and wrapped his bandana around his leg. It might hold for a short time.

He looked along the north wall upslope toward the front of the church. He could see and hear voices and shots to his right at the Consolidated Virginia works. But there was no sign of Brown. Will flipped open his magazine but only had time to load two more rounds in from his belt as he limped up the side of the building toward the front entrance. That meant he had three rounds in his gun. They'd have to do. He held his gun out in front of him as he moved. The red line in the dirt told him Brown had taken the same path.

Will hesitated at the front corner of the church. He had no idea if Beth was alive or dead. He feared the worst. If she had survived, he thought he'd have heard her say something more. That she had been silent was not good. He peeked around toward the front door but saw no one. There were no puddles in the trail of blood, only intermittent red footprints. Without small pools of blood in spots, Will surmised that Brown had kept moving. The signs pointed to Brown heading right into the house of worship. Will followed the red footprints but stood for a moment at the main door to the church. He listened for any sounds. Then he heard voices.

"Leave him alone!" It was a woman's voice. "He's a priest!"

"He's gonna be a dead priest real quick if he keeps struggling."

Will could tell the male voice was Brown. He ducked into the foyer through the main door. Brown shot at Will just as he dove behind the last row of pews at the rear of the nave. Will looked up again over the top of the thick oak pew. Brown shot again just as Will ducked. That was four shots for Brown; only two were left unless he'd had time to reload, which based on the tracks he'd seen Will thought unlikely. In his dive into the church, Will caught a quick glimpse of Brown, who was still holding his shoulder. The grasp of his shoulder confirmed the chance that Brown reloaded was unlikely. Will had three rounds left.

"Rancher, stand up now or the priest dies."

"You are in a place of God."

Will recognized the voice of Fr. Cecconi.

"I'm here holding the gun, priest. God is nowhere near."

Will knelt and looked low around a pew up the center aisle. He didn't linger but pulled back around behind the pew. Brown was behind Fr. Cecconi. Sr. Charity was on the other side of the altar. Even in his quick look, he could see that Brown was struggling physically. He was bent over, and there were dark stains down half of his shirt and jacket. He had the look of a cornered animal. No telling how that animal might react in these circumstances.

"Stand up, rancher. I'm not gonna wait. The priest is dead if you don't stand."

Will knew if he stood, he'd be a wide-open target. But he knew a man like Brown would shoot Fr. Cecconi. He couldn't let that happen. Will rose slowly with his gun still in his right hand at his side, pointed down to the floor.

Brown moved further behind Fr. Cecconi, using him as a shield. There was no part of Brown visible around the priest except his head. Brown and Fr. Cecconi were still in front of the altar. Will was about sixty feet away from the man, but he could see the sweat on his flushed face. The wound was having an effect. The loss of blood was probably making it difficult to keep focused. The more he could delay, the better the chance of an opening. Brown's gun was behind the priest, probably jammed into his spine. But that was not a good spot when facing down another gun-hand.

"I'm listening, Brown."

"Hold your gun in your two fingers and raise up your right arm where I can see you drop it."

Another mistake, thought Will.

"Alright, move the priest away first. I don't want you to accidentally pull off a round and hit him."

"You don't get it, rancher. You don't set the terms here. Let me see you drop your gun."

Precious seconds passed. With each delay, Brown would lose more blood.

Will slowly raised his right arm forward before him. He held the trigger guard with his thumb and forefinger. His right arm was extended in the direction of Brown as he kept walking right at the man, closing the distance with each step.

"That's right, rancher. Let me see it. That's good. Now drop it."

"It's right there Brown, you can see it." He kept walking. He was now close to thirty feet from Brown and Fr. Cecconi.

"Drop it, drop it now or the priest is dead."

In a singular movement Will spun the gun around in his hand, aimed, and shot Brown hitting him flush in the cheekbone. Brown fell back against the altar in something close to a sitting position. Fr.

Cecconi was now to the side and out of the direct line of fire. Will had two rounds left. Instinct more than thought moved Will up the main aisle of the church. After two steps, he shot the now exposed Brown. Two more steps, and he pulled off another round. Both found their mark in the slumped man's chest. But Brown's eyes still had life. Brown tried to raise up his gun, and Will remembered the man still had two rounds left. *Stupid. I should have saved a round until I got closer.* Will had let his emotions get the better of him. This was the man who took Luke and Sean and might have killed Beth. Those two last shots were for them. Brown raised up his gun in a trembling hand. Will simply looked at him. If he were going to shoot, there was nothing Will could do about it.

"No more." The voice was Fr. Cecconi's. Fr. Cecconi kicked at Brown's lifting arm, separating the gun from his weakened grip. The gun skidded across the marble floor. Brown's eyes stared at Will for an instant and then closed. He was dead.

Will sat in a heap in the first row pew next to the aisle. He stared at the dead man. In a tone devoid of emotion, he said, "Father, I am sorry for shooting a gun here in your church." Will's eyes never left the dead man. "I would normally say that I was sorry for killing a man, but I am not sorry at all about shooting this one, nor the one behind him on the altar."

Will's head slumped as his elbows caught his upper body weight on his knees. He looked up at the priest. "She's dead, isn't she? I loved her but never told her so. I should have held her close long ago, Father, but I didn't. Now she's gone." Will ended with a drop of his head and looked at the floor between his feet.

Fr. Cecconi looked at Will. "I believe Beth is still alive. Sr. Charity went up to check on her after this man fell through the ceiling. She was on her way back to get some wet rags to clean Beth's wounds. Battered and bruised as she is, she's alive, laying still up in the bell tower."

Will's face, body, and entire being lifted as if raised from some dark depth. He had collapsed down on this oak pew bleeding scarlet hope out of his own body, crushed by the thought Beth was dead. Life had no prospect of light had she passed. "She's alive?"

"Yes. Go to her. She needs to be held. She needs to see what I see in your face here."

Will turned and began running to the stairs.

"But for God's sake be careful of the floor!"

"Father, you should be careful how you use our Lord's name." Sr. Charity had a school nun's disciplinary expression on her face. But she grinned. "Did you see his face, Father? Pure joy. He loves her, doesn't he?"

"Yes, there is love in this building. Can't deny it."

"You saved her by ringing the bell. What made you think of that?"

"That ray of sunlight hit the bell and reflected right down in my face. I'd have to be daft not to have then realized ringing the bell would startle the man. Remarkable, a single ray of light on a cloud covered day."

"And where do you think that ray of light came from?"

Fr. Cecconi was still looking in Will's direction toward the stairs. "I think you know, Sister. You had asked why we've been tested. I cannot answer the why, but I think I can affirm that if the test were to find out if there was any love left in this world, the answer was found in Will Toal's face. I think He sent the horsemen and later changed His mind. But someone had to earn it. Will Toal earned it, maybe for all of us. He's the one good man Lot could not find. It's a theme I can use in Sunday's homily."

Fr. Cecconi turned to face Sr. Charity. "Let's clean up the altar."

Chapter Thirty-Seven

1873 March
Virginia City, NV

John Mackay sat in the Washoe Club. The day was quiet, a marked change from the events of the recent past. James Fair again sat next to him. Both men had come to relax. Both felt they deserved a respite. Then word came about today's newspaper: an article of special importance would be in the Territorial Enterprise. Now the two sat in their respective club chair reading with heightened anticipation. Pages fanned out before them.

They were reading the advanced copies of De Quille's article. Both were going as fast as they could to get to the ultimate conclusion printed by De Quille. Though both started at the same time, Mackay had always struggled with the English language. He read far slower than Fair.

Fair virtually threw down his copy of the paper and stood. He turned and looked down at Mackay.

"So, John. Looks like your idea of taking De Quille down into the mine has borne fruit. Have you finished the article yet?"

"I'm close. I haven't finished it yet, but it looks quite good so far."

"Quite good? That's all you would say? I think it's fabulous. It couldn't have come out any better if we'd written it ourselves."

"He did like the quality of the ore and says his three assay's confirmed it is of the highest grade."

"That's all well and good, but the best part is his description of the size. He goes into great detail to describe the size. I'm going to spoil your reading. Just head to the last sentence. He calls it the Big Bonanza. He calls us the Bonanza Kings. Doesn't get much better than that."

Mackay smiled, "Yes, I suppose it is what he describes, the Big Bonanza."

Fair returned the smile, the satisfaction. "Grant should be happy."

Mackay set down his paper. "Yes, Grant should be happy. Now maybe we can mine some ore and get the country back on its feet."

*****

Bishop Manogue had finally arrived back in Virginia City, freeing Fr. Cecconi to return home. The Archbishop of San Francisco had required his stay be extended far longer than originally anticipated. Fr. Cecconi smiled as he remembered the bishop first walking into his burned-out place of worship.

"I leave for close to a month and look what you've done to my church!"

"It was a terrible fire, Bishop. We are lucky we saved what we could."

Sr. Charity had stood nearby and looked frozen in fear as she tried to defend the current state of affairs, no doubt preferring to be anywhere else in the world other than standing before her upset bishop. But the bishop had then smiled. Fr. Cecconi recalled his own immediate relief.

"I speak in jest. It sounds to me that both you and Fr. Cecconi have done a remarkable job of providing for our parishioners in a time of great need. You are a credit to your orders. I will tell the archbishop as much."

"It was a trying time, Bishop." Sr. Charity's frozen exterior had begun to melt just a bit, enough to allow a tentative comment.

Then the Bishop had said, "From what I heard and read in the papers, it was not just *trying*. It sounded more like an ordeal, a tribulation the likes of which we've not seen before. First flood, then fire, then murder, then a shoot-out. People were dispossessed. The mines were almost lost in the blaze. What wasn't washed away in the deluge was later reduced to ash in the conflagration."

Fr. Cecconi had responded. "The reports you read were accurate, but the combination of the events magnified the effect for those in the middle of it."

Manogue nodded. "I am sure that unless you were here to experience it firsthand, one could not understand the difficulties faced."

The bishop then asked the most interesting question. "Father, don't you find it curious that two of the men you saw riding out of the horizon weeks ago ended up dead at our altar?"

"I did find it most curious, but after giving it much thought, maybe it was quite appropriate."

Bishop Manogue nodded. "Maybe it *was* quite appropriate."

*****

Fr. Cecconi had taken his time riding home. He'd spent the night in Mound House but now hoped to make Carson City by the end of the day. Around his shoulders hung a cassock which had been clean at journey's start but now smelled of sweat and horse. His body sagged more than usual as he rode, a combination of exhaustion and relief. He thought about the ten years of college he'd been required to attend before he could be ordained as a Jesuit. Those years included a strong dose of theology. The constant sway of the horse's gait rocked his consciousness to the border of sleep. But even in this state of diminished intellectual inhibition, thoughts of these last few weeks would not rest.

Was there anything in that long period of education he could draw from to make sense of what had transpired? As he left Virginia City, there was a hum of activity to rebuild the city. It would rise again.

Humanity's history encompassed cycle after cycle of death and renewal. Several religions, his own included, revered such cycles. The Catholic and Protestant faiths believed in the renewal of baptism: a dying to then be risen. Buddhists, Hindus, and even Native Americans believed in forms of cessation followed by a new cycle of life. In these recent weeks, had he just witnessed another of humanity's rebirths?

His horse stopped at the top of a crest overlooking the Carson Valley, a natural hiatus. It was a small rise but high enough to see all the way to the crest of the snow-covered peaks on the west side of the valley. That snow provided water to keep the valley green almost year-round. But here in the approach of spring, it was greener than ever. He could see specks of cattle grazing. In the far distance stood the small town of Carson City with the dome of the legislature shining in the sunlight. It was all surrounded by ever spreading grass, a pervasive verdant green.

Speaking as if he wanted someone else to hear, he said, "I had harbored doubts about the future when I saw those four horsemen. But this valley never looked more like Eden than right now."

Father Cecconi made the sign of the cross. It seemed appropriate for reasons he could not completely explain. He reached down to stroke the fur at the base of his mount's neck, consciously focused on the touch of another being. He spoke to the animal as if it were one of his flock. "We were almost here at the same spot some weeks ago on the way to Virginia City when we stopped to see that small dust cloud to the east. I made the sign of the cross that day in fear. Based on what followed, that fear was justified. But today, here on that same rise but now looking west, I feel a new beginning. I feel hope."

His heels touched his old horse in a silent instruction to move ahead and follow the road back to his regular parish. He wondered how many times he'd tell the story of Will Toal and Virginia City.

Chapter Thirty-Eight

1873 March
Toal Ranch- Jack's Valley, NV

Will stood up from dinner. Scents of cooling cooked meat wafted throughout the room that functioned as both a place to eat and collect. He saw Beth watch his movements as if trying to read his mind by physical action. They had spent two days in the Mackay Mansion waiting for Beth to recover enough to ride. But she had wanted to get back home to Luke and Sean. Will did too. It'd been over two weeks since they'd left the mansion. Beth was physically recovered; at least, she looked fine to Will. But she'd been cool, distant. He'd wondered if there wasn't some mental injury that would take longer to heal. He'd seen it in the war. Men who'd been injured might recover physically, but their heads were never the same. Beth had been through a war.

Will watched Beth from across the table and waited for everyone to finish their meal. Hoping she would agree, he suggested, "It's a warm night for this time of year. Let's take a walk."

Beth offered a questioning look at María, who immediately knew why.

"Go, *Señora*, I will take care of the dishes and Juan will see to the *Niño*s."

Beth rose, "Juan brought the boys all the way back from Mound House by himself, but he's probably going to find it more difficult to get them into bed."

Juan rose from the table and looked at the twins, "Ah *Señora,* Juan is a man of many talents."

Apparently comfortable with the arrangements, Beth then swiveled standing next to the table to cast Will an indiscernible yet feminine look. He noticed a faint crinkles form at the corner of her mouth. It could be the start of a smile, something he had not seen in days if not weeks.

"Let me get a shawl."

He stood just outside the doorway until she joined him.

"You look like you're staring out into space."

Will turned. The light inside silhouetted her figure in the doorway. His eyes lingered on the vision until he stumbled out of his temporary trance. "I was looking at the spot we might build the new bunkhouse. With the money Mr. Mackay gave us, we can build something that might sleep four or five men."

"Gave *us* money?" There was a bit of query in Beth's manner.

Will responded in a matter of fact of tone. "Yes, us. You were sitting right there when he said it. He wanted us, both of us, to have the money."

"It was certainly nice of Mr. Mackay to insist."

"I told him Sam Brown obviously wasn't going to get it nor any of his men, so he should take it back. But Mackay is a man who is used to getting his way. It was impossible to refuse him."

"He seemed most thankful for what you'd done. He acted as if it wasn't a lot of money, but the offer sounded heartfelt to me. He was most gracious. And I loved his house. I certainly wouldn't have gone to Paris if I was his wife. I'd never leave that house."

"It was big, I'll give it that."

Luke and Sean ran up to Beth as she stood next to Will. "Can we go to the barn? We want to brush the horses."

Beth shook her head. "No, it's dark. You know you're not supposed to be in the barn in the dark."

Disappointment registered on both faces. A voice came from within the house.

"*Niño's* come to the house. It is time for sleep. You must get ready. Juan, you must get them back in to the casa. If you no do this easy job, how are you ever to take care of your own little vaquero?"

Everyone could see the startled look on Juan's unsuspecting face. Evidently, Maria might have some news to deliver later.

Beth then reached for the boys. "Here, give me a hug, and run along to María." Beth lifted first one and then the other in a big hug. Will watched as they trudged into the house somewhat unhappily.

Will tried to hide a look of puzzlement. "They do mind María. She says go, and they go. I say go, and they ask, 'why?'"

"That's because they know how to manipulate their father. You would have let them go to the barn and brush the horses."

"Horses could always use a good brush."

"Like I said, the boys know how to control you."

"I've faced gunmen who don't question my intentions as much."

"They're your boys, not some gunmen."

Thinking to change the subject, Will reached for Beth's hand. He hadn't done that in some time. "Let's walk out to the Carson River."

"To the river?" A full smile now spread across her face. He knew immediately that smile was for him. He pulled her closer and dropped her hand but reached out and put his arm around her waist. Though it had been years since he'd held Beth this way, it seemed natural to him.

She did not resist. In fact, he felt her lean a little more into his side. The sensation was stirring.

Trying to seem casual though his heartbeat increased with each step, Will offered, "Remember our walk out here on another evening several years ago?"

She looked at him with a sarcastic smile. "Do you think I would forget?"

"We ended up making a couple of babies on that walk."

They reached the bank of the river and stopped. On their trip to this same spot years before, Will remembered Beth had been the one to push intimacy. She made no such move here tonight. But it had been his suggestion to walk here to this place, this special place between them.

He looked up. "Stars again. There were lots of stars that night. And the moon was special."

"Of course. I will never forget the sliver of the moon winking at us."

"Tonight, the moon looks huge, like a big eye watching."

"Will Toal, you will never be a poet." She grinned as she said it.

Will turned to Beth and took both of her hands and sank to one knee. He looked up directly into her eyes. She could not conceal a tiny gasp of anticipation.

"Elizabeth Armstrong, will you marry me? I love you, always have. The shoot-out in the church finally made it clear that I never want to lose you. You are as much a part of me as are our sons. I want to take care of you and them for the rest of our days if you'll have me."

Will watched as what initially looked like shock melted into a knowing smile. Moisture began to build in her eyes. She slowly dropped to her knees and looked him in the face.

"Will Toal, you sure took your time. But right now, I'm the happiest I've been in my life. Yes, I will marry you. The sooner the better."

Will grinned. "Maybe we can make some more babies. A girl would be nice."

"It could be another set of twins."

As he did those years ago, Will took off his jacket and laid it between them. He stood to his full height and pulled Beth to him in a long overdue embrace. He wrapped his arms around her and kissed her deeply. The contours of her figure pressed against him. He felt the quickening of her breath and sensed her longing too. Emotions pent up for years soared to the surface. He pulled away to look again to make sure his earlier question met with her approval. Her eyes and the smile told him all he needed to know. He began to unbutton her bodice.

"The moon may keep watching with its big eye."

Beth smiled and flipped the hair away from her face. "Let him watch."

From the Author

FACT FROM FICTION

As I indicate in my previous book *Railroaded*, I have always admired the works of Steve Berry. He picks wonderful historical events, each one possessed with a bit of mystery. Then he weaves fascinating stories creating more intrigue on top of the true history. At the conclusion of each of his books, Mr. Berry includes a section acknowledging fictional additions and points out the often-surprising facts. The following is my humble attempt to imitate Mr. Berry and identify some of the events in the *Silver City Reckoning* story which actually did take place.

CHAPTER 1

Bishop Patrick Manogue was a miner, priest, and, later, a bishop. He was born in Kilkenny, Ireland, migrating to America to join the Gold Rush. Unlike most, he had great success but used his newfound money to pay his way back to France to study in the Saint-Sulpice Seminary. He returned to Nevada, which was in great need of priests, and was then assigned to Virginia City. It was Bishop Manogue who would ultimately supervise the construction of St. Mary's of the Mountains Catholic Church, which still stands today. (See *Nevada's Bonanza Church Saint Mary's in the Mountains* by Virgil Bucchianeri, p. 15-16). But there was no Fr. Cecconi, S.J.

The four horsemen of the story spring forth from biblical imagery:

Then I saw when the Lamb broke one of the seven seals, and I heard one of the four living creatures saying as with a voice of thunder, 'Come.' I looked, and behold, a white horse, and he who sat on it had a bow; and a crown was given to him, and he went out conquering and to conquer.

—Revelation 6:1-2

Then another horse came out, a fiery red one. Its rider was given power to take peace from the earth and to make people kill each other. To him was given a large sword.

—Revelation 6:4

When the Lamb opened the third seal, I heard the third living creature say, "Come!" I looked, and there before me was a black horse! Its rider was holding a pair of scales in his hand.

—Revelation 6:5

When the Lamb opened the fourth seal, I head the voice of the fourth living creature say, "Come!" I looked up and saw a horse whose color was pale green. Its rider was named Death, and his companion was the Grave.

—Revelations 6:7-8

Sam Brown was one of the most vicious outlaws in the history of both Virginia City and neighboring Carson City. Known to have murdered at least six men in broad daylight and many in front of numerous witnesses, it was thought he had committed several others. He met his demise when he was gunned down with a shotgun by a citizen who was described as "easy going" on the streets of Virginia City. The citizen later commented, "enough was enough." (See *Virginia City and the Silver Region of the Comstock Lode* by Douglas McDonald, p. 61).

As further evidence of the vicious nature of Sam Brown, the following was written by Dan DeQuille, a newspaper reporter for the Virginia City Territorial Enterprise:

"In order to signalize his arrival and let it be known that he was no *King Log*, Sam Brown committed a murder soon after reaching Virginia [City]. He picked a quarrel one night in a saloon with a man who was so drunk that he did not know what he was saying, ripped him up with his bowie-knife, killing him instantly; then, wiping his knife on the leg of his pantaloons, walked across the saloon, lay down on a bench and went to sleep. . . . Sam had then killed about fifteen men, doubtless much in the same way as he killed the last man." See *The Big Bonanza* by Dan Dequille, American Publishing, Co. Hartford, CT. 1876.

CHAPTER 2

Millard Luce Cattle Co. is a thinly veiled name change for the Miller Lux Cattle Co. as outlined in more detail in my book *Railroaded*, Book 1 in the Will Toal series. Run by meticulous Henry Miller, the company, upon his death, owned over a million acres of cattle ranches from Oregon into Nevada and down as far south as Bakersfield, CA. (See *The Cattle King: The Biography of Henry Miller,* By Edward F. Treadwell c. 1931. San Francisco: Western Tanager Press 1981).

Joseph R. Walker was one of the true mountain men. I have attempted to summarize the extraordinary exploits of this straightforward, humble man. His initial travels from the Rockies to California and back were chronicled by a scribe appointed by Benjamin Bonneville: Zenas Leonard. (See *Adventures of a Mountain Man* by Zenas Leonard). For a wonderful, detailed history of Joe Walker's life, see *Westering Man: The Life of Joseph Walker, by Bill Gilbert. (See also the article "The Fur Trade Role In Western Expansion" by Ned Eddins).*

CHAPTER 3

John William Mackay (pronounced Mackie) was the mining genius and operations leader of the four investors who became known as the Bonanza Kings. The four were principals in a company called Flood &

O'Brien based in San Francisco. But the real source of their wealth originated in a series of Virginia City silver mines purchased at the suggestion of Mackay. I have tried to accurately portray Mackay's personality and strengths both in business acumen, as a co-worker, and leader of men. He and Jack O'Brien did walk from Downieville to Virginia City and, upon arrival, had but fifty cents between them. Mackay told the story over and over through the years of O'Brien throwing that coin away before they reached town. But Mackay never found it funny. (See The Bonanza King by Gregory Crouch. Scribner).

The Washoe Club was a club of the wealthiest men in Virginia City at the height of the Comstock Lode. It was, and still is, located at 112 S. C Street in downtown Virginia City. While quite exclusive in 1873, today, anyone can walk in and see the same wall hangings from the 1870s, including a picture of the globe that might have provided inspiration Club members who amassed extraordinary sums of money.

CHAPTER 6

The Mackay Mansion was built in 1860 for a young George Hearst (Father of William Randolph Hearst and San Simeon fame) when he was indeed the superintendent of the Gould and Curry Mine just as represented in my story. Descriptions of the home are also as accurate as I can be. I personally have been in the house twice. It now stands as something of a museum and historical residence. Anyone can enter and marvel at the preservation of 1870's life of a millionaire. However, while I have John Mackay living in the mansion in 1873, he did not buy the property until 1875 after the great fire when his previous home was burned. I have changed those dates for my own purpose here in the story.

John Mackay married Marie Louise Bryant in 1867. Mackay had managed his money to enter into a partnership with J.M. Walker to buy the Bullion Mine in 1863. It did not do well, but the two then bought the Kentuck Mine during the stock depression of 1865. A minor bonanza found at the Kentuck brought Mackay his first million dollars. He bought out Walker for six hundred thousand dollars, a princely sum in the day. With some of the remainder, Mackay built a small frame house at the corner of Taylor and Howard streets in which he and Marie lived. Marie hated Virginia City. She thought it much too uncivilized. Mackay was anything but ostentatious. He was much the opposite. Yet he loved his wife dearly by all accounts. While it is difficult to read the mind of someone long since passed, Mackay might have bought this grandiose house built by Hearst to make Marie happy. It did not work. She would leave Virginia City and move to Paris where Mackay would build her an even more luxurious mansion in which she would live for two decades, holding lavish parties, hosting all manner of rich and royal. *(See Douglas McDonald's Virginia City and the Silver Region of the Comstock Lode, p. 98).*

I have no information regarding any relationship between John Mackay and Henry Miller of the Miller Lux Cattle Co. While both were pillars of the San Francisco financial world at that time, this connection is purely fiction of my own creation.

The Big Bonanza ore find occurred just about the time as described in the story. The massive discovery, coupled with the crash created by the Coinage Act, made for extraordinarily volatile times in a city and set of markets that were already the most unpredictable the world had ever seen. This combination of events in the history of the West originally drew me to the story. Before the Big Bonanza, the biggest vein found in the Comstock happened at the Ophir. Described as approximately fifteen to twenty-one feet in diameter, it made its owners a fortune. To give some context as to the magnanimity of the Big Bonanza, the vein of extremely high-grade ore found by Mackay and Fair ended up being over two hundred feet in diameter with estimates as high as six hundred feet across in some places and thousands of feet long. The Big Bonanza dwarfed other mineral finds throughout the history of mining in the United States up to present day.

It was common practice on the Comstock for mine owners to keep miners down in the mine after the discovery of a new vein. The temptation of stock speculation at a time and place without restriction of insider trading was just too great. Stories of stock manipulation both in the local Virginia City markets and the San Francisco markets are legend. The inflation of the stock price from sixty-two dollars to six-hundred and seventy-five dollars in the Savage Mine, which took place in 1872 by keeping men down in the shafts, did take place as represented in the story. *(See Douglas McDonald's Virginia City and the Silver Region of the Comstock Lode, p. 111)*. But Mackay and Fair never wanted to play the stock speculation game. They wanted to make their money from mining operations. I have no information that Mackay held his crew below grade after the discovery of the Big Bonanza, but I have used this fairly common practice in a manner I speculate Mackay might have done while providing for his men, always an utmost concern of Mackay. The use of the practice here by Mackay is purely for purposes of my story to create a second level of the two-week time limitation to match the timing for Will Toal's requirement to generate cash to get his sons back.

Duane Bliss is described accurately. He came to both Carson and Virginia City and worked in the Bank of California under William Sharon and later left to create the Carson Tahoe Lumber & Fluming Co. along with Darius Ogden Mills, another historic California financier.

CHAPTER 9

The practice of square setting open space after ore had been mined originated in Virginia City. The original mines, the Mexican, Ophir, and Yellow Jacket, tried to work from slanted entry shafts supported by standard timbers along the way. But ore veins were too big, and the mining process required the removal of tons of dirt mixed in with the ore. Huge unsupported holes were left. As the soil was soft, collapses were common. No one could devise a solution until Philip Deidesheimer, a German-trained mining engineer, was called in to inspect the Ophir in 1860. He devised a system of wooden cubes eight feet square and made of twelve-inch by twelve-inch timbers. As soon as enough material was removed to create that large a space, the timbers were placed in such a manner that no nails or bolts were required. The system was first used in the Ophir in 1861 with success. Soon, the entire Comstock used the same system. It became a requirement for any of the mining unions before they would allow their men down below the surface. Deidesheimer never patented his invention. He intentionally gave it to all the different mines for the benefit of the miner's safety. As the Comstock ultimately disgorged over $1.5 billion dollars in 1870's money, Deidesheimer walked away from a fortune. *(See Douglas McDonald's Virginia City and the Silver Region of the Comstock Lode, p. 64-65).*

Fair and Mackay did use a telegraphic code to communicate with Jim Flood and William O'Brien at their brokerage office on Montgomery Street in San Francisco. Again, in a world with no limitation on insider information, Jim Flood was free to use advanced knowledge to the financial advantage of the Bonanza Kings in the San Francisco Markets, and he did so frequently. William Sharon, the force behind the Bank of California, used the practice to an even higher degree in both Virginia City and San Francisco. *(See The Bonanza King by Gregory Crouch).*

There was a vigilante-like group in Virginia City known as the 601s. A secretive group, they stepped in when law enforcement failed to effectuate what the public thought was appropriate justice. Two trouble causing men were asked by the 601s to leave after various criminal activity went unpunished. The group would place a note on one of the felonious individual's door or tent flap stating, "Leave, 601s." The first man so notified did not leave. He was found hung from a rope at the top of the mine entrance where he had been employed as a symbol for all to see. A note was pinned to the body which simply read "601s." The second man notified immediately left town after the hanging. Word got around, and serious crime was remarkably diminished in Virginia City for years, especially when compared to the complete lawlessness found in other mining towns, such as Tombstone and Bodie. *(See Douglas McDonald's Virginia City and the Silver Region of the Comstock Lode, p. 60-62).*

CHAPTER 10

William Ralston and William Sharon were partners, along with Darius O. Mills, in creating and incorporating the Bank of California. This bank was the main force financing the early Comstock capital needs, which were substantial. As indicated in the book, Ralston was the builder of the Palace Hotel on Market Street in San Francisco, which still exists. But it broke him financially. Ralston ultimately finished the Palace in 1875 but at a total cost of over five million dollars. *(See "A Brief Illustrated History of the Palace Hotel of San Francisco" by Bruce C. Cooper).*

The Bank of California's loss of the Consolidated and California Mines, thereby missing out on the Big Bonanza, also contributed to Ralston's eventual financial demise. Soon after the announcement of the Big Bonanza, the Bank of California started a slow steady decline. Ralston continued to suffer the combined losses from both the bank and the Palace. In early 1875, he put his affairs in order, left his office, and went swimming in the San Francisco Bay. His body washed up two days later. *(See Douglas McDonald's Virginia City and the Silver Region of the Comstock Lode, p. 30-31).*

The Coinage Act (officially termed the Mint Act) of 1873 was indeed finally passed and signed into law by President Ulysses S. Grant on February 12, 1873, just as represented in the story. While it passed with little fanfare and almost no debate, following its passage came tremendous accusations of bribery, fraud, and legislative manipulation. The Comstock Lode already flooded the international markets with silver. The actual value of the metal in a silver dollar had dropped to seventy-five cents. Governments were dealing with a run on their gold reserves as financial money markets started buying silver dollars only to purchase gold coin of supposed equal value but saving twenty-five cents per dollar in the process. Germany reacted by demonetizing silver to protect their gold. The United States followed suit. However, the result upset financial markets even more than if they had left the bimetal standard intact. There was a severe crash of 1873 and a resultant depression which lasted almost ten years. *(See Neil Carothers' Fractional Money: A History of the Small Coins and Fractional Paper Currency of the United States, p. 249).*

William Sharon was indeed the president of the Bank of California. I have tried to be faithful to the history of his activities in Virginia City regarding the Bank of California, the mines he took over, the stamping and milling operations, the Virginia & Truckee Railroad he built, and his interactions with Mackay. It was indeed Sharon who gave Mackay permission to use the Gould's shaft to begin his crosscut, which eventually found the Big Bonanza. Sharon thought that by making the offer, he gave Mackay a length of rope with which to hang himself financially. He has been quoted to have said, "I'll help those Irishmen lose some of their Hale & Norcross money" just as represented in the story.

It is one of the most interesting ironies in history that this man who was so competitive and responsible for so much of the initial capitalization of Virginia City's entire mining business was the one who gave Mackay the opportunity to find what became the largest body of valuable metallic ore ever found in United States' history. *(See Douglas McDonald's Virginia City and the Silver Region of the Comstock Lode, p. 29).*

Samuel Clemens, aka Mark Twain, did work at the Virginia City Territorial Enterprise newspaper from about 1862 to 1864. During his time at the Enterprise, Clemens took on the pen name Mark Twain. Both he and William Wright, aka Dan De Quille, wrote humor for the paper. De Quille would later write the seminal story of the Virginia City mining heyday called "The Bonanza Kings" both financed and promoted by Mark Twain. But De Quille never achieved the fame Twain did. It is Dan De DeQuille who tells the tale of how Clemens came to be known by his pen name as represented in the story. De Quille remained in Virginia City for over thirty years. He saw the beginnings of the bonanza and stayed until everything had completely played out. *(See Douglas McDonald's Virginia City and the Silver Region of the Comstock Lode, p. 68-70).*

Mark Twain did leave Virginia City for San Francisco circa 1864 to avoid a duel challenge from James Laird, who championed a woman Twain had insulted in an article. The ensuing buildup was carried by papers all the way to San Francisco. Anticipation for the upcoming event became so intense that Twain could not simply decline. So, he left town. *(See Douglas McDonald's Virginia City and the Silver Region of the Comstock Lode, p. 69-70).* He did return some ten years later, about the time of our story here. But he did not report on the Big Bonanza.

CHAPTER 12

Julia Bulette, an English-born woman, did reside in a rented house at the corner of Union and D Street. She was what one might call a sophisticated courtesan. The regular working girls stayed in tent cribs further toward the north and end of town on D Street. Julia was a huge contributor to the volunteer fire department. Despite her obvious stain on social standing, she became an honorary member of Engine Co. 1. Below is a picture of Julia with an honorary helmet from Engine Co. 1.

CHAPTER 13

The Coinage Act did cause a crash first in the mining markets beginning on February 25, 1873, but ultimately spread to a massive global downturn. A worldwide depression lasted for over ten years. The drop in price for the Consolidated and California mining operations were as represented in the story. *(See The Bonanza King by Gregory Crouch).*

CHAPTER 17

Virginia City did experience a massive fire but it did not occur at the time represented. The Great fire started on October 26,1875. It started in a lodging house. I have altered the date to fit the story here. Many lives were lost. It took the community several months if not a full year to recover. It devastated an entire one-half square mile of the central city. The fire fighters had to use dynamite to destroy swaths of buildings in order to stop the fire. Most of the mines were covered but the Ophir did have fire head down its shaft for over four hundred feet. Over ten million dollars-worth of damage was done. Over two thousand people were left homeless. All the buildings in the central city were burned to the ground. None were saved as in our story. But the rebuilding began immediately. Many of the business used brick and mortar in the rebuild and those buildings stand today.

CHAPTER 19

St. Mary's, then a wood church, burned completely in the great fire of 1875. During the fire, John Mackay did personally work to seal the collar of the Consolidated. While doing so, one of the nuns from St. Mary's did come up to John Mackay while he worked frantically to seal the mine, asking if he could help save the church. He uttered the words as stated in the story. The church's brick structure described in the story was actually built after the Great Fire. Mackay was the main contributor funding the rebuild of the church, which still exists in the same form today. (See *Virginia City and the Silver Region of the Comstock Lode* by Douglas McDonald, *p. 31-38).*

CHAPTER 23

The Molinelli Hotel was probably the fanciest hotel in Virginia City before the fire. It was burned completely to the ground as in the story here. A much larger and much more luxurious hotel called the International was constructed near the original location of the Molinelli. The

International served as the most sophisticated hotel between San Francisco and St. Louis for almost seventy years.

The telegram from President Grant to John Mackay is my own fiction. However, Grant would later comment that signing the Coinage Act was a mistake. Grant did visit Virginia City as the guest of John Mackay. However, he did not arrive until after he served out his last term as president. Grant and his wife took a trip, a world tour, after he left office. One of his first stops was Virginia City. I could not find out how or why, but somehow, during his stay, he obtained stock in some of the Mackay mines, which quickly generated a profit in excess of twenty-five thousand dollars for the ex-president. That would be the equivalent of four hundred fifty-four thousand dollars in 2020 money. Grant used the money and the vast bulk of his own personal funds to finance a trip, which for two and a half years literally did take both he and his wife around the world. At the end of the trip, Grant was broke. He returned to New York where his daughter lived. In his later years, suffering from cancer of the throat, he started his memoirs, which would ultimately be a financial success. But Grant would not live to enjoy those fruits. He died in Wilton, New York, virtually penniless, so much so that ex-soldiers helped pay for his funeral.

Below is a picture of U.S. Grant along with his wife as they made their way into the mines with John Mackay and James Fair in 1879. President Grant and his wife are in the center. Mackay is to the far left and Fair is to the far right.

CHAPTER 25

William Sharon did conceive, finance, and execute the construction of the Virginia & Truckee Railroad. Before the railroad, all supplies came into the town via wagons drawn by either teams of horses, mules, or oxen. The ore was carried out of town to the stamp mills along the Carson River in and about the city of Mound House for processing also via wagon. The V & T changed all of that. Sharon and the Bank of California owned up to seven mines at one time in Virginia City. He also owned several stamp mills. Silver ore had to be processed in these stamp mills before it could be reduced to bullion. With the construction of the V & T, he came close to monopolizing the entire processing of silver ore and the supply of Virginia City itself. He was always Mackay's biggest competitor. (*See Douglas McDonald's Virginia City and the Silver Region of the Comstock Lode pp. 19-31).*

Ralston and Sharon comment on the fact that the Carson City lumber yard for Duane Bliss's Carson Tahoe Lumber & Fluming Co. was at least a mile long stacked with both rough cut ten- and twelve-inch timbers for square setting. However, old pictures of that lumber yard also show lumber of every other length and width for building and roofing. Ultimately, Bliss and his lumber company owned almost twenty-one miles of the eastern shore of Lake Tahoe, which was virtually clear-cut to fill the lumber yard. Bliss's son and later generations lost most of their Tahoe land holdings in the crash of 1929. But the demand for lumber made Duane Bliss one of the richest men in Carson City. (See the picture below which shows the Carson Tahoe lumber yard in Carson City).

The V & T engine houses were impressive. The horseshoe-shaped main structure was roughly two hundred by three hundred feet and built out of the same native sandstone as the Capitol, the Mint, and other buildings around town. The engine works were designed by Abraham Curry, an early settler of Genoa and Carson City. Curry was one of the most prominent citizens of the budding Nevada Territory. Starting as the owner-partner of a general store, and later hotels, he rode the immigration onslaught following the discovery of the silver bonanza to become the first commissioner of the Mint and de facto Lt. Governor of the Territory. When statehood was approved, Curry donated ten acres for the construction of the State Capitol building. In his later years, he supervised construction of the V & T Railroad depot and engine house. When the engine house was completed, there were eleven full-size bays where a locomotive could be brought in for repairs or maintenance. The building also housed an iron foundry and fabrication shop that built machinery not only for the railroad but for other businesses in the area.

Church bells and flagpoles were just some of the items constructed here along with railroad parts.

As the years went on, mining activity decreased on the Comstock, and the V & T moved on to hauling passengers and agricultural freight to stay viable, even opening a line to Douglas County. But as the railroad declined and sold off its engines, the shops were needed less and less.

The picture below was taken in 1939, right around the time service to Virginia City stopped. There are seven engines here, which was probably the entire roster of the V & T at the time. The paint shops and foundry had already been closed, and parts of the building were falling into disuse. By the time the photo was taken, the Virginia & Truckee was a dying railroad.

The railroad was dying, but it was not dead yet. Service to Virginia City may have stopped in 1939, but the railroad still ran daily routes to Minden and Reno. It wasn't until 1950 that the line was finally shut down and the last of the equipment sold. The rails were pulled up soon after, and the shop building shuttered.

The building was already in deteriorating shape in 1950 and being abandoned didn't help any. Over the next few decades, neglect produced more decay, the roof caved in, the doors rusted, and wild animals took up residence. By the 1980s, the building was seen as a public hazard, and although there was interest from preservationists to save it, nobody was coming forward with any money to do the necessary renovations.

In the late 1980s, time finally ran out for the old V & T shops. The building was torn down, dismantled brick by brick. The sandstone blocks were sent to Napa Valley to build a winery. The land they sat on, two full city blocks now surrounded by hotels and shopping, was put up for sale. (See *The Silver Short Line: A History of the Virginia & Truckee Railroad*, by Ted Wurm and Harre W. Demoro). The V & T was actually a separate business venture from the Bank of California and the mining interests of William Sharon, Darius Ogden Mills, and William Ralston. The ownership of the mines that the bank foreclosed on was all consolidated in a company called the Union Mill & Mining Co. The Bank of California and the V & T were separate, stand-alone companies though owned principally by the same three investors. I have combined the ownership as per the conversation between Sharon and Ralston for simplicity.

CHAPTER 28

Duane Bliss did start a small bank with money he made from a mining stake in California. That bank did merge with William Sharon's Bank of California. Sharon did appoint Bliss to obtain easements of rights of way for the V & T Railroad running from Virginia City down to Mound House then on to Carson City and ultimately on to Lake Crossing (Reno). Bliss did return to Massachusetts to marry his betrothed, Elizabeth née Tobey, and returned to the West Coast. It is also true that while Back East and tending to his marriage, Bliss' holdings evaporated. It is my invention that the reason for this revolved around William Sharon and the Bank of California.

The information in this chapter identifying the original founders of the Carson and Tahoe Lumber & Fluming Co.'s founders is taken from the actual company records which have been digitized by the University of Reno. Those records can be accessed online.

CHAPTER 29

An enterprising man thought the desert climate would be conducive to using camels as beasts of burden in the early days of Virginia City. There was also a tremendous need for material to be carried from Carson City to Virginia City before the railroad was built. But the camels were unsuited for the terrain. The sage brush wreaked havoc with their feet. Being a place of regularly inebriated clusters of men, legend has it that a group sipping alcoholic libations came up with the grand idea that if they could not be used as beasts of burden, then they should have camel races on which they could place bets. The races continued for only a short time but they were later revived in more recent days as a tourist attraction. Virginia City still holds camel races every summer.

The Knights of Pythias was a fraternal order for those who did not qualify for membership in the Freemasons. This would have included any Catholics, such as Kevin Hurley of our story. The Knights still exist today.

CHAPTER 31

Julia Bulette referenced above in Chapter 12 was killed in her home at the corner of Union and D Street on January 20, 1867. John Millian was seen leaving the house shortly before it was discovered Julia was dead. Millian was apprehended and charged for the murder. He was tried, sentenced, and later hung for the murder of Ms. Bulette on April 24, 1868. I have changed the timing to fit the story line. *(See Douglas*

McDonald's Virginia City and the Silver Region of the Comstock Lode pp. 74-75).

CHAPTER 32

Mackay and Fair did take Dan De Quille down into the Consolidated Virginia and California Mine to show him the size, nature, and quality of the major ore find. It was extraordinarily rare for any mine owner to take a reporter down below the surface to verify a new find. De Quille wrote a famous article about the amazing discovery, describing in detail the magnitude and magnificent quality of the ore. It was in this same article that he coined the name of the four owners of the Consolidated as the "Bonanza Kings."

CHAPTER 33

In the chapter, Mackay explains to De Quille that each miner takes two candles down the shaft each day. He also talks about their need to conserve. If you take the current day tour down the Belcher Mine in downtown Virginia City, the guide will tell you about the candles and how the men worked in pairs and tried to conserve their tallow. One man would hold a six- to eight-foot hexagonal drill bit on his shoulder pointed straight out and level into the ore body while his working buddy swung a fourteen-pound, full length sledgehammer to strike the drill bit only inches away from the holder's head. One small miss and a neck or head was destroyed. And the only light they had to make sure those strikes hit the drill bit would have come from a single candle. That was true trust.

For years, the main problem the mine owners faced was water. Not just cold water but hot water at the lower depths. Virginia City saw multiple new innovations in hydro pumps. Massive steam driven pumps usually ran twenty-four hours a day just to keep up with the ever-present flooding. But it was not enough. Adolph Sutro saw profit in the problem. He came up with the idea that if he drilled a crosscut below any other crosscut, then he could set up access tunnels to almost all the mines along the Comstock and drain the water by simple gravity. Of course, he would charge for the drainage.

The mine owners were spending hundreds of thousands of 1870's dollars on their newest and innovative pumps sucking the water to the surface to be discarded. Using simple gravity seemed like a much better idea. Sutro started drilling his tunnel into the lower side of Mt. Davidson in 1865. He found major opposition with the mine owners initially as they wished to protect their standing with creditors who helped finance huge capital investments in pumps. More importantly, they controlled the outflow from their own mines. They did not have to pay anyone to drain, just pump. But Sutro was obsessed. He had a profitable mill plant that mysteriously burned, leaving him wealthy on the insurance payout. (See *Virginia City and the Silver Region of the Comstock Lode* by Douglas McDonald, p. 86). He used the money to start financing the tunnel. But the local opposition forced him to go to the government. At great personal expense, he went political. The Sutro Tunnel Act was passed by US Congress in 1866, which mandated that the tunnel be built and mandated that mine owners must pay drainage fees to Sutro.

William Sharon was probably the most powerful opponent to Sutro. He viewed the tunnel as a potential alternative to the V & T Railroad he had built for ore transport down toward the Carson River where all the mills were. Sharon worried that if Sutro could drain water via gravity, he might also create rail systems within his tunnels into the mines to roll out the ore using that same gravity. Finally, after years of drilling, Sutro got his tunnel connected to the Savage Mine at a depth of one thousand six hundred feet directly below Virginia City.

Sutro eventually made a deal with Mackay for drainage, but it wasn't until sometime in 1878, long after the current story line. Sutro devised a devilish method of payment for the fluid drained out of each mine. His drainage fee was set in terms of tons of ore raised to the surface. Mackay paid Sutro Tunnel Co. one dollar per ton of all ore raised from the mines if the quality of the ore was assayed at forty dollars a ton or less and two dollars for every ton if the quality of the ore was assayed at more than forty dollars a ton. Sutro Tunnel Co. was paid for every ton of ore raised out of the Comstock. At its peak, the Sutro Tunnel drained four million gallons of water per day and generated ten thousand dollars per day in revenue. (See *The Comstock Lode 1849-1888* by Hubert Howe Bancroft).

But Sutro foresaw the time when the ore would run out. He took his profits for what he felt were the last glory years of the bonanza and sold his stock at the company's height. He then invested in San Francisco property. The concept of the Sutro drainage tunnel was another of the pioneering ideas generated by the vast wealth of the Comstock Lode. Its blueprint was used later at the Argo Gold Mine in Idaho Springs, CO.

About the Author

J.L. Crafts was raised on the outskirts of a very large city in Southern California. Thankfully, back in those days the very distant outskirts of that city still included open spaces and small ranches. As a young boy he worked wrangling horses on one of those ranches learning to rope, ride and train one of the most magnificent animals our planet has to offer. Those early years created a lifelong connection with, not only horses, but with the west of the 1800's. College led to law school followed by over thirty years of trying cases to juries up and down the state of California. Speaking to juries in a simple directness, he did what he could to elicit facts and arguments wherever possible through stories of life in the saddle and open spaces. He now spends his days creating those stories on the page and enjoys every minute of it.

Coming Soon!

J.L. CRAFTS
CLEAR CUT JUSTICE
A WILL TOAL NOVEL

When a bomb explodes in a sawmill near Glenbrook Harbor, the residents and businessmen on the shores of Lake Tahoe are left reeling. Will Toal and his wife, Beth, are caught in the deadly, fiery fragments of the devastating explosion, and Beth is severely injured…

In a race against time, Will is forced to work with an old nemesis, private investigator Dale Paris, to try to stop the arsonists and save the sawmills from disaster. Can they stop the bloodshed? At any price, Will is determined to have **CLEAR CUT JUSTICE**…

For more information
visit: www.SpeakingVolumes.us

Now Available!

A WILL TOAL NOVEL

**For more information
visit:** www.SpeakingVolumes.us

Now Available!

AWARD WINNING AUTHOR
MARK WARREN

For more information
visit: www.SpeakingVolumes.us